WHAT'S WRONG WITH BEING CRABBY?

Copr. © 1952 United Feature Syndicate, Inc.

PEANUTS CLASSICS

Dr. Beagle and Mr. Hyde
Fly, You Stupid Kite, Fly!
How Long, Great Pumpkin, How Long?
It's Great to Be a Superstar
Kiss Her, You Blockhead!
My Anxieties Have Anxieties
Speak Softly, and Carry a Beagle
There Goes the Shutout
Summers Fly, Winters Walk
Thank Goodness for People
The Beagle Has Landed
What Makes You Think You're Happy?
And a Woodstock in a Birch Tree
A Smile Makes a Lousy Umbrella
The Mad Punter Strikes Again
There's a Vulture Outside
Here Comes the April Fool!
What Makes Musicians So Sarcastic?
A Kiss on the Nose Turns Anger Aside
It's Hard Work Being Bitter
I'm Not Your Sweet Babboo!
Stop Snowing on My Secretary
Always Stick Up for the Underbird
What's Wrong with Being Crabby?
Don't Hassle Me with Your Sighs, Chuck
The Way of the Fussbudget Is Not Easy
You're Weird, Sir!
It's a Long Way to Tipperary
Who's the Funny-Looking Kid with the Big
Nose?
Sunday's Fun Day, Charlie Brown
You're Out of Your Mind, Charlie Brown!
You're the Guest of Honor, Charlie Brown
You Can't Win, Charlie Brown
Peanuts Every Sunday
The Unsinkable Charlie Brown
Good Grief, More Peanuts
You've Come a Long Way, Charlie Brown
The Cheshire Beagle
Duck, Here Comes Another Day!
Sarcasm Does Not Become You, Ma'am
Nothing Echoes Like an Empty Mailbox
I Heard A D Minus Call Me

WHAT'S WRONG WITH BEING CRABBY?

by Charles M. Schulz

An Owl Book
Henry Holt and Company/New York

Henry Holt and Company, LLC
Publishers since 1866
115 West 18th Street
New York, New York 10011

Henry Holt® is a registered
trademark of Henry Holt and Company, LLC.

Distributed in Canada by H. B. Fenn and Company Ltd.

Library of Congress Catalog Card Number: 92-54437

ISBN 0-8050-2400-X (An Owl Book: pbk.)

Henry Holt books are available for special promotions
and premiums. For details contact: Director, Special Markets.

Originally published by Holt, Rinehart and Winston in 1964
as *As You Like It, Charlie Brown*. Published in an expanded edition
under the title *What's Wrong with Being Crabby?* in 1976 and
included strips from *Sunday's Fun Day, Charlie Brown*,
published in 1965 by Holt, Rinehart and Winston.

New Owl Book Edition 1992

Printed in the United States of America

7 9 10 8 6

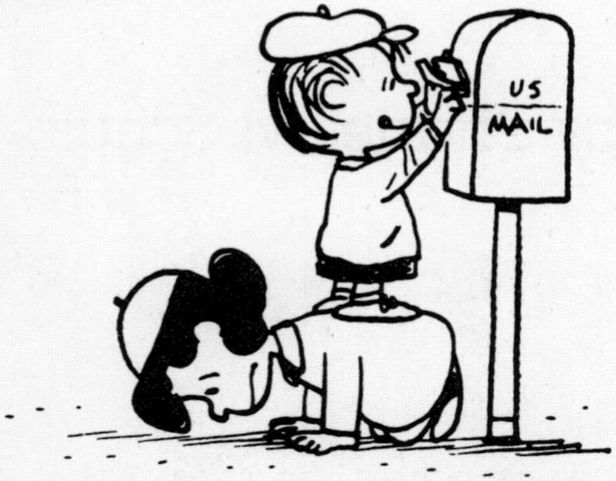
US
MAIL

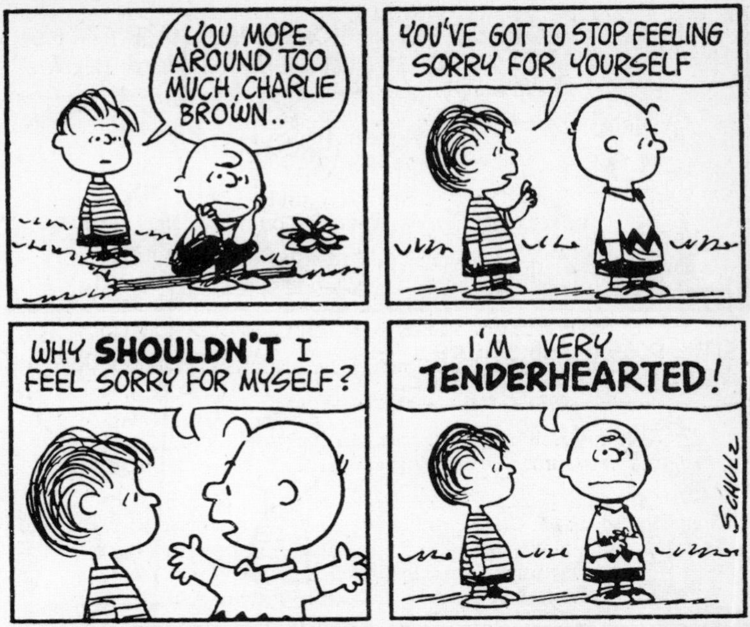
YOU MOPE AROUND TOO MUCH, CHARLIE BROWN..
YOU'VE GOT TO STOP FEELING SORRY FOR YOURSELF
WHY SHOULDN'T I FEEL SORRY FOR MYSELF?
I'M VERY TENDERHEARTED!
SCHULZ

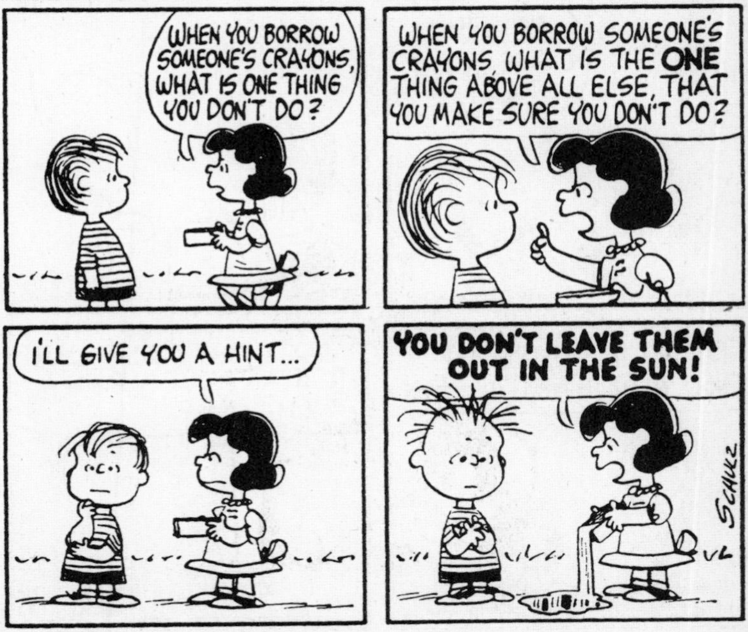
WHEN YOU BORROW SOMEONE'S CRAYONS, WHAT IS ONE THING YOU DON'T DO?
WHEN YOU BORROW SOMEONE'S CRAYONS, WHAT IS THE ONE THING ABOVE ALL ELSE, THAT YOU MAKE SURE YOU DON'T DO?
I'LL GIVE YOU A HINT...
YOU DON'T LEAVE THEM OUT IN THE SUN!
SCHULZ

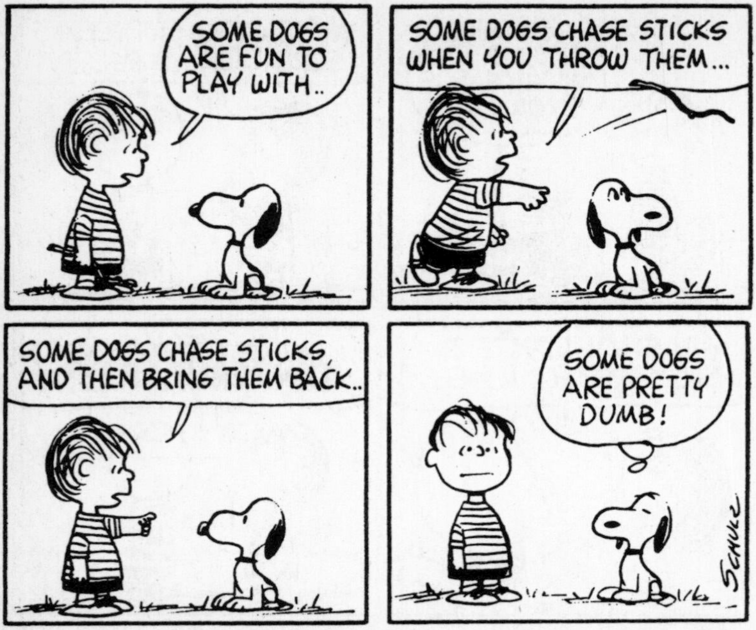
SOME DOGS ARE FUN TO PLAY WITH..
SOME DOGS CHASE STICKS WHEN YOU THROW THEM...
SOME DOGS CHASE STICKS, AND THEN BRING THEM BACK..
SOME DOGS ARE PRETTY DUMB!
SCHULZ

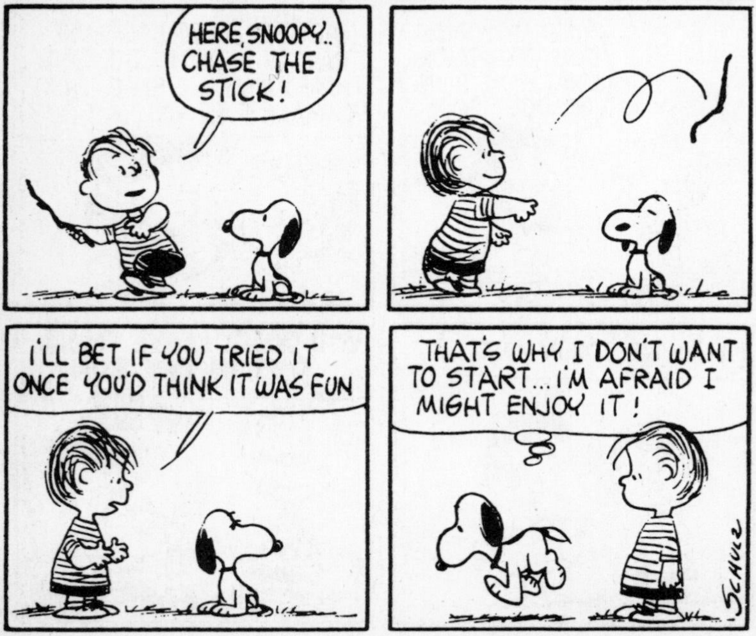
HERE, SNOOPY.. CHASE THE STICK!
I'LL BET IF YOU TRIED IT ONCE YOU'D THINK IT WAS FUN
THAT'S WHY I DON'T WANT TO START... I'M AFRAID I MIGHT ENJOY IT!
SCHULZ

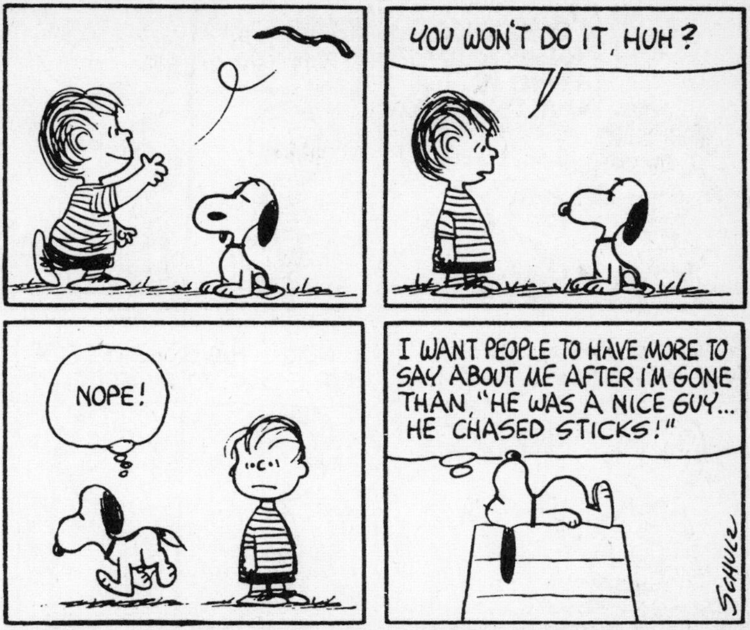
YOU WON'T DO IT, HUH?
NOPE!
I WANT PEOPLE TO HAVE MORE TO SAY ABOUT ME AFTER I'M GONE THAN, "HE WAS A NICE GUY... HE CHASED STICKS!"
SCHULZ

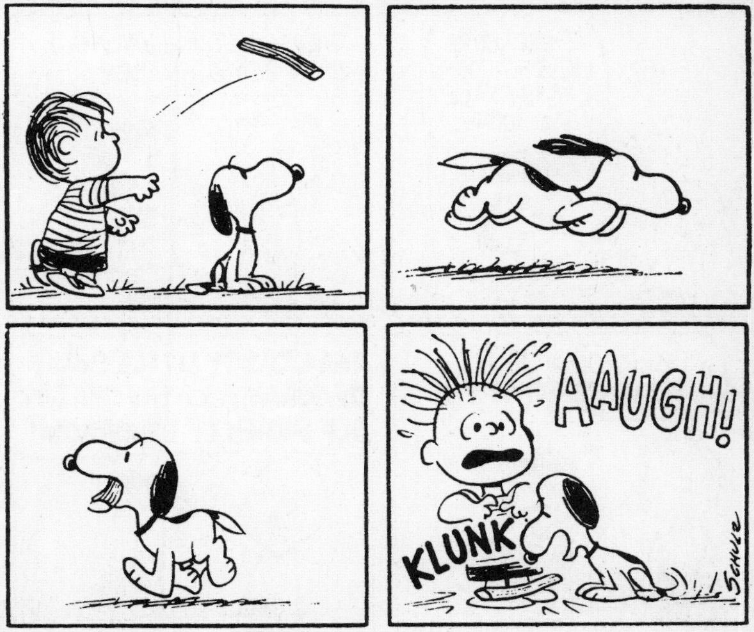
AAUGH!
KLUNK
SCHULZ

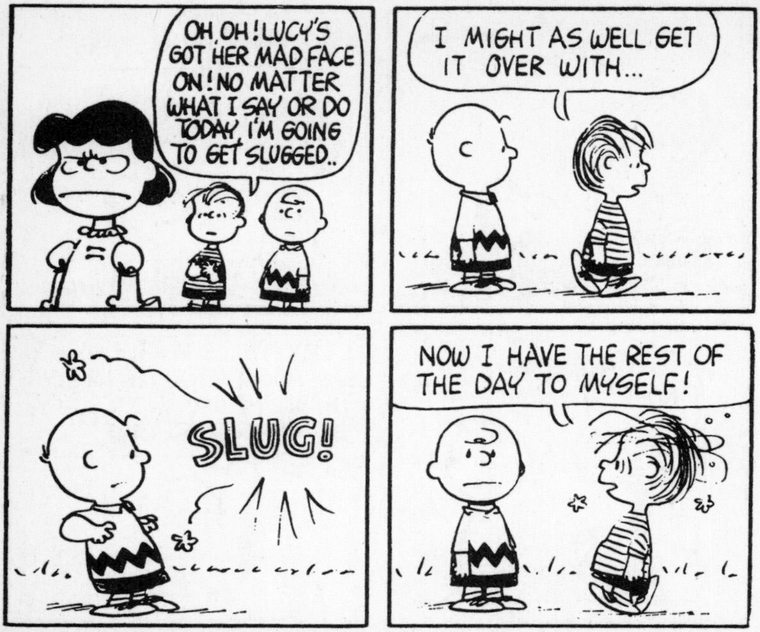

OH, OH! LUCY'S GOT HER MAD FACE ON! NO MATTER WHAT I SAY OR DO TODAY, I'M GOING TO GET SLUGGED..
I MIGHT AS WELL GET IT OVER WITH...
SLUG!
NOW I HAVE THE REST OF THE DAY TO MYSELF!

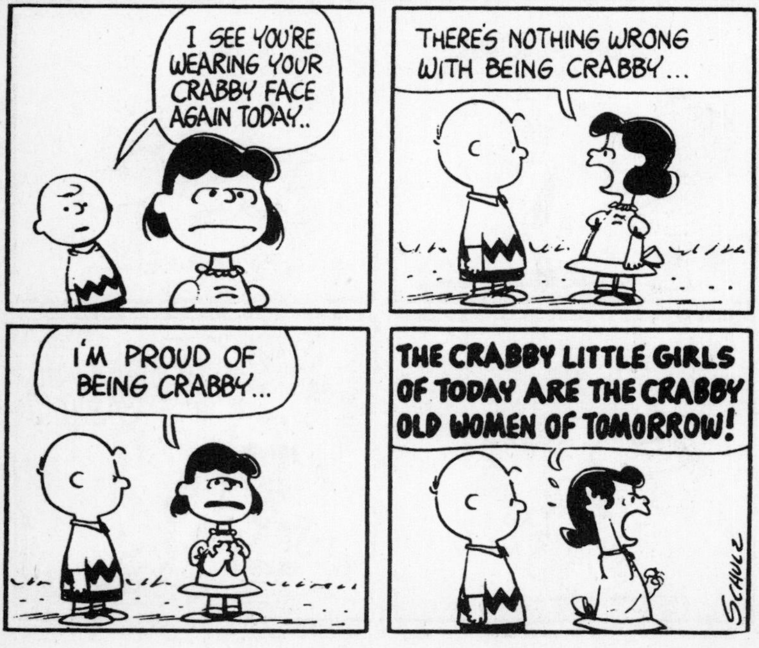

I SEE YOU'RE WEARING YOUR CRABBY FACE AGAIN TODAY..
THERE'S NOTHING WRONG WITH BEING CRABBY...
I'M PROUD OF BEING CRABBY...
THE CRABBY LITTLE GIRLS OF TODAY ARE THE CRABBY OLD WOMEN OF TOMORROW!
SCHULZ

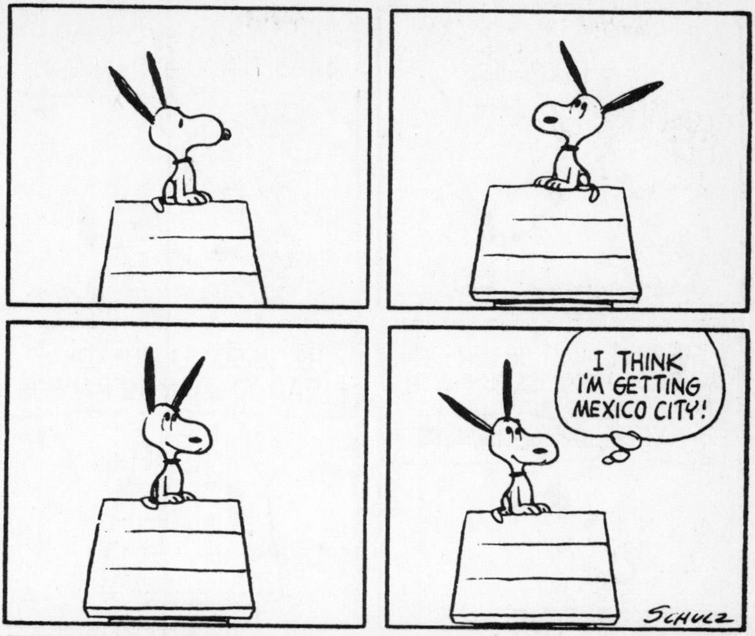
I THINK I'M GETTING MEXICO CITY!

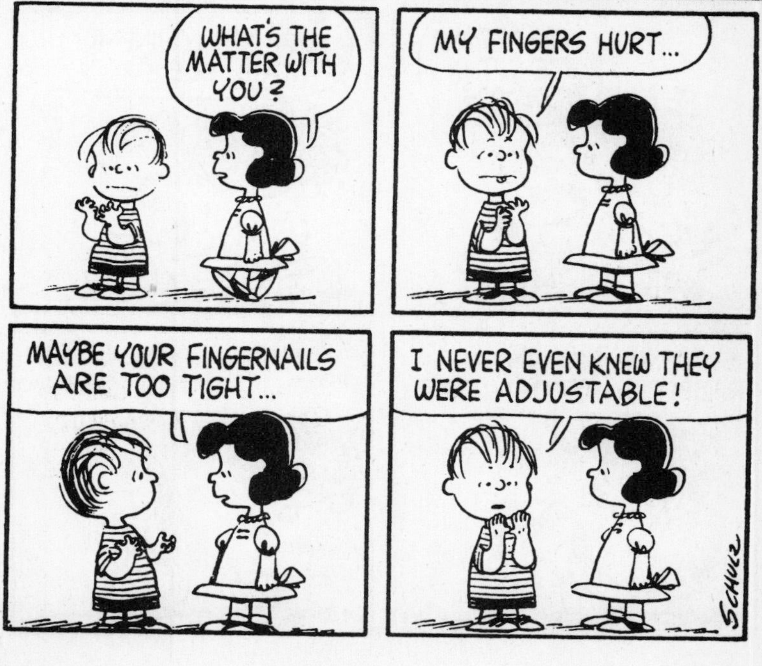
WHAT'S THE MATTER WITH YOU?
MY FINGERS HURT...
MAYBE YOUR FINGERNAILS ARE TOO TIGHT...
I NEVER EVEN KNEW THEY WERE ADJUSTABLE!

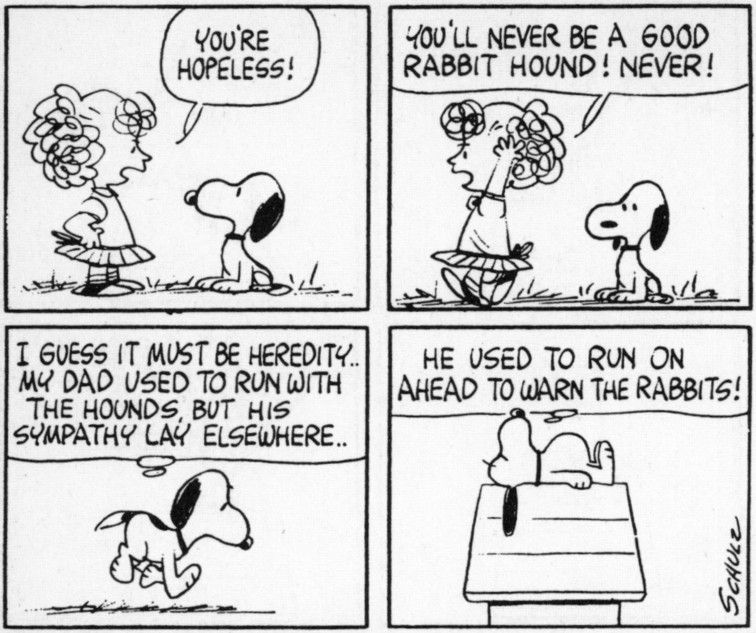
YOU'RE HOPELESS!
YOU'LL NEVER BE A GOOD RABBIT HOUND! NEVER!
I GUESS IT MUST BE HEREDITY.. MY DAD USED TO RUN WITH THE HOUNDS, BUT HIS SYMPATHY LAY ELSEWHERE..
HE USED TO RUN ON AHEAD TO WARN THE RABBITS!
SCHULZ

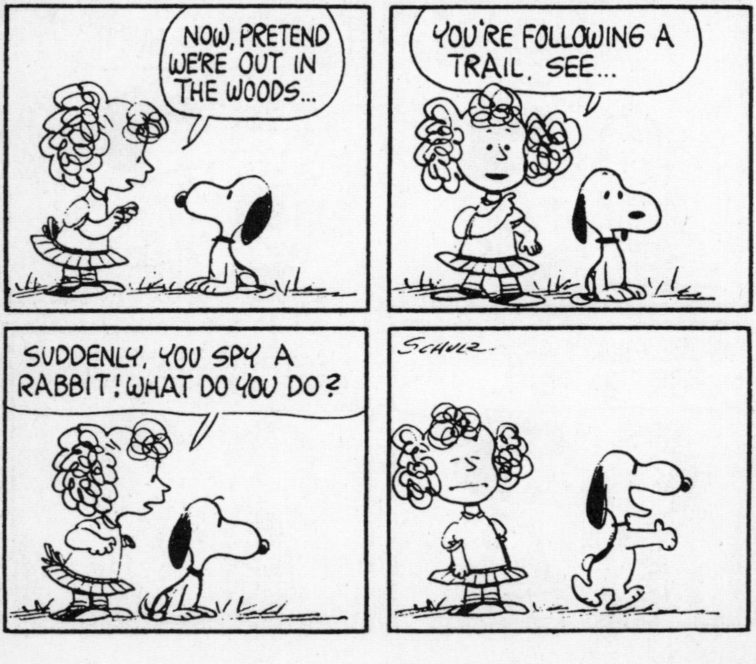
NOW, PRETEND WE'RE OUT IN THE WOODS...
YOU'RE FOLLOWING A TRAIL, SEE...
SUDDENLY, YOU SPY A RABBIT! WHAT DO YOU DO?
SCHULZ

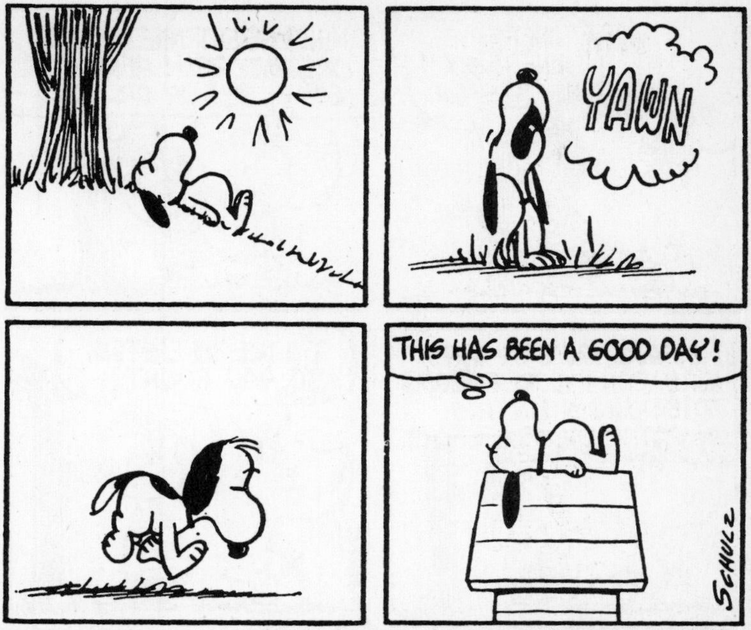
YAWN
THIS HAS BEEN A GOOD DAY!
SCHULZ

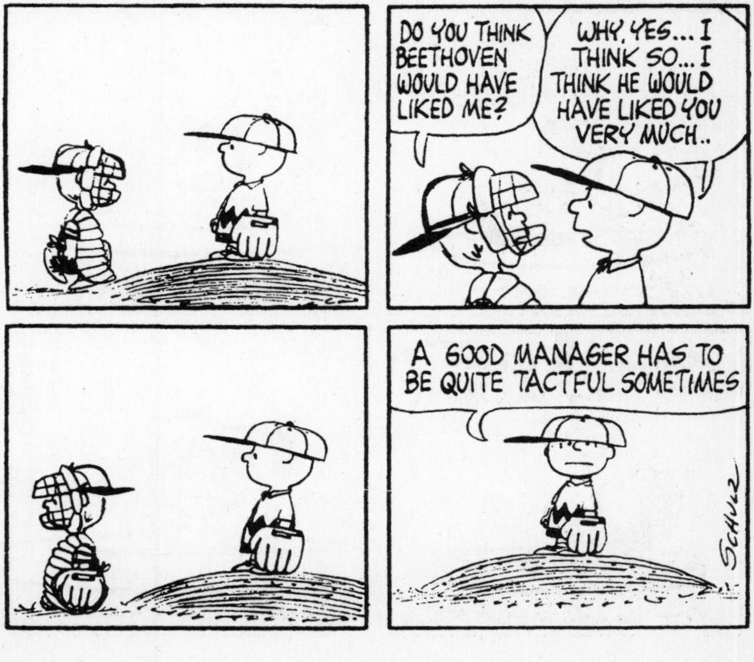
DO YOU THINK BEETHOVEN WOULD HAVE LIKED ME?
WHY, YES... I THINK SO... I THINK HE WOULD HAVE LIKED YOU VERY MUCH..
A GOOD MANAGER HAS TO BE QUITE TACTFUL SOMETIMES
SCHULZ

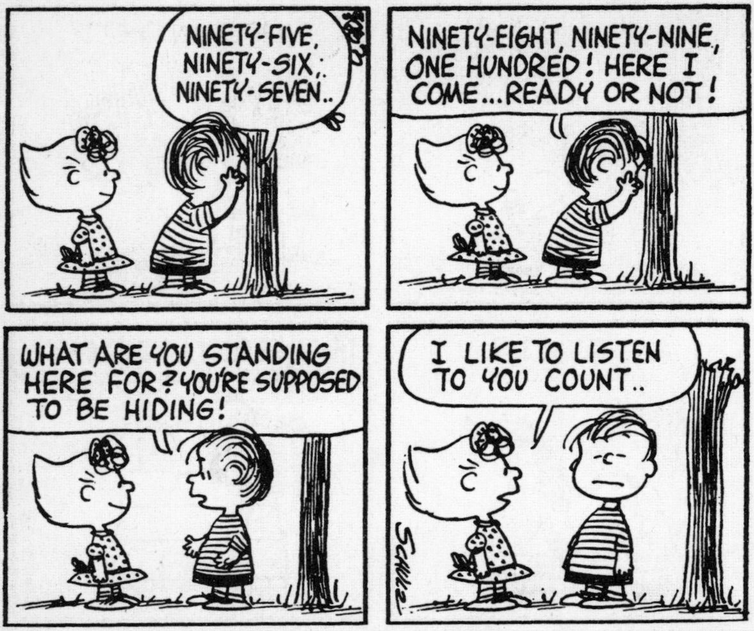
NINETY-FIVE, NINETY-SIX, NINETY-SEVEN..
NINETY-EIGHT, NINETY-NINE, ONE HUNDRED! HERE I COME...READY OR NOT!
WHAT ARE YOU STANDING HERE FOR? YOU'RE SUPPOSED TO BE HIDING!
I LIKE TO LISTEN TO YOU COUNT..
SCHULZ

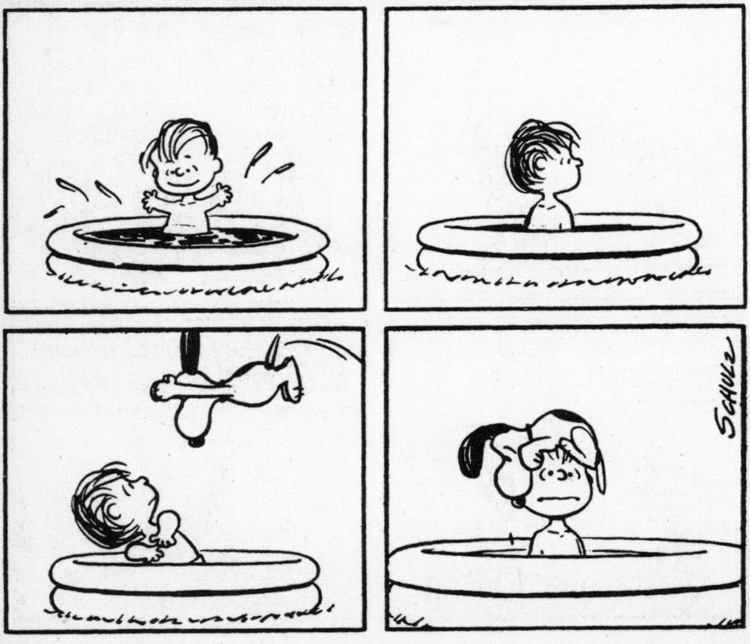
SCHULZ

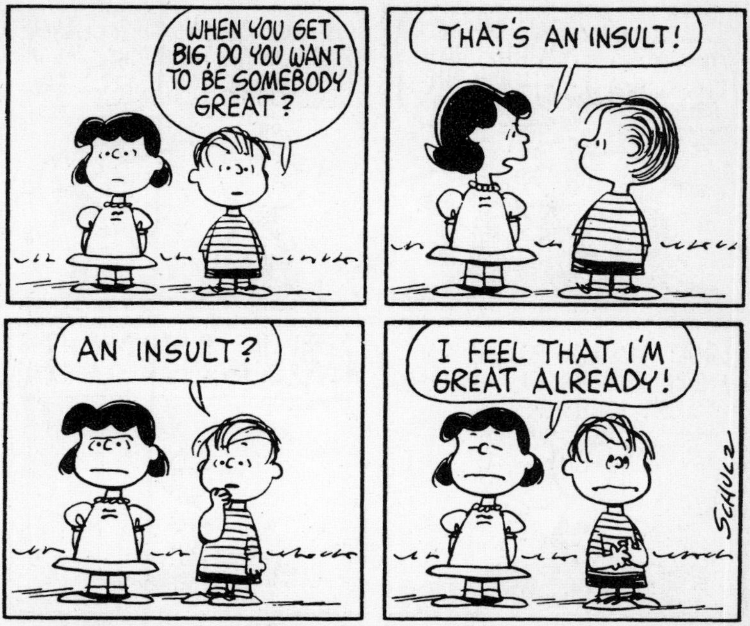
WHEN YOU GET BIG, DO YOU WANT TO BE SOMEBODY GREAT?
THAT'S AN INSULT!
AN INSULT?
I FEEL THAT I'M GREAT ALREADY!
SCHULZ

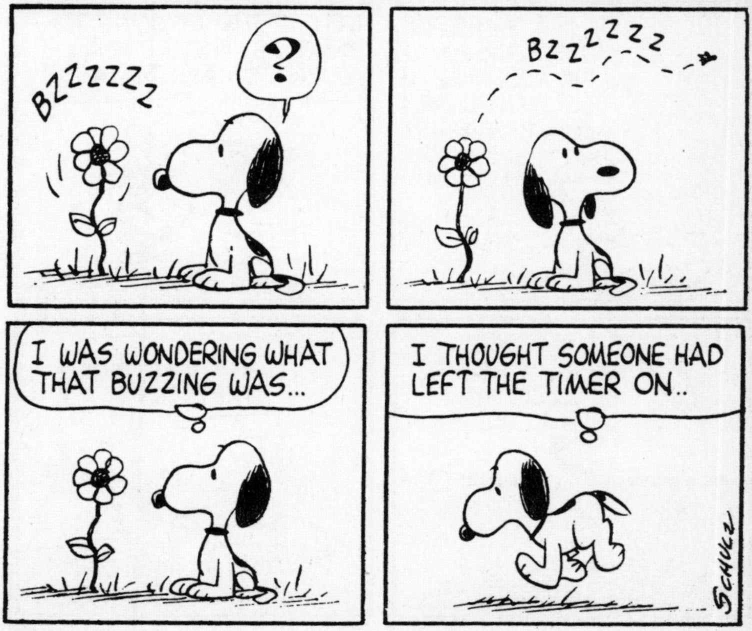
BZZZZZZ
?
BZZZZZZ
I WAS WONDERING WHAT THAT BUZZING WAS...
I THOUGHT SOMEONE HAD LEFT THE TIMER ON..
SCHULZ

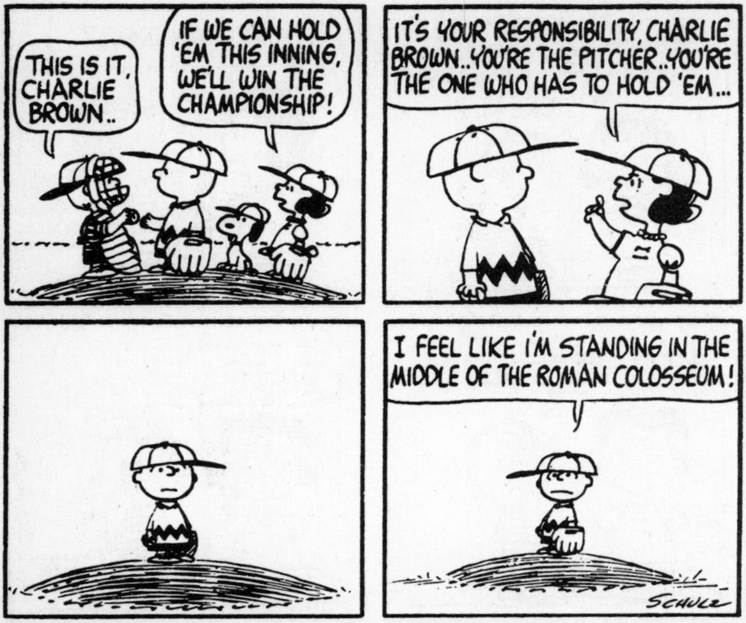
THIS IS IT, CHARLIE BROWN..
IF WE CAN HOLD 'EM THIS INNING, WE'LL WIN THE CHAMPIONSHIP!
IT'S YOUR RESPONSIBILITY, CHARLIE BROWN..YOU'RE THE PITCHER..YOU'RE THE ONE WHO HAS TO HOLD 'EM...
I FEEL LIKE I'M STANDING IN THE MIDDLE OF THE ROMAN COLOSSEUM!
SCHULZ

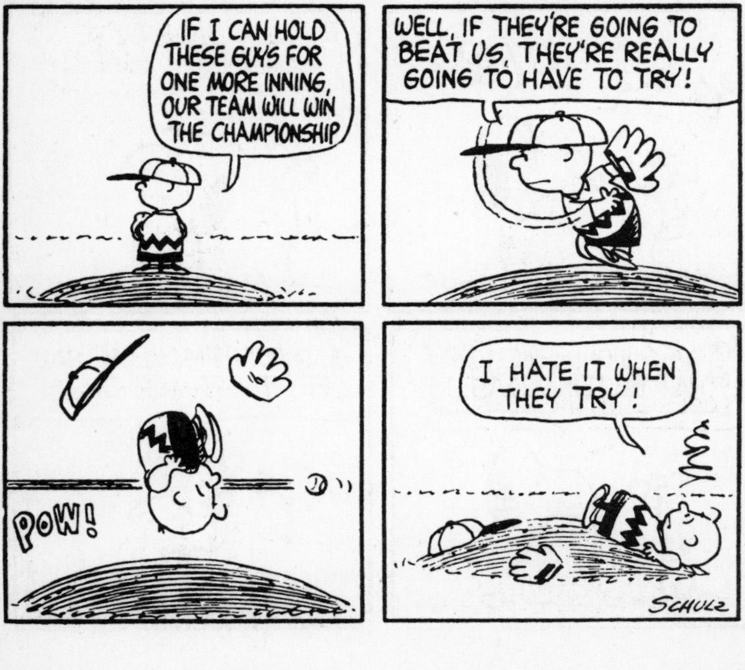
IF I CAN HOLD THESE GUYS FOR ONE MORE INNING, OUR TEAM WILL WIN THE CHAMPIONSHIP
WELL, IF THEY'RE GOING TO BEAT US, THEY'RE REALLY GOING TO HAVE TO TRY!
POW!
I HATE IT WHEN THEY TRY!
SCHULZ

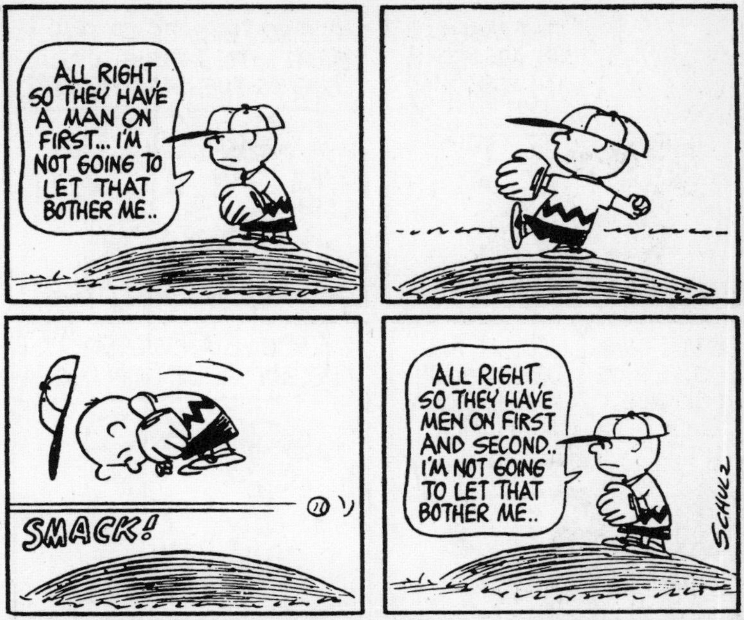
ALL RIGHT, SO THEY HAVE A MAN ON FIRST... I'M NOT GOING TO LET THAT BOTHER ME..
SMACK!
ALL RIGHT, SO THEY HAVE MEN ON FIRST AND SECOND.. I'M NOT GOING TO LET THAT BOTHER ME..
SCHULZ

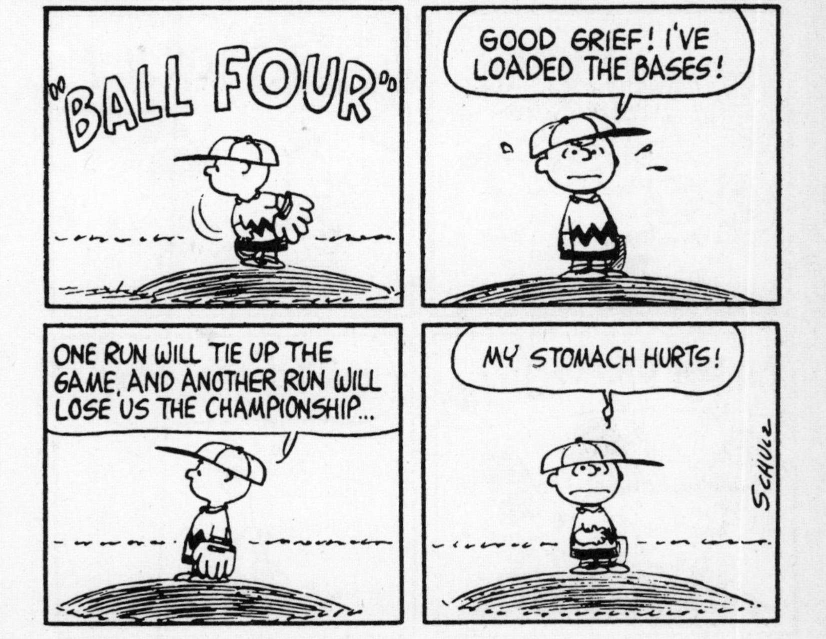
"BALL FOUR"
GOOD GRIEF! I'VE LOADED THE BASES!
ONE RUN WILL TIE UP THE GAME, AND ANOTHER RUN WILL LOSE US THE CHAMPIONSHIP...
MY STOMACH HURTS!
SCHULZ

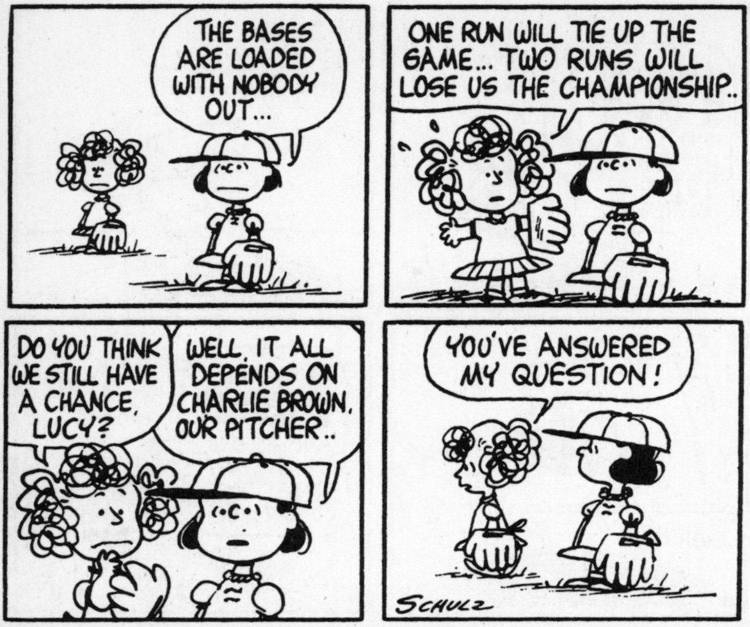
THE BASES ARE LOADED WITH NOBODY OUT...
ONE RUN WILL TIE UP THE GAME... TWO RUNS WILL LOSE US THE CHAMPIONSHIP..
DO YOU THINK WE STILL HAVE A CHANCE, LUCY?
WELL, IT ALL DEPENDS ON CHARLIE BROWN, OUR PITCHER..
YOU'VE ANSWERED MY QUESTION!
SCHULZ

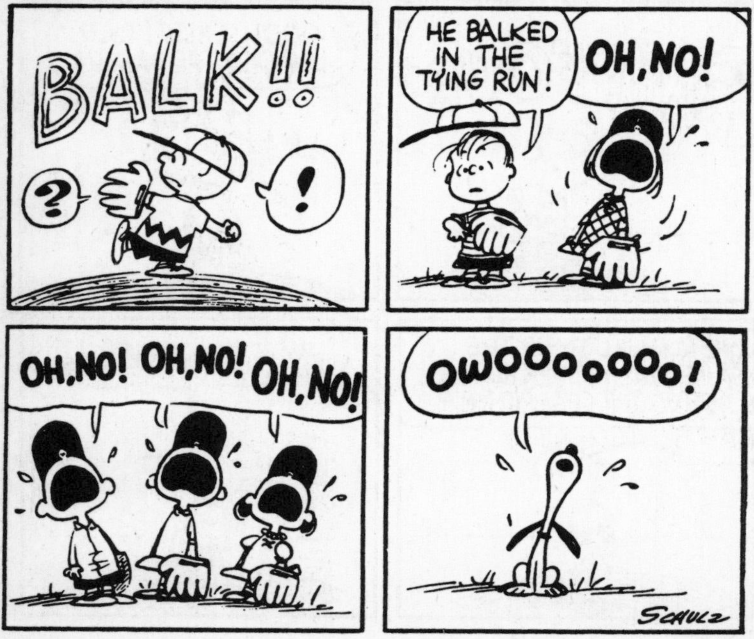
BALK!!
?
!
HE BALKED IN THE TYING RUN!
OH, NO!
OH, NO! OH, NO! OH, NO!
OWOOOOOOOO!
SCHULZ

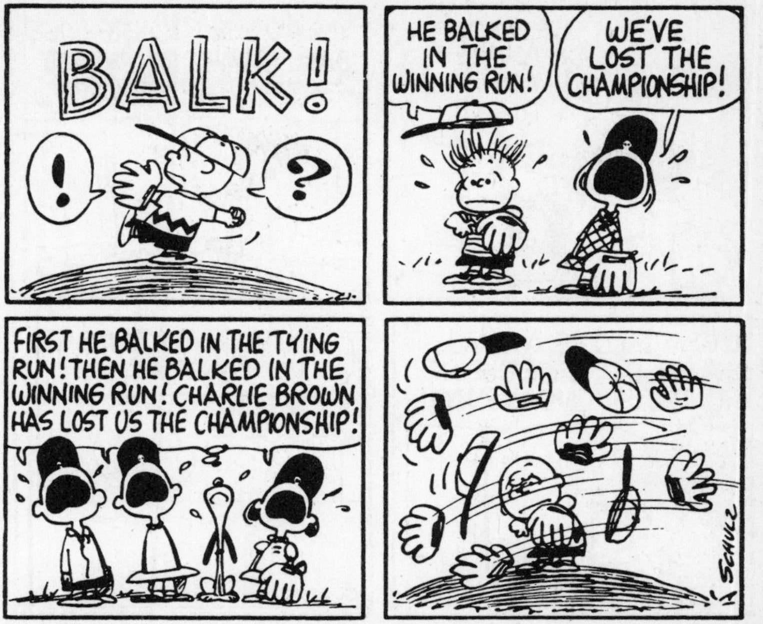
BALK!
!
?
HE BALKED IN THE WINNING RUN!
WE'VE LOST THE CHAMPIONSHIP!
FIRST HE BALKED IN THE TYING RUN! THEN HE BALKED IN THE WINNING RUN! CHARLIE BROWN HAS LOST US THE CHAMPIONSHIP!
SCHULZ

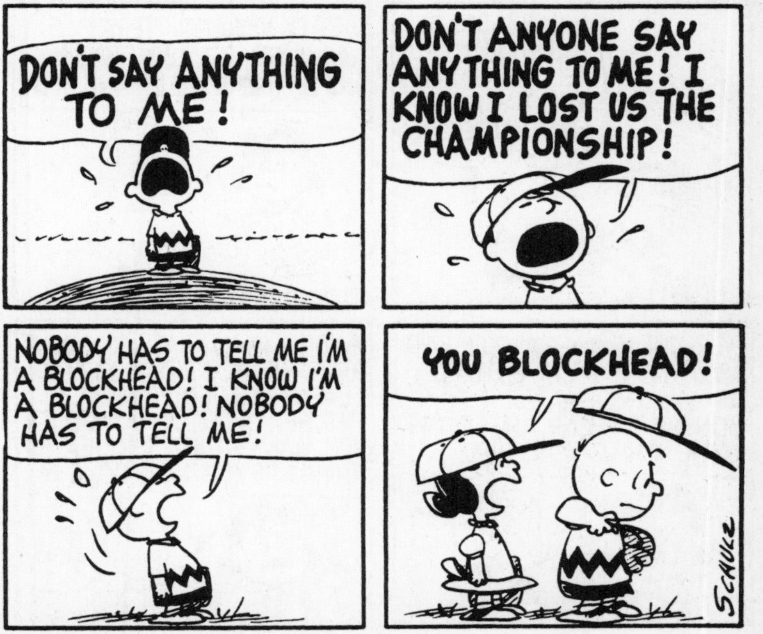
DON'T SAY ANYTHING TO ME!
DON'T ANYONE SAY ANYTHING TO ME! I KNOW I LOST US THE CHAMPIONSHIP!
NOBODY HAS TO TELL ME I'M A BLOCKHEAD! I KNOW I'M A BLOCKHEAD! NOBODY HAS TO TELL ME!
YOU BLOCKHEAD!
SCHULZ

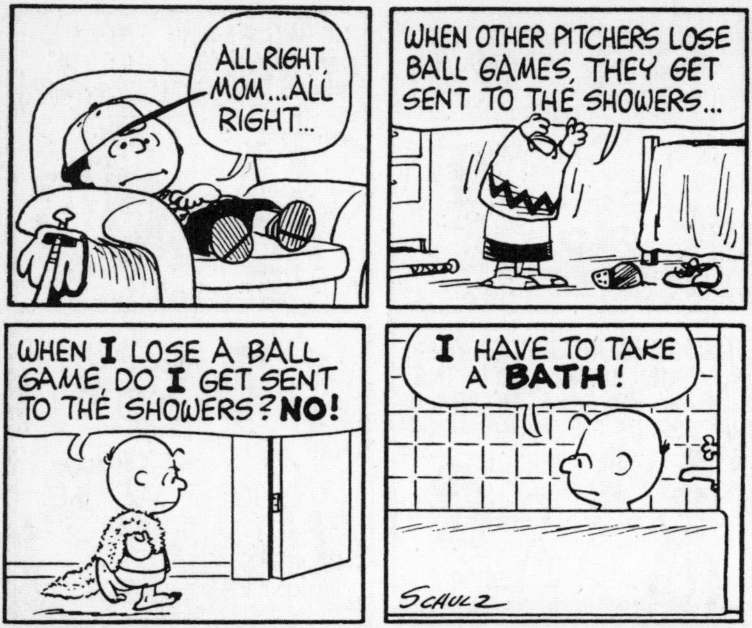
ALL RIGHT, MOM...ALL RIGHT...
WHEN OTHER PITCHERS LOSE BALL GAMES, THEY GET SENT TO THE SHOWERS...
WHEN I LOSE A BALL GAME, DO I GET SENT TO THE SHOWERS? NO!
I HAVE TO TAKE A BATH!
SCHULZ

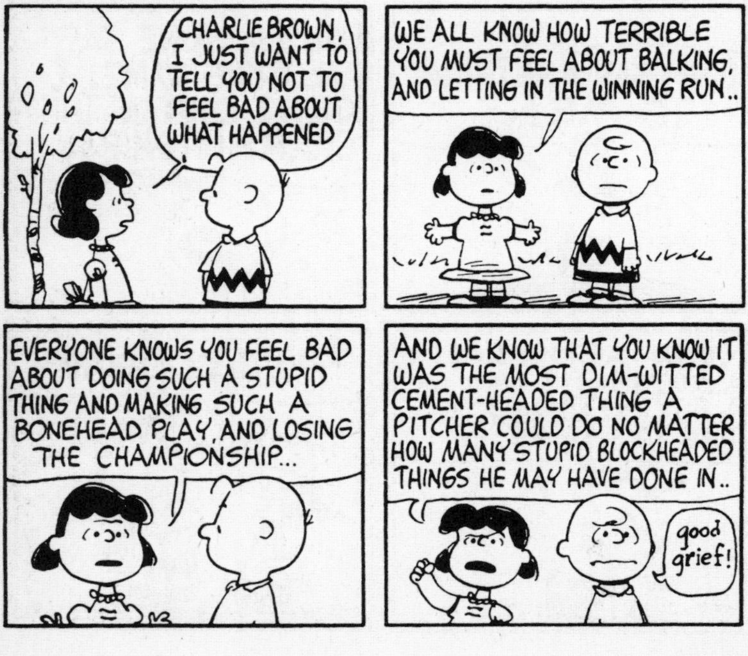
CHARLIE BROWN, I JUST WANT TO TELL YOU NOT TO FEEL BAD ABOUT WHAT HAPPENED
WE ALL KNOW HOW TERRIBLE YOU MUST FEEL ABOUT BALKING, AND LETTING IN THE WINNING RUN..
EVERYONE KNOWS YOU FEEL BAD ABOUT DOING SUCH A STUPID THING AND MAKING SUCH A BONEHEAD PLAY, AND LOSING THE CHAMPIONSHIP...
AND WE KNOW THAT YOU KNOW IT WAS THE MOST DIM-WITTED CEMENT-HEADED THING A PITCHER COULD DO NO MATTER HOW MANY STUPID BLOCKHEADED THINGS HE MAY HAVE DONE IN..
good grief!

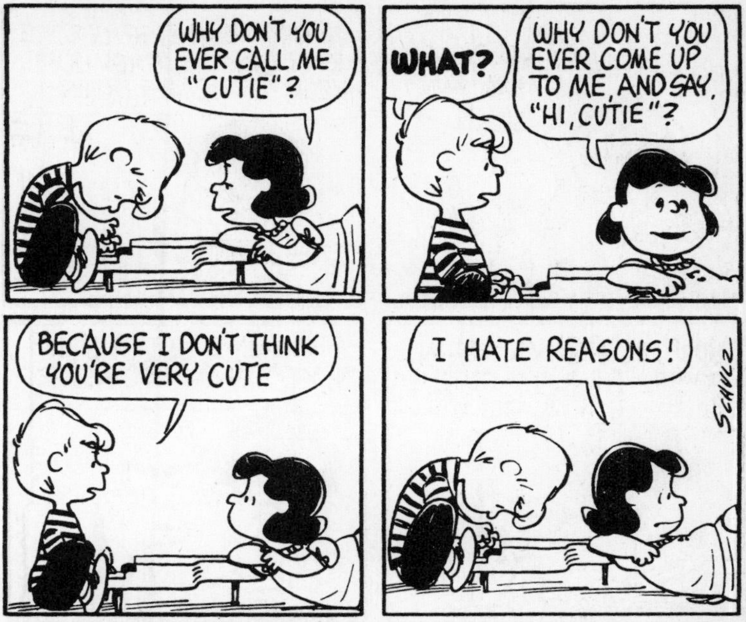
WHY DON'T YOU EVER CALL ME "CUTIE"?
WHAT?
WHY DON'T YOU EVER COME UP TO ME, AND SAY, "HI, CUTIE"?
BECAUSE I DON'T THINK YOU'RE VERY CUTE
I HATE REASONS!
SCHULZ

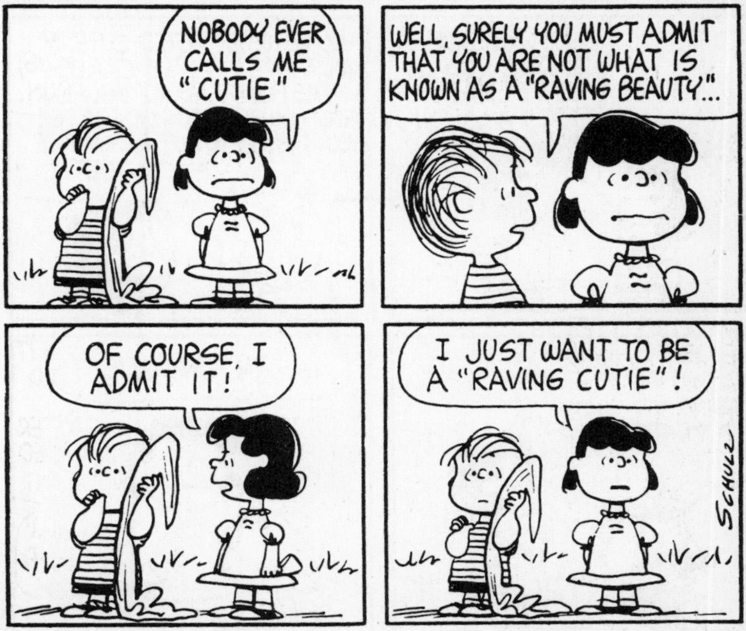
NOBODY EVER CALLS ME "CUTIE"
WELL, SURELY YOU MUST ADMIT THAT YOU ARE NOT WHAT IS KNOWN AS A "RAVING BEAUTY"...
OF COURSE, I ADMIT IT!
I JUST WANT TO BE A "RAVING CUTIE"!
SCHULZ

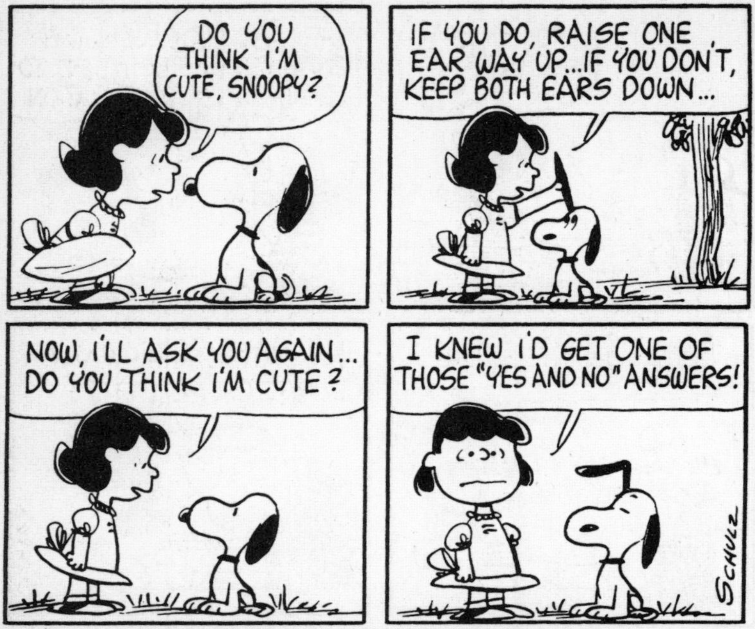
DO YOU THINK I'M CUTE, SNOOPY?
IF YOU DO, RAISE ONE EAR WAY UP...IF YOU DON'T, KEEP BOTH EARS DOWN...
NOW, I'LL ASK YOU AGAIN... DO YOU THINK I'M CUTE?
I KNEW I'D GET ONE OF THOSE "YES AND NO" ANSWERS!
SCHULZ

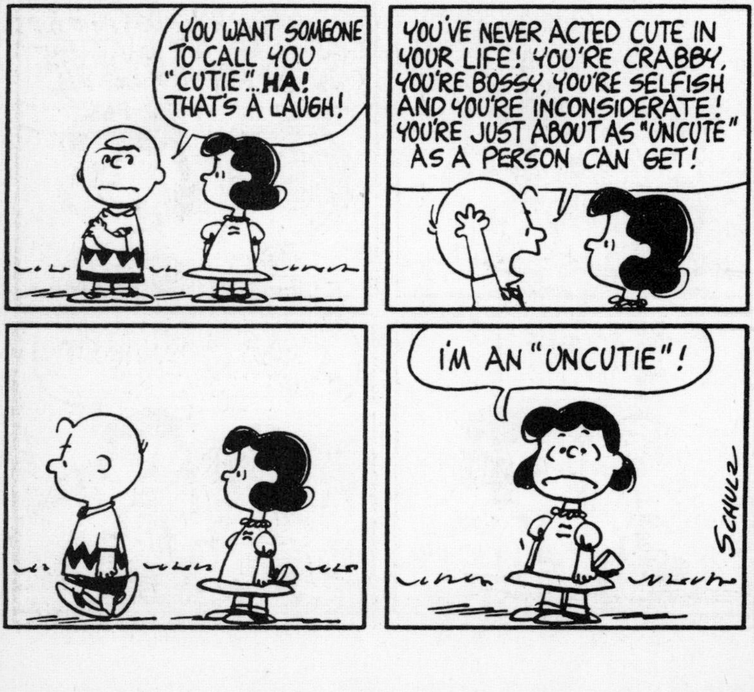
YOU WANT SOMEONE TO CALL YOU "CUTIE"...HA! THAT'S A LAUGH!
YOU'VE NEVER ACTED CUTE IN YOUR LIFE! YOU'RE CRABBY, YOU'RE BOSSY, YOU'RE SELFISH AND YOU'RE INCONSIDERATE! YOU'RE JUST ABOUT AS "UNCUTE" AS A PERSON CAN GET!
I'M AN "UNCUTIE"!
SCHULZ

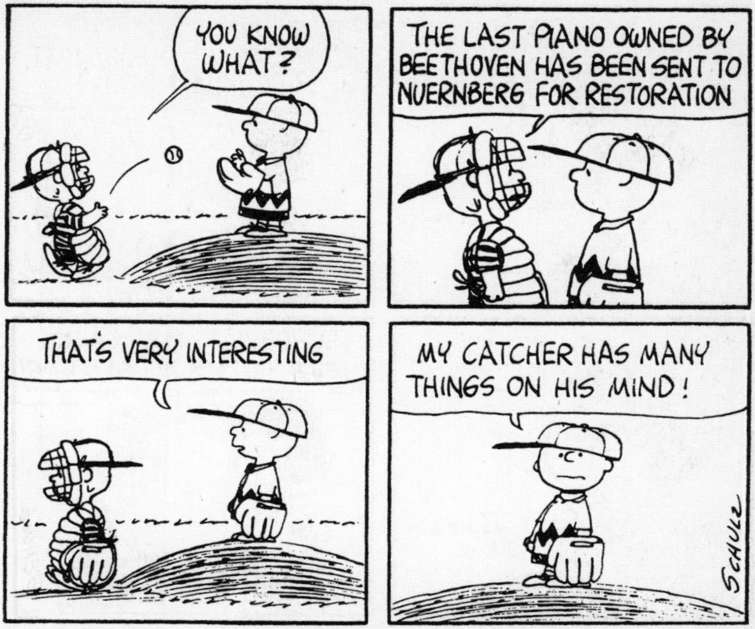
YOU KNOW WHAT?
THE LAST PIANO OWNED BY BEETHOVEN HAS BEEN SENT TO NUERNBERG FOR RESTORATION
THAT'S VERY INTERESTING
MY CATCHER HAS MANY THINGS ON HIS MIND!
SCHULZ

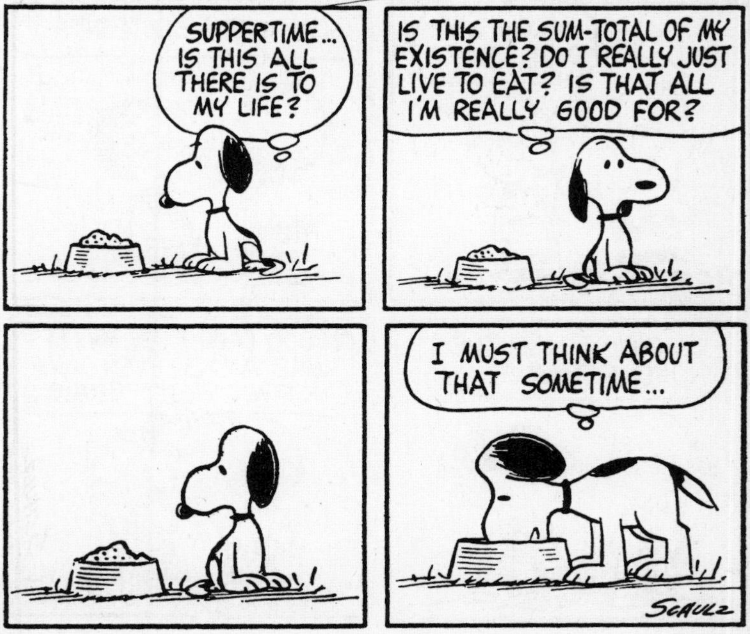
SUPPERTIME... IS THIS ALL THERE IS TO MY LIFE?
IS THIS THE SUM-TOTAL OF MY EXISTENCE? DO I REALLY JUST LIVE TO EAT? IS THAT ALL I'M REALLY GOOD FOR?
I MUST THINK ABOUT THAT SOMETIME...
SCHULZ

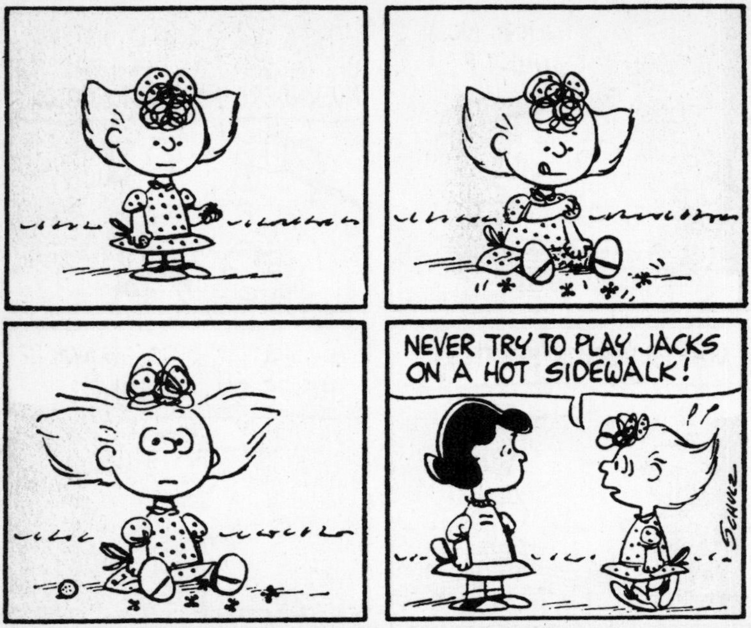
NEVER TRY TO PLAY JACKS ON A HOT SIDEWALK!
SCHULZ

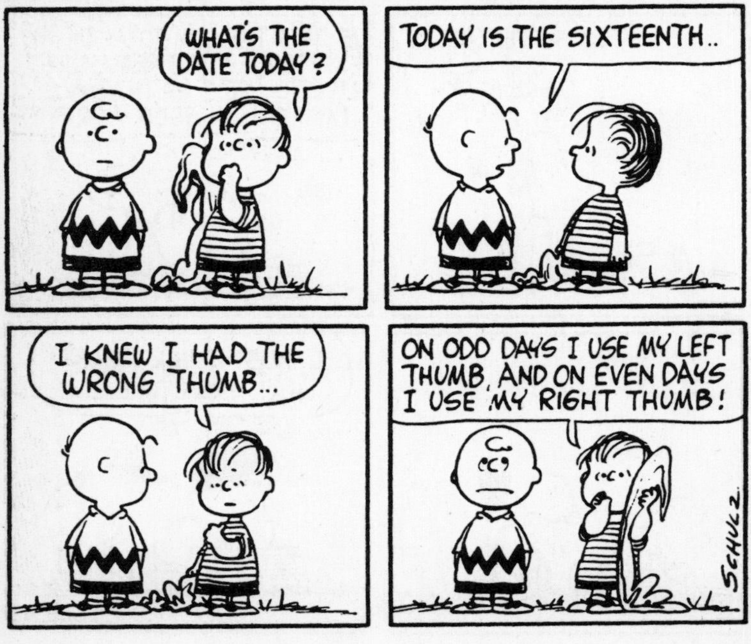
WHAT'S THE DATE TODAY?
TODAY IS THE SIXTEENTH..
I KNEW I HAD THE WRONG THUMB...
ON ODD DAYS I USE MY LEFT THUMB, AND ON EVEN DAYS I USE MY RIGHT THUMB!
SCHULZ

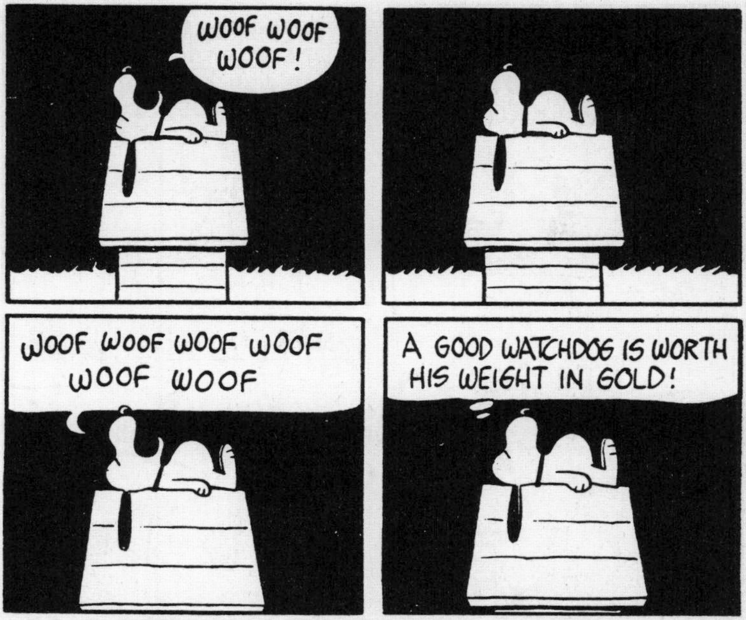
WOOF WOOF WOOF!
WOOF WOOF WOOF WOOF WOOF WOOF
A GOOD WATCHDOG IS WORTH HIS WEIGHT IN GOLD!

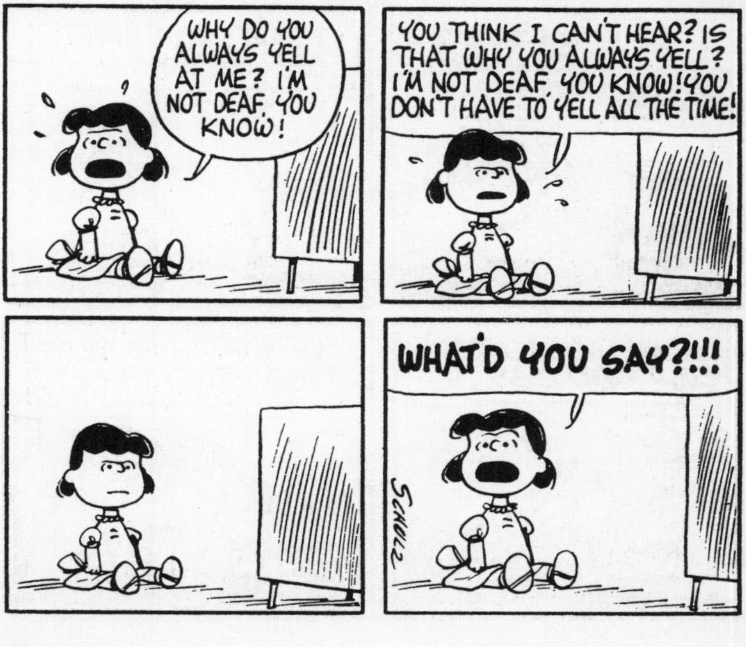
WHY DO YOU ALWAYS YELL AT ME? I'M NOT DEAF, YOU KNOW!
YOU THINK I CAN'T HEAR? IS THAT WHY YOU ALWAYS YELL? I'M NOT DEAF, YOU KNOW! YOU DON'T HAVE TO YELL ALL THE TIME!
SCHULZ
WHAT'D YOU SAY?!!!

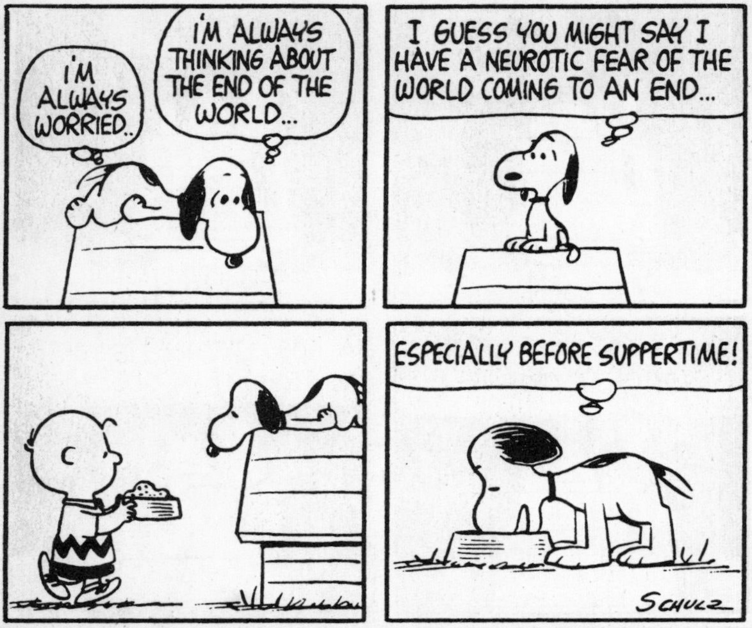
I'M ALWAYS WORRIED..
I'M ALWAYS THINKING ABOUT THE END OF THE WORLD...
I GUESS YOU MIGHT SAY I HAVE A NEUROTIC FEAR OF THE WORLD COMING TO AN END...
ESPECIALLY BEFORE SUPPERTIME!
SCHULZ

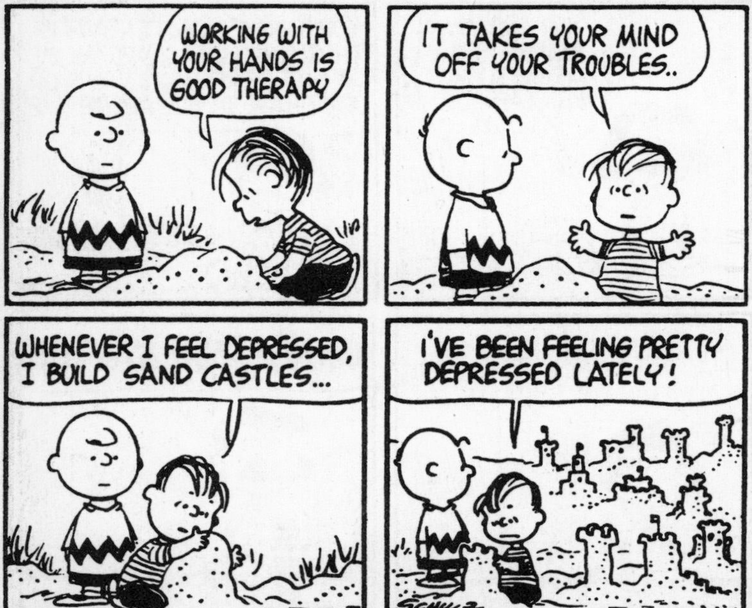
WORKING WITH YOUR HANDS IS GOOD THERAPY
IT TAKES YOUR MIND OFF YOUR TROUBLES..
WHENEVER I FEEL DEPRESSED, I BUILD SAND CASTLES...
I'VE BEEN FEELING PRETTY DEPRESSED LATELY!
SCHULZ

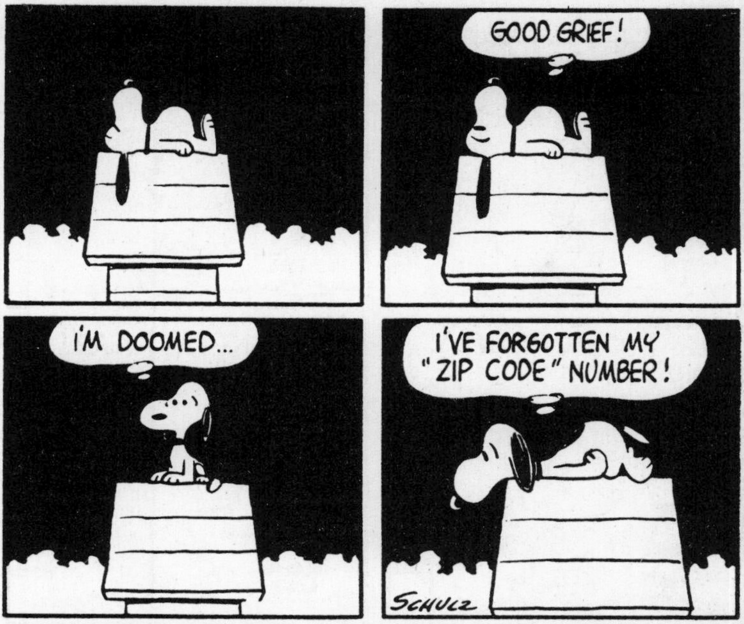
GOOD GRIEF!
I'M DOOMED...
I'VE FORGOTTEN MY "ZIP CODE" NUMBER!
SCHULZ

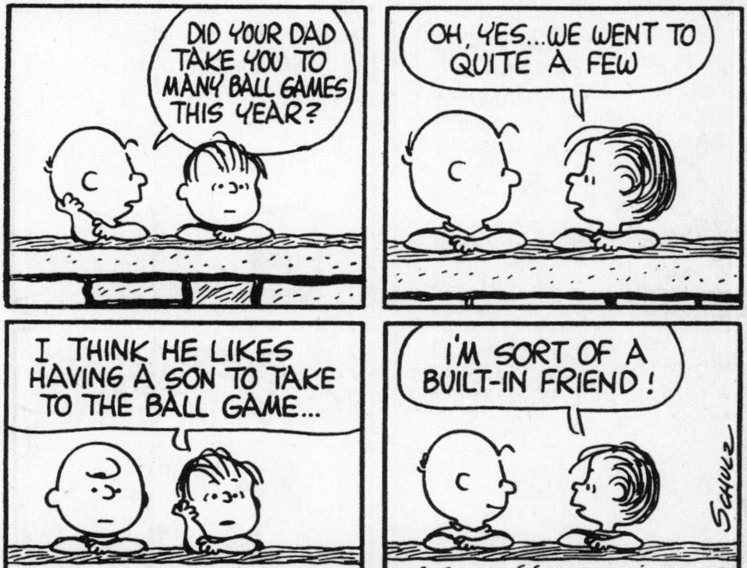
DID YOUR DAD TAKE YOU TO MANY BALL GAMES THIS YEAR?
OH, YES...WE WENT TO QUITE A FEW
I THINK HE LIKES HAVING A SON TO TAKE TO THE BALL GAME...
I'M SORT OF A BUILT-IN FRIEND!
SCHULZ

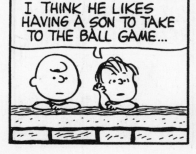

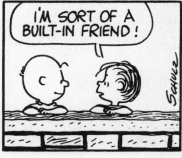

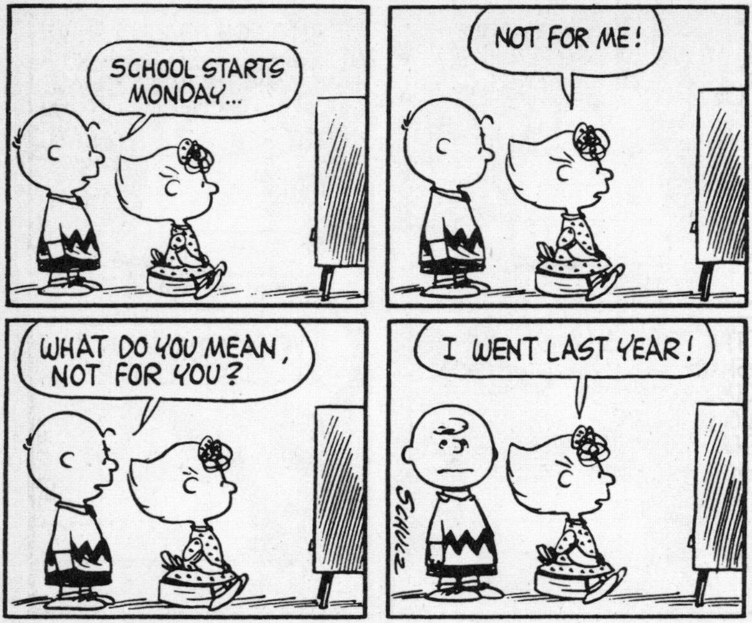
SCHOOL STARTS MONDAY...
NOT FOR ME!
WHAT DO YOU MEAN, NOT FOR YOU?
I WENT LAST YEAR!
SCHULZ

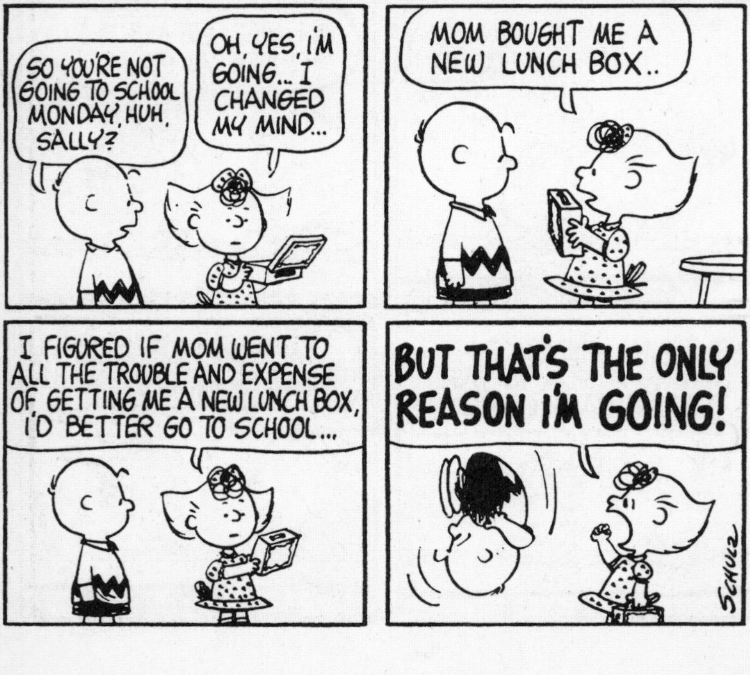
SO YOU'RE NOT GOING TO SCHOOL MONDAY, HUH, SALLY?
OH, YES, I'M GOING... I CHANGED MY MIND...
MOM BOUGHT ME A NEW LUNCH BOX..
I FIGURED IF MOM WENT TO ALL THE TROUBLE AND EXPENSE OF GETTING ME A NEW LUNCH BOX, I'D BETTER GO TO SCHOOL...
BUT THAT'S THE ONLY REASON I'M GOING!
SCHULZ

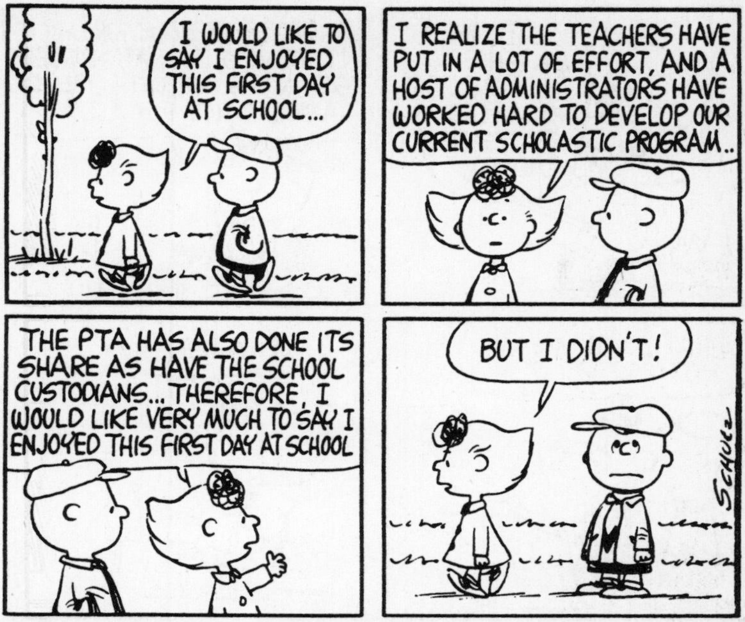
I WOULD LIKE TO SAY I ENJOYED THIS FIRST DAY AT SCHOOL...
I REALIZE THE TEACHERS HAVE PUT IN A LOT OF EFFORT, AND A HOST OF ADMINISTRATORS HAVE WORKED HARD TO DEVELOP OUR CURRENT SCHOLASTIC PROGRAM..
THE PTA HAS ALSO DONE ITS SHARE AS HAVE THE SCHOOL CUSTODIANS... THEREFORE, I WOULD LIKE VERY MUCH TO SAY I ENJOYED THIS FIRST DAY AT SCHOOL
BUT I DIDN'T!
SCHULZ

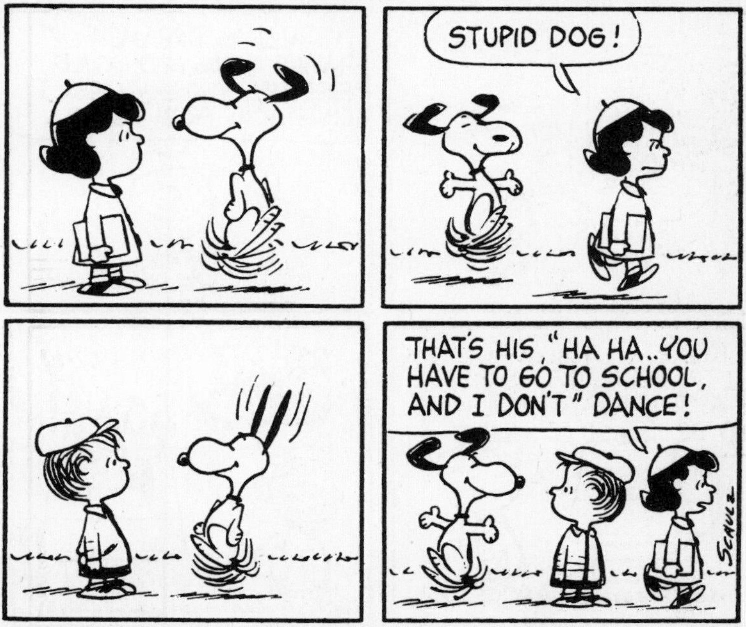
STUPID DOG!
THAT'S HIS, "HA HA..YOU HAVE TO GO TO SCHOOL, AND I DON'T" DANCE!
SCHULZ

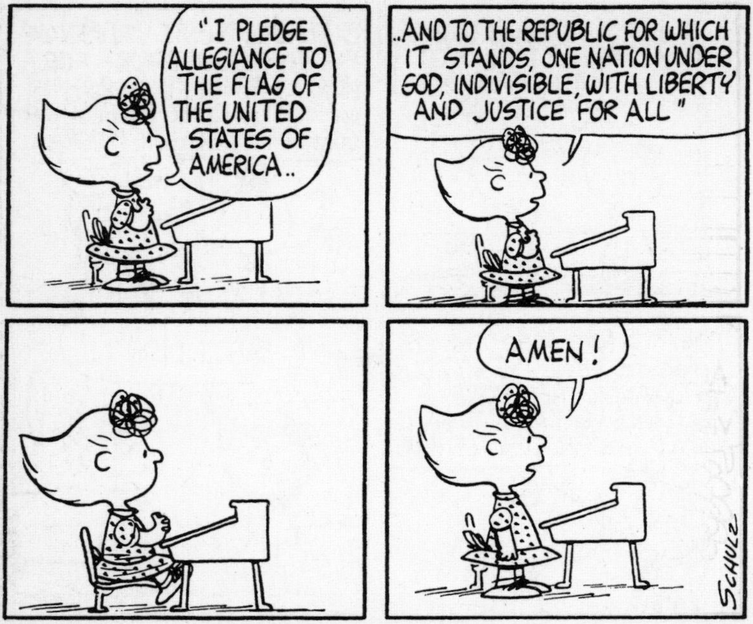
"I PLEDGE ALLEGIANCE TO THE FLAG OF THE UNITED STATES OF AMERICA..
..AND TO THE REPUBLIC FOR WHICH IT STANDS, ONE NATION UNDER GOD, INDIVISIBLE, WITH LIBERTY AND JUSTICE FOR ALL"
AMEN!
SCHULZ

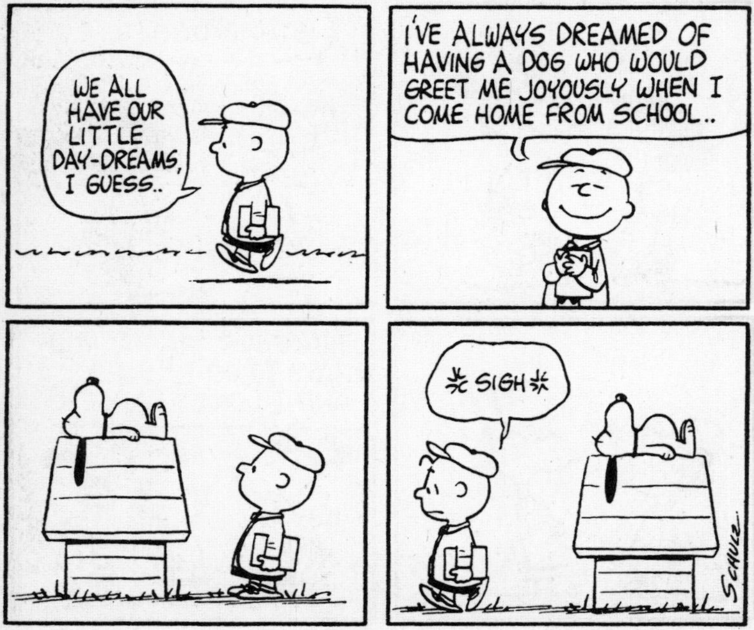
WE ALL HAVE OUR LITTLE DAY-DREAMS, I GUESS..
I'VE ALWAYS DREAMED OF HAVING A DOG WHO WOULD GREET ME JOYOUSLY WHEN I COME HOME FROM SCHOOL..
SIGH
SCHULZ

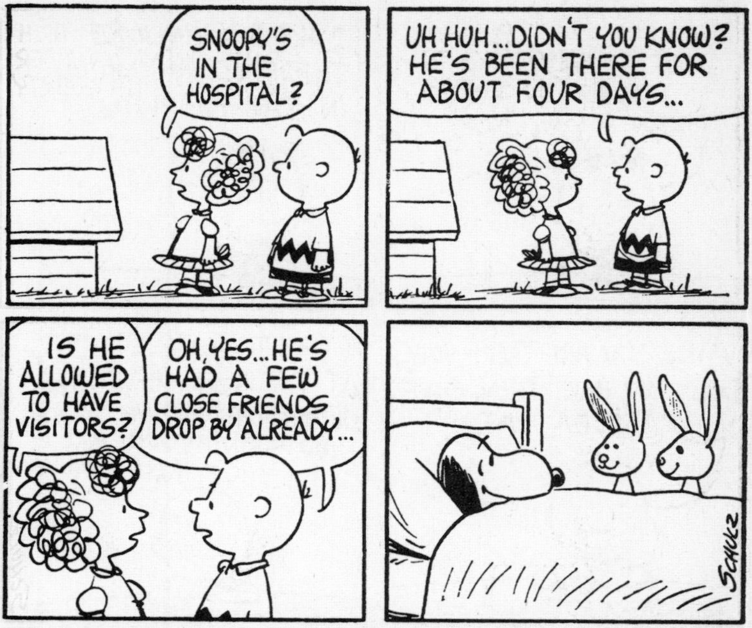
SNOOPY'S IN THE HOSPITAL?
UH HUH...DIDN'T YOU KNOW? HE'S BEEN THERE FOR ABOUT FOUR DAYS...
IS HE ALLOWED TO HAVE VISITORS?
OH, YES...HE'S HAD A FEW CLOSE FRIENDS DROP BY ALREADY...
SCHULZ

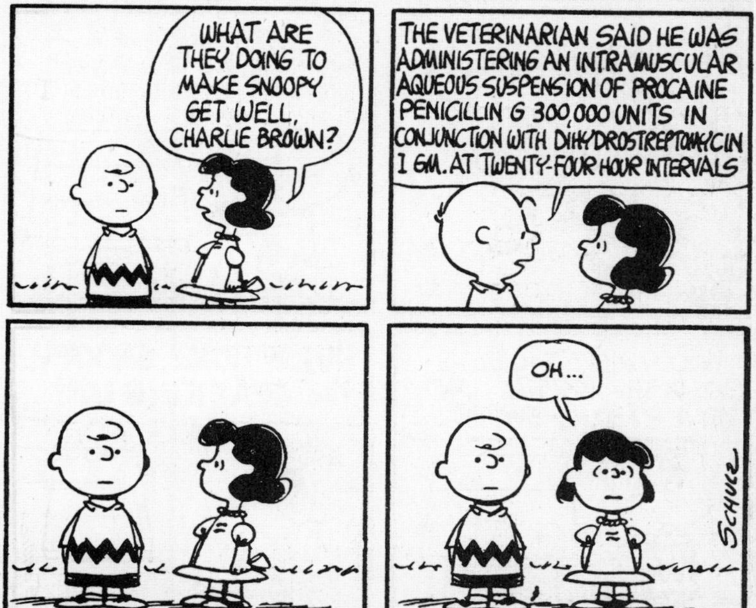
WHAT ARE THEY DOING TO MAKE SNOOPY GET WELL, CHARLIE BROWN?
THE VETERINARIAN SAID HE WAS ADMINISTERING AN INTRAMUSCULAR AQUEOUS SUSPENSION OF PROCAINE PENICILLIN G 300,000 UNITS IN CONJUNCTION WITH DIHYDROSTREPTOMYCIN 1 GM. AT TWENTY-FOUR HOUR INTERVALS
OH...
SCHULZ

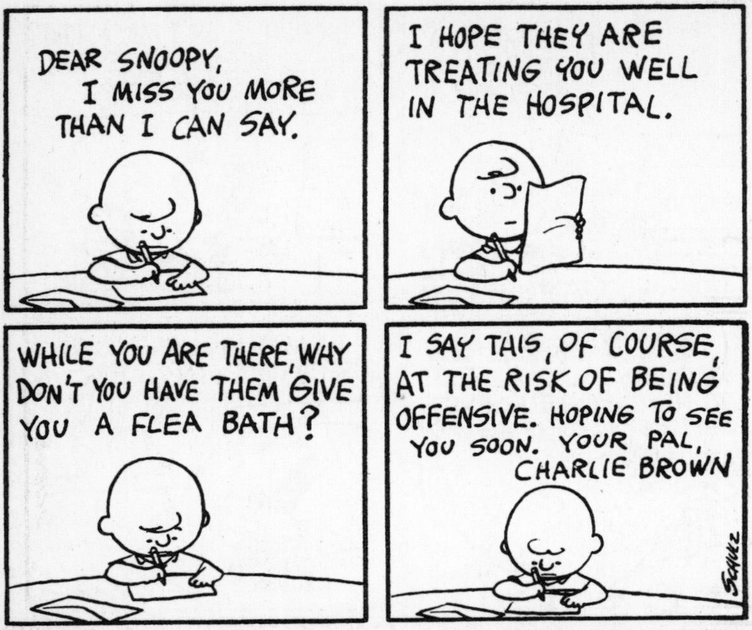
DEAR SNOOPY,
I MISS YOU MORE THAN I CAN SAY.
I HOPE THEY ARE TREATING YOU WELL IN THE HOSPITAL.
WHILE YOU ARE THERE, WHY DON'T YOU HAVE THEM GIVE YOU A FLEA BATH?
I SAY THIS, OF COURSE, AT THE RISK OF BEING OFFENSIVE. HOPING TO SEE YOU SOON. YOUR PAL,
CHARLIE BROWN
SCHULZ

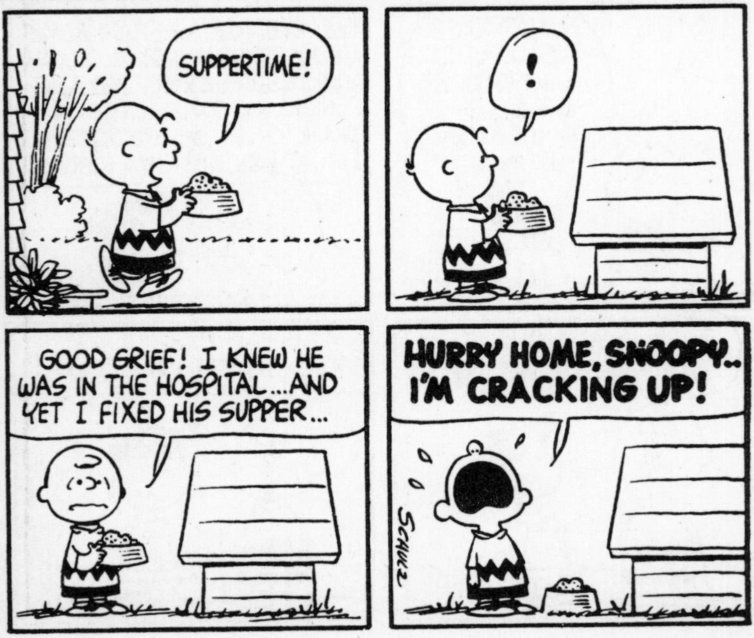
SUPPERTIME!
!
GOOD GRIEF! I KNEW HE WAS IN THE HOSPITAL...AND YET I FIXED HIS SUPPER...
HURRY HOME, SNOOPY.. I'M CRACKING UP!
SCHULZ

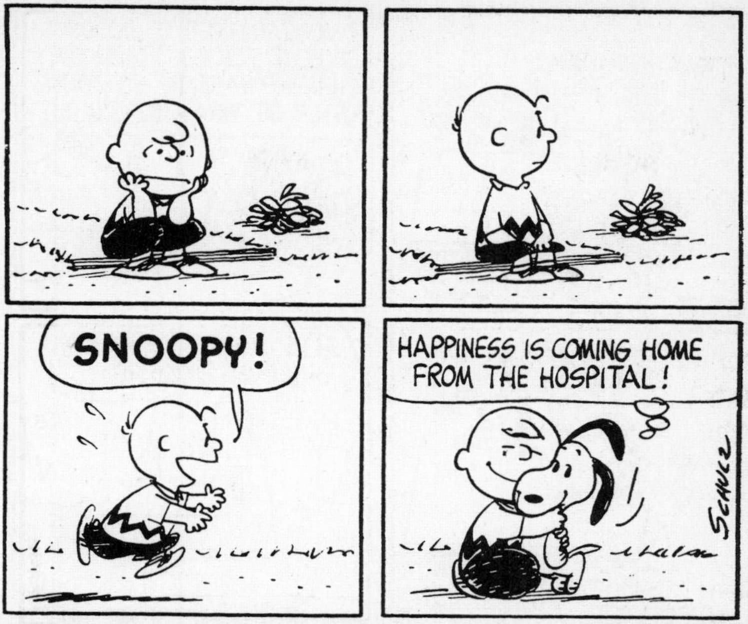
SNOOPY!
HAPPINESS IS COMING HOME FROM THE HOSPITAL!
SCHULZ

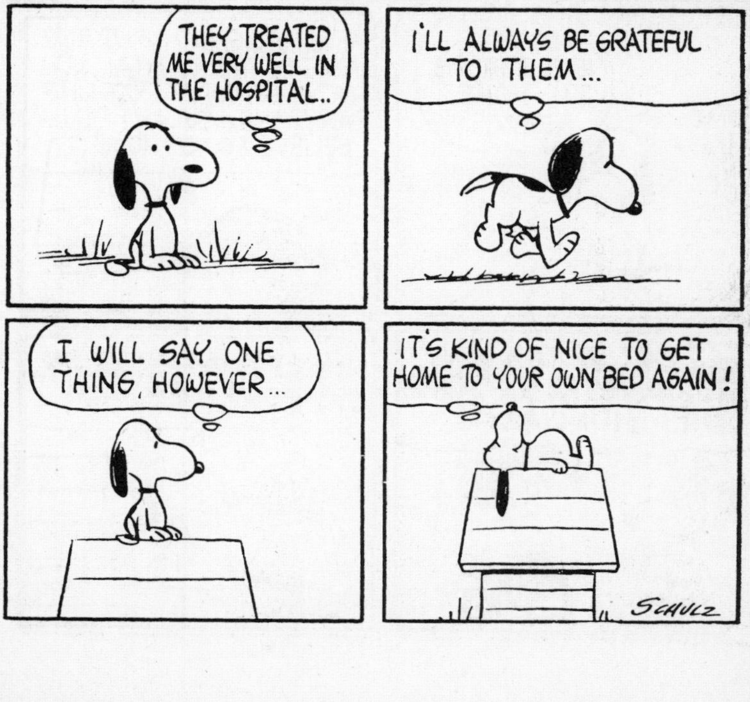
THEY TREATED ME VERY WELL IN THE HOSPITAL..
I'LL ALWAYS BE GRATEFUL TO THEM...
I WILL SAY ONE THING, HOWEVER...
IT'S KIND OF NICE TO GET HOME TO YOUR OWN BED AGAIN!
SCHULZ

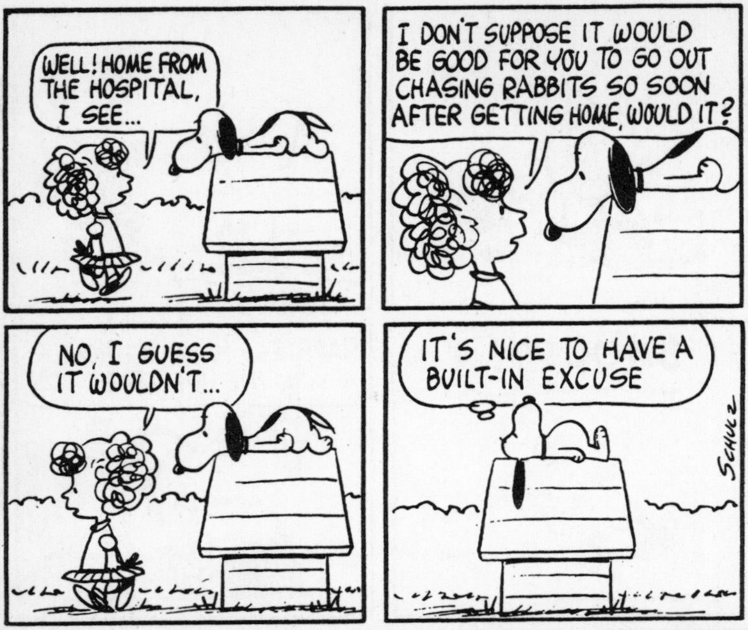
WELL! HOME FROM THE HOSPITAL, I SEE...
I DON'T SUPPOSE IT WOULD BE GOOD FOR YOU TO GO OUT CHASING RABBITS SO SOON AFTER GETTING HOME, WOULD IT?
NO, I GUESS IT WOULDN'T...
IT'S NICE TO HAVE A BUILT-IN EXCUSE
SCHULZ

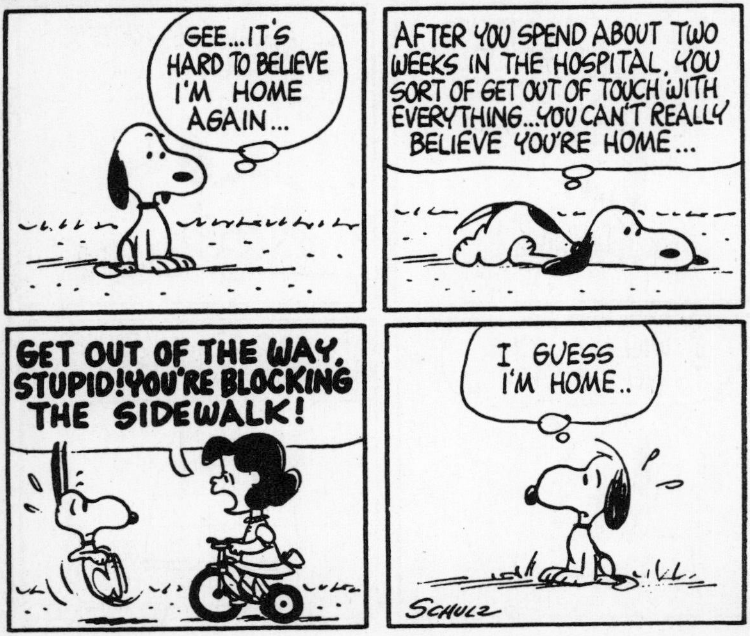
GEE...IT'S HARD TO BELIEVE I'M HOME AGAIN...
AFTER YOU SPEND ABOUT TWO WEEKS IN THE HOSPITAL, YOU SORT OF GET OUT OF TOUCH WITH EVERYTHING...YOU CAN'T REALLY BELIEVE YOU'RE HOME...
GET OUT OF THE WAY, STUPID! YOU'RE BLOCKING THE SIDEWALK!
I GUESS I'M HOME..
SCHULZ

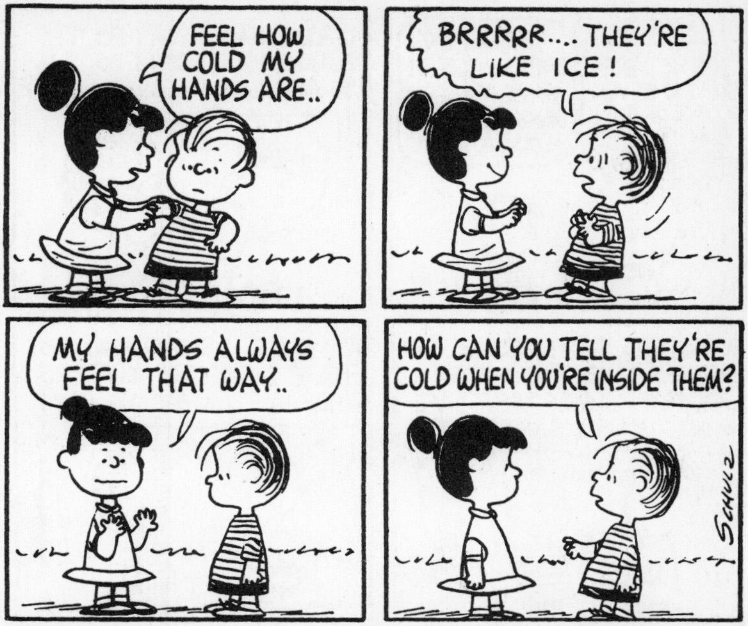
FEEL HOW COLD MY HANDS ARE..
BRRRRR.... THEY'RE LIKE ICE!
MY HANDS ALWAYS FEEL THAT WAY..
HOW CAN YOU TELL THEY'RE COLD WHEN YOU'RE INSIDE THEM?
SCHULZ

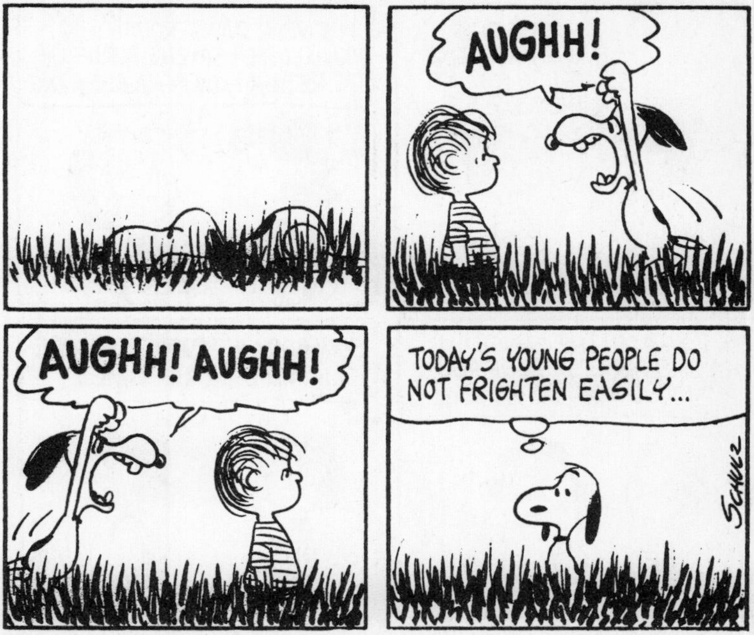
AUGHH!
AUGHH! AUGHH!
TODAY'S YOUNG PEOPLE DO NOT FRIGHTEN EASILY...
SCHULZ

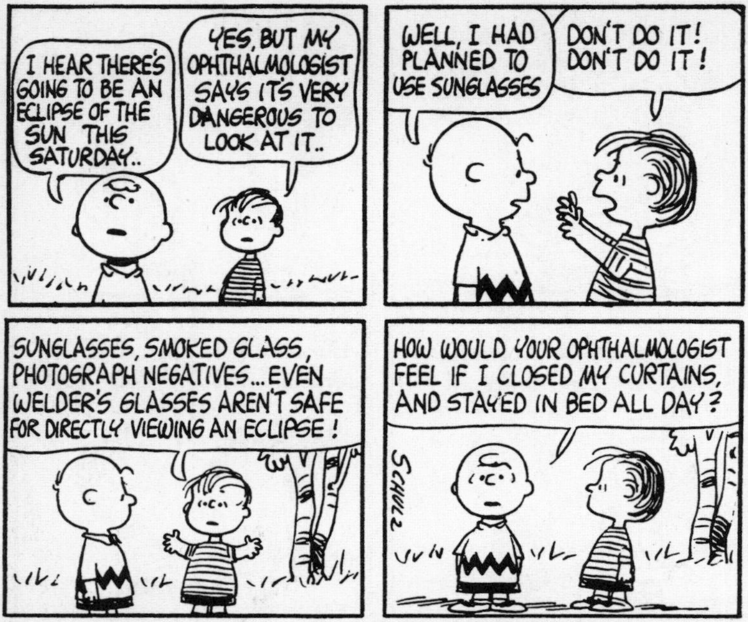
I HEAR THERE'S GOING TO BE AN ECLIPSE OF THE SUN THIS SATURDAY..
YES, BUT MY OPHTHALMOLOGIST SAYS IT'S VERY DANGEROUS TO LOOK AT IT..
WELL, I HAD PLANNED TO USE SUNGLASSES
DON'T DO IT! DON'T DO IT!
SUNGLASSES, SMOKED GLASS, PHOTOGRAPH NEGATIVES...EVEN WELDER'S GLASSES AREN'T SAFE FOR DIRECTLY VIEWING AN ECLIPSE!
HOW WOULD YOUR OPHTHALMOLOGIST FEEL IF I CLOSED MY CURTAINS, AND STAYED IN BED ALL DAY?
SCHULZ

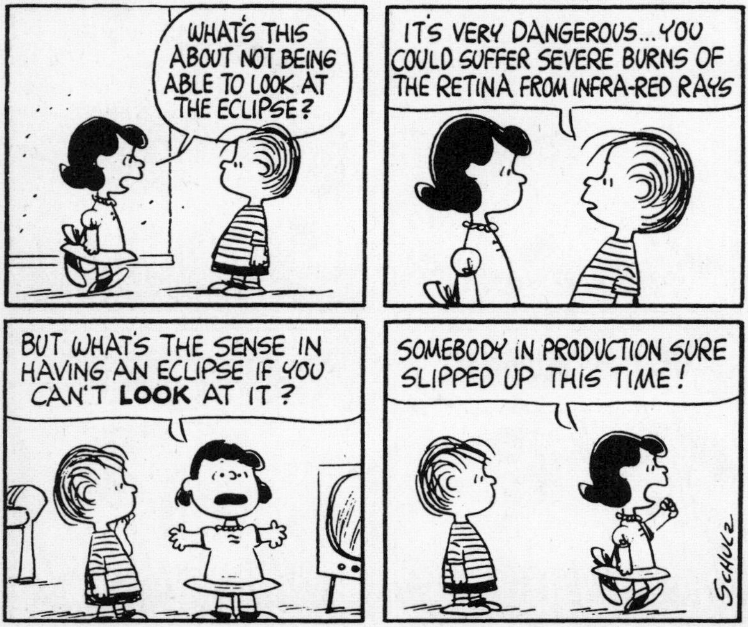
WHAT'S THIS ABOUT NOT BEING ABLE TO LOOK AT THE ECLIPSE?
IT'S VERY DANGEROUS...YOU COULD SUFFER SEVERE BURNS OF THE RETINA FROM INFRA-RED RAYS
BUT WHAT'S THE SENSE IN HAVING AN ECLIPSE IF YOU CAN'T LOOK AT IT?
SOMEBODY IN PRODUCTION SURE SLIPPED UP THIS TIME!
SCHULZ

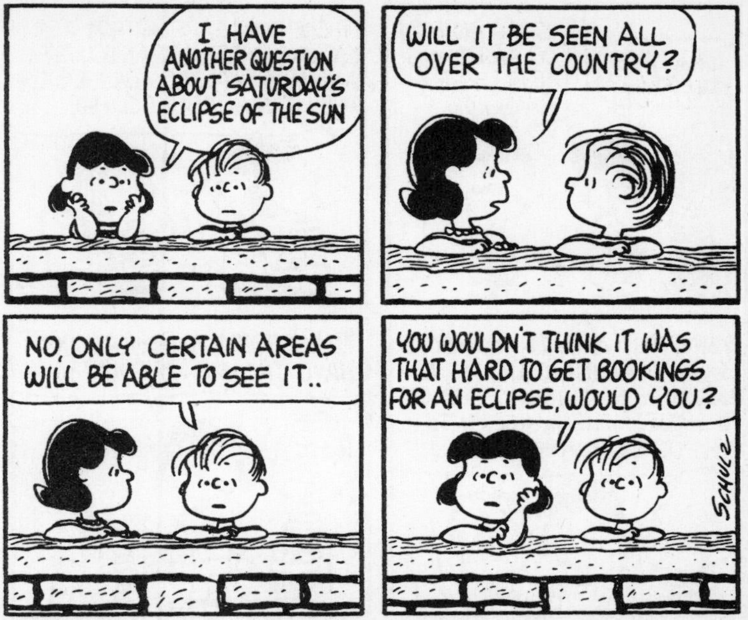
I HAVE ANOTHER QUESTION ABOUT SATURDAY'S ECLIPSE OF THE SUN
WILL IT BE SEEN ALL OVER THE COUNTRY?
NO, ONLY CERTAIN AREAS WILL BE ABLE TO SEE IT..
YOU WOULDN'T THINK IT WAS THAT HARD TO GET BOOKINGS FOR AN ECLIPSE, WOULD YOU?
SCHULZ

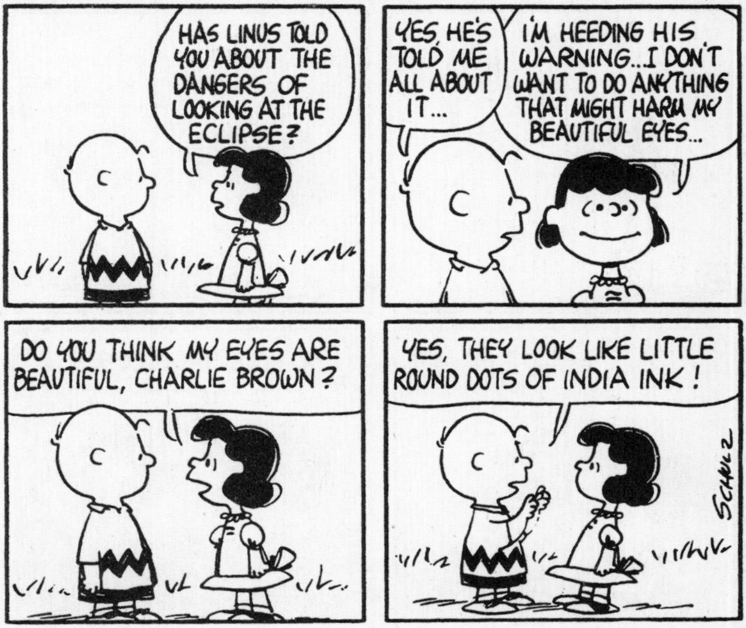
HAS LINUS TOLD YOU ABOUT THE DANGERS OF LOOKING AT THE ECLIPSE?
YES, HE'S TOLD ME ALL ABOUT IT...
I'M HEEDING HIS WARNING...I DON'T WANT TO DO ANYTHING THAT MIGHT HARM MY BEAUTIFUL EYES...
DO YOU THINK MY EYES ARE BEAUTIFUL, CHARLIE BROWN?
YES, THEY LOOK LIKE LITTLE ROUND DOTS OF INDIA INK!
SCHULZ

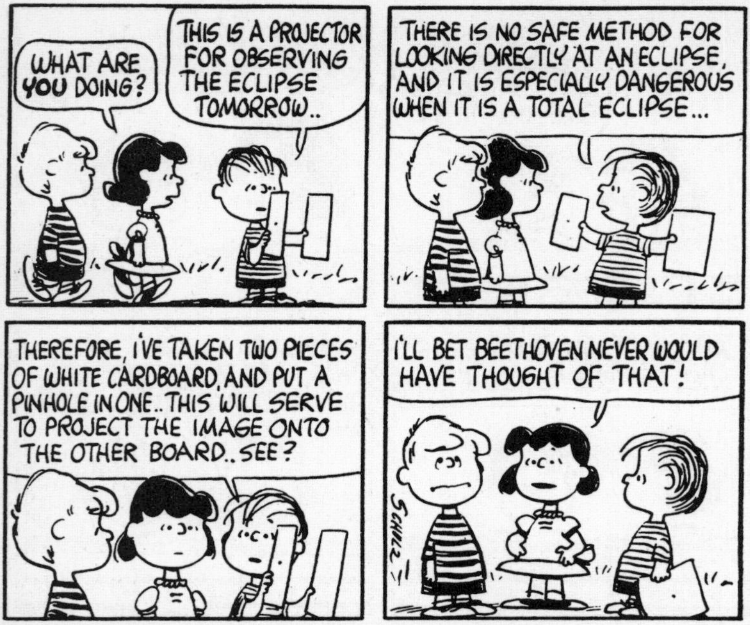
WHAT ARE YOU DOING?
THIS IS A PROJECTOR FOR OBSERVING THE ECLIPSE TOMORROW..
THERE IS NO SAFE METHOD FOR LOOKING DIRECTLY AT AN ECLIPSE, AND IT IS ESPECIALLY DANGEROUS WHEN IT IS A TOTAL ECLIPSE...
THEREFORE, I'VE TAKEN TWO PIECES OF WHITE CARDBOARD, AND PUT A PINHOLE IN ONE.. THIS WILL SERVE TO PROJECT THE IMAGE ONTO THE OTHER BOARD.. SEE?
I'LL BET BEETHOVEN NEVER WOULD HAVE THOUGHT OF THAT!

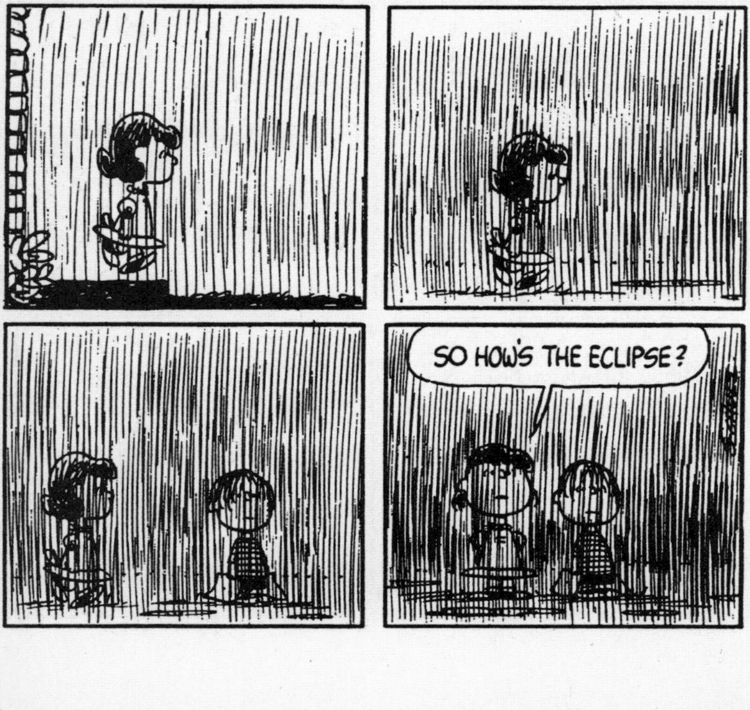
SO HOW'S THE ECLIPSE?

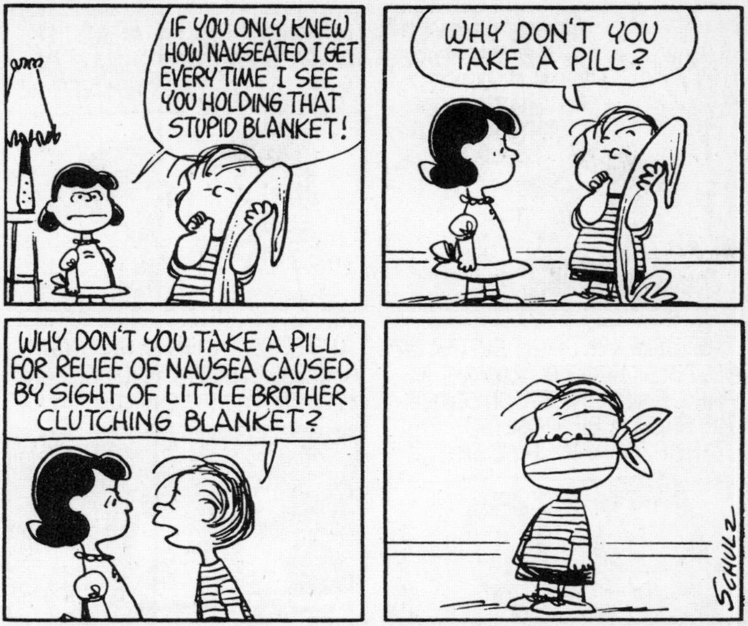
IF YOU ONLY KNEW HOW NAUSEATED I GET EVERY TIME I SEE YOU HOLDING THAT STUPID BLANKET!
WHY DON'T YOU TAKE A PILL?
WHY DON'T YOU TAKE A PILL FOR RELIEF OF NAUSEA CAUSED BY SIGHT OF LITTLE BROTHER CLUTCHING BLANKET?
SCHULZ

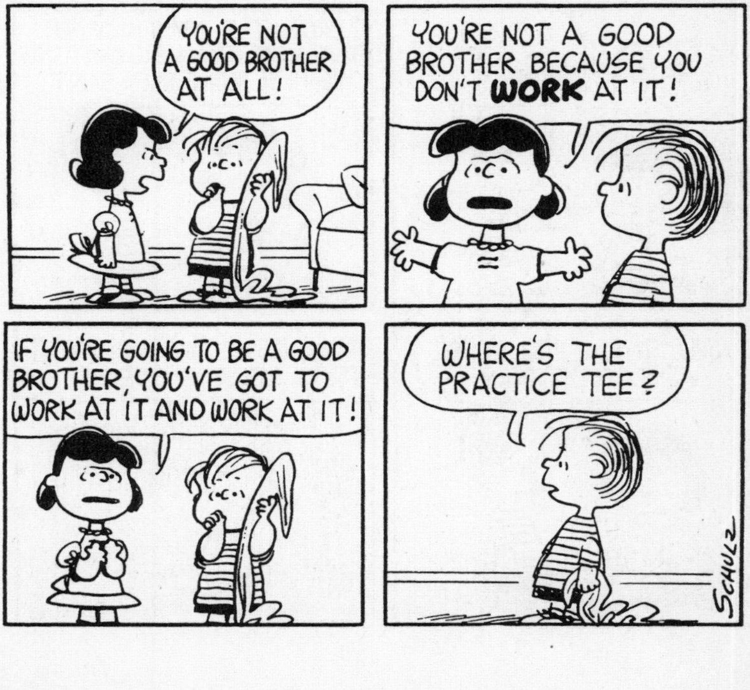
YOU'RE NOT A GOOD BROTHER AT ALL!
YOU'RE NOT A GOOD BROTHER BECAUSE YOU DON'T **WORK** AT IT!
IF YOU'RE GOING TO BE A GOOD BROTHER, YOU'VE GOT TO WORK AT IT AND WORK AT IT!
WHERE'S THE PRACTICE TEE?
SCHULZ

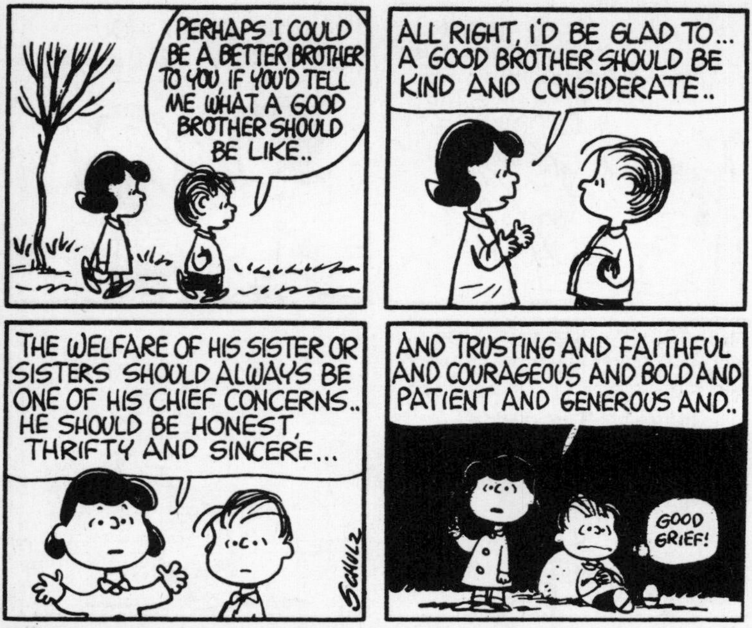
PERHAPS I COULD BE A BETTER BROTHER TO YOU, IF YOU'D TELL ME WHAT A GOOD BROTHER SHOULD BE LIKE..
ALL RIGHT, I'D BE GLAD TO... A GOOD BROTHER SHOULD BE KIND AND CONSIDERATE..
THE WELFARE OF HIS SISTER OR SISTERS SHOULD ALWAYS BE ONE OF HIS CHIEF CONCERNS.. HE SHOULD BE HONEST, THRIFTY AND SINCERE...
SCHULZ
AND TRUSTING AND FAITHFUL AND COURAGEOUS AND BOLD AND PATIENT AND GENEROUS AND..
GOOD GRIEF!

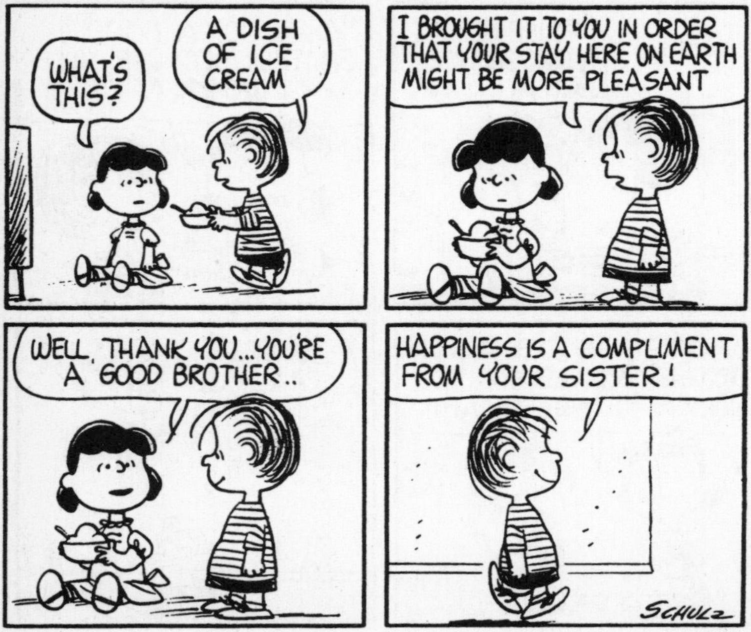
WHAT'S THIS?
A DISH OF ICE CREAM
I BROUGHT IT TO YOU IN ORDER THAT YOUR STAY HERE ON EARTH MIGHT BE MORE PLEASANT
WELL, THANK YOU...YOU'RE A GOOD BROTHER..
HAPPINESS IS A COMPLIMENT FROM YOUR SISTER!
SCHULZ

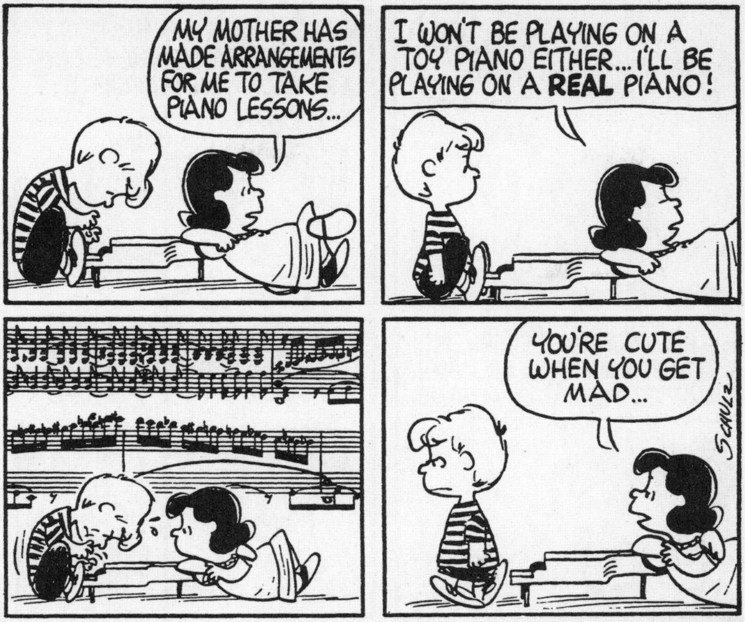
MY MOTHER HAS MADE ARRANGEMENTS FOR ME TO TAKE PIANO LESSONS...
I WON'T BE PLAYING ON A TOY PIANO EITHER... I'LL BE PLAYING ON A **REAL** PIANO!
YOU'RE CUTE WHEN YOU GET MAD...
SCHULZ

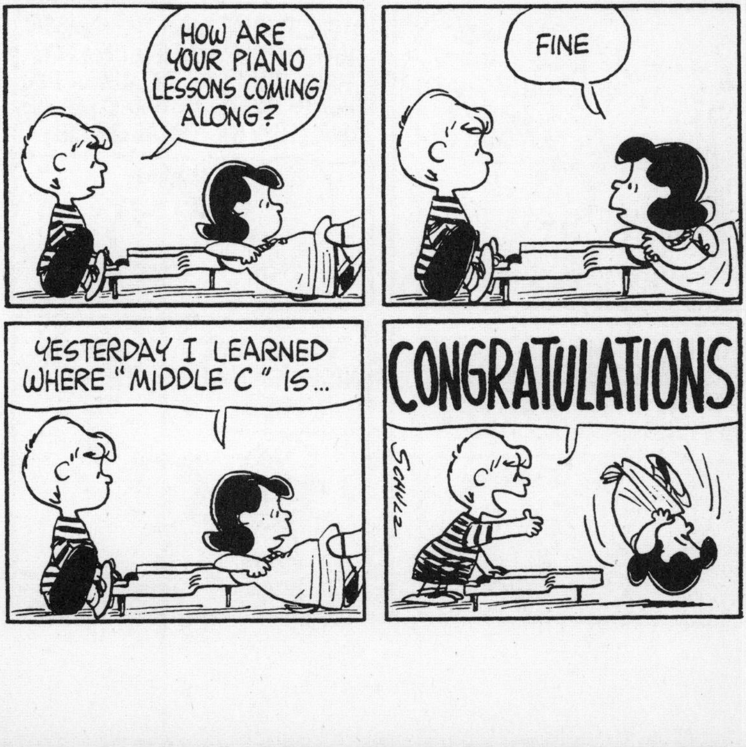
HOW ARE YOUR PIANO LESSONS COMING ALONG?
FINE
YESTERDAY I LEARNED WHERE "MIDDLE C" IS...
CONGRATULATIONS
SCHULZ

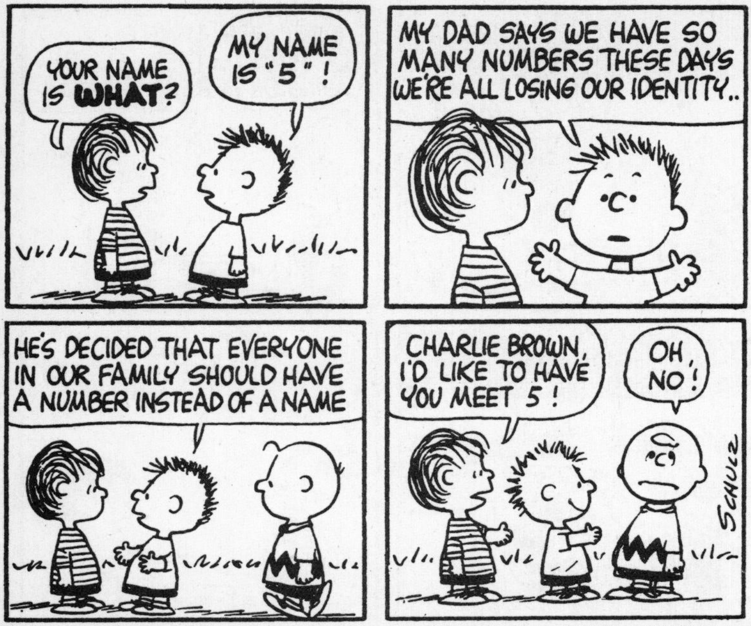
YOUR NAME IS WHAT?
MY NAME IS "5"!
MY DAD SAYS WE HAVE SO MANY NUMBERS THESE DAYS WE'RE ALL LOSING OUR IDENTITY..
HE'S DECIDED THAT EVERYONE IN OUR FAMILY SHOULD HAVE A NUMBER INSTEAD OF A NAME
CHARLIE BROWN, I'D LIKE TO HAVE YOU MEET 5!
OH NO!
SCHULZ

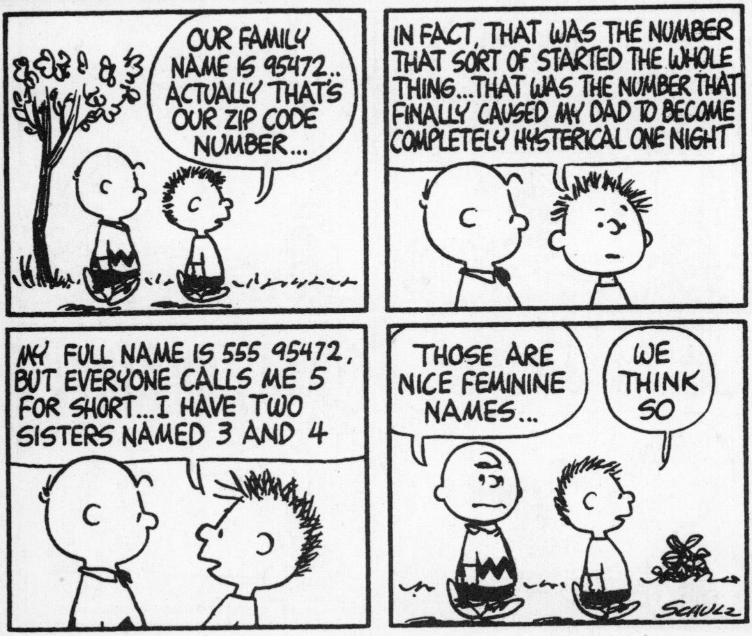
OUR FAMILY NAME IS 95472.. ACTUALLY THAT'S OUR ZIP CODE NUMBER...
IN FACT, THAT WAS THE NUMBER THAT SORT OF STARTED THE WHOLE THING...THAT WAS THE NUMBER THAT FINALLY CAUSED MY DAD TO BECOME COMPLETELY HYSTERICAL ONE NIGHT
MY FULL NAME IS 555 95472, BUT EVERYONE CALLS ME 5 FOR SHORT...I HAVE TWO SISTERS NAMED 3 AND 4
THOSE ARE NICE FEMININE NAMES...
WE THINK SO
SCHULZ

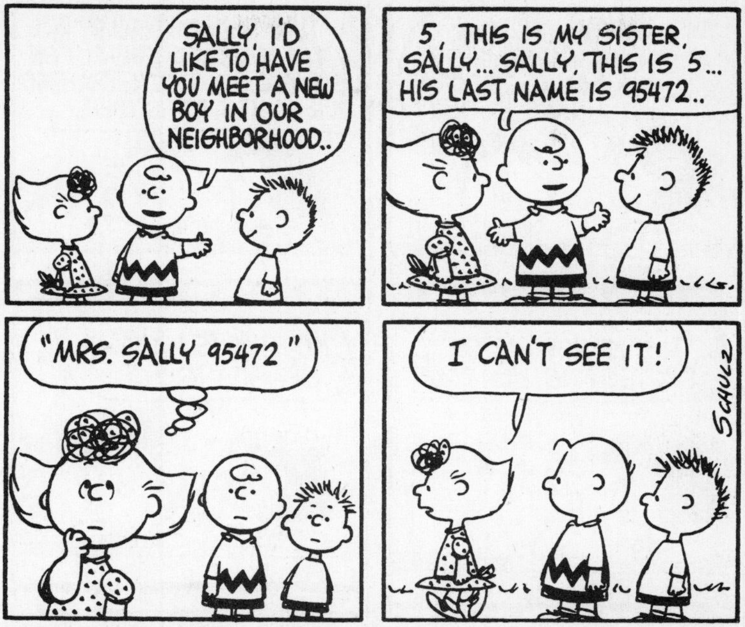
SALLY, I'D LIKE TO HAVE YOU MEET A NEW BOY IN OUR NEIGHBORHOOD..
5, THIS IS MY SISTER, SALLY... SALLY, THIS IS 5... HIS LAST NAME IS 95472..
"MRS. SALLY 95472"
I CAN'T SEE IT!
SCHULZ

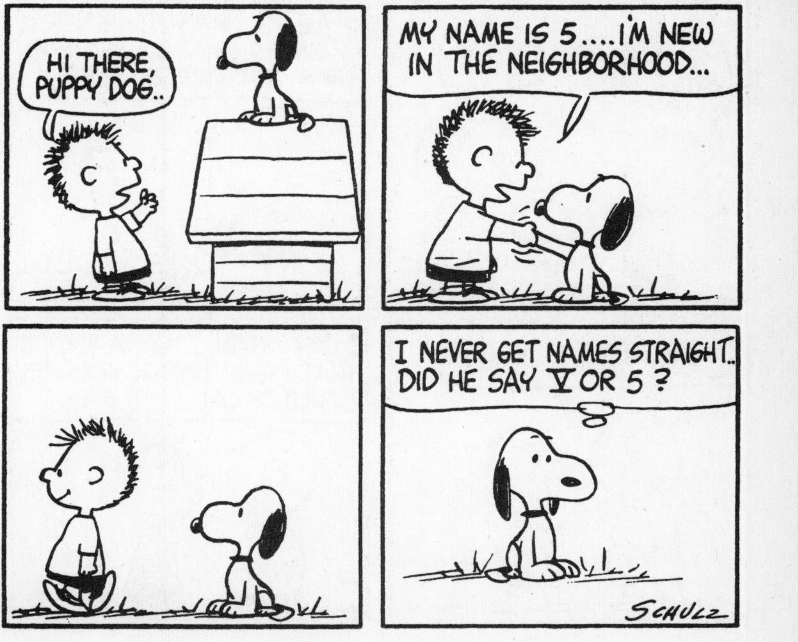
HI THERE, PUPPY DOG..
MY NAME IS 5.....I'M NEW IN THE NEIGHBORHOOD...
I NEVER GET NAMES STRAIGHT.. DID HE SAY V OR 5 ?
SCHULZ

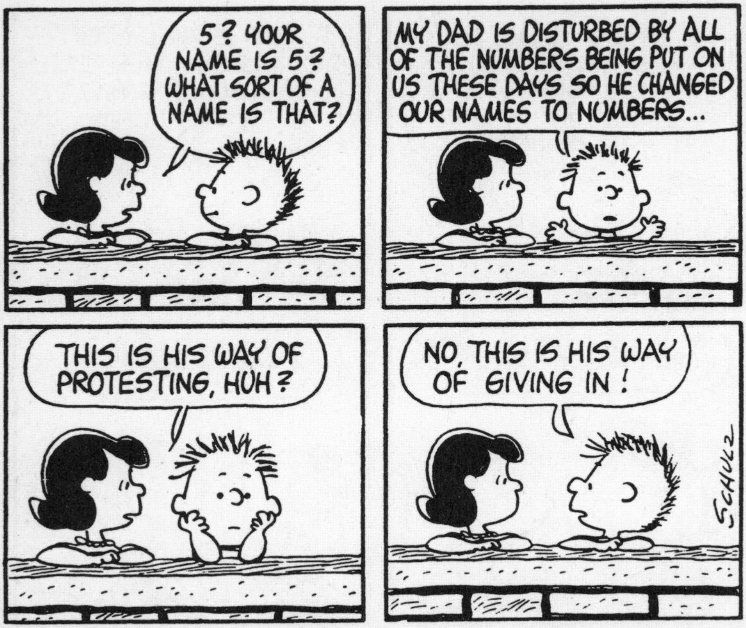
5? YOUR NAME IS 5? WHAT SORT OF A NAME IS THAT?
MY DAD IS DISTURBED BY ALL OF THE NUMBERS BEING PUT ON US THESE DAYS SO HE CHANGED OUR NAMES TO NUMBERS...
THIS IS HIS WAY OF PROTESTING, HUH?
NO, THIS IS HIS WAY OF GIVING IN!
SCHULZ

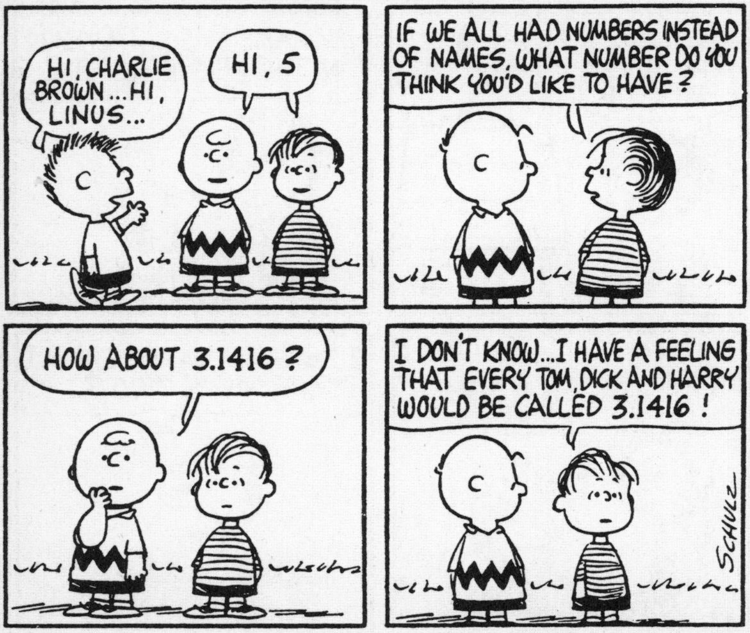
HI, CHARLIE BROWN...HI, LINUS...
HI, 5
IF WE ALL HAD NUMBERS INSTEAD OF NAMES, WHAT NUMBER DO YOU THINK YOU'D LIKE TO HAVE?
HOW ABOUT 3.1416?
I DON'T KNOW...I HAVE A FEELING THAT EVERY TOM, DICK AND HARRY WOULD BE CALLED 3.1416!
SCHULZ

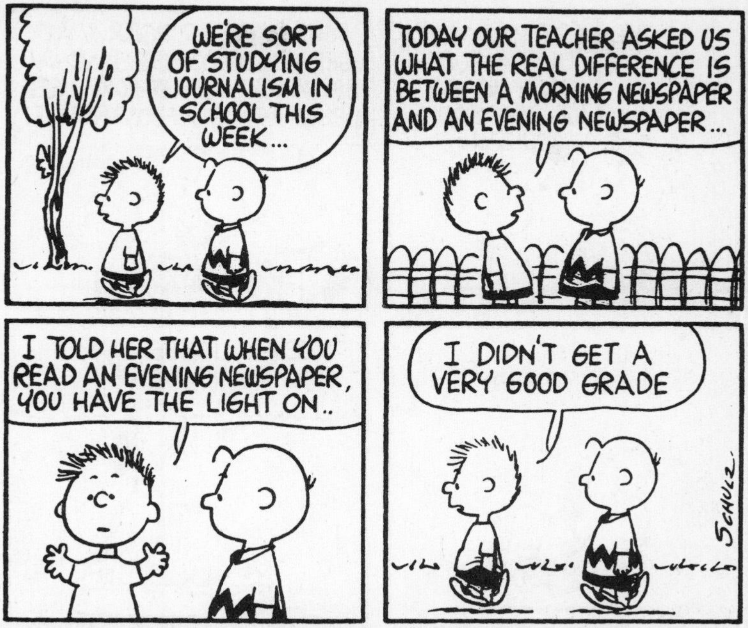
WE'RE SORT OF STUDYING JOURNALISM IN SCHOOL THIS WEEK...
TODAY OUR TEACHER ASKED US WHAT THE REAL DIFFERENCE IS BETWEEN A MORNING NEWSPAPER AND AN EVENING NEWSPAPER...
I TOLD HER THAT WHEN YOU READ AN EVENING NEWSPAPER, YOU HAVE THE LIGHT ON..
I DIDN'T GET A VERY GOOD GRADE
SCHULZ

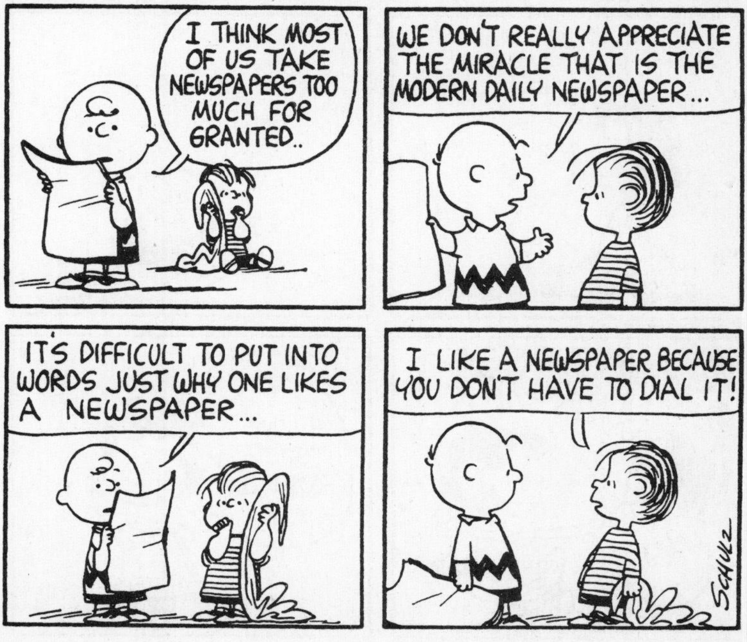
I THINK MOST OF US TAKE NEWSPAPERS TOO MUCH FOR GRANTED..
WE DON'T REALLY APPRECIATE THE MIRACLE THAT IS THE MODERN DAILY NEWSPAPER...
IT'S DIFFICULT TO PUT INTO WORDS JUST WHY ONE LIKES A NEWSPAPER...
I LIKE A NEWSPAPER BECAUSE YOU DON'T HAVE TO DIAL IT!
SCHULZ

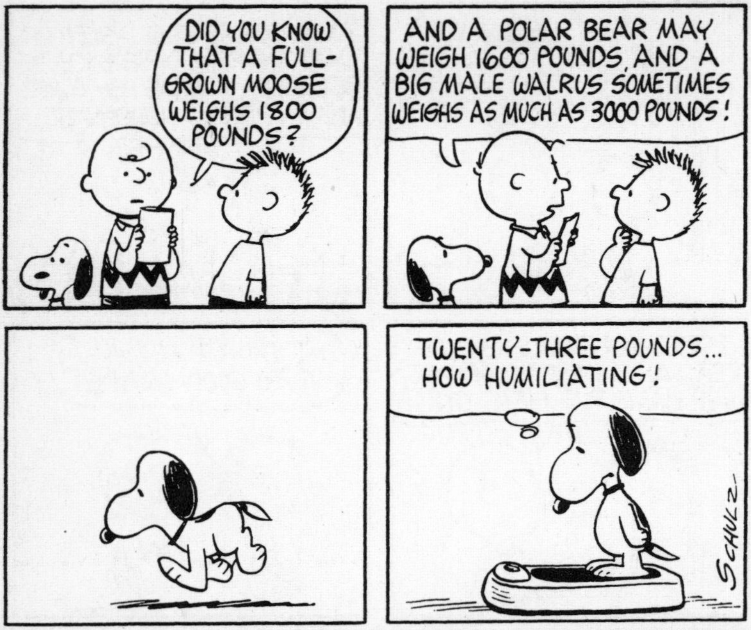
DID YOU KNOW THAT A FULL-GROWN MOOSE WEIGHS 1800 POUNDS?
AND A POLAR BEAR MAY WEIGH 1600 POUNDS, AND A BIG MALE WALRUS SOMETIMES WEIGHS AS MUCH AS 3000 POUNDS!
TWENTY-THREE POUNDS... HOW HUMILIATING!
SCHULZ

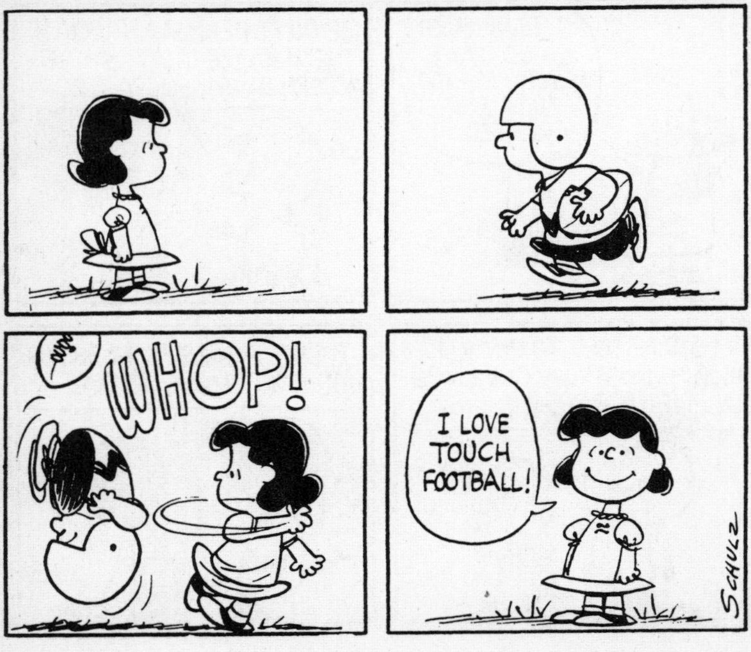
WHOP!
I LOVE TOUCH FOOTBALL!
SCHULZ

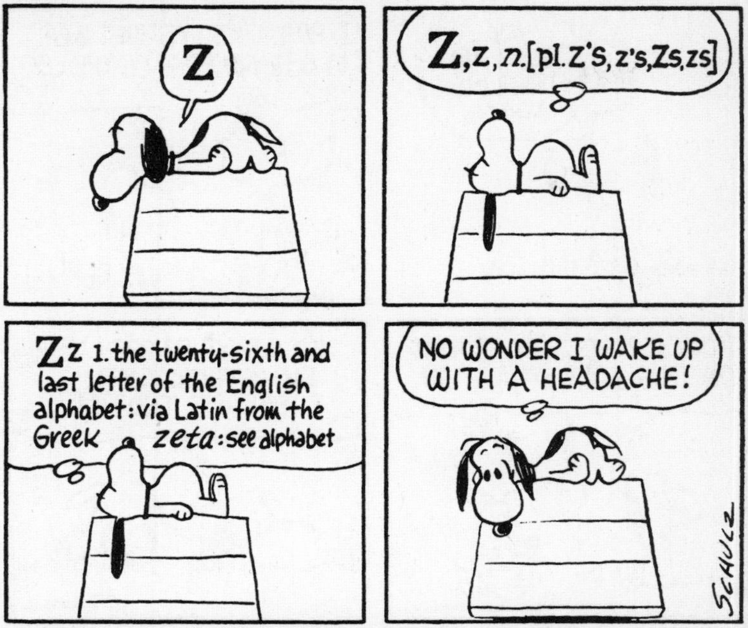
Z
Z,z,n.[pl.Z's,z's,Zs,zs]
Zz 1. the twenty-sixth and last letter of the English alphabet: via Latin from the Greek zeta: see alphabet
NO WONDER I WAKE UP WITH A HEADACHE!
SCHULZ

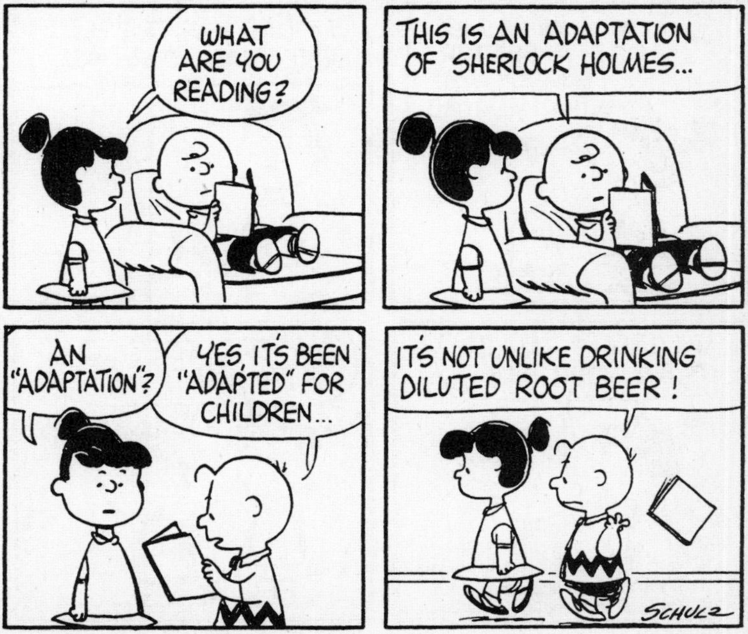
WHAT ARE YOU READING?
THIS IS AN ADAPTATION OF SHERLOCK HOLMES...
AN "ADAPTATION"?
YES, IT'S BEEN "ADAPTED" FOR CHILDREN...
IT'S NOT UNLIKE DRINKING DILUTED ROOT BEER!
SCHULZ

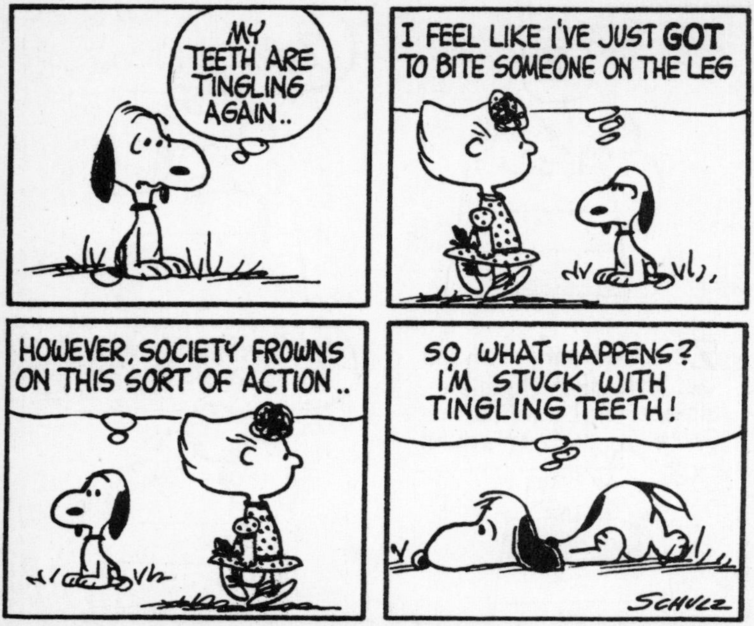
MY TEETH ARE TINGLING AGAIN..
I FEEL LIKE I'VE JUST GOT TO BITE SOMEONE ON THE LEG
HOWEVER, SOCIETY FROWNS ON THIS SORT OF ACTION..
SO WHAT HAPPENS? I'M STUCK WITH TINGLING TEETH!
SCHULZ

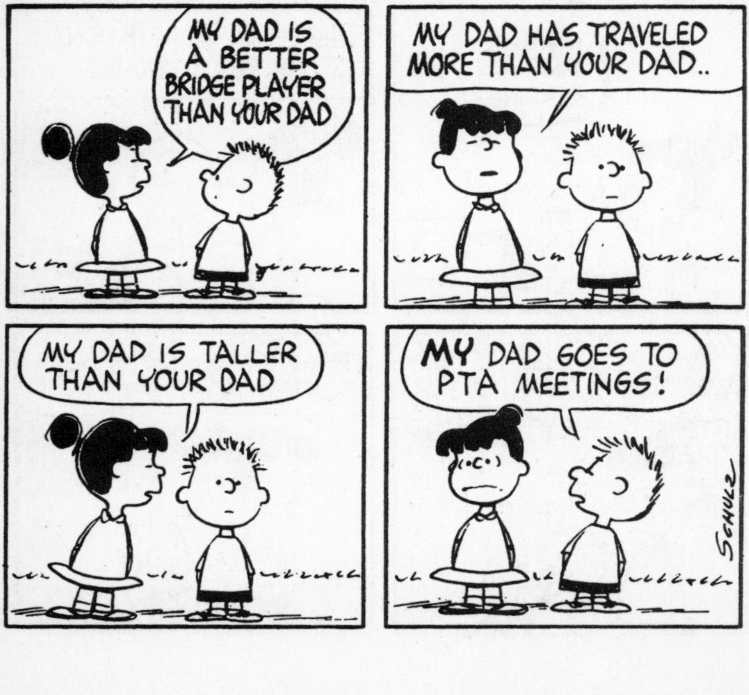
MY DAD IS A BETTER BRIDGE PLAYER THAN YOUR DAD
MY DAD HAS TRAVELED MORE THAN YOUR DAD..
MY DAD IS TALLER THAN YOUR DAD
MY DAD GOES TO PTA MEETINGS!
SCHULZ

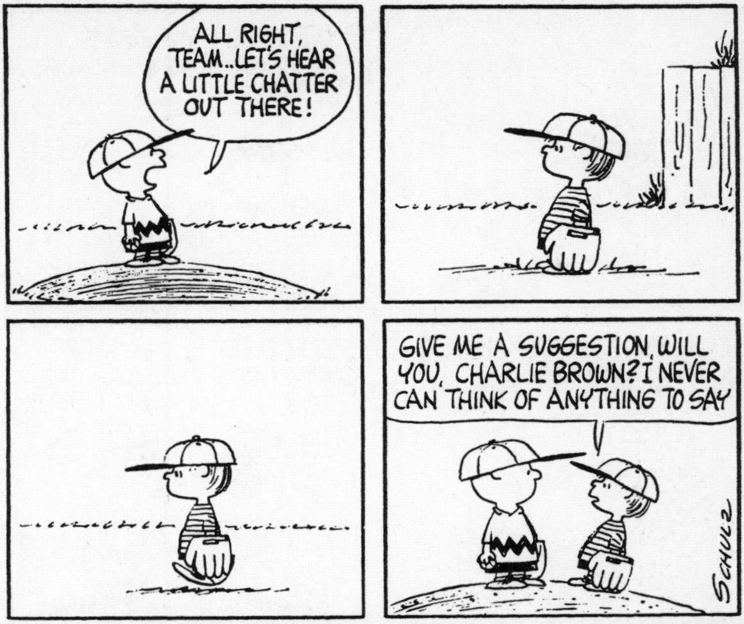
ALL RIGHT, TEAM..LET'S HEAR A LITTLE CHATTER OUT THERE!
GIVE ME A SUGGESTION, WILL YOU, CHARLIE BROWN? I NEVER CAN THINK OF ANYTHING TO SAY
SCHULZ

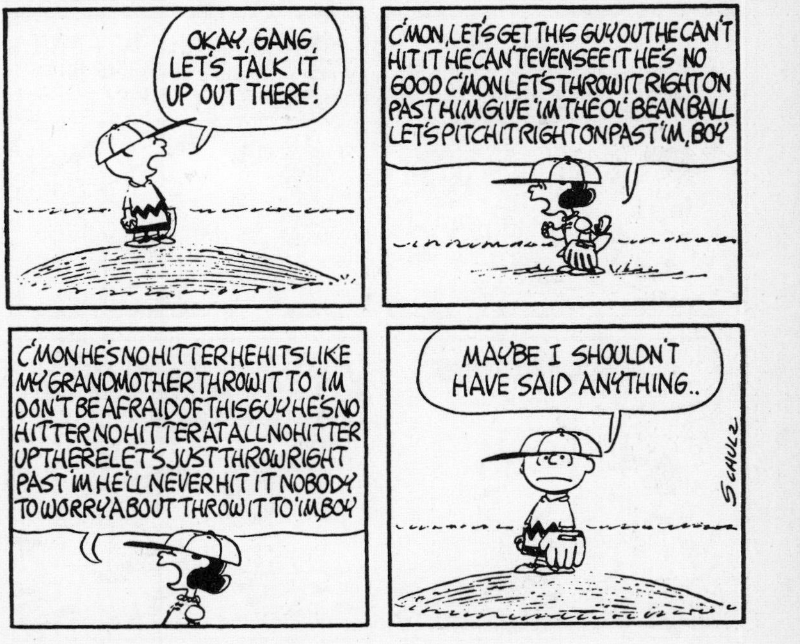
OKAY, GANG, LET'S TALK IT UP OUT THERE!
C'MON,LET'SGETTHISGUYOUTHECAN'T HITITHECAN'TEVENSEEIT HE'S NO GOOD C'MONLET'STHROWITRIGHTON PASTHIMGIVE 'IMTHEOL' BEANBALL LET'SPITCHITRIGHTONPAST'IM,BOY
C'MONHE'SNOHITTERHEHITSLIKE MYGRANDMOTHERTHROWITTO'IM DON'TBEAFRAIDOFTHISGUYHE'SNO HITTERNOHITTERATALLNOHITTER UPTHERELET'SJUSTTHROWRIGHT PAST'IMHE'LLNEVERHITITNOBODY TOWORRYABOUTTHROWITTO'IM,BOY
MAYBE I SHOULDN'T HAVE SAID ANYTHING..
SCHULZ

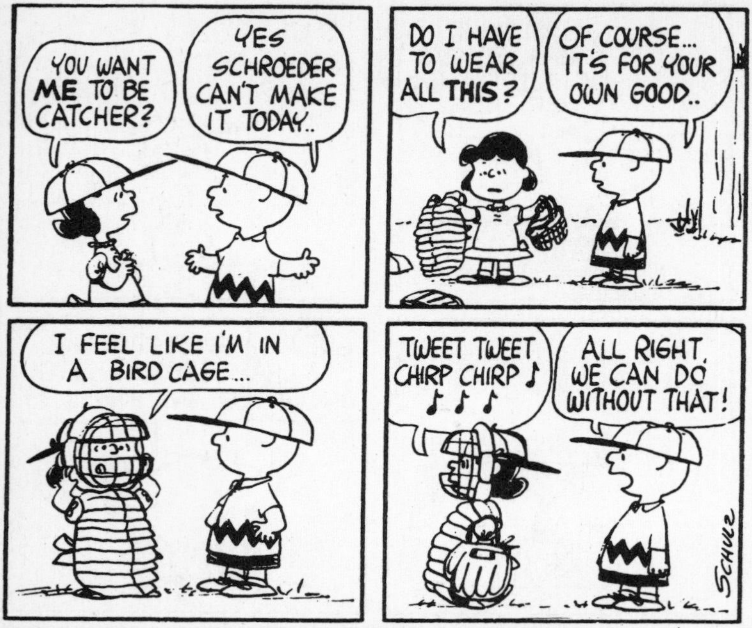
YOU WANT **ME** TO BE CATCHER?
YES SCHROEDER CAN'T MAKE IT TODAY..
DO I HAVE TO WEAR ALL **THIS**?
OF COURSE... IT'S FOR YOUR OWN GOOD..
I FEEL LIKE I'M IN A BIRD CAGE...
TWEET TWEET CHIRP CHIRP ♪ ♪ ♪ ♪
ALL RIGHT, WE CAN DO WITHOUT THAT!
SCHULZ

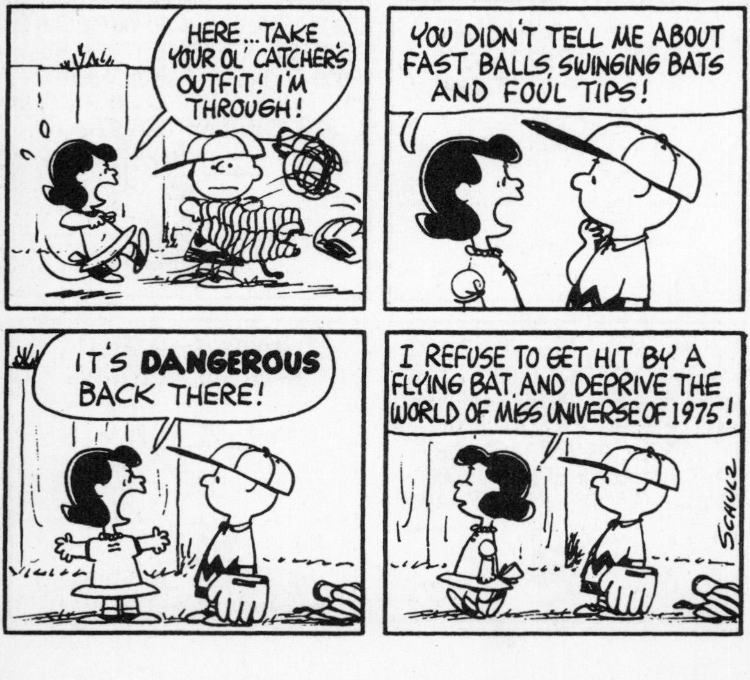
HERE...TAKE YOUR OL' CATCHER'S OUTFIT! I'M THROUGH!
YOU DIDN'T TELL ME ABOUT FAST BALLS, SWINGING BATS AND FOUL TIPS!
IT'S **DANGEROUS** BACK THERE!
I REFUSE TO GET HIT BY A FLYING BAT, AND DEPRIVE THE WORLD OF MISS UNIVERSE OF 1975!
SCHULZ

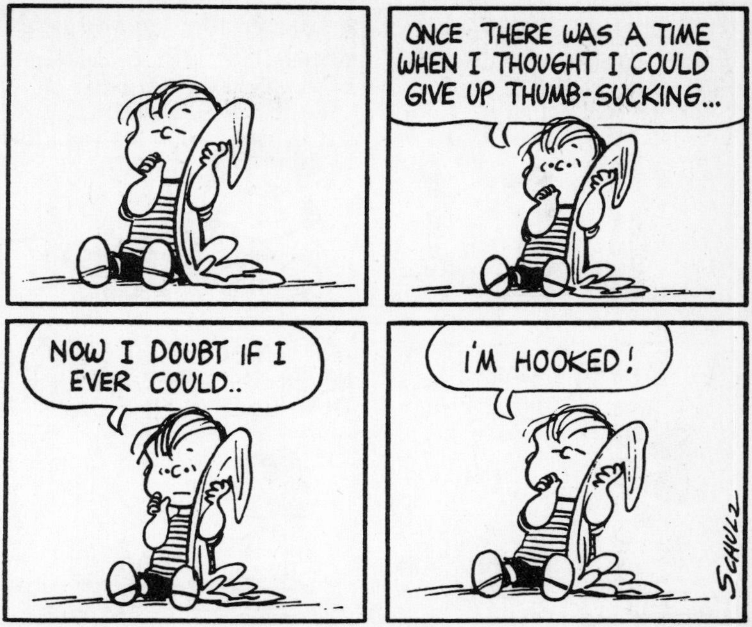
ONCE THERE WAS A TIME WHEN I THOUGHT I COULD GIVE UP THUMB-SUCKING...
NOW I DOUBT IF I EVER COULD..
I'M HOOKED!
SCHULZ

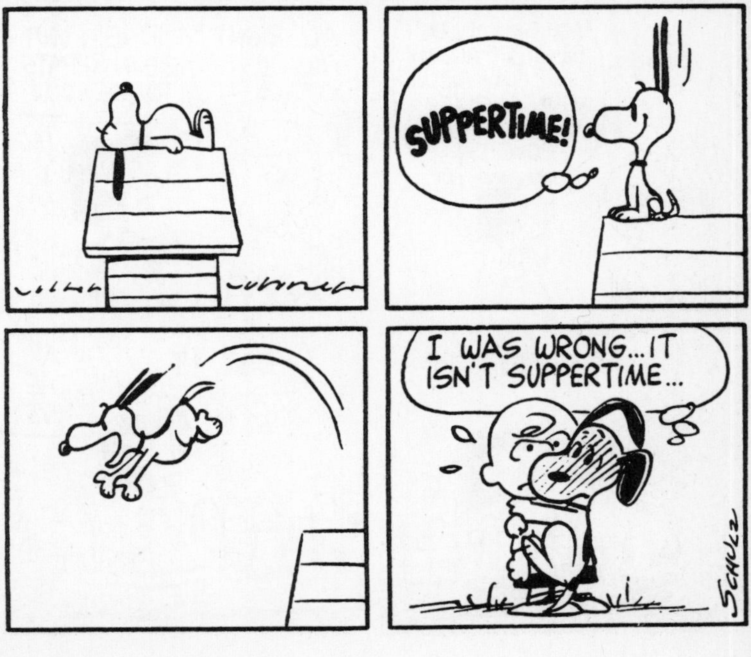
SUPPERTIME!
I WAS WRONG...IT ISN'T SUPPERTIME...
SCHULZ

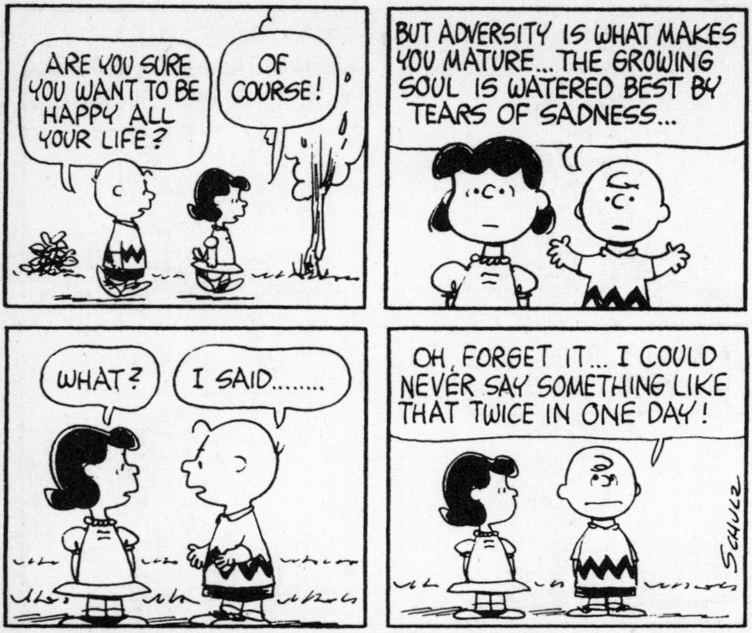
ARE YOU SURE YOU WANT TO BE HAPPY ALL YOUR LIFE?
OF COURSE!
BUT ADVERSITY IS WHAT MAKES YOU MATURE... THE GROWING SOUL IS WATERED BEST BY TEARS OF SADNESS...
WHAT?
I SAID........
OH, FORGET IT... I COULD NEVER SAY SOMETHING LIKE THAT TWICE IN ONE DAY!
SCHULZ

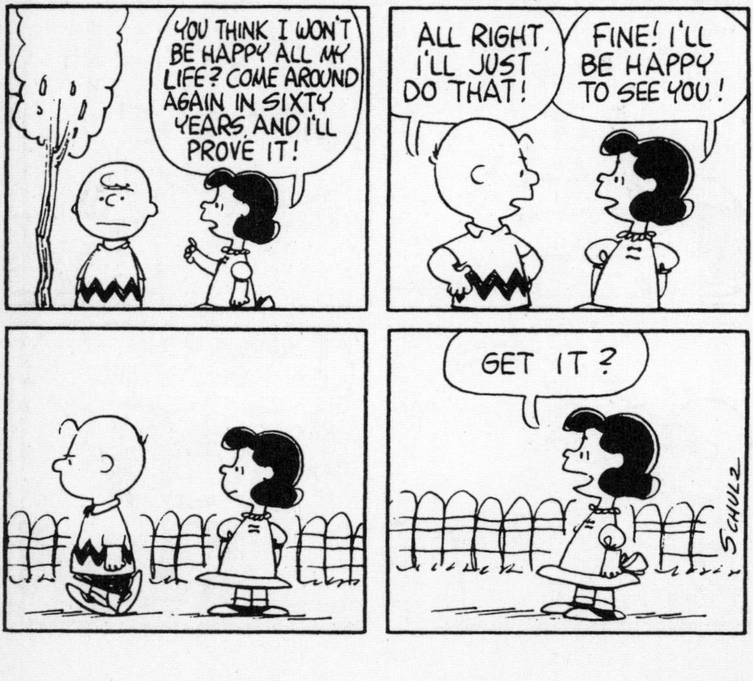
YOU THINK I WON'T BE HAPPY ALL MY LIFE? COME AROUND AGAIN IN SIXTY YEARS, AND I'LL PROVE IT!
ALL RIGHT, I'LL JUST DO THAT!
FINE! I'LL BE HAPPY TO SEE YOU!
GET IT?
SCHULZ

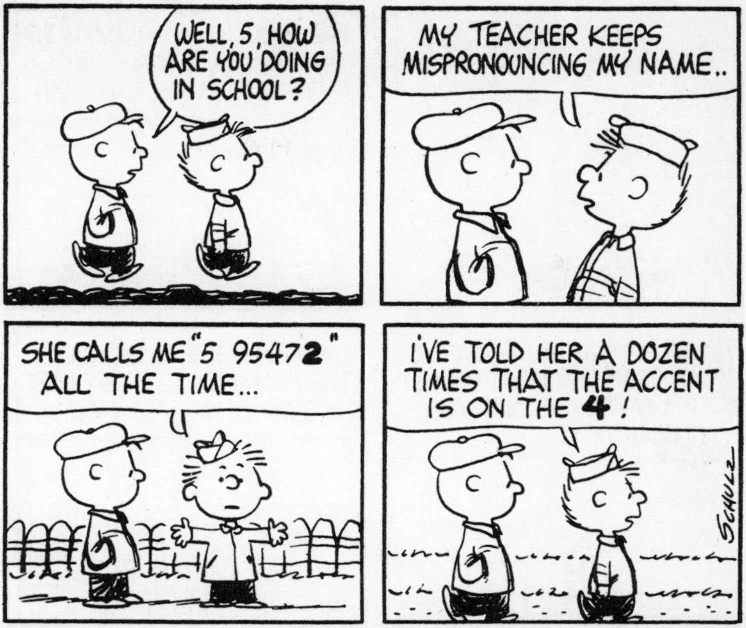
WELL, 5, HOW ARE YOU DOING IN SCHOOL?
MY TEACHER KEEPS MISPRONOUNCING MY NAME..
SHE CALLS ME "5 95472" ALL THE TIME...
I'VE TOLD HER A DOZEN TIMES THAT THE ACCENT IS ON THE 4!
SCHULZ

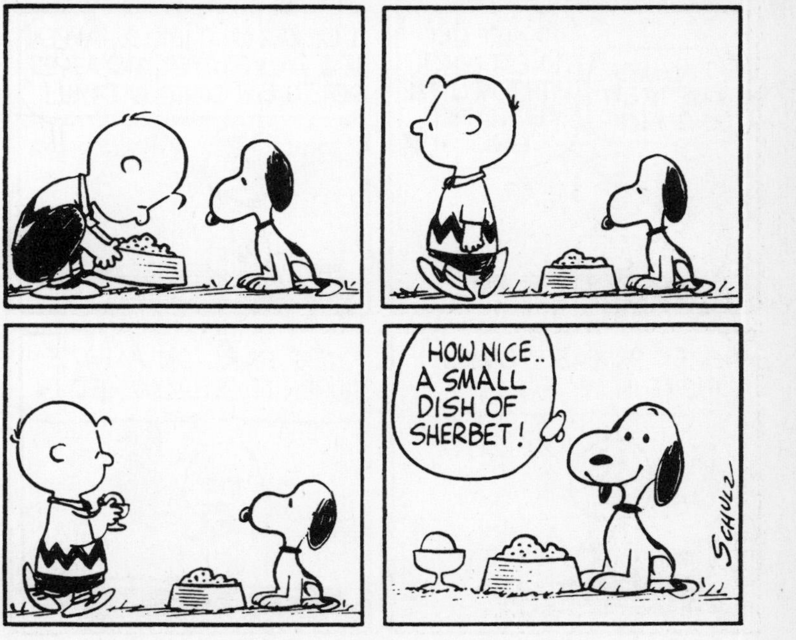
HOW NICE.. A SMALL DISH OF SHERBET!
SCHULZ

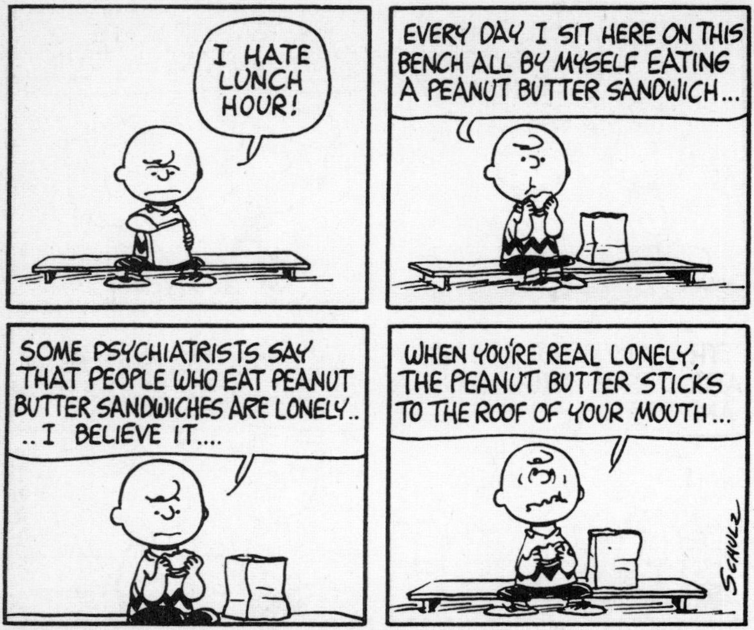
I HATE LUNCH HOUR!
EVERY DAY I SIT HERE ON THIS BENCH ALL BY MYSELF EATING A PEANUT BUTTER SANDWICH...
SOME PSYCHIATRISTS SAY THAT PEOPLE WHO EAT PEANUT BUTTER SANDWICHES ARE LONELY.. ..I BELIEVE IT....
WHEN YOU'RE REAL LONELY, THE PEANUT BUTTER STICKS TO THE ROOF OF YOUR MOUTH...
SCHULZ

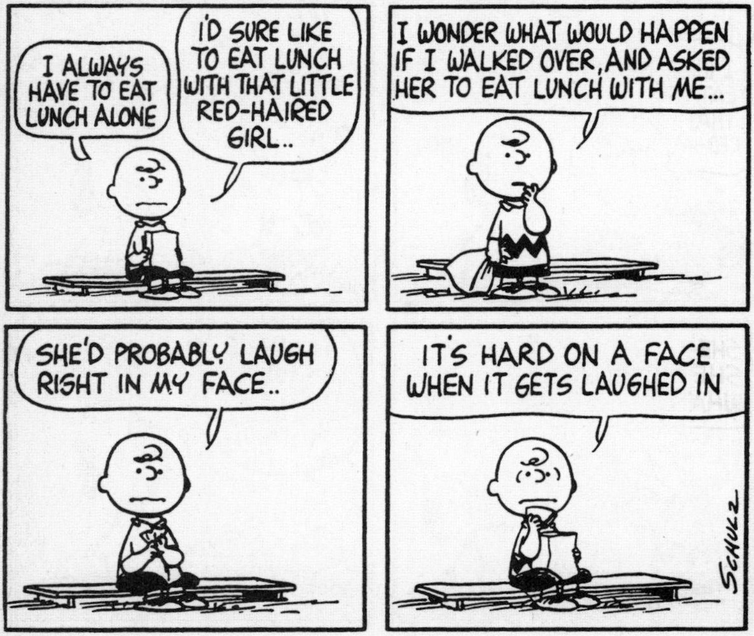
I ALWAYS HAVE TO EAT LUNCH ALONE
I'D SURE LIKE TO EAT LUNCH WITH THAT LITTLE RED-HAIRED GIRL..
I WONDER WHAT WOULD HAPPEN IF I WALKED OVER, AND ASKED HER TO EAT LUNCH WITH ME...
SHE'D PROBABLY LAUGH RIGHT IN MY FACE..
IT'S HARD ON A FACE WHEN IT GETS LAUGHED IN
SCHULZ

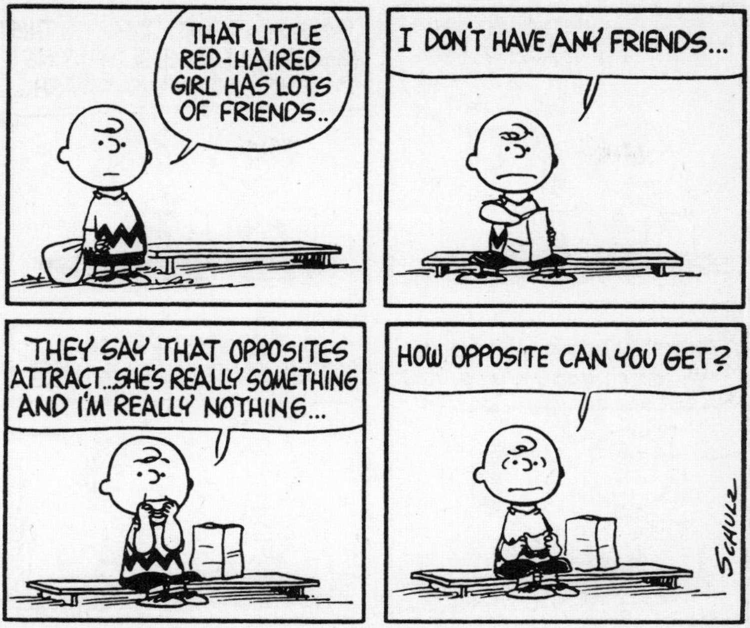
THAT LITTLE RED-HAIRED GIRL HAS LOTS OF FRIENDS..
I DON'T HAVE ANY FRIENDS...
THEY SAY THAT OPPOSITES ATTRACT...SHE'S REALLY SOMETHING AND I'M REALLY NOTHING...
HOW OPPOSITE CAN YOU GET?
SCHULZ

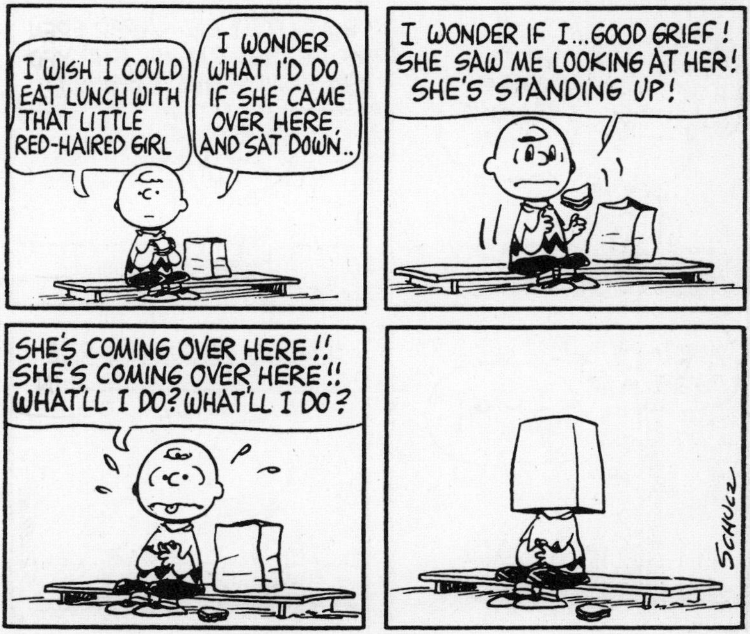
I WISH I COULD EAT LUNCH WITH THAT LITTLE RED-HAIRED GIRL
I WONDER WHAT I'D DO IF SHE CAME OVER HERE AND SAT DOWN..
I WONDER IF I...GOOD GRIEF! SHE SAW ME LOOKING AT HER! SHE'S STANDING UP!
SHE'S COMING OVER HERE!! SHE'S COMING OVER HERE!! WHAT'LL I DO? WHAT'LL I DO?
SCHULZ

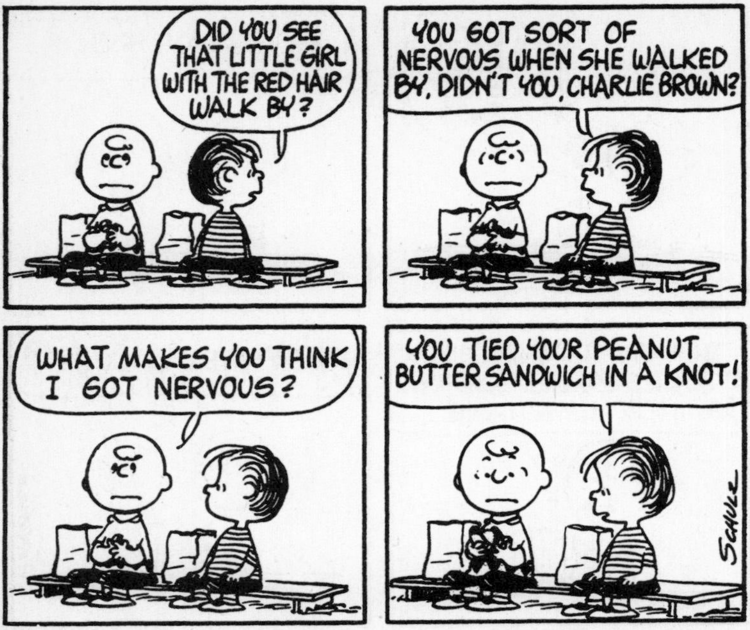
DID YOU SEE THAT LITTLE GIRL WITH THE RED HAIR WALK BY?
YOU GOT SORT OF NERVOUS WHEN SHE WALKED BY, DIDN'T YOU, CHARLIE BROWN?
WHAT MAKES YOU THINK I GOT NERVOUS?
YOU TIED YOUR PEANUT BUTTER SANDWICH IN A KNOT!
SCHULZ

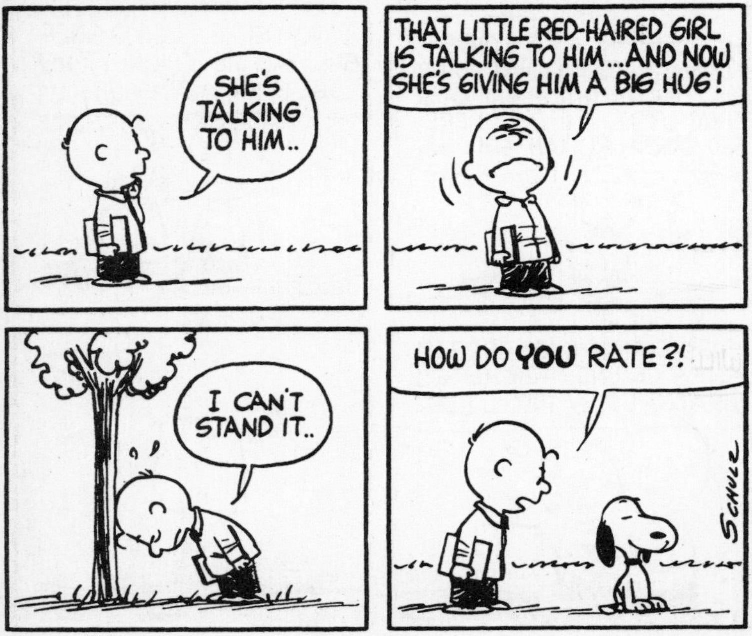
SHE'S TALKING TO HIM..
THAT LITTLE RED-HAIRED GIRL IS TALKING TO HIM...AND NOW SHE'S GIVING HIM A BIG HUG!
I CAN'T STAND IT..
HOW DO **YOU** RATE?!
SCHULZ

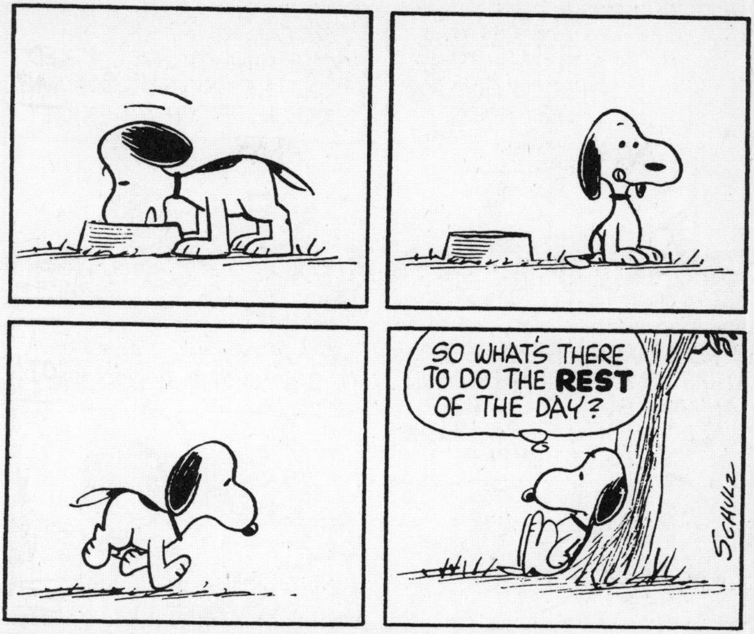
SO WHAT'S THERE TO DO THE **REST** OF THE DAY?
SCHULZ

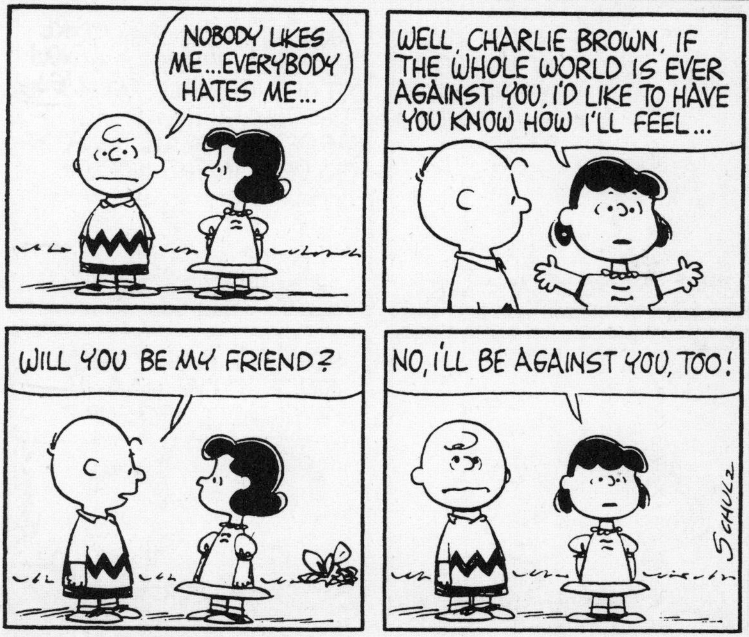
NOBODY LIKES ME...EVERYBODY HATES ME...
WELL, CHARLIE BROWN, IF THE WHOLE WORLD IS EVER AGAINST YOU, I'D LIKE TO HAVE YOU KNOW HOW I'LL FEEL...
WILL YOU BE MY FRIEND?
NO, I'LL BE AGAINST YOU, TOO!
SCHULZ

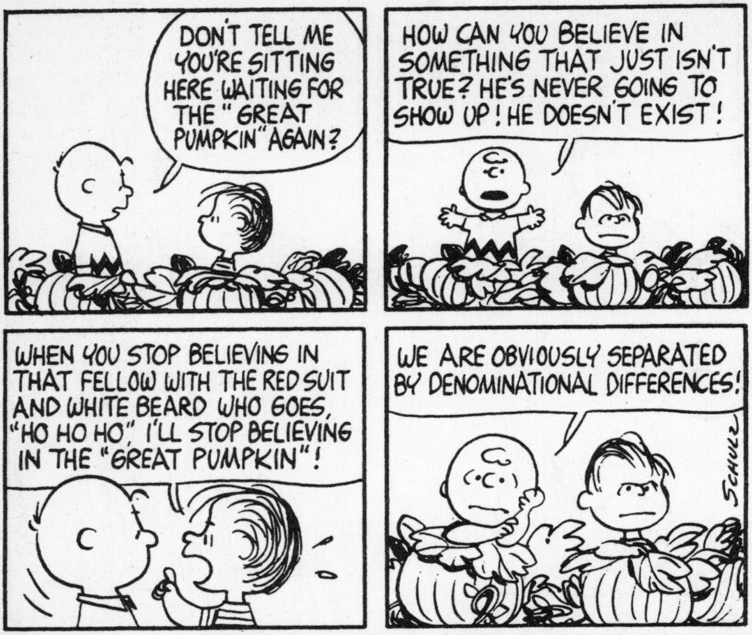
DON'T TELL ME YOU'RE SITTING HERE WAITING FOR THE "GREAT PUMPKIN" AGAIN?
HOW CAN YOU BELIEVE IN SOMETHING THAT JUST ISN'T TRUE? HE'S NEVER GOING TO SHOW UP! HE DOESN'T EXIST!
WHEN YOU STOP BELIEVING IN THAT FELLOW WITH THE RED SUIT AND WHITE BEARD WHO GOES, "HO HO HO," I'LL STOP BELIEVING IN THE "GREAT PUMPKIN"!
WE ARE OBVIOUSLY SEPARATED BY DENOMINATIONAL DIFFERENCES!
SCHULZ

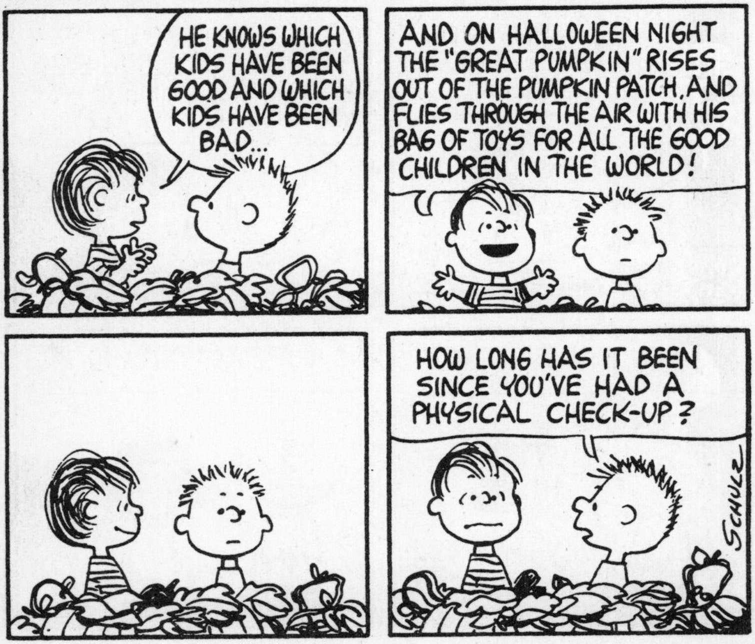
HE KNOWS WHICH KIDS HAVE BEEN GOOD AND WHICH KIDS HAVE BEEN BAD...
AND ON HALLOWEEN NIGHT THE "GREAT PUMPKIN" RISES OUT OF THE PUMPKIN PATCH, AND FLIES THROUGH THE AIR WITH HIS BAG OF TOYS FOR ALL THE GOOD CHILDREN IN THE WORLD!
HOW LONG HAS IT BEEN SINCE YOU'VE HAD A PHYSICAL CHECK-UP?
SCHULZ

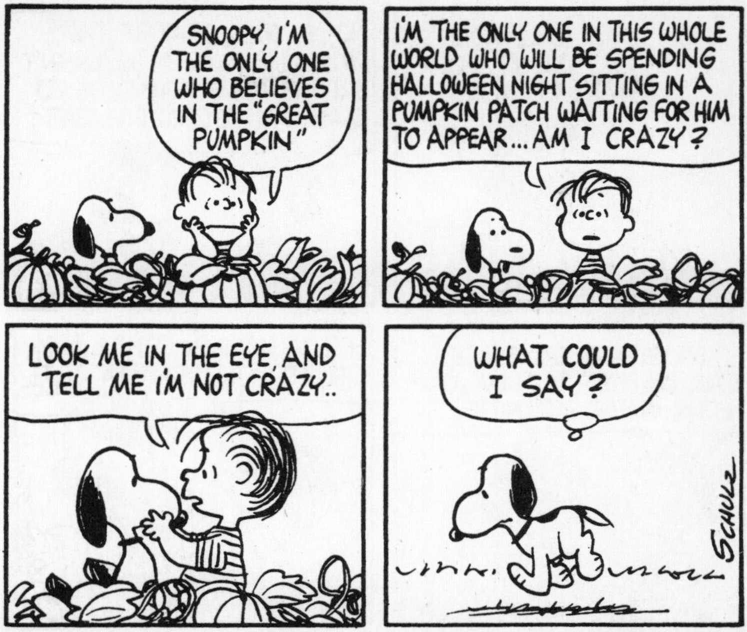
SNOOPY, I'M THE ONLY ONE WHO BELIEVES IN THE "GREAT PUMPKIN"
I'M THE ONLY ONE IN THIS WHOLE WORLD WHO WILL BE SPENDING HALLOWEEN NIGHT SITTING IN A PUMPKIN PATCH WAITING FOR HIM TO APPEAR... AM I CRAZY?
LOOK ME IN THE EYE, AND TELL ME I'M NOT CRAZY..
WHAT COULD I SAY?
SCHULZ

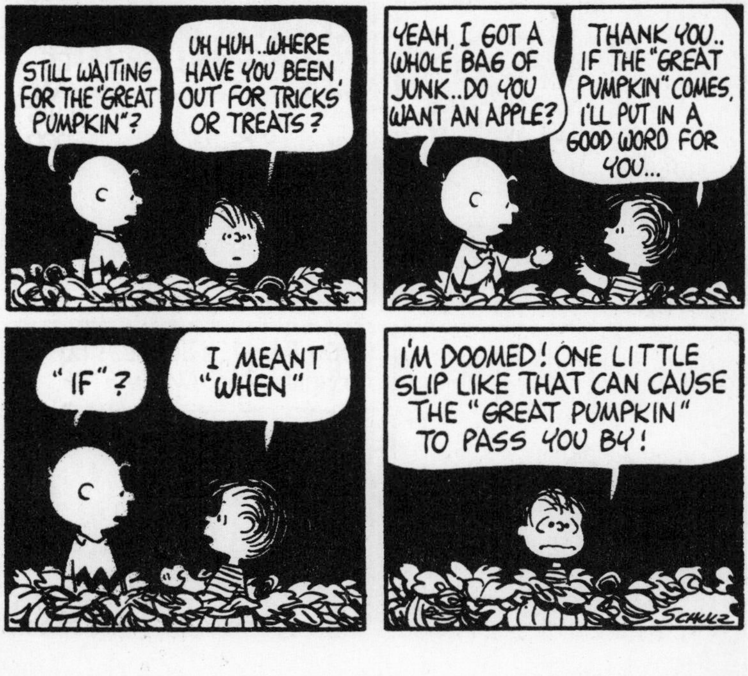
STILL WAITING FOR THE "GREAT PUMPKIN"?
UH HUH..WHERE HAVE YOU BEEN, OUT FOR TRICKS OR TREATS?
YEAH, I GOT A WHOLE BAG OF JUNK..DO YOU WANT AN APPLE?
THANK YOU.. IF THE "GREAT PUMPKIN" COMES, I'LL PUT IN A GOOD WORD FOR YOU...
"IF"?
I MEANT "WHEN"
I'M DOOMED! ONE LITTLE SLIP LIKE THAT CAN CAUSE THE "GREAT PUMPKIN" TO PASS YOU BY!
SCHULZ

WELL, HOW DID IT GO LAST NIGHT?

NOT SO GOOD...I SAT OUT THERE UNTIL FOUR O'CLOCK IN THE MORNING, BUT THE "GREAT PUMPKIN" NEVER CAME...I ALMOST FROZE TO DEATH..

I GUESS A PUMPKIN PATCH CAN BE PRETTY COLD AT FOUR IN THE MORNING..

ESPECIALLY WHEN IT HAS BEEN CHILLED WITH DISAPPOINTMENT

OH, "GREAT PUMPKIN" YOU'VE LET ME DOWN AGAIN!

I'LL NEVER BELIEVE IN YOU AGAIN! NEVER!

DON'T LISTEN TO ME..I DON'T KNOW WHAT I'M SAYING!

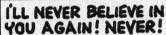

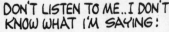

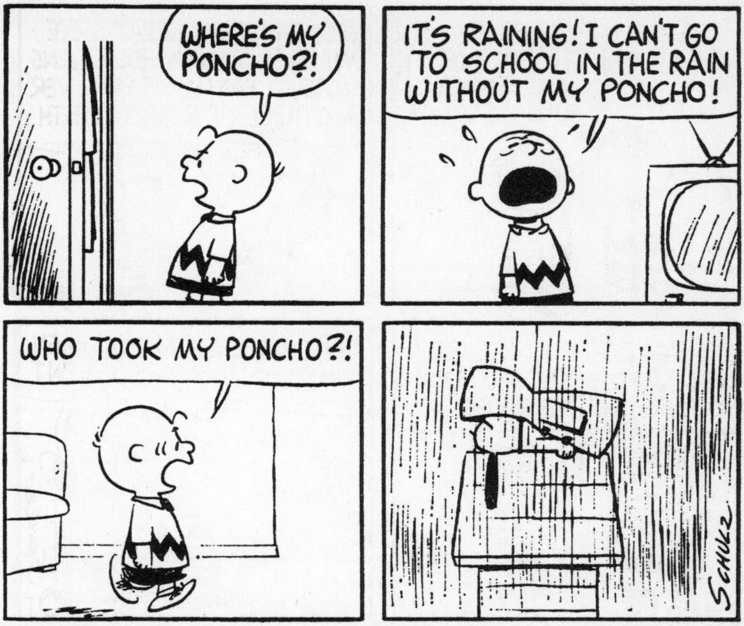
WHERE'S MY PONCHO?!
IT'S RAINING! I CAN'T GO TO SCHOOL IN THE RAIN WITHOUT MY PONCHO!
WHO TOOK MY PONCHO?!
SCHULZ

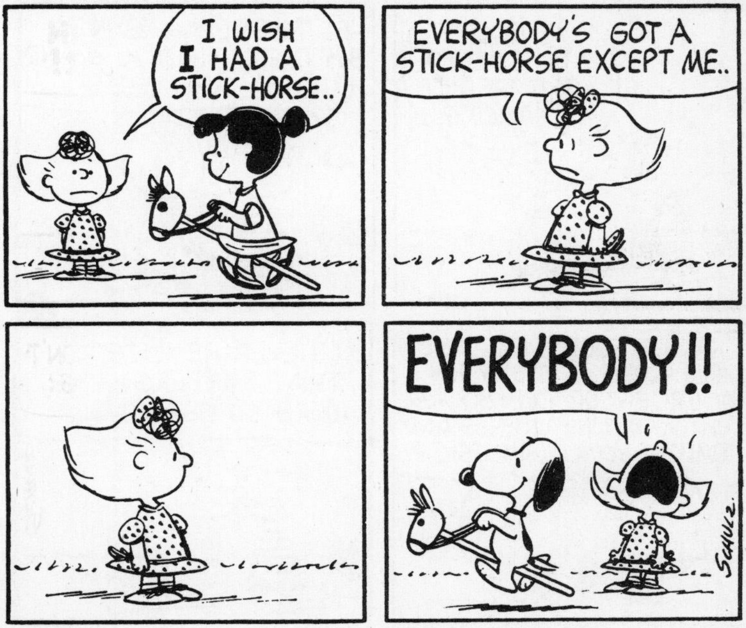
I WISH I HAD A STICK-HORSE..
EVERYBODY'S GOT A STICK-HORSE EXCEPT ME..
EVERYBODY!!
SCHULZ

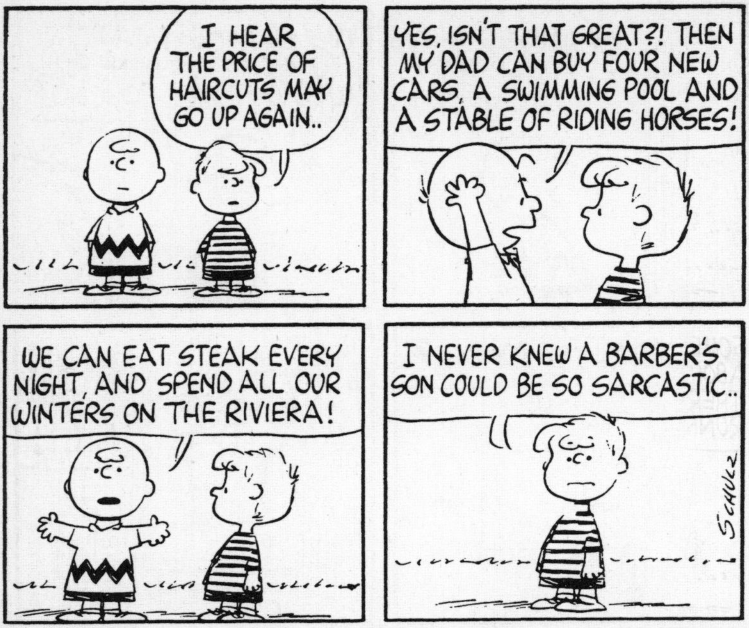
I HEAR THE PRICE OF HAIRCUTS MAY GO UP AGAIN..
YES, ISN'T THAT GREAT?! THEN MY DAD CAN BUY FOUR NEW CARS, A SWIMMING POOL AND A STABLE OF RIDING HORSES!
WE CAN EAT STEAK EVERY NIGHT, AND SPEND ALL OUR WINTERS ON THE RIVIERA!
I NEVER KNEW A BARBER'S SON COULD BE SO SARCASTIC..
SCHULZ

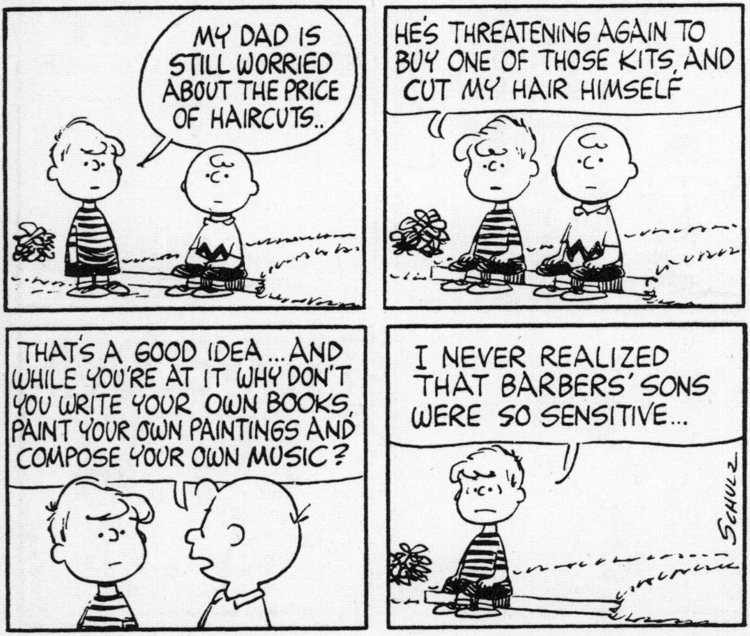
MY DAD IS STILL WORRIED ABOUT THE PRICE OF HAIRCUTS..
HE'S THREATENING AGAIN TO BUY ONE OF THOSE KITS, AND CUT MY HAIR HIMSELF
THAT'S A GOOD IDEA ... AND WHILE YOU'RE AT IT WHY DON'T YOU WRITE YOUR OWN BOOKS, PAINT YOUR OWN PAINTINGS AND COMPOSE YOUR OWN MUSIC?
I NEVER REALIZED THAT BARBERS' SONS WERE SO SENSITIVE...
SCHULZ

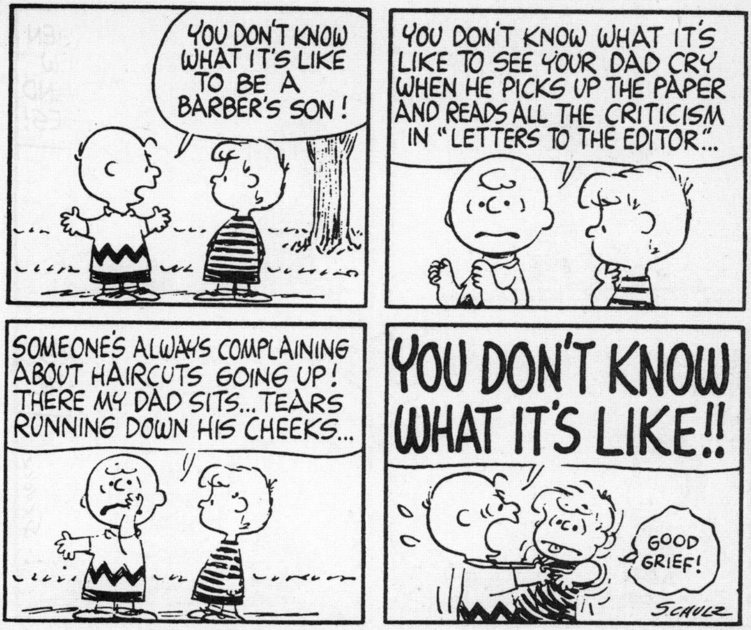
YOU DON'T KNOW WHAT IT'S LIKE TO BE A BARBER'S SON!
YOU DON'T KNOW WHAT IT'S LIKE TO SEE YOUR DAD CRY WHEN HE PICKS UP THE PAPER AND READS ALL THE CRITICISM IN "LETTERS TO THE EDITOR"...
SOMEONE'S ALWAYS COMPLAINING ABOUT HAIRCUTS GOING UP! THERE MY DAD SITS... TEARS RUNNING DOWN HIS CHEEKS...
YOU DON'T KNOW WHAT IT'S LIKE!!
GOOD GRIEF!
SCHULZ

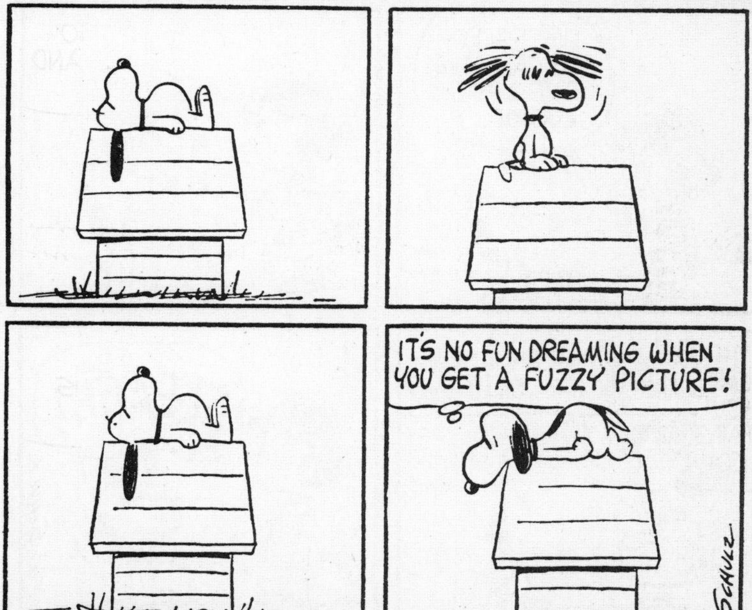
IT'S NO FUN DREAMING WHEN YOU GET A FUZZY PICTURE!
SCHULZ

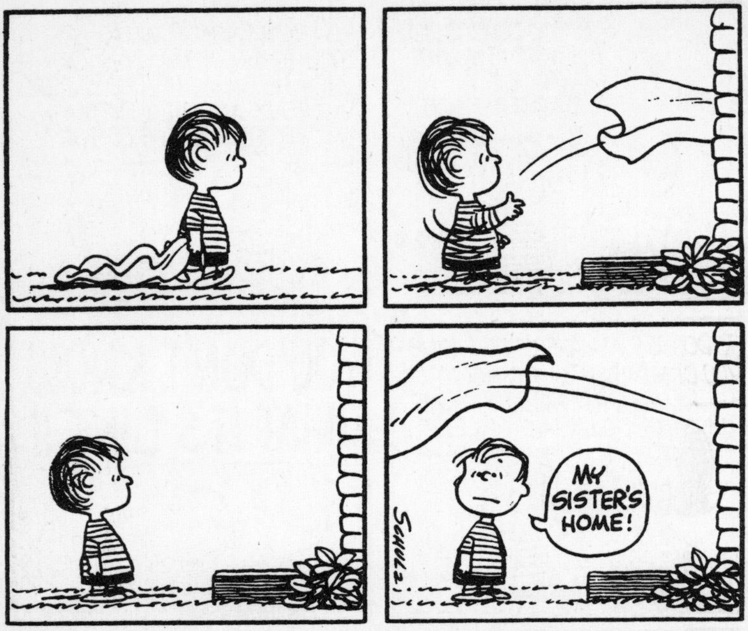
MY SISTER'S HOME!
SCHULZ

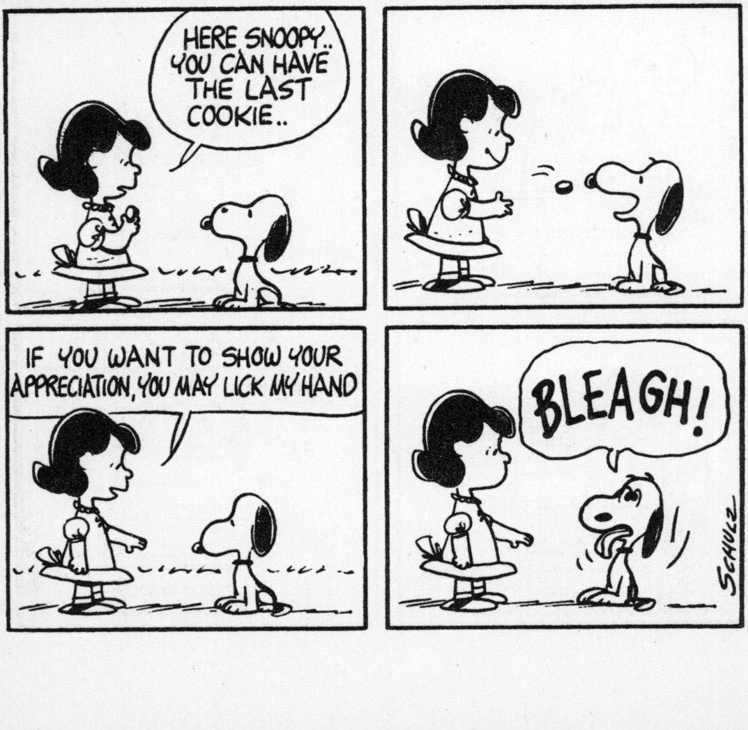
HERE SNOOPY.. YOU CAN HAVE THE LAST COOKIE..
IF YOU WANT TO SHOW YOUR APPRECIATION, YOU MAY LICK MY HAND
BLEAGH!
SCHULZ

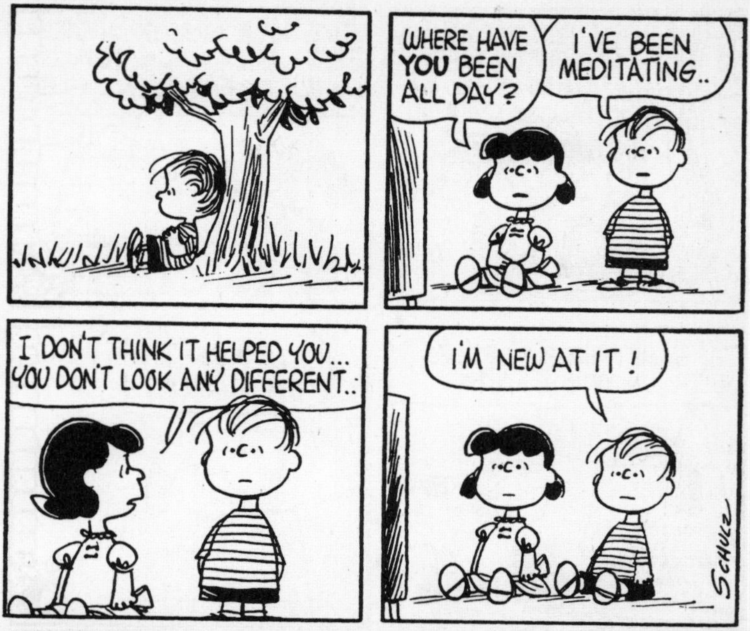
WHERE HAVE **YOU** BEEN ALL DAY?
I'VE BEEN MEDITATING..
I DON'T THINK IT HELPED YOU... YOU DON'T LOOK ANY DIFFERENT..
I'M NEW AT IT!
SCHULZ

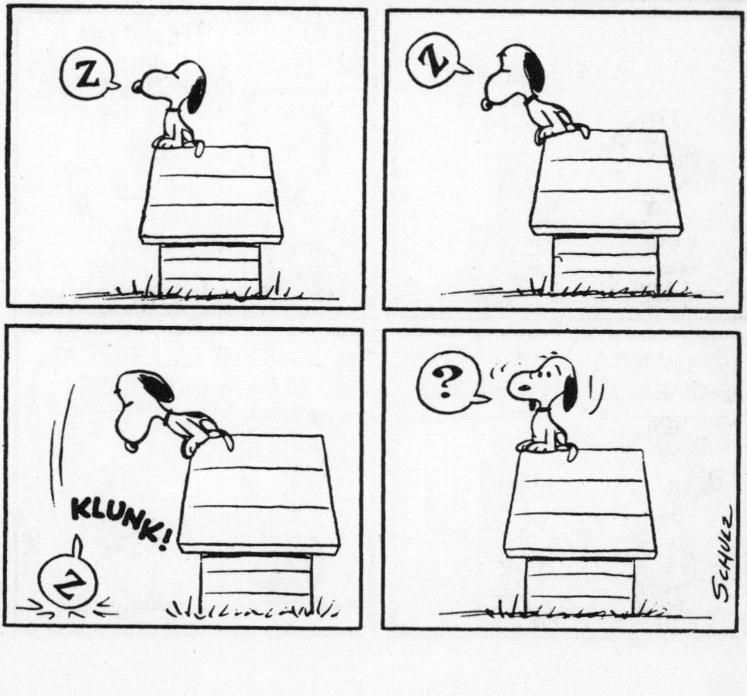
Z
Z
KLUNK!
Z
?
SCHULZ

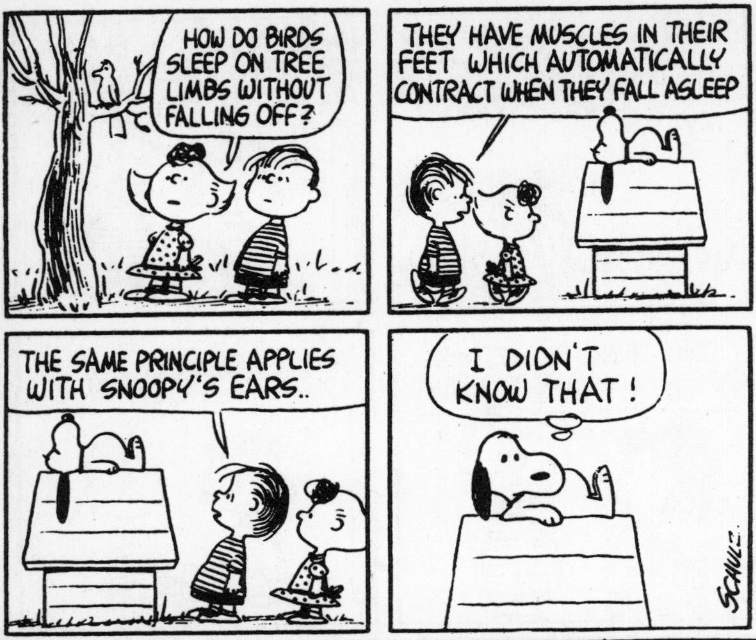
HOW DO BIRDS SLEEP ON TREE LIMBS WITHOUT FALLING OFF?
THEY HAVE MUSCLES IN THEIR FEET WHICH AUTOMATICALLY CONTRACT WHEN THEY FALL ASLEEP
THE SAME PRINCIPLE APPLIES WITH SNOOPY'S EARS..
I DIDN'T KNOW THAT!
SCHULZ

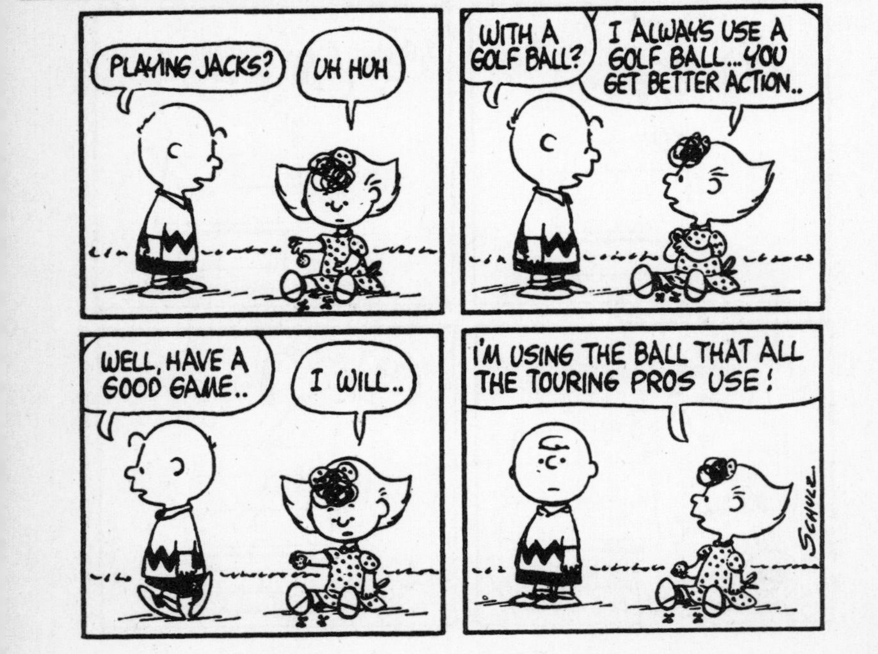
PLAYING JACKS?
UH HUH
WITH A GOLF BALL?
I ALWAYS USE A GOLF BALL...YOU GET BETTER ACTION..
WELL, HAVE A GOOD GAME..
I WILL..
I'M USING THE BALL THAT ALL THE TOURING PROS USE!
SCHULZ

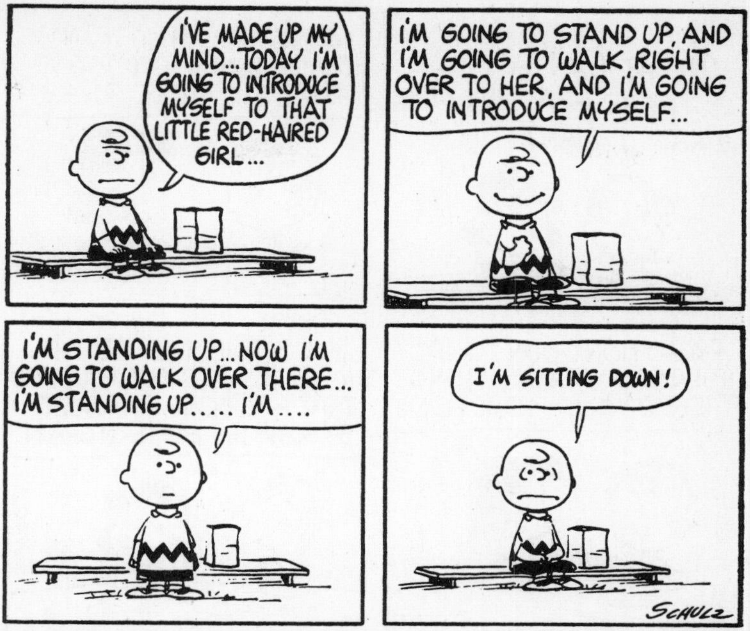
I'VE MADE UP MY MIND...TODAY I'M GOING TO INTRODUCE MYSELF TO THAT LITTLE RED-HAIRED GIRL...
I'M GOING TO STAND UP, AND I'M GOING TO WALK RIGHT OVER TO HER, AND I'M GOING TO INTRODUCE MYSELF...
I'M STANDING UP...NOW I'M GOING TO WALK OVER THERE... I'M STANDING UP..... I'M....
I'M SITTING DOWN!
SCHULZ

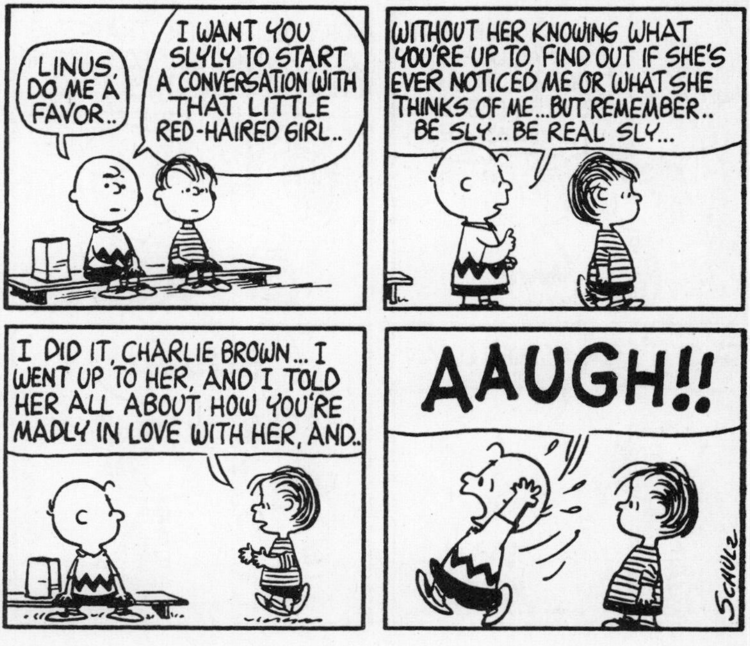
LINUS, DO ME A FAVOR..
I WANT YOU SLYLY TO START A CONVERSATION WITH THAT LITTLE RED-HAIRED GIRL..
WITHOUT HER KNOWING WHAT YOU'RE UP TO, FIND OUT IF SHE'S EVER NOTICED ME OR WHAT SHE THINKS OF ME...BUT REMEMBER.. BE SLY... BE REAL SLY...
I DID IT, CHARLIE BROWN... I WENT UP TO HER, AND I TOLD HER ALL ABOUT HOW YOU'RE MADLY IN LOVE WITH HER, AND..
AAUGH!!
SCHULZ

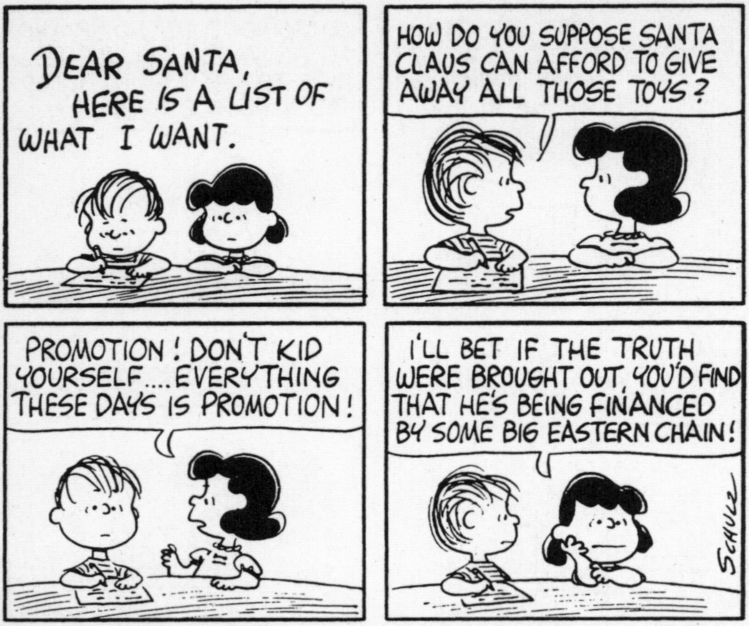
DEAR SANTA, HERE IS A LIST OF WHAT I WANT.
HOW DO YOU SUPPOSE SANTA CLAUS CAN AFFORD TO GIVE AWAY ALL THOSE TOYS?
PROMOTION! DON'T KID YOURSELF.... EVERYTHING THESE DAYS IS PROMOTION!
I'LL BET IF THE TRUTH WERE BROUGHT OUT, YOU'D FIND THAT HE'S BEING FINANCED BY SOME BIG EASTERN CHAIN!
SCHULZ

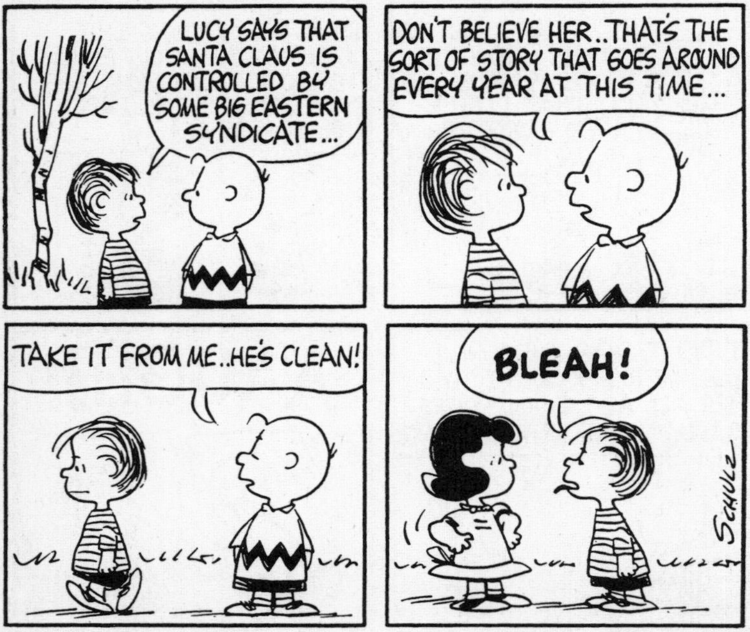
LUCY SAYS THAT SANTA CLAUS IS CONTROLLED BY SOME BIG EASTERN SYNDICATE...
DON'T BELIEVE HER..THAT'S THE SORT OF STORY THAT GOES AROUND EVERY YEAR AT THIS TIME...
TAKE IT FROM ME..HE'S CLEAN!
BLEAH!
SCHULZ

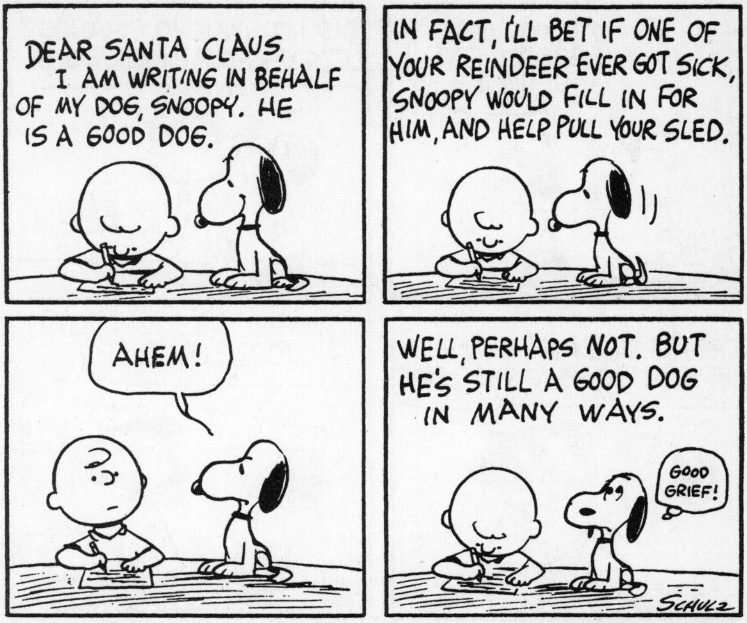
DEAR SANTA CLAUS,
I AM WRITING IN BEHALF OF MY DOG, SNOOPY. HE IS A GOOD DOG.
IN FACT, I'LL BET IF ONE OF YOUR REINDEER EVER GOT SICK, SNOOPY WOULD FILL IN FOR HIM, AND HELP PULL YOUR SLED.
AHEM!
WELL, PERHAPS NOT. BUT HE'S STILL A GOOD DOG IN MANY WAYS.
GOOD GRIEF!
SCHULZ

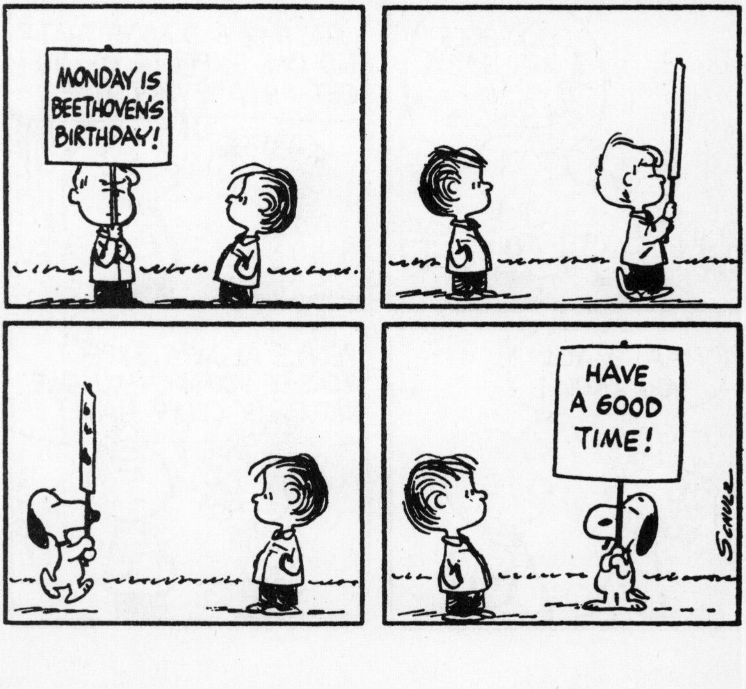
MONDAY IS BEETHOVEN'S BIRTHDAY!
HAVE A GOOD TIME!
SCHULZ

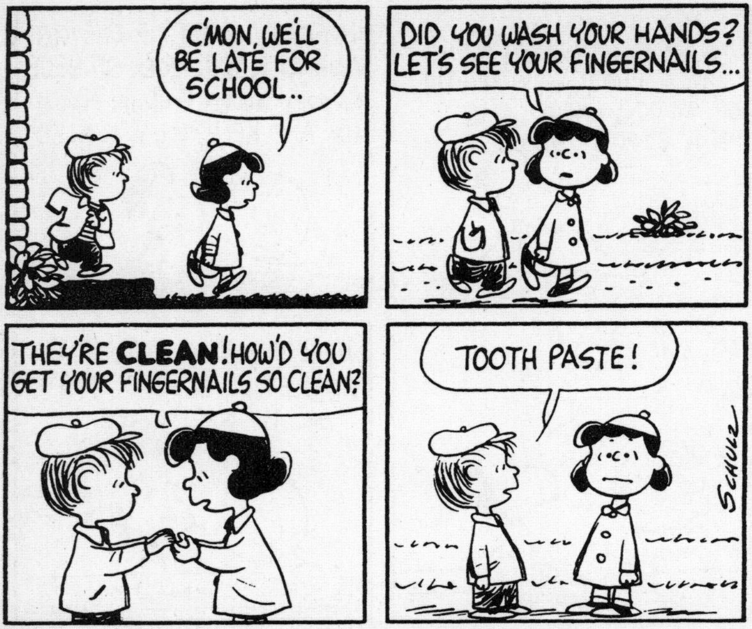
C'MON, WE'LL BE LATE FOR SCHOOL..
DID YOU WASH YOUR HANDS? LET'S SEE YOUR FINGERNAILS...
THEY'RE **CLEAN**! HOW'D YOU GET YOUR FINGERNAILS SO CLEAN?
TOOTH PASTE!
SCHULZ

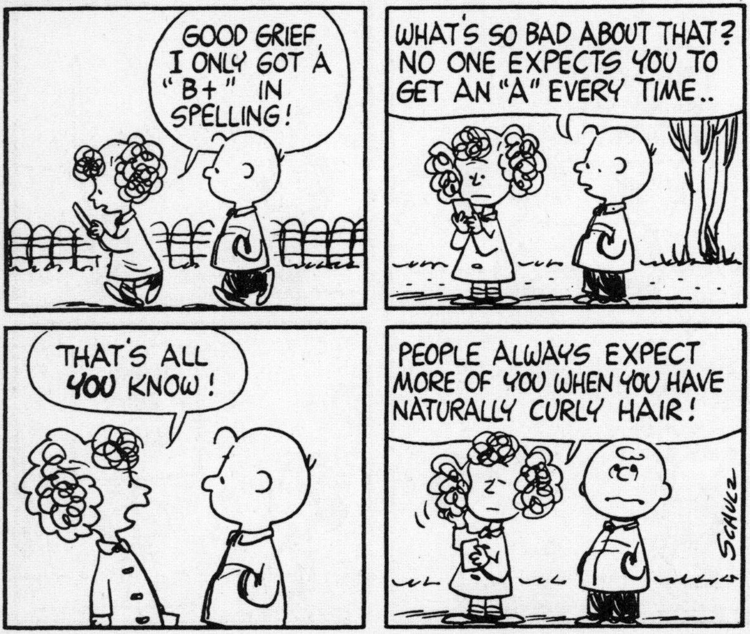
GOOD GRIEF, I ONLY GOT A "B+" IN SPELLING!
WHAT'S SO BAD ABOUT THAT? NO ONE EXPECTS YOU TO GET AN "A" EVERY TIME..
THAT'S ALL ***YOU*** KNOW!
PEOPLE ALWAYS EXPECT MORE OF YOU WHEN YOU HAVE NATURALLY CURLY HAIR!
SCHULZ

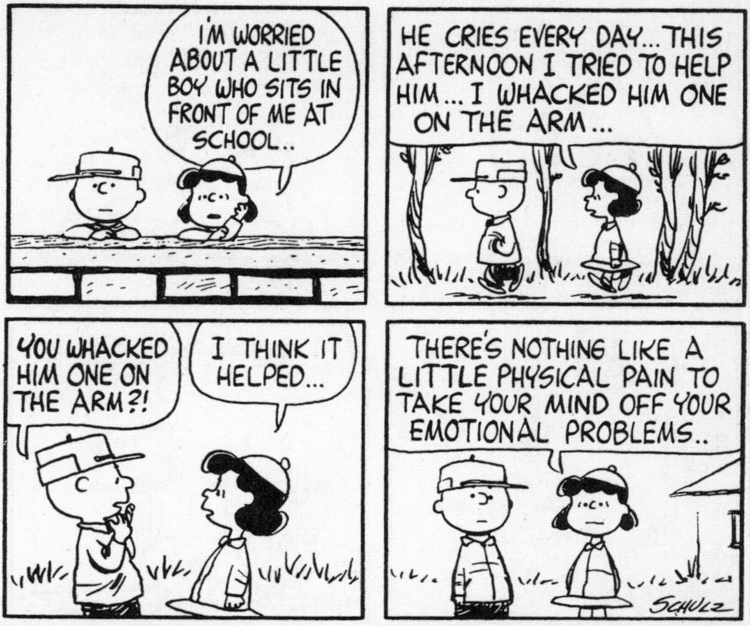
I'M WORRIED ABOUT A LITTLE BOY WHO SITS IN FRONT OF ME AT SCHOOL..
HE CRIES EVERY DAY... THIS AFTERNOON I TRIED TO HELP HIM... I WHACKED HIM ONE ON THE ARM...
YOU WHACKED HIM ONE ON THE ARM?!
I THINK IT HELPED...
THERE'S NOTHING LIKE A LITTLE PHYSICAL PAIN TO TAKE YOUR MIND OFF YOUR EMOTIONAL PROBLEMS..
SCHULZ

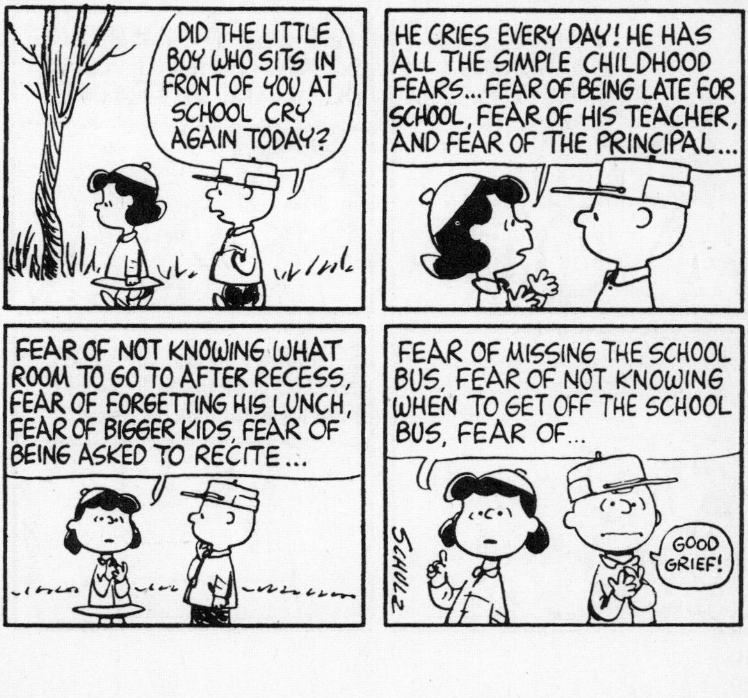
DID THE LITTLE BOY WHO SITS IN FRONT OF YOU AT SCHOOL CRY AGAIN TODAY?
HE CRIES EVERY DAY! HE HAS ALL THE SIMPLE CHILDHOOD FEARS... FEAR OF BEING LATE FOR SCHOOL, FEAR OF HIS TEACHER, AND FEAR OF THE PRINCIPAL...
FEAR OF NOT KNOWING WHAT ROOM TO GO TO AFTER RECESS, FEAR OF FORGETTING HIS LUNCH, FEAR OF BIGGER KIDS, FEAR OF BEING ASKED TO RECITE...
FEAR OF MISSING THE SCHOOL BUS, FEAR OF NOT KNOWING WHEN TO GET OFF THE SCHOOL BUS, FEAR OF...
SCHULZ
GOOD GRIEF!

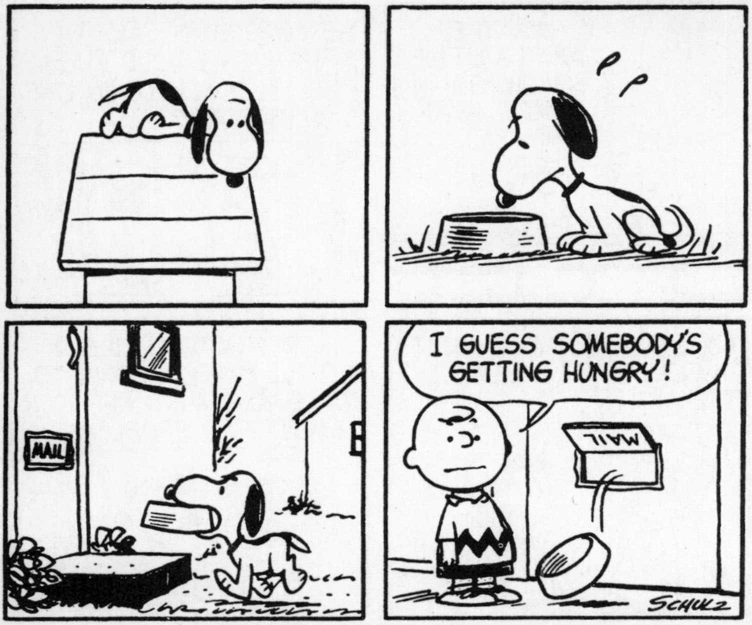
MAIL
I GUESS SOMEBODY'S GETTING HUNGRY!
SCHULZ

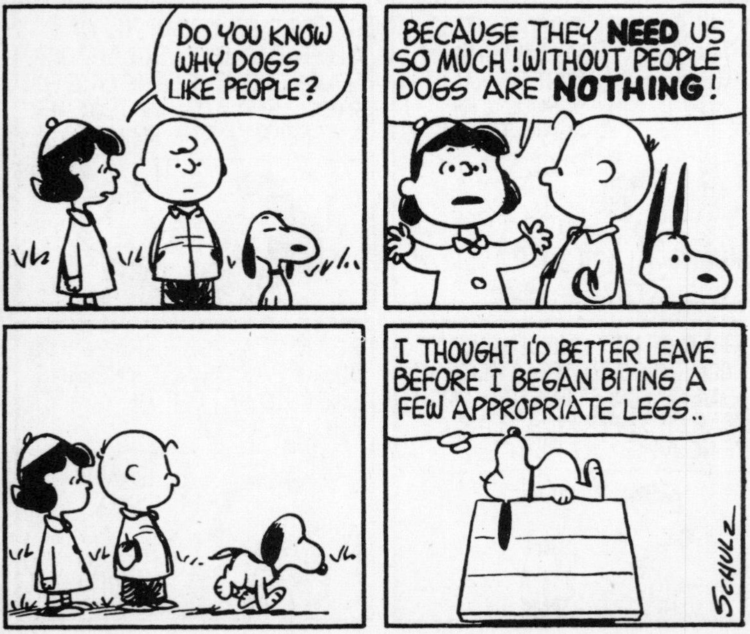
DO YOU KNOW WHY DOGS LIKE PEOPLE?
BECAUSE THEY **NEED** US SO MUCH! WITHOUT PEOPLE DOGS ARE **NOTHING**!
I THOUGHT I'D BETTER LEAVE BEFORE I BEGAN BITING A FEW APPROPRIATE LEGS..
SCHULZ

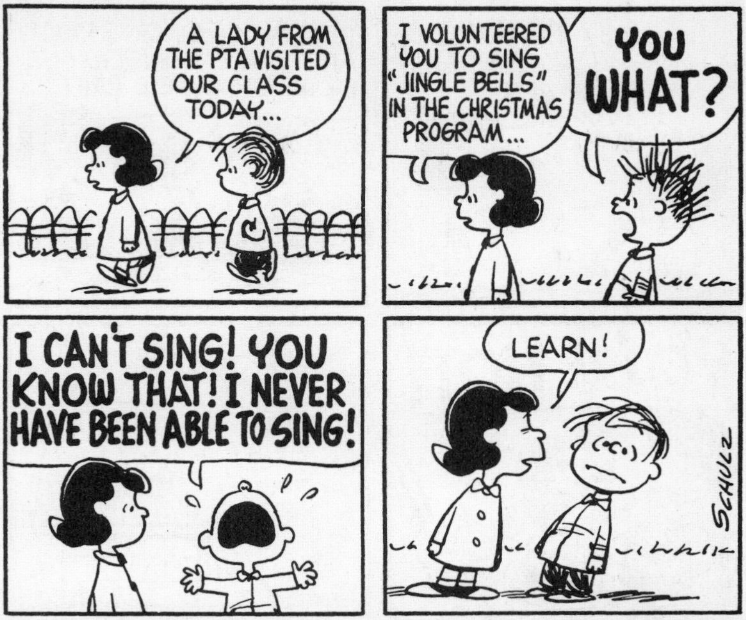

A LADY FROM THE PTA VISITED OUR CLASS TODAY...
I VOLUNTEERED YOU TO SING "JINGLE BELLS" IN THE CHRISTMAS PROGRAM...
YOU WHAT?
I CAN'T SING! YOU KNOW THAT! I NEVER HAVE BEEN ABLE TO SING!
LEARN!
SCHULZ

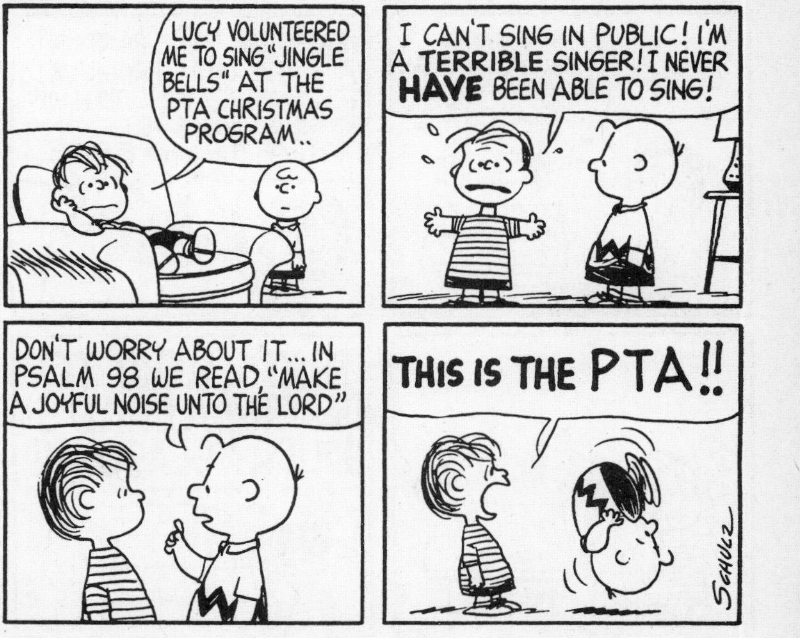

LUCY VOLUNTEERED ME TO SING "JINGLE BELLS" AT THE PTA CHRISTMAS PROGRAM..
I CAN'T SING IN PUBLIC! I'M A TERRIBLE SINGER! I NEVER HAVE BEEN ABLE TO SING!
DON'T WORRY ABOUT IT... IN PSALM 98 WE READ, "MAKE A JOYFUL NOISE UNTO THE LORD"
THIS IS THE PTA!!
SCHULZ

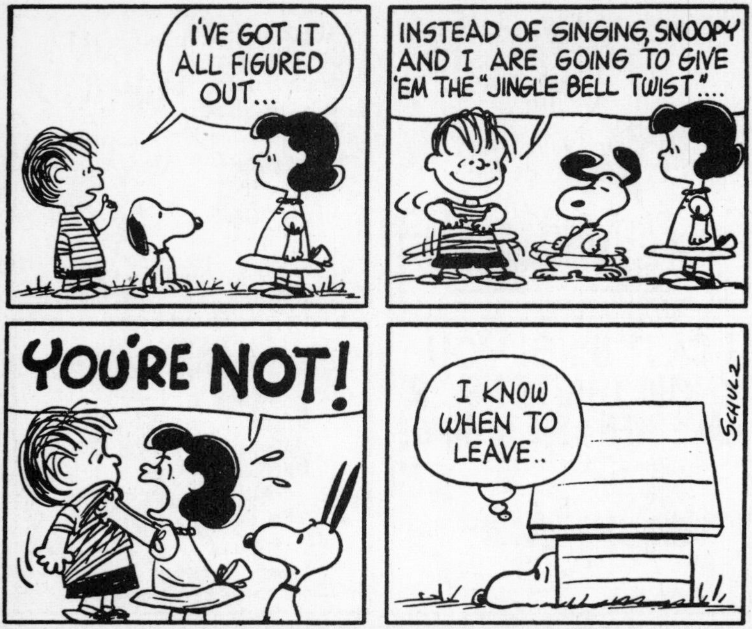
I'VE GOT IT ALL FIGURED OUT...
INSTEAD OF SINGING, SNOOPY AND I ARE GOING TO GIVE 'EM THE "JINGLE BELL TWIST"....
YOU'RE NOT!
I KNOW WHEN TO LEAVE..
SCHULZ

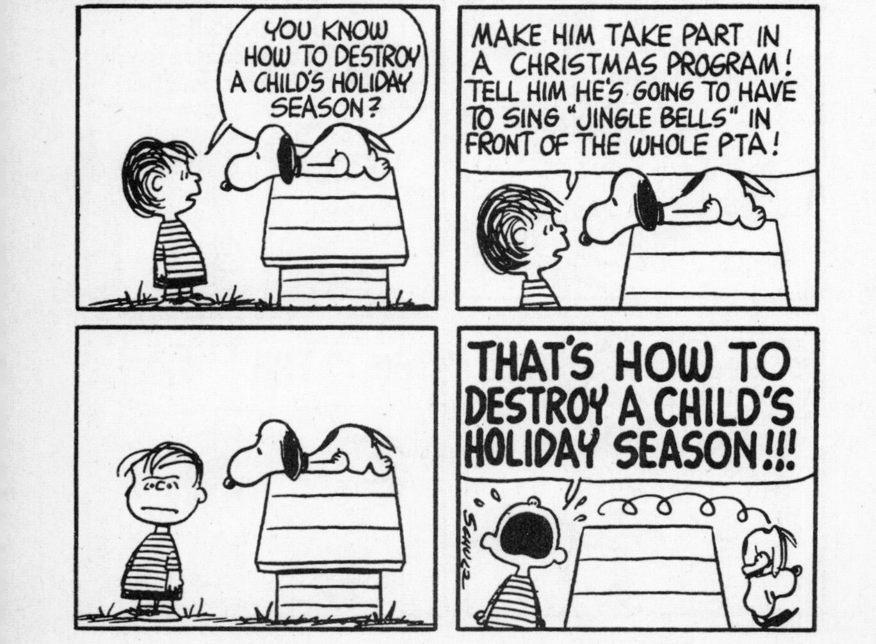
YOU KNOW HOW TO DESTROY A CHILD'S HOLIDAY SEASON?
MAKE HIM TAKE PART IN A CHRISTMAS PROGRAM! TELL HIM HE'S GOING TO HAVE TO SING "JINGLE BELLS" IN FRONT OF THE WHOLE PTA!
THAT'S HOW TO DESTROY A CHILD'S HOLIDAY SEASON!!!
SCHULZ

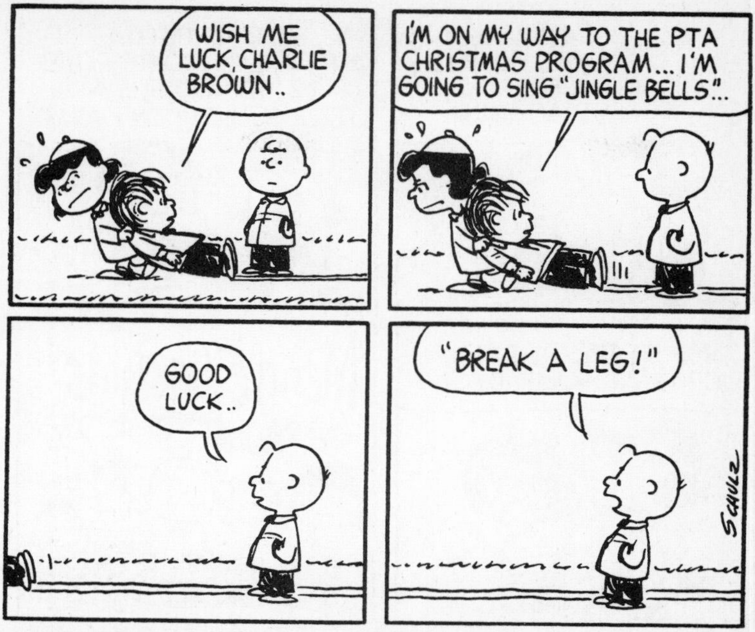
WISH ME LUCK, CHARLIE BROWN..
I'M ON MY WAY TO THE PTA CHRISTMAS PROGRAM... I'M GOING TO SING "JINGLE BELLS"..
GOOD LUCK..
"BREAK A LEG!"
SCHULZ

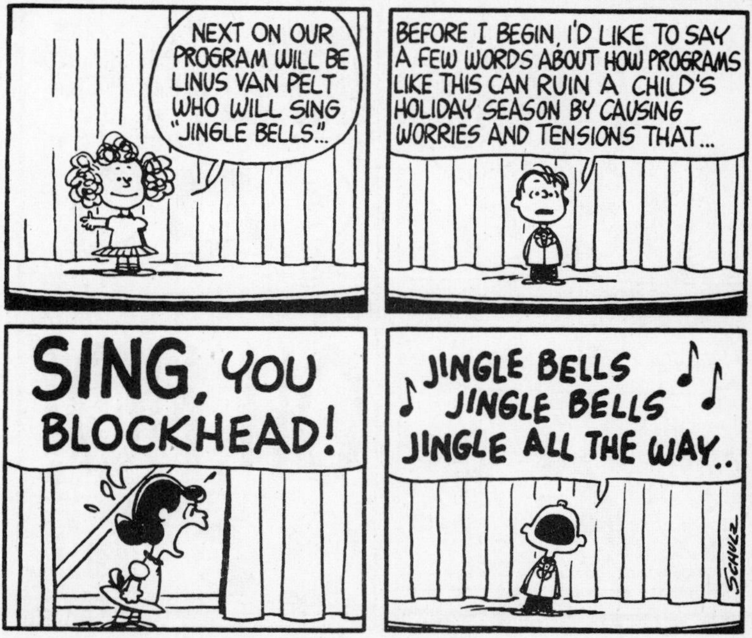
NEXT ON OUR PROGRAM WILL BE LINUS VAN PELT WHO WILL SING "JINGLE BELLS"..
BEFORE I BEGIN, I'D LIKE TO SAY A FEW WORDS ABOUT HOW PROGRAMS LIKE THIS CAN RUIN A CHILD'S HOLIDAY SEASON BY CAUSING WORRIES AND TENSIONS THAT...
SING, YOU BLOCKHEAD!
JINGLE BELLS
JINGLE BELLS
JINGLE ALL THE WAY..
SCHULZ

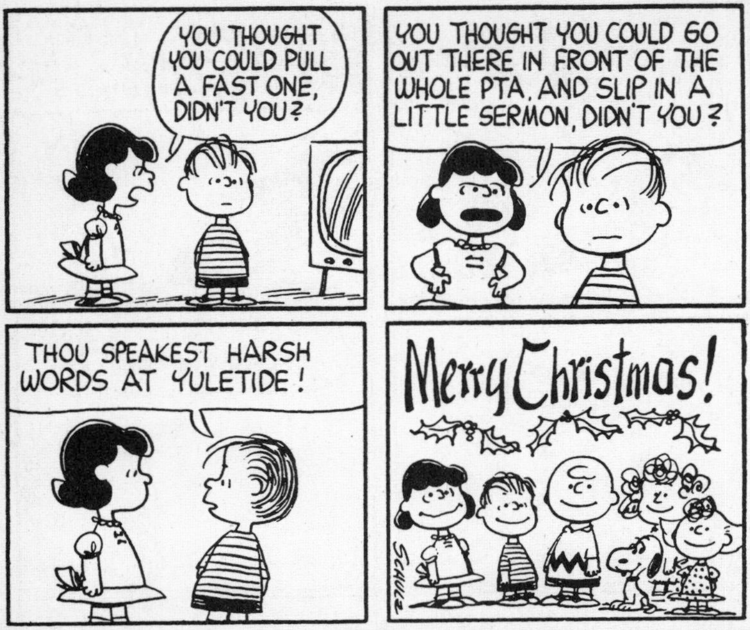
YOU THOUGHT YOU COULD PULL A FAST ONE, DIDN'T YOU?
YOU THOUGHT YOU COULD GO OUT THERE IN FRONT OF THE WHOLE PTA, AND SLIP IN A LITTLE SERMON, DIDN'T YOU?
THOU SPEAKEST HARSH WORDS AT YULETIDE!
Merry Christmas!
SCHULZ

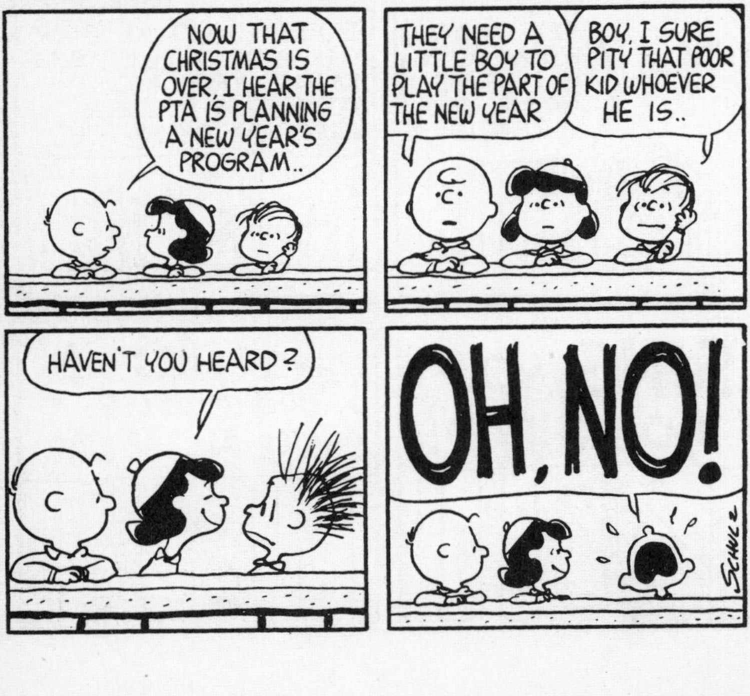
NOW THAT CHRISTMAS IS OVER, I HEAR THE PTA IS PLANNING A NEW YEAR'S PROGRAM..
THEY NEED A LITTLE BOY TO PLAY THE PART OF THE NEW YEAR
BOY, I SURE PITY THAT POOR KID WHOEVER HE IS..
HAVEN'T YOU HEARD?
OH, NO!
SCHULZ

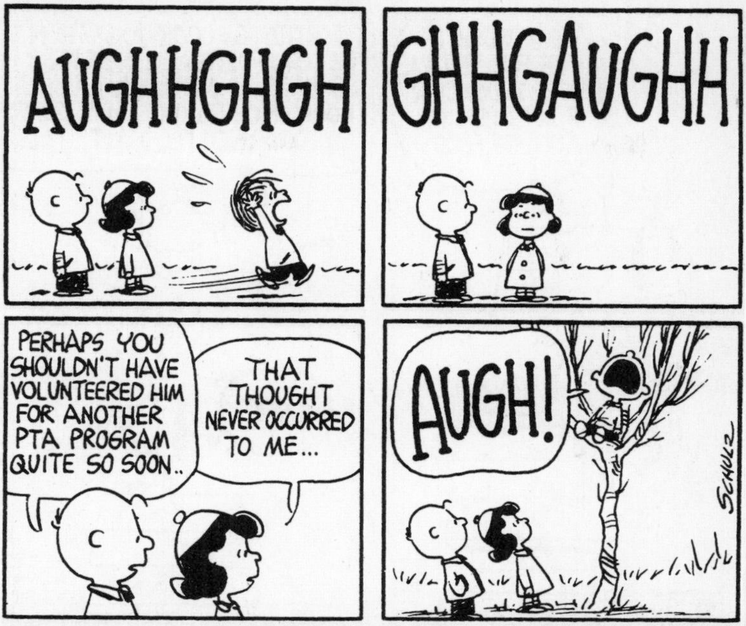
AUGHHGHGH
GHHGAUGHH
PERHAPS YOU SHOULDN'T HAVE VOLUNTEERED HIM FOR ANOTHER PTA PROGRAM QUITE SO SOON..
THAT THOUGHT NEVER OCCURRED TO ME...
AUGH!
SCHULZ

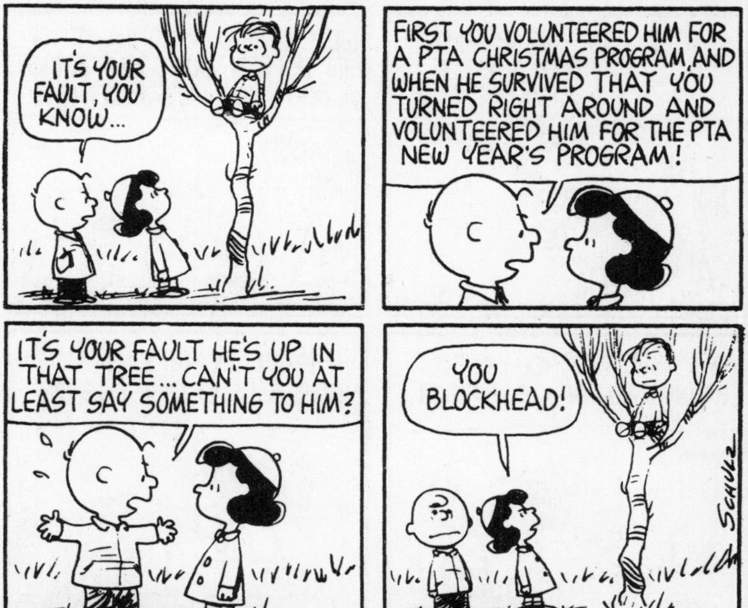
IT'S YOUR FAULT, YOU KNOW...
FIRST YOU VOLUNTEERED HIM FOR A PTA CHRISTMAS PROGRAM, AND WHEN HE SURVIVED THAT YOU TURNED RIGHT AROUND AND VOLUNTEERED HIM FOR THE PTA NEW YEAR'S PROGRAM!
IT'S YOUR FAULT HE'S UP IN THAT TREE... CAN'T YOU AT LEAST SAY SOMETHING TO HIM?
YOU BLOCKHEAD!
SCHULZ

I WONDER IF IT'S SUPPERTIME YET...I WONDER IF MY DISH IS FULL OF FOOD..
I HATE TO LOOK AND THEN BE DISAPPOINTED...IT'S BETTER TO WAIT...WHO CAN WAIT? I'LL LOOK..NO! I WON'T....I'VE GOT TO LOOK...NO! I'LL WAIT...I'LL..
RATS!
SCHULZ

I'VE ALWAYS BEEN SORT OF AFRAID OF DOGS...
WELL, IF YOU DON'T WANT TO GET BITTEN, JUST DON'T BOTHER A DOG WHILE HE'S EATING...
AND WHATEVER YOU DO, DON'T GET INVOLVED IN A DOG FIGHT..
IN FACT, DON'T EVEN GO NEAR A LOUD DISCUSSION!
SCHULZ

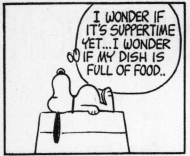

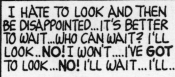

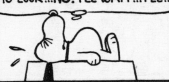

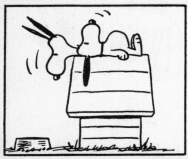

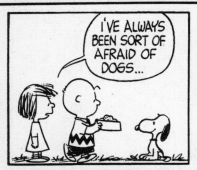

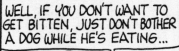

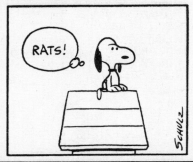

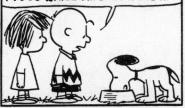

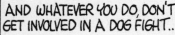

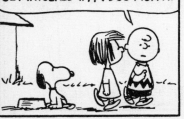

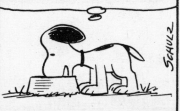

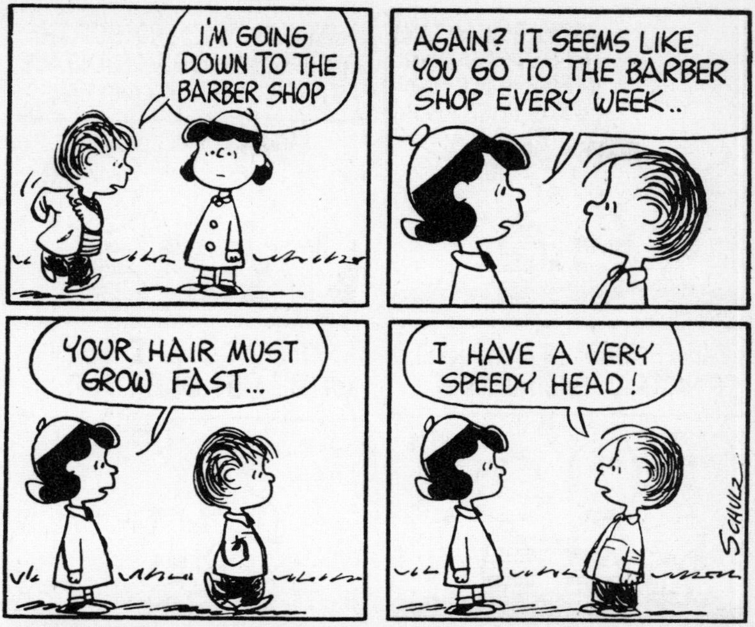
I'M GOING DOWN TO THE BARBER SHOP
AGAIN? IT SEEMS LIKE YOU GO TO THE BARBER SHOP EVERY WEEK..
YOUR HAIR MUST GROW FAST...
I HAVE A VERY SPEEDY HEAD!
SCHULZ

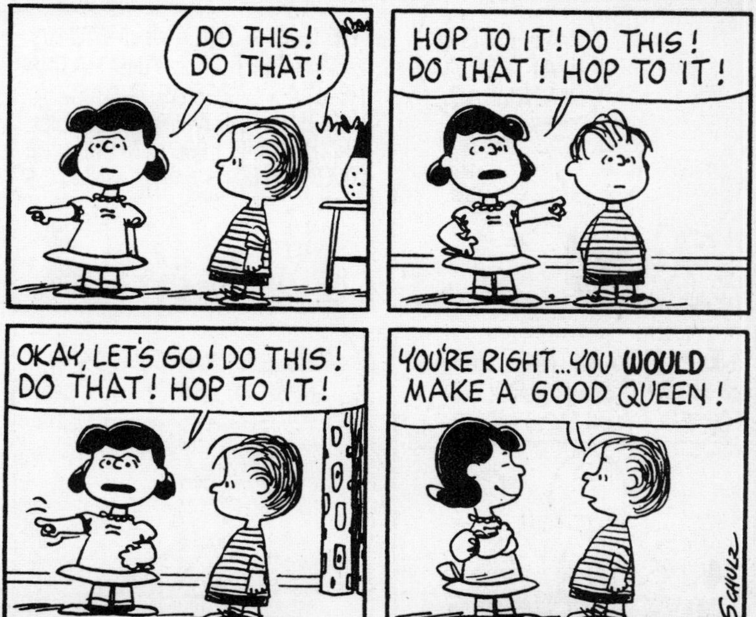
DO THIS! DO THAT!
HOP TO IT! DO THIS! DO THAT! HOP TO IT!
OKAY, LET'S GO! DO THIS! DO THAT! HOP TO IT!
YOU'RE RIGHT...YOU **WOULD** MAKE A GOOD QUEEN!
SCHULZ

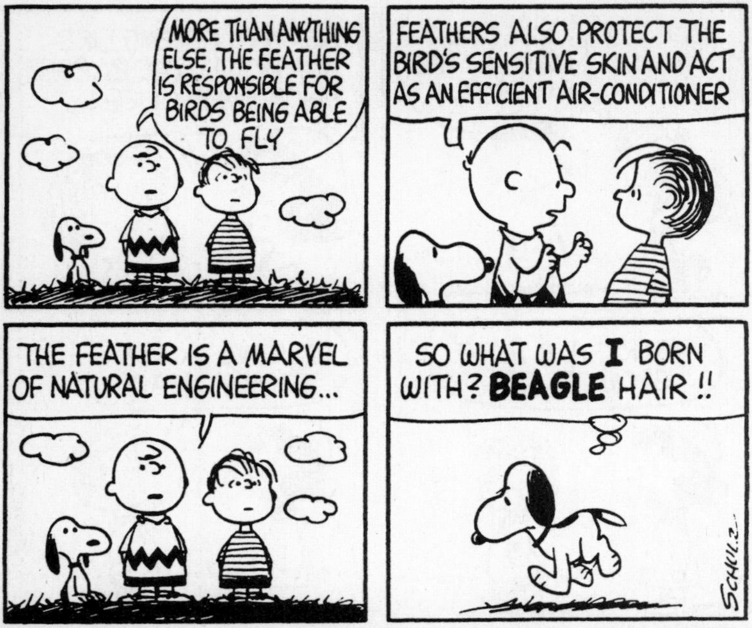
MORE THAN ANYTHING ELSE, THE FEATHER IS RESPONSIBLE FOR BIRDS BEING ABLE TO FLY
FEATHERS ALSO PROTECT THE BIRD'S SENSITIVE SKIN AND ACT AS AN EFFICIENT AIR-CONDITIONER
THE FEATHER IS A MARVEL OF NATURAL ENGINEERING...
SO WHAT WAS I BORN WITH? BEAGLE HAIR!!
SCHULZ

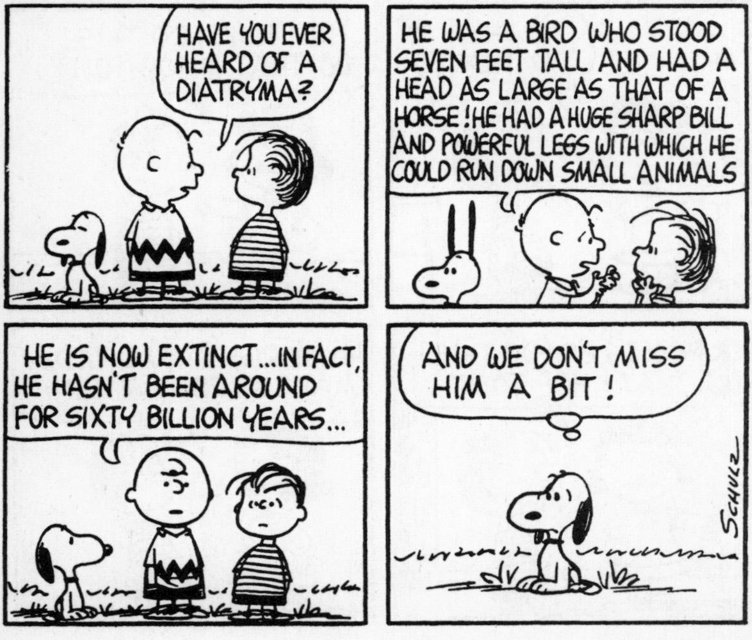
HAVE YOU EVER HEARD OF A DIATRYMA?
HE WAS A BIRD WHO STOOD SEVEN FEET TALL AND HAD A HEAD AS LARGE AS THAT OF A HORSE! HE HAD A HUGE SHARP BILL AND POWERFUL LEGS WITH WHICH HE COULD RUN DOWN SMALL ANIMALS
HE IS NOW EXTINCT...IN FACT, HE HASN'T BEEN AROUND FOR SIXTY BILLION YEARS...
AND WE DON'T MISS HIM A BIT!
SCHULZ

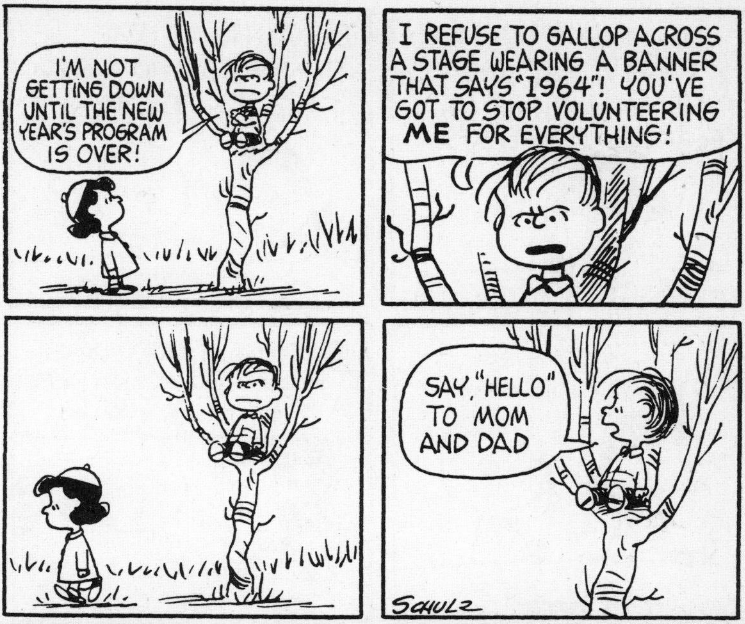
I'M NOT GETTING DOWN UNTIL THE NEW YEAR'S PROGRAM IS OVER!
I REFUSE TO GALLOP ACROSS A STAGE WEARING A BANNER THAT SAYS "1964"! YOU'VE GOT TO STOP VOLUNTEERING **ME** FOR EVERYTHING!
SAY, "HELLO" TO MOM AND DAD
SCHULZ

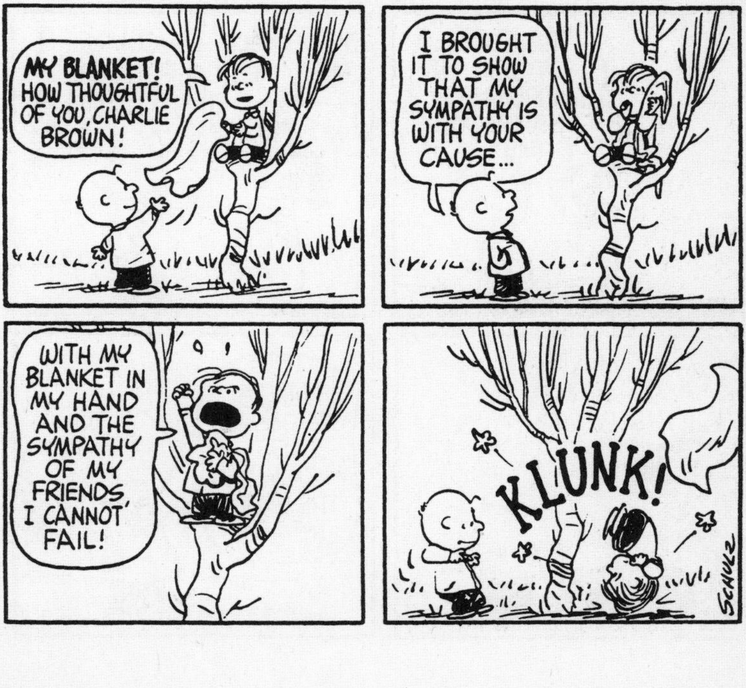
MY BLANKET! HOW THOUGHTFUL OF YOU, CHARLIE BROWN!
I BROUGHT IT TO SHOW THAT MY SYMPATHY IS WITH YOUR CAUSE...
WITH MY BLANKET IN MY HAND AND THE SYMPATHY OF MY FRIENDS, I CANNOT FAIL!
KLUNK!
SCHULZ

TO WHOM IT MAY CONCERN, I AM WRITING IN REGARD TO GOOD DAYS.
I WANT THREE HUNDRED AND SIXTY FIVE OF THEM.
IF YOU WANT GOOD DAYS, IT'S BEST TO ORDER THEM A YEAR AT A TIME!
SCHULZ

THERE! I'VE JUST SENT IN MY ORDER FOR 365 GOOD DAYS..
US MAIL
BY "GOOD," OF COURSE, I MEAN GOOD FOR ME!
THAT'S GREAT! SHE'S JUST PRE-EMPTED THE WHOLE YEAR!
SCHULZ

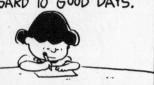

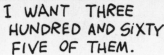

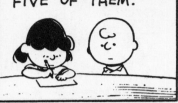

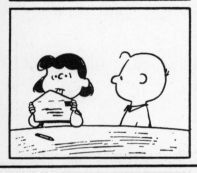

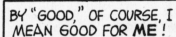

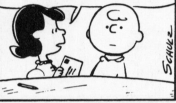

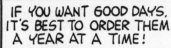

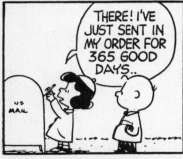

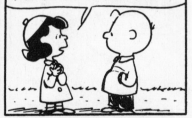

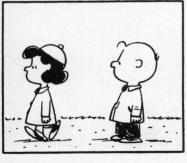

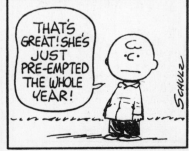

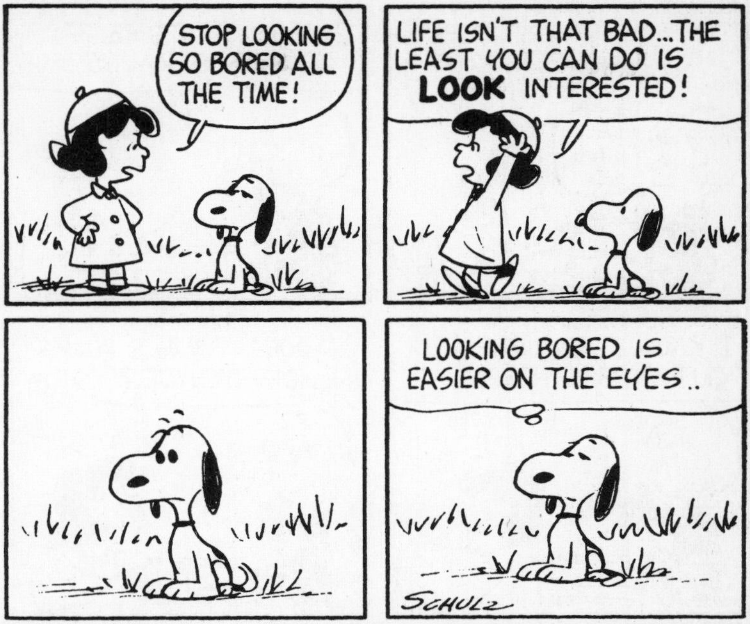
STOP LOOKING SO BORED ALL THE TIME!
LIFE ISN'T THAT BAD...THE LEAST YOU CAN DO IS **LOOK** INTERESTED!
LOOKING BORED IS EASIER ON THE EYES..
SCHULZ

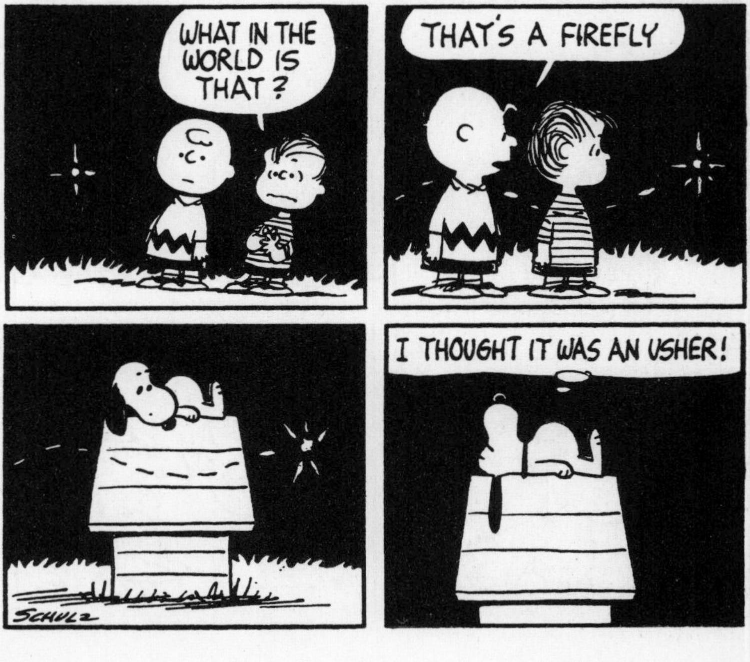
WHAT IN THE WORLD IS THAT?
THAT'S A FIREFLY
SCHULZ
I THOUGHT IT WAS AN USHER!

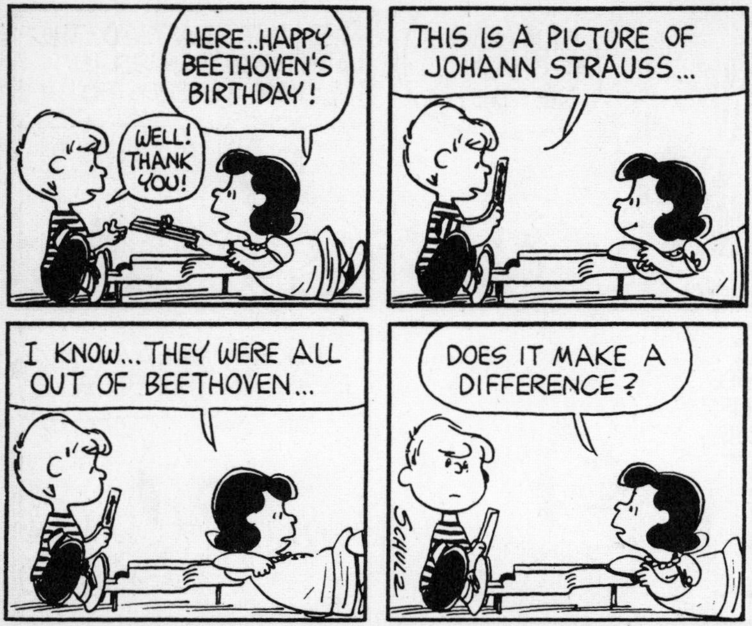
HERE..HAPPY BEETHOVEN'S BIRTHDAY!
WELL! THANK YOU!
THIS IS A PICTURE OF JOHANN STRAUSS...
I KNOW...THEY WERE ALL OUT OF BEETHOVEN...
DOES IT MAKE A DIFFERENCE?
SCHULZ

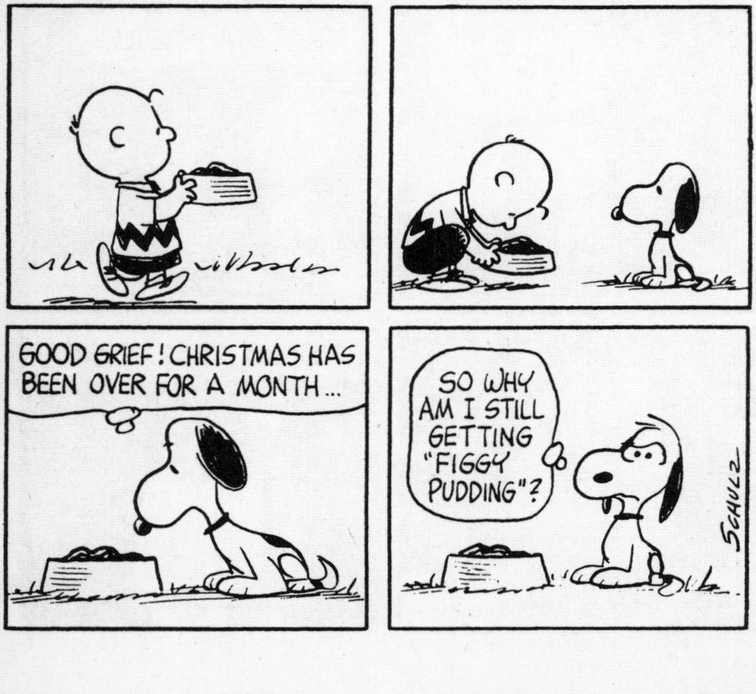
GOOD GRIEF! CHRISTMAS HAS BEEN OVER FOR A MONTH...
SO WHY AM I STILL GETTING "FIGGY PUDDING"?
SCHULZ

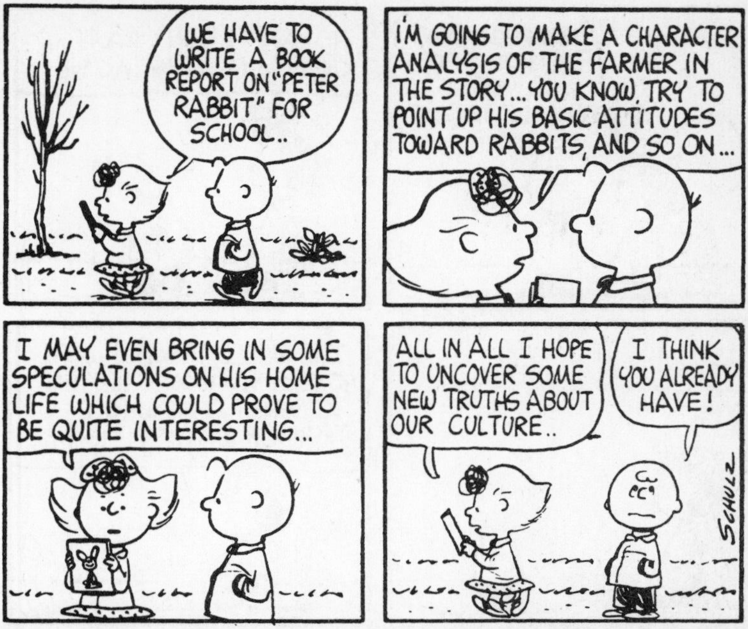
WE HAVE TO WRITE A BOOK REPORT ON "PETER RABBIT" FOR SCHOOL..
I'M GOING TO MAKE A CHARACTER ANALYSIS OF THE FARMER IN THE STORY... YOU KNOW, TRY TO POINT UP HIS BASIC ATTITUDES TOWARD RABBITS, AND SO ON...
I MAY EVEN BRING IN SOME SPECULATIONS ON HIS HOME LIFE WHICH COULD PROVE TO BE QUITE INTERESTING...
ALL IN ALL I HOPE TO UNCOVER SOME NEW TRUTHS ABOUT OUR CULTURE..
I THINK YOU ALREADY HAVE!
SCHULZ

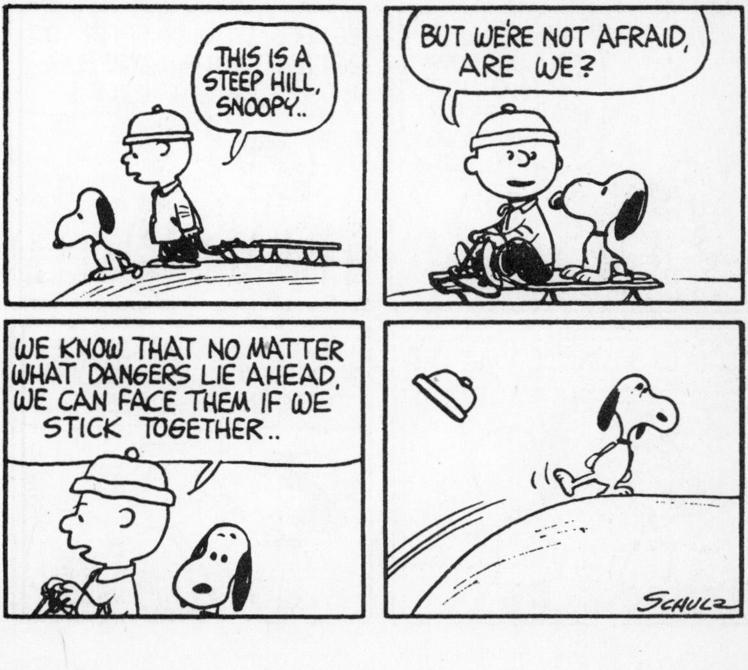
THIS IS A STEEP HILL, SNOOPY..
BUT WE'RE NOT AFRAID, ARE WE?
WE KNOW THAT NO MATTER WHAT DANGERS LIE AHEAD, WE CAN FACE THEM IF WE STICK TOGETHER..
SCHULZ

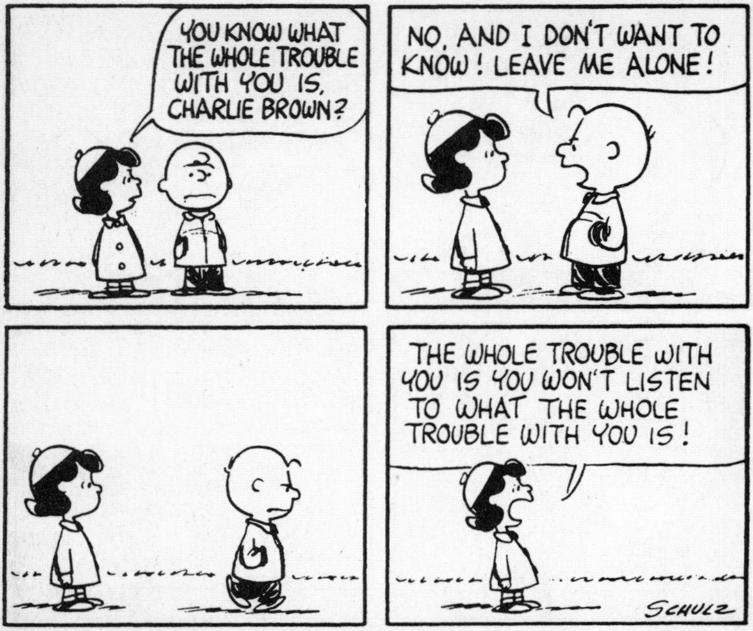
YOU KNOW WHAT THE WHOLE TROUBLE WITH YOU IS, CHARLIE BROWN?
NO, AND I DON'T WANT TO KNOW! LEAVE ME ALONE!
THE WHOLE TROUBLE WITH YOU IS YOU WON'T LISTEN TO WHAT THE WHOLE TROUBLE WITH YOU IS!
SCHULZ

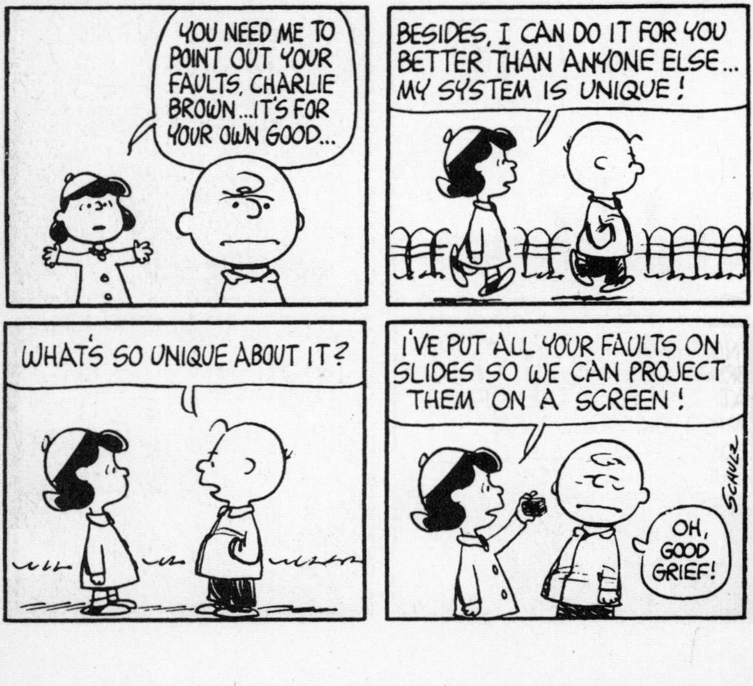
YOU NEED ME TO POINT OUT YOUR FAULTS, CHARLIE BROWN...IT'S FOR YOUR OWN GOOD...
BESIDES, I CAN DO IT FOR YOU BETTER THAN ANYONE ELSE... MY SYSTEM IS UNIQUE!
WHAT'S SO UNIQUE ABOUT IT?
I'VE PUT ALL YOUR FAULTS ON SLIDES SO WE CAN PROJECT THEM ON A SCREEN!
OH, GOOD GRIEF!
SCHULZ

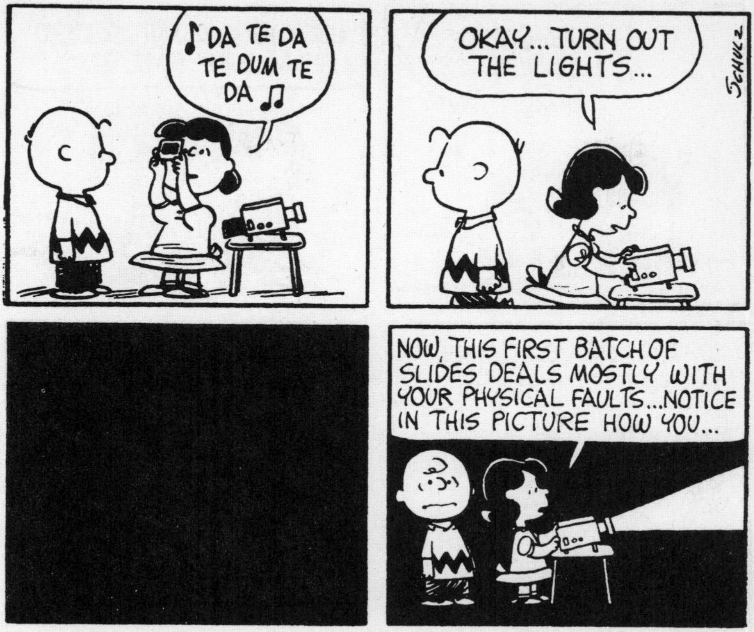
DA TE DA TE DUM TE DA
OKAY... TURN OUT THE LIGHTS...
SCHULZ
NOW, THIS FIRST BATCH OF SLIDES DEALS MOSTLY WITH YOUR PHYSICAL FAULTS...NOTICE IN THIS PICTURE HOW YOU...

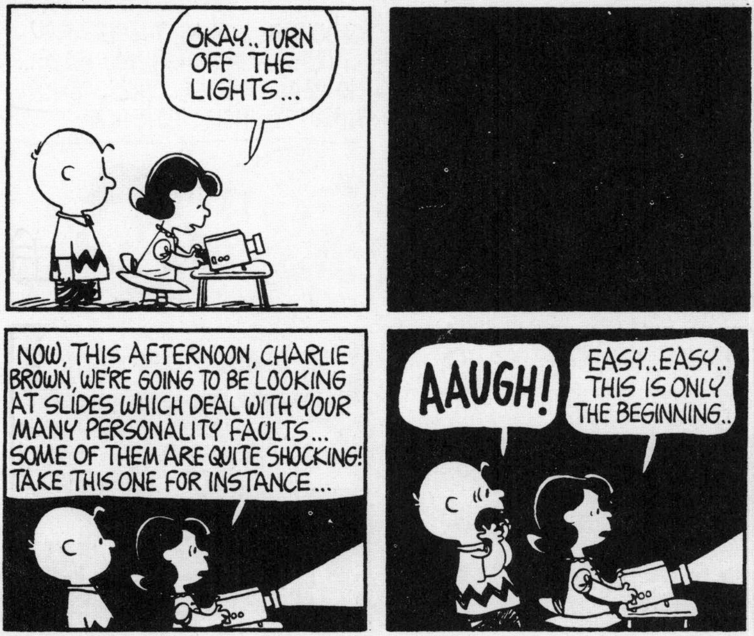
OKAY..TURN OFF THE LIGHTS...
NOW, THIS AFTERNOON, CHARLIE BROWN, WE'RE GOING TO BE LOOKING AT SLIDES WHICH DEAL WITH YOUR MANY PERSONALITY FAULTS... SOME OF THEM ARE QUITE SHOCKING! TAKE THIS ONE FOR INSTANCE...
AAUGH!
EASY..EASY.. THIS IS ONLY THE BEGINNING..

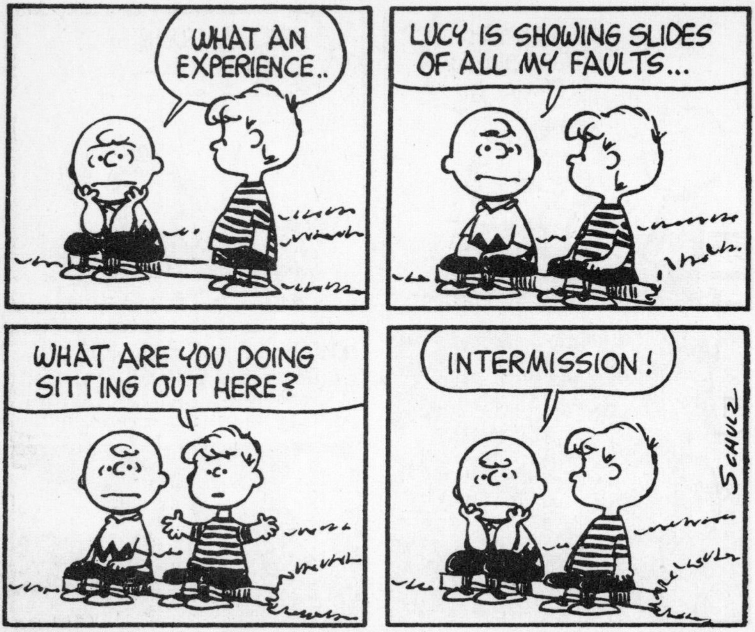
WHAT AN EXPERIENCE..
LUCY IS SHOWING SLIDES OF ALL MY FAULTS...
WHAT ARE YOU DOING SITTING OUT HERE?
INTERMISSION!
SCHULZ

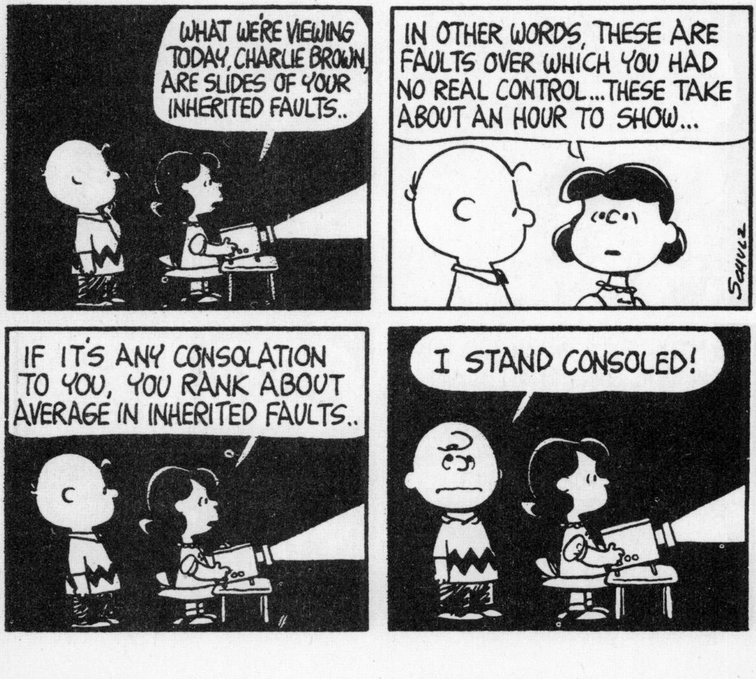
WHAT WE'RE VIEWING TODAY, CHARLIE BROWN, ARE SLIDES OF YOUR INHERITED FAULTS..
IN OTHER WORDS, THESE ARE FAULTS OVER WHICH YOU HAD NO REAL CONTROL...THESE TAKE ABOUT AN HOUR TO SHOW...
SCHULZ
IF IT'S ANY CONSOLATION TO YOU, YOU RANK ABOUT AVERAGE IN INHERITED FAULTS..
I STAND CONSOLED!

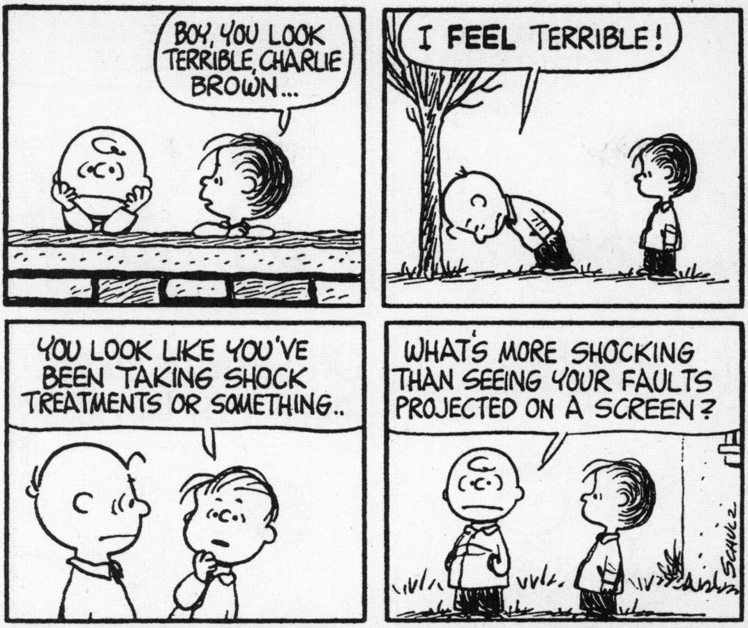
BOY, YOU LOOK TERRIBLE, CHARLIE BROWN...
I FEEL TERRIBLE!
YOU LOOK LIKE YOU'VE BEEN TAKING SHOCK TREATMENTS OR SOMETHING..
WHAT'S MORE SHOCKING THAN SEEING YOUR FAULTS PROJECTED ON A SCREEN?
SCHULZ

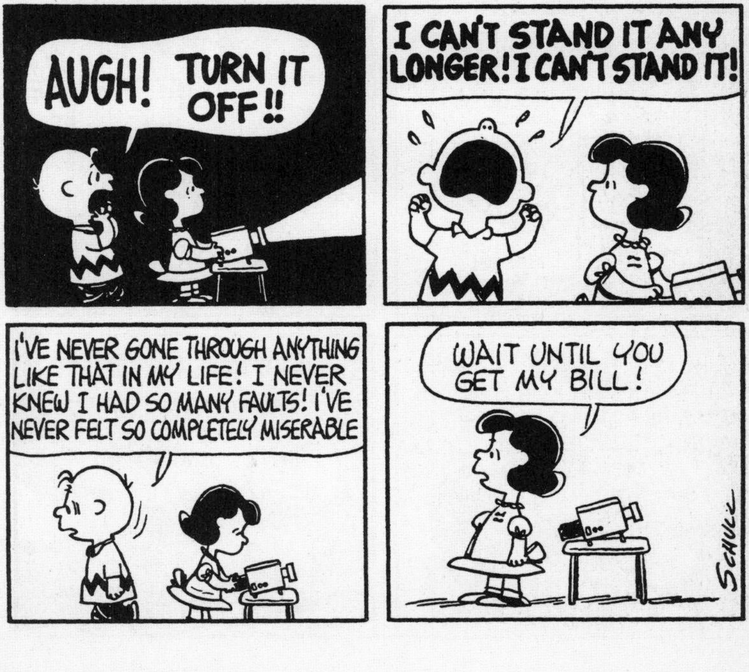
AUGH! TURN IT OFF!!
I CAN'T STAND IT ANY LONGER! I CAN'T STAND IT!
I'VE NEVER GONE THROUGH ANYTHING LIKE THAT IN MY LIFE! I NEVER KNEW I HAD SO MANY FAULTS! I'VE NEVER FELT SO COMPLETELY MISERABLE
WAIT UNTIL YOU GET MY BILL!
SCHULZ

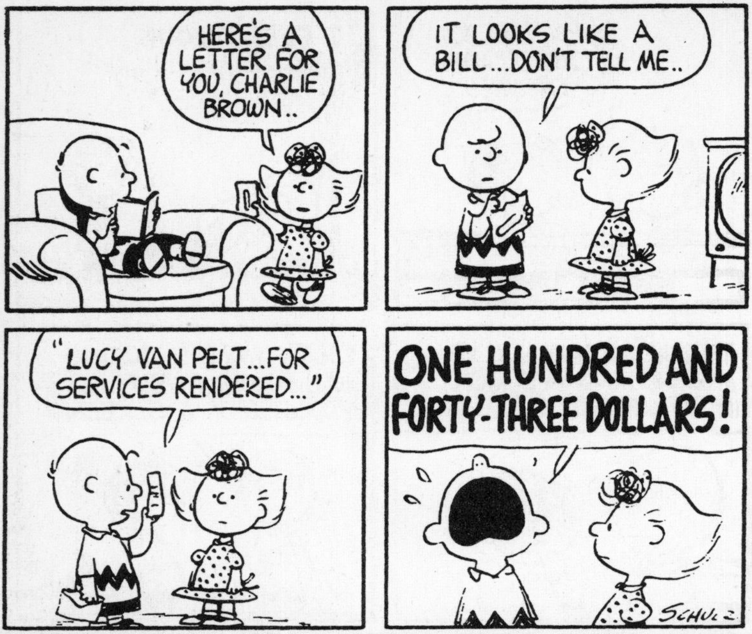
HERE'S A LETTER FOR YOU, CHARLIE BROWN..
IT LOOKS LIKE A BILL...DON'T TELL ME..
"LUCY VAN PELT...FOR SERVICES RENDERED..."
ONE HUNDRED AND FORTY-THREE DOLLARS!
SCHULZ

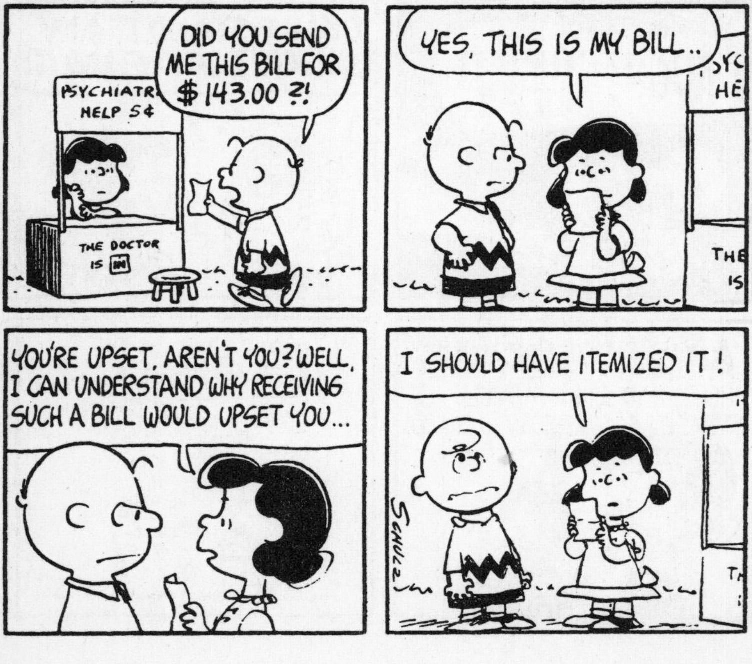
PSYCHIATR
HELP 5¢
THE DOCTOR IS IN
DID YOU SEND ME THIS BILL FOR $143.00 ?!
YES, THIS IS MY BILL..
YOU'RE UPSET, AREN'T YOU? WELL, I CAN UNDERSTAND WHY RECEIVING SUCH A BILL WOULD UPSET YOU...
I SHOULD HAVE ITEMIZED IT!
SCHULZ

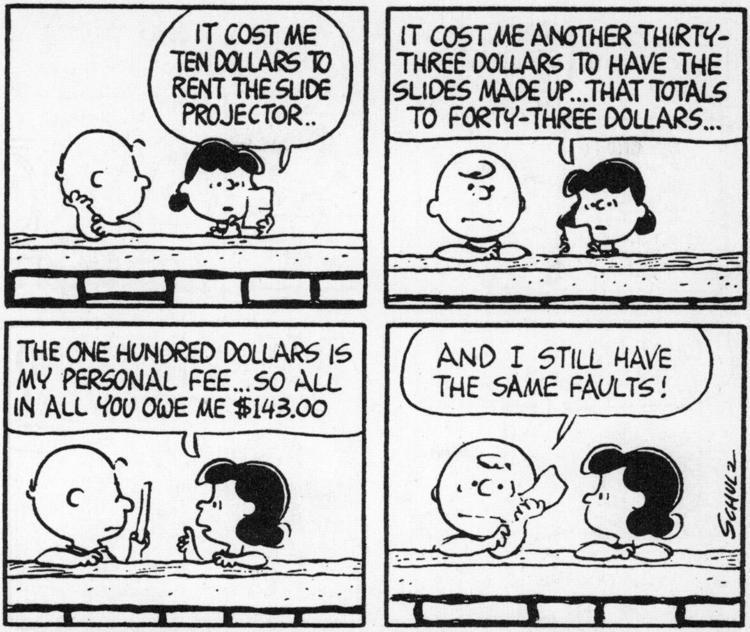
IT COST ME TEN DOLLARS TO RENT THE SLIDE PROJECTOR..
IT COST ME ANOTHER THIRTY-THREE DOLLARS TO HAVE THE SLIDES MADE UP...THAT TOTALS TO FORTY-THREE DOLLARS...
THE ONE HUNDRED DOLLARS IS MY PERSONAL FEE...SO ALL IN ALL YOU OWE ME $143.00
AND I STILL HAVE THE SAME FAULTS!
SCHULZ

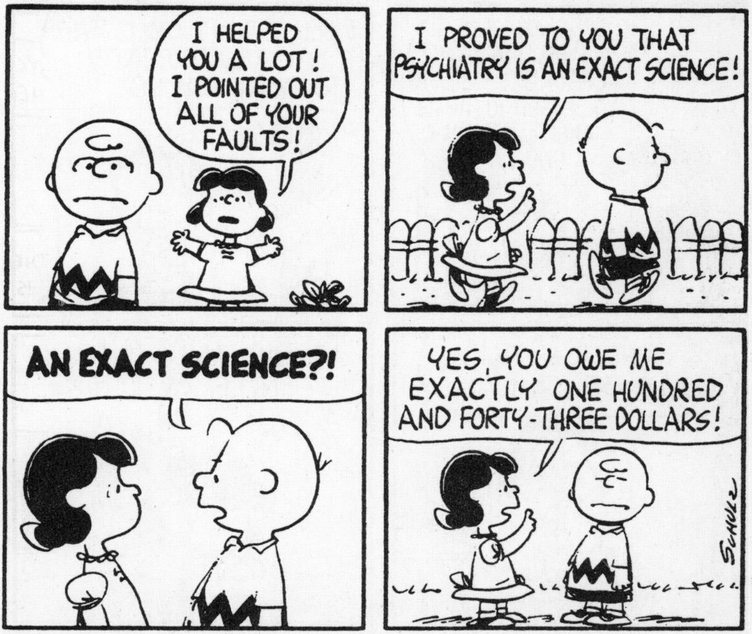
I HELPED YOU A LOT! I POINTED OUT ALL OF YOUR FAULTS!
I PROVED TO YOU THAT PSYCHIATRY IS AN EXACT SCIENCE!
AN EXACT SCIENCE?!
YES, YOU OWE ME EXACTLY ONE HUNDRED AND FORTY-THREE DOLLARS!
SCHULZ

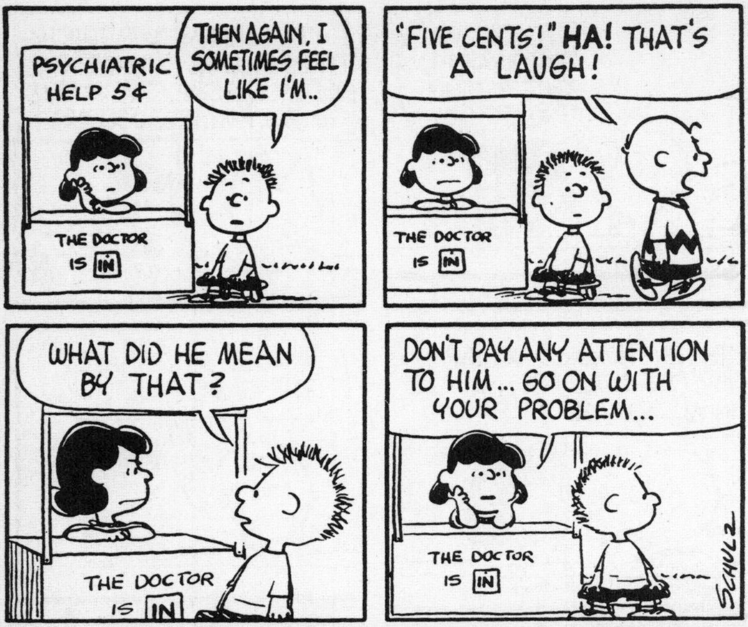
PSYCHIATRIC HELP 5¢
THE DOCTOR IS IN
THEN AGAIN, I SOMETIMES FEEL LIKE I'M..
"FIVE CENTS!" HA! THAT'S A LAUGH!
THE DOCTOR IS IN
WHAT DID HE MEAN BY THAT?
THE DOCTOR IS IN
DON'T PAY ANY ATTENTION TO HIM... GO ON WITH YOUR PROBLEM...
THE DOCTOR IS IN
SCHULZ

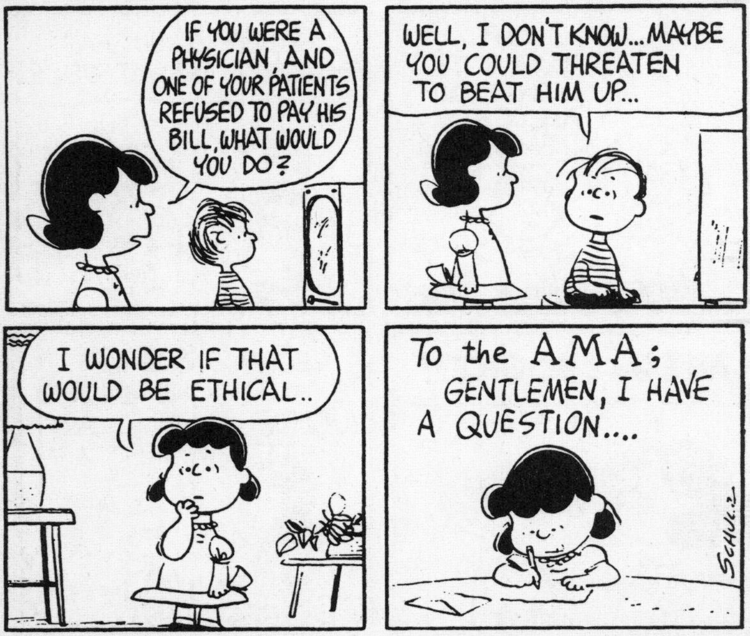
IF YOU WERE A PHYSICIAN, AND ONE OF YOUR PATIENTS REFUSED TO PAY HIS BILL, WHAT WOULD YOU DO?
WELL, I DON'T KNOW...MAYBE YOU COULD THREATEN TO BEAT HIM UP...
I WONDER IF THAT WOULD BE ETHICAL..
To the AMA;
GENTLEMEN, I HAVE A QUESTION....
SCHULZ

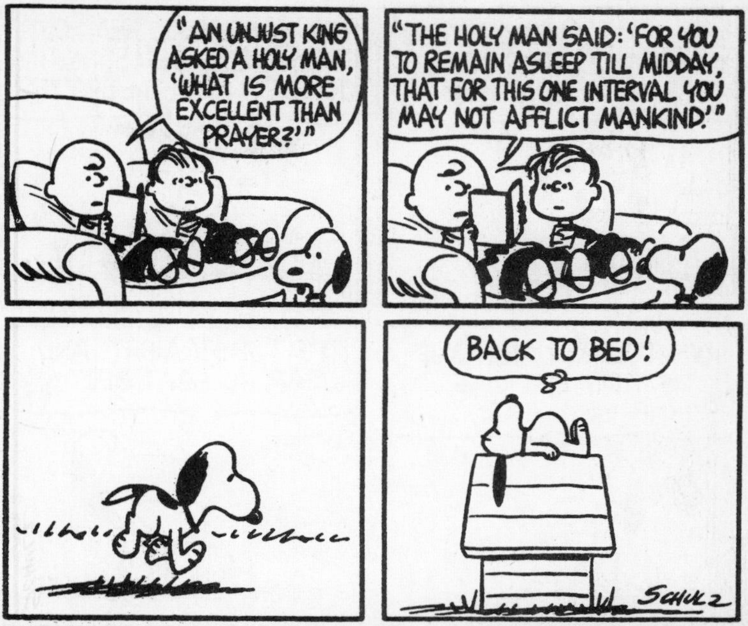
"AN UNJUST KING ASKED A HOLY MAN, 'WHAT IS MORE EXCELLENT THAN PRAYER?'"
"THE HOLY MAN SAID: 'FOR YOU TO REMAIN ASLEEP TILL MIDDAY, THAT FOR THIS ONE INTERVAL YOU MAY NOT AFFLICT MANKIND.'"
BACK TO BED!
SCHULZ

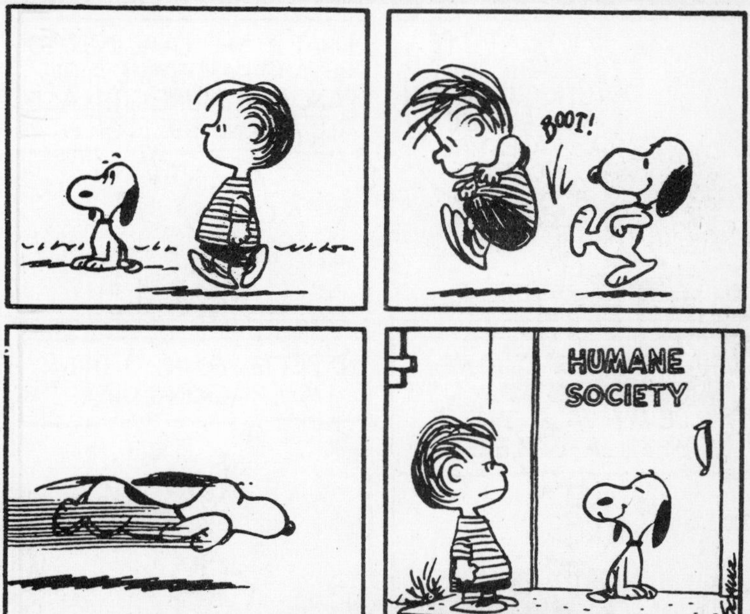
BOOT!
HUMANE SOCIETY

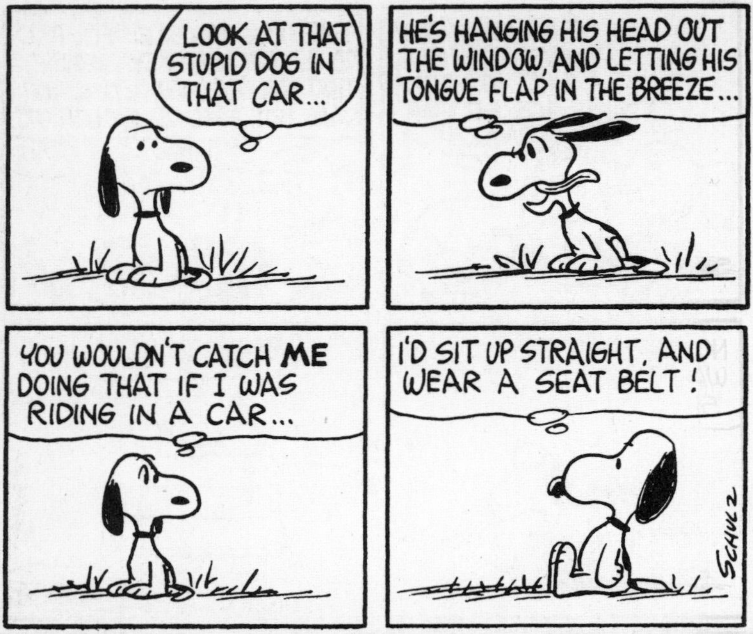
LOOK AT THAT STUPID DOG IN THAT CAR...
HE'S HANGING HIS HEAD OUT THE WINDOW, AND LETTING HIS TONGUE FLAP IN THE BREEZE...
YOU WOULDN'T CATCH **ME** DOING THAT IF I WAS RIDING IN A CAR...
I'D SIT UP STRAIGHT, AND WEAR A SEAT BELT!
SCHULZ

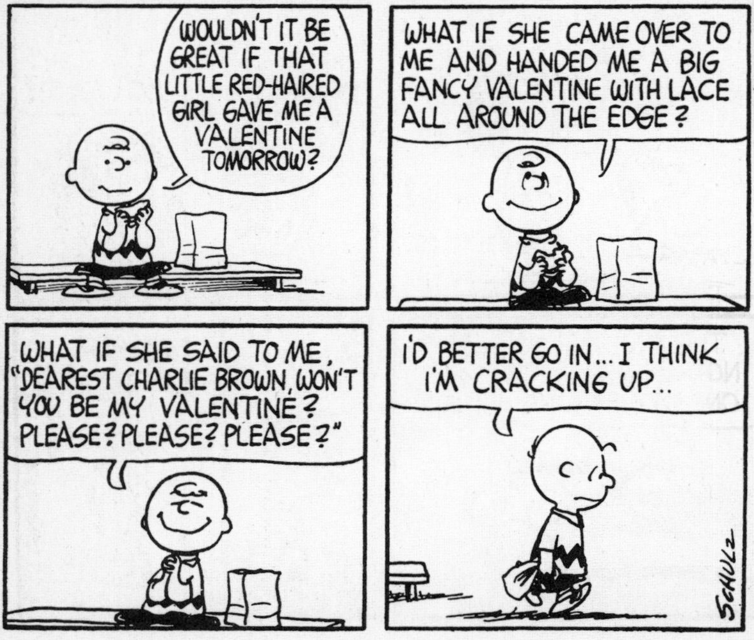
WOULDN'T IT BE GREAT IF THAT LITTLE RED-HAIRED GIRL GAVE ME A VALENTINE TOMORROW?
WHAT IF SHE CAME OVER TO ME AND HANDED ME A BIG FANCY VALENTINE WITH LACE ALL AROUND THE EDGE?
WHAT IF SHE SAID TO ME, "DEAREST CHARLIE BROWN, WON'T YOU BE MY VALENTINE? PLEASE? PLEASE? PLEASE?"
I'D BETTER GO IN... I THINK I'M CRACKING UP...
SCHULZ

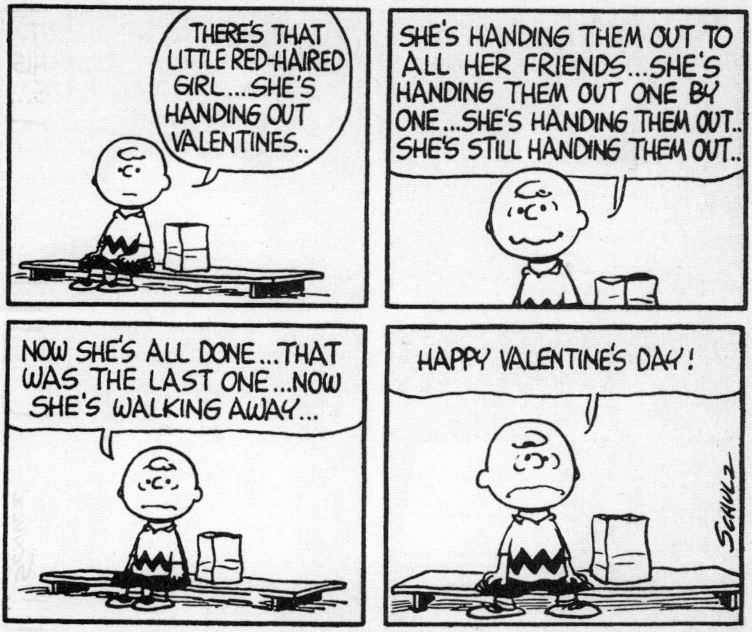
THERE'S THAT LITTLE RED-HAIRED GIRL....SHE'S HANDING OUT VALENTINES..
SHE'S HANDING THEM OUT TO ALL HER FRIENDS...SHE'S HANDING THEM OUT ONE BY ONE....SHE'S HANDING THEM OUT.. SHE'S STILL HANDING THEM OUT..
NOW SHE'S ALL DONE...THAT WAS THE LAST ONE...NOW SHE'S WALKING AWAY...
HAPPY VALENTINE'S DAY!
SCHULZ

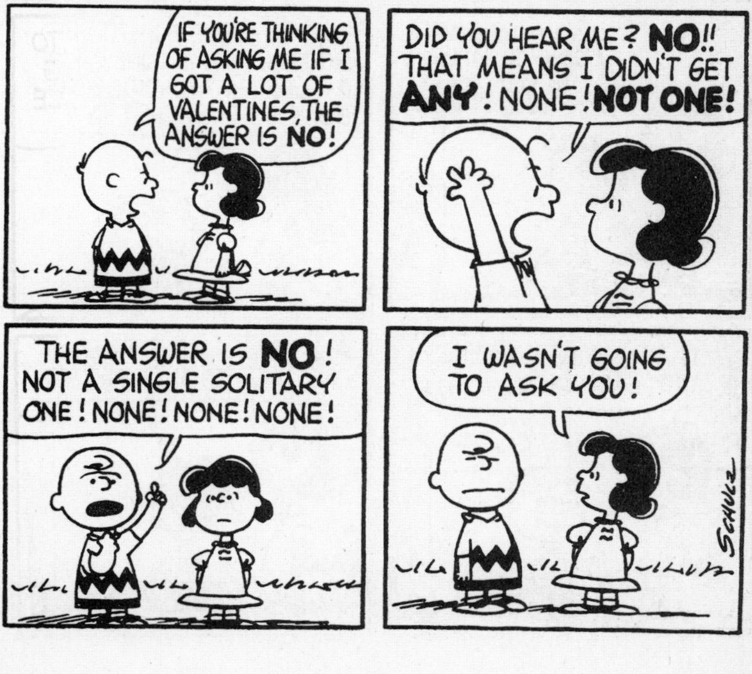
IF YOU'RE THINKING OF ASKING ME IF I GOT A LOT OF VALENTINES, THE ANSWER IS NO!
DID YOU HEAR ME? NO!! THAT MEANS I DIDN'T GET ANY! NONE! NOT ONE!
THE ANSWER IS NO! NOT A SINGLE SOLITARY ONE! NONE! NONE! NONE!
I WASN'T GOING TO ASK YOU!
SCHULZ

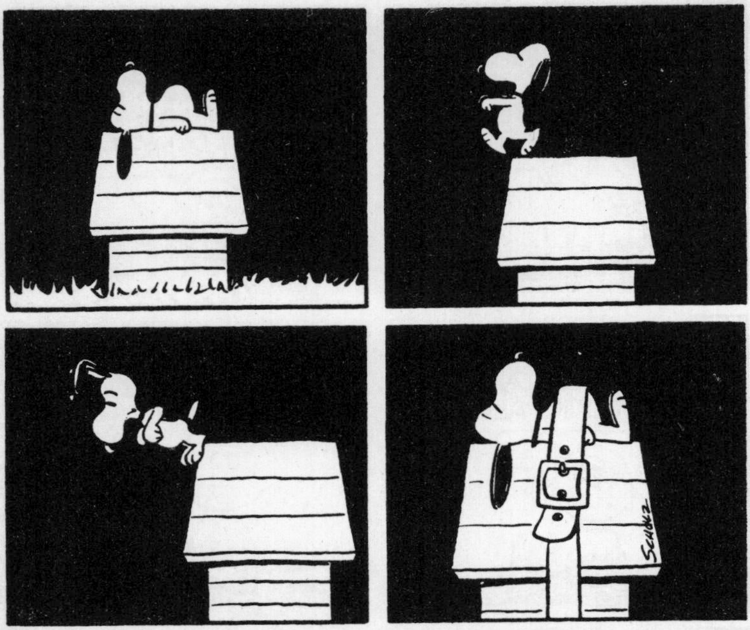

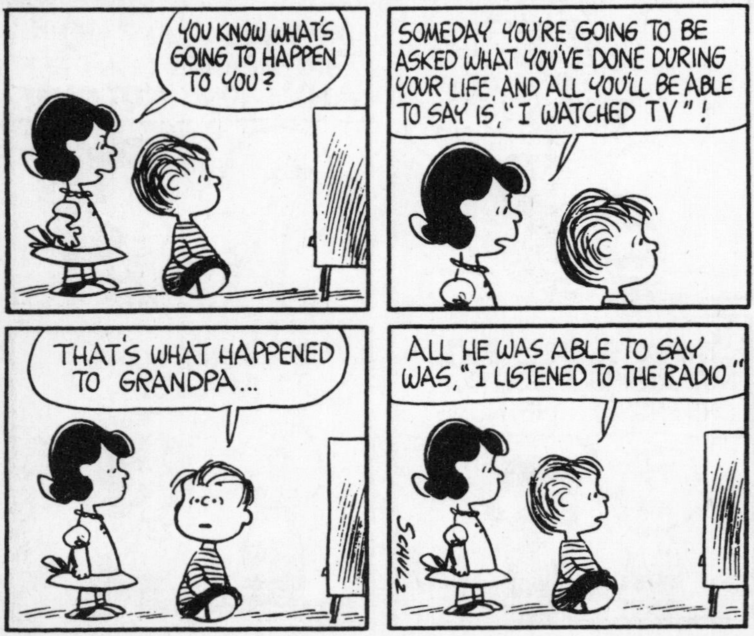
YOU KNOW WHAT'S GOING TO HAPPEN TO YOU?
SOMEDAY YOU'RE GOING TO BE ASKED WHAT YOU'VE DONE DURING YOUR LIFE, AND ALL YOU'LL BE ABLE TO SAY IS, "I WATCHED TV"!
THAT'S WHAT HAPPENED TO GRANDPA...
ALL HE WAS ABLE TO SAY WAS, "I LISTENED TO THE RADIO"
SCHULZ

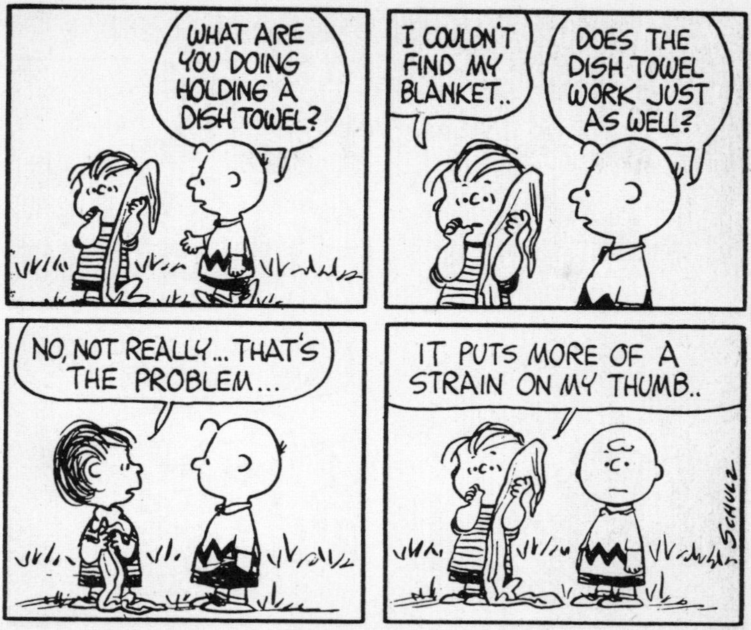
WHAT ARE YOU DOING HOLDING A DISH TOWEL?
I COULDN'T FIND MY BLANKET..
DOES THE DISH TOWEL WORK JUST AS WELL?
NO, NOT REALLY... THAT'S THE PROBLEM...
IT PUTS MORE OF A STRAIN ON MY THUMB..
SCHULZ

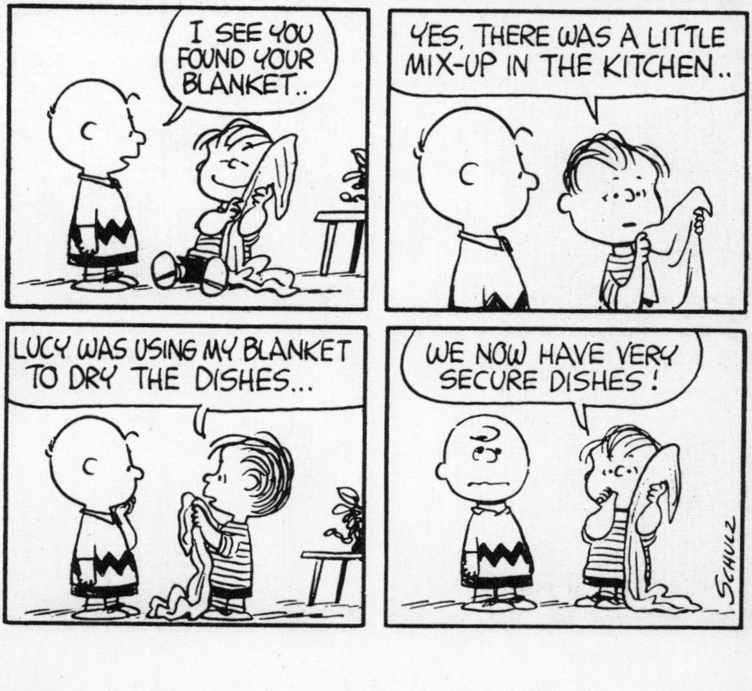
I SEE YOU FOUND YOUR BLANKET..
YES, THERE WAS A LITTLE MIX-UP IN THE KITCHEN..
LUCY WAS USING MY BLANKET TO DRY THE DISHES...
WE NOW HAVE VERY SECURE DISHES!
SCHULZ

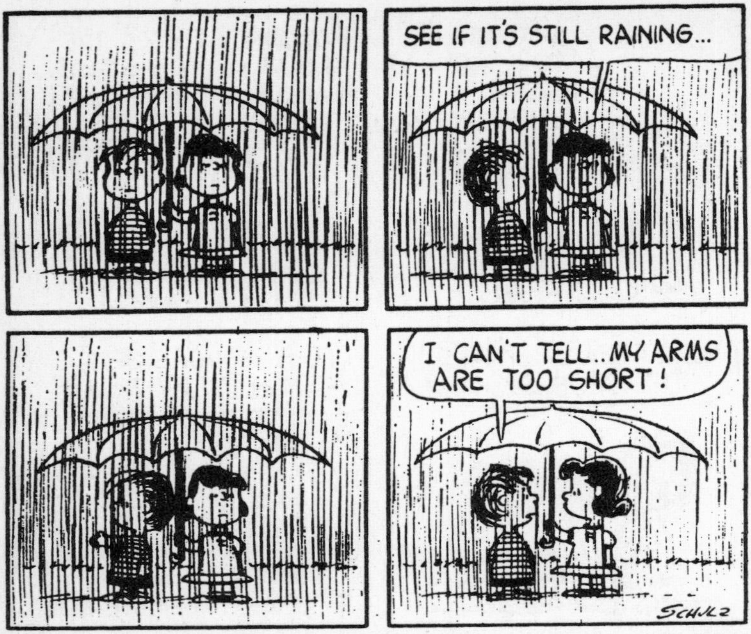
SEE IF IT'S STILL RAINING...
I CAN'T TELL..MY ARMS ARE TOO SHORT!
SCHULZ

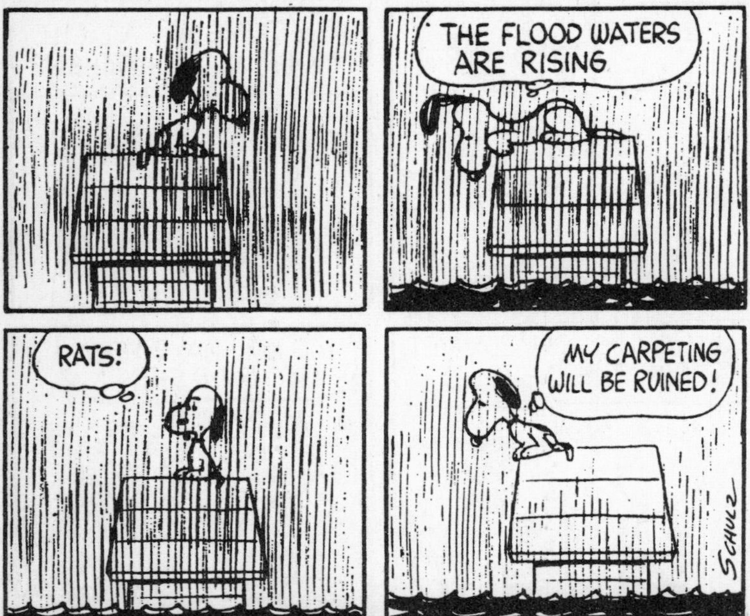
THE FLOOD WATERS ARE RISING
RATS!
MY CARPETING WILL BE RUINED!
SCHULZ

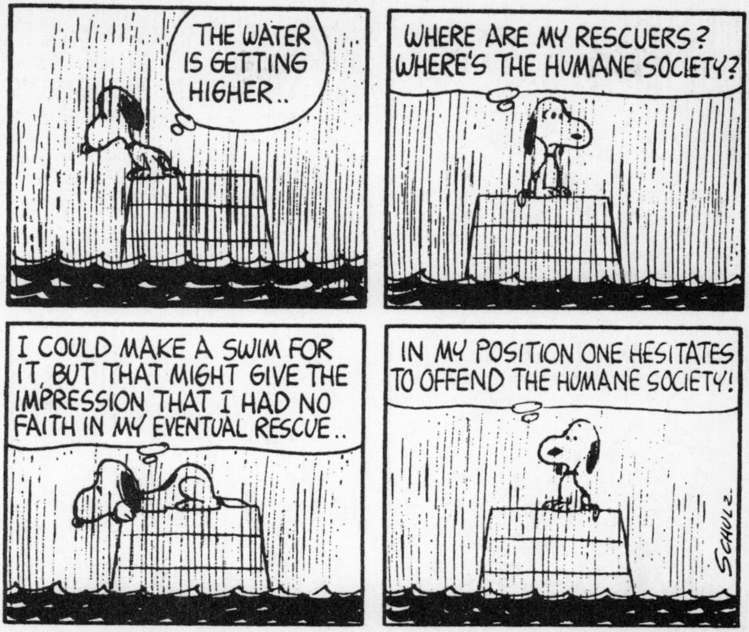
THE WATER IS GETTING HIGHER..
WHERE ARE MY RESCUERS? WHERE'S THE HUMANE SOCIETY?
I COULD MAKE A SWIM FOR IT, BUT THAT MIGHT GIVE THE IMPRESSION THAT I HAD NO FAITH IN MY EVENTUAL RESCUE..
IN MY POSITION ONE HESITATES TO OFFEND THE HUMANE SOCIETY!
SCHULZ

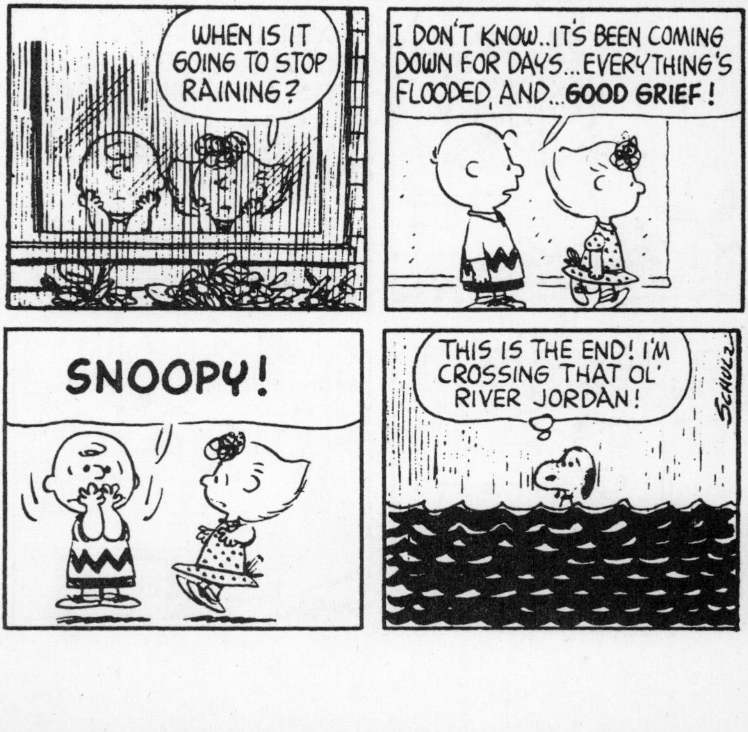
WHEN IS IT GOING TO STOP RAINING?
I DON'T KNOW..IT'S BEEN COMING DOWN FOR DAYS...EVERYTHING'S FLOODED, AND...GOOD GRIEF!
SNOOPY!
THIS IS THE END! I'M CROSSING THAT OL' RIVER JORDAN!
SCHULZ

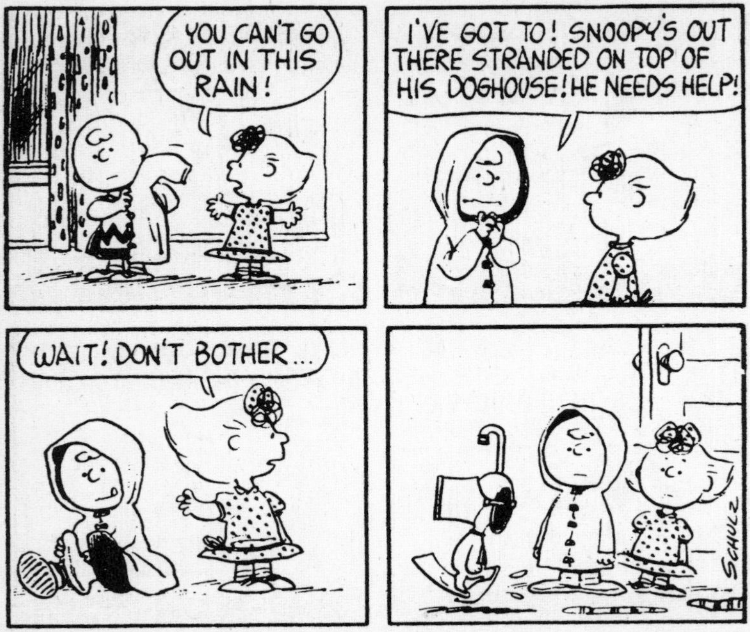
YOU CAN'T GO OUT IN THIS RAIN!
I'VE GOT TO! SNOOPY'S OUT THERE STRANDED ON TOP OF HIS DOGHOUSE! HE NEEDS HELP!
WAIT! DON'T BOTHER...
SCHULZ

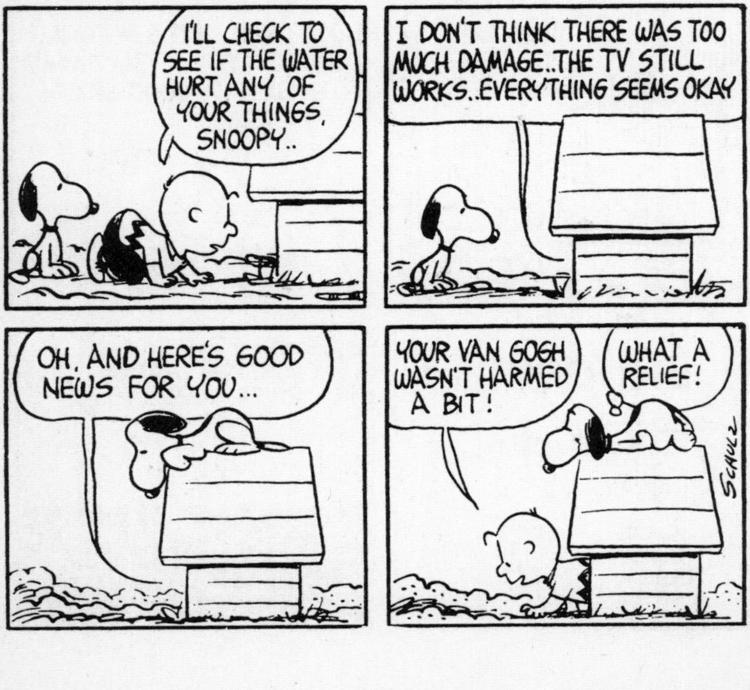
I'LL CHECK TO SEE IF THE WATER HURT ANY OF YOUR THINGS, SNOOPY..
I DON'T THINK THERE WAS TOO MUCH DAMAGE..THE TV STILL WORKS..EVERYTHING SEEMS OKAY
OH, AND HERE'S GOOD NEWS FOR YOU...
YOUR VAN GOGH WASN'T HARMED A BIT!
WHAT A RELIEF!
SCHULZ

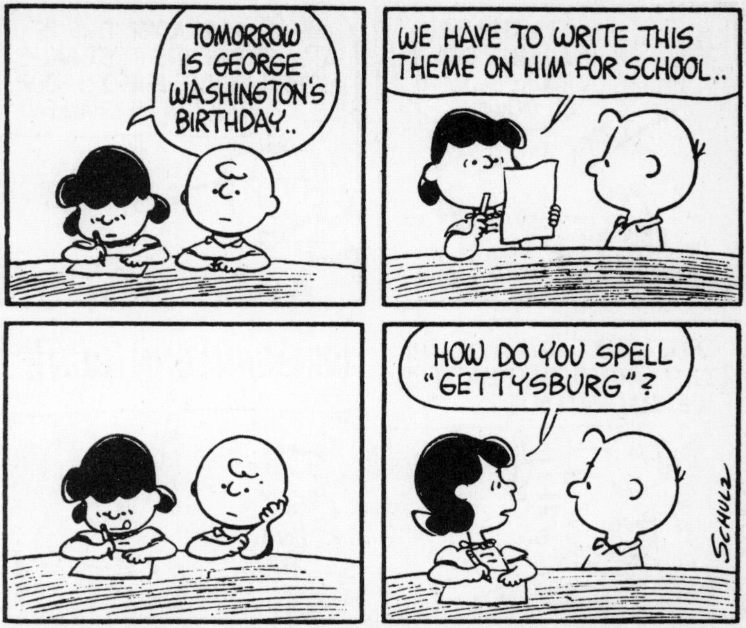
TOMORROW IS GEORGE WASHINGTON'S BIRTHDAY..
WE HAVE TO WRITE THIS THEME ON HIM FOR SCHOOL..
HOW DO YOU SPELL "GETTYSBURG"?
SCHULZ

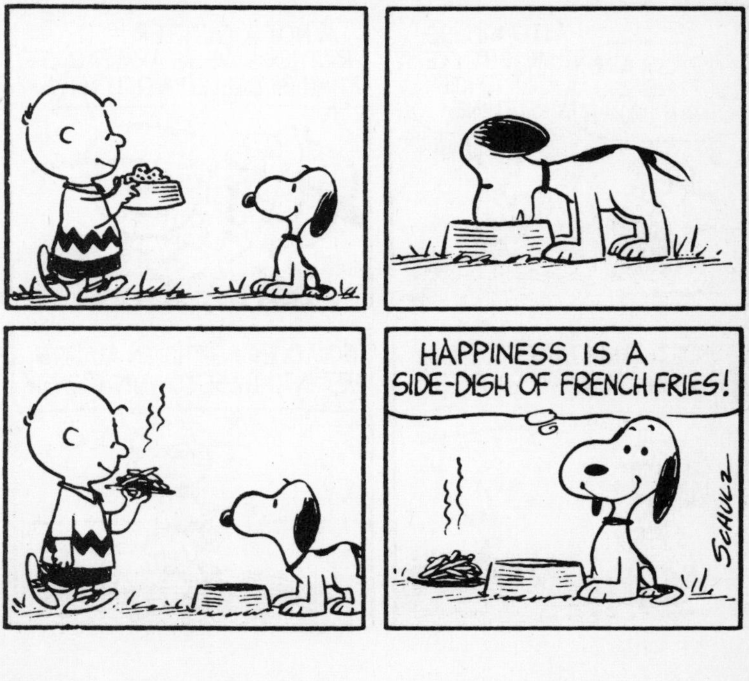
HAPPINESS IS A SIDE-DISH OF FRENCH FRIES!
SCHULZ

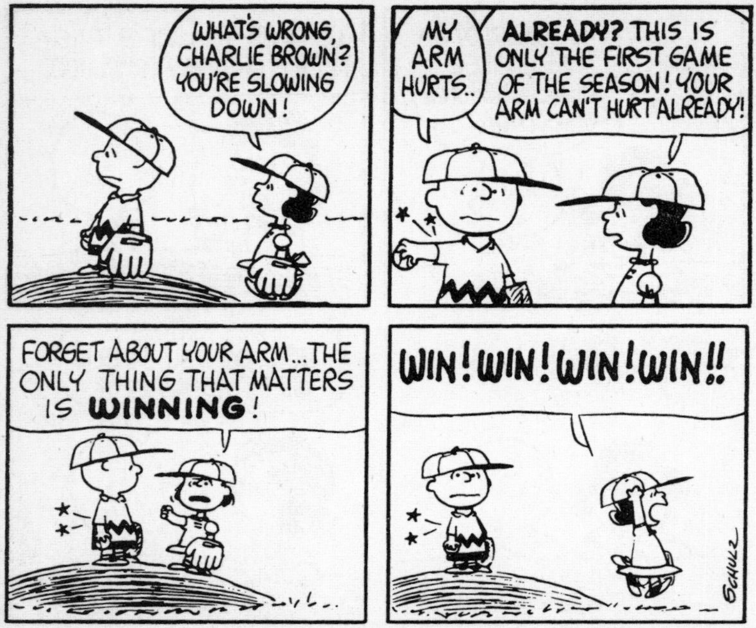
WHAT'S WRONG, CHARLIE BROWN? YOU'RE SLOWING DOWN!
MY ARM HURTS..
ALREADY? THIS IS ONLY THE FIRST GAME OF THE SEASON! YOUR ARM CAN'T HURT ALREADY!
FORGET ABOUT YOUR ARM... THE ONLY THING THAT MATTERS IS **WINNING**!
WIN! WIN! WIN! WIN!!
SCHULZ

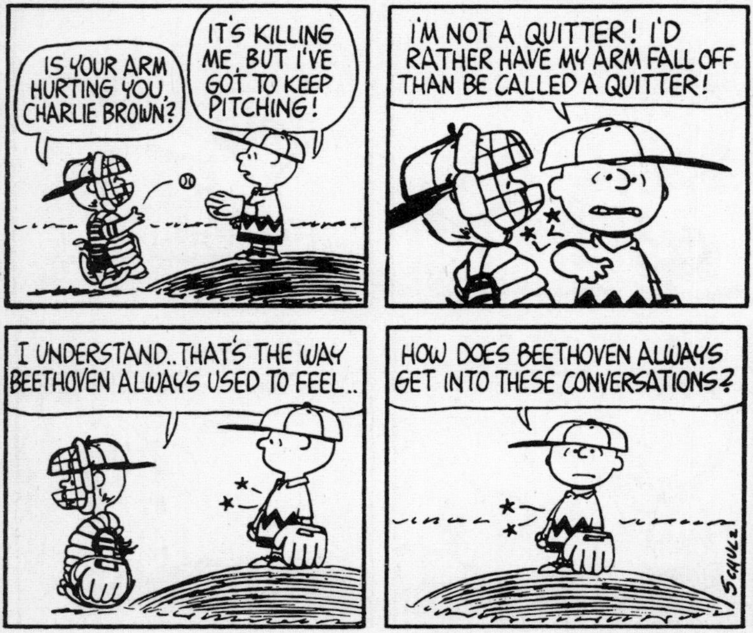
IS YOUR ARM HURTING YOU, CHARLIE BROWN?
IT'S KILLING ME, BUT I'VE GOT TO KEEP PITCHING!
I'M NOT A QUITTER! I'D RATHER HAVE MY ARM FALL OFF THAN BE CALLED A QUITTER!
I UNDERSTAND.. THAT'S THE WAY BEETHOVEN ALWAYS USED TO FEEL..
HOW DOES BEETHOVEN ALWAYS GET INTO THESE CONVERSATIONS?
SCHULZ

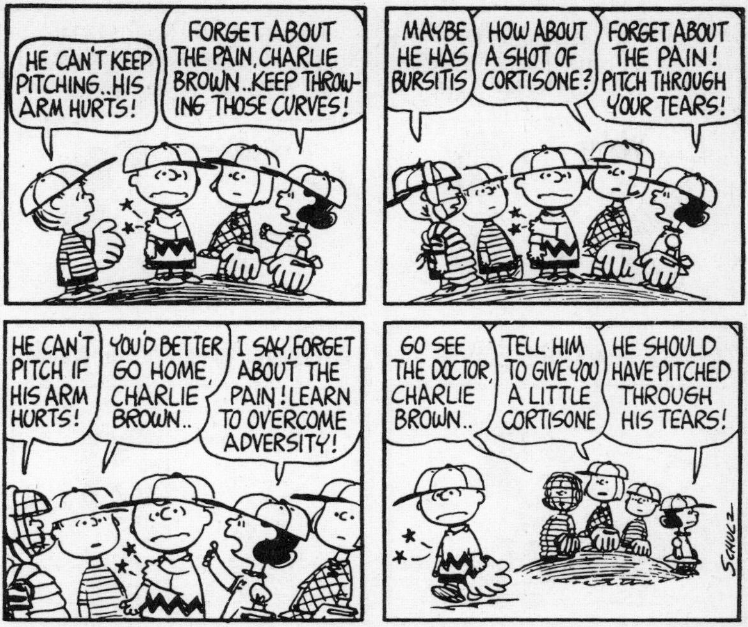
HE CAN'T KEEP PITCHING..HIS ARM HURTS!
FORGET ABOUT THE PAIN, CHARLIE BROWN..KEEP THROWING THOSE CURVES!
MAYBE HE HAS BURSITIS
HOW ABOUT A SHOT OF CORTISONE?
FORGET ABOUT THE PAIN! PITCH THROUGH YOUR TEARS!
HE CAN'T PITCH IF HIS ARM HURTS!
YOU'D BETTER GO HOME, CHARLIE BROWN..
I SAY, FORGET ABOUT THE PAIN! LEARN TO OVERCOME ADVERSITY!
GO SEE THE DOCTOR, CHARLIE BROWN..
TELL HIM TO GIVE YOU A LITTLE CORTISONE
HE SHOULD HAVE PITCHED THROUGH HIS TEARS!
SCHULZ

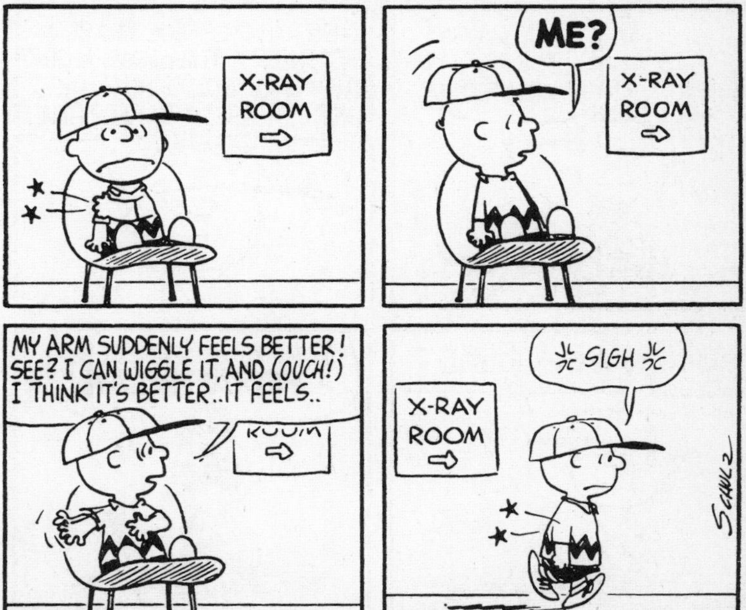
X-RAY ROOM
ME?
X-RAY ROOM
MY ARM SUDDENLY FEELS BETTER! SEE? I CAN WIGGLE IT, AND (OUCH!) I THINK IT'S BETTER..IT FEELS..
SIGH
X-RAY ROOM
SCHULZ

WELL, I FOUND OUT WHAT'S WRONG WITH MY ARM..
I'VE GOT "LITTLE LEAGUER'S ELBOW"!
YOU'VE GOT WHAT?
"LITTLE LEAGUER'S ELBOW"
A LOUSY PLAYER LIKE YOU?!
SCHULZ

I'M ALWAYS BEING HUMILIATED!
WHEN A BIG-LEAGUE PLAYER GETS HURT, THEY HAVE A GUY THEY CALL "DOC" WHO RUSHES ONTO THE FIELD TO HELP HIM
WHAT HAPPENS TO ME?
I HAVE TO GO SEE A PEDIATRICIAN!
SCHULZ

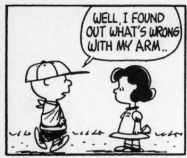

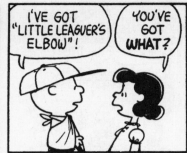

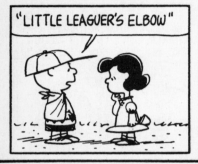

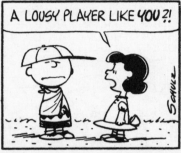

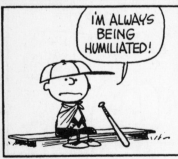

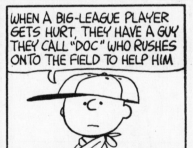

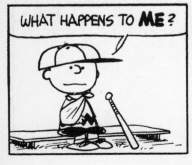

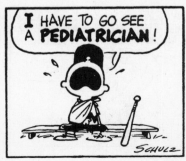

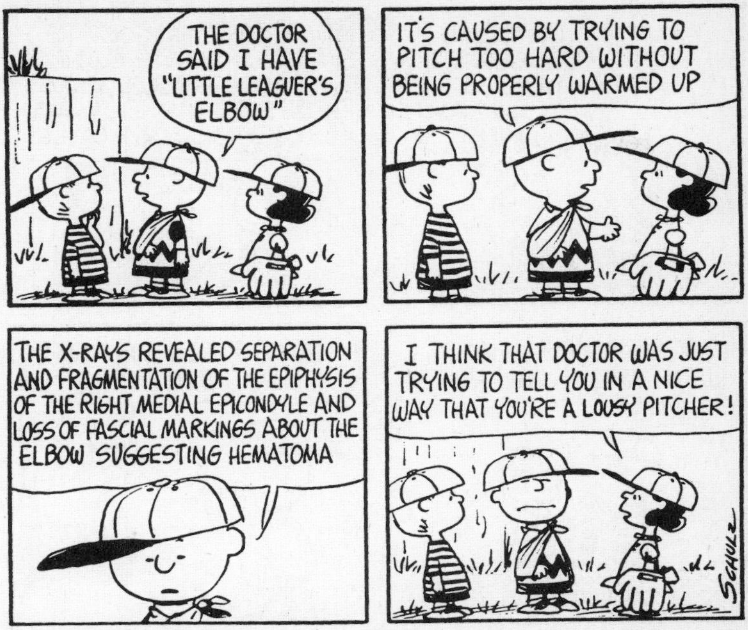
THE DOCTOR SAID I HAVE "LITTLE LEAGUER'S ELBOW"
IT'S CAUSED BY TRYING TO PITCH TOO HARD WITHOUT BEING PROPERLY WARMED UP
THE X-RAYS REVEALED SEPARATION AND FRAGMENTATION OF THE EPIPHYSIS OF THE RIGHT MEDIAL EPICONDYLE AND LOSS OF FASCIAL MARKINGS ABOUT THE ELBOW SUGGESTING HEMATOMA
I THINK THAT DOCTOR WAS JUST TRYING TO TELL YOU IN A NICE WAY THAT YOU'RE A LOUSY PITCHER!
SCHULZ

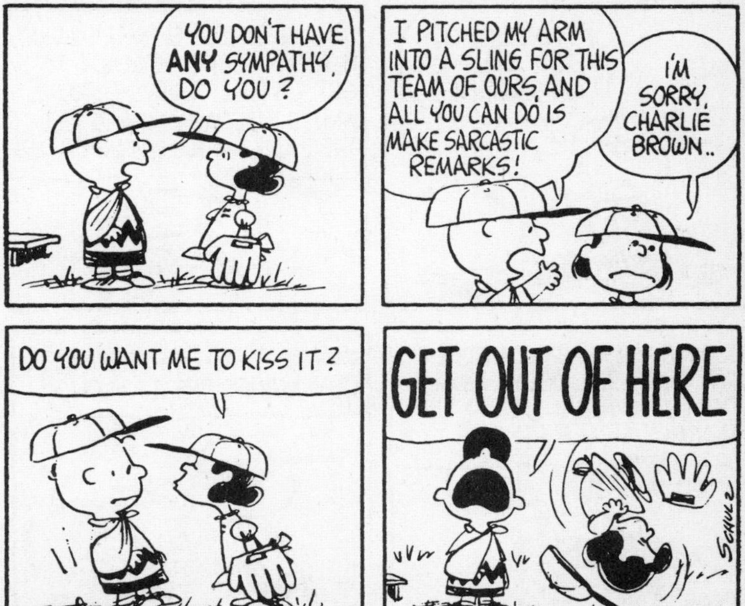
YOU DON'T HAVE ANY SYMPATHY, DO YOU?
I PITCHED MY ARM INTO A SLING FOR THIS TEAM OF OURS, AND ALL YOU CAN DO IS MAKE SARCASTIC REMARKS!
I'M SORRY, CHARLIE BROWN..
DO YOU WANT ME TO KISS IT?
GET OUT OF HERE
SCHULZ

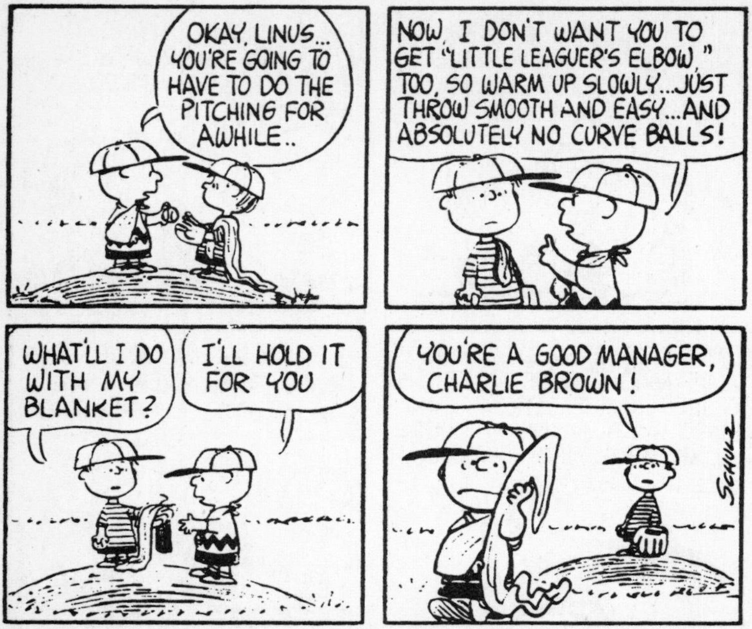
OKAY, LINUS... YOU'RE GOING TO HAVE TO DO THE PITCHING FOR AWHILE..
NOW, I DON'T WANT YOU TO GET "LITTLE LEAGUER'S ELBOW," TOO, SO WARM UP SLOWLY...JUST THROW SMOOTH AND EASY...AND ABSOLUTELY NO CURVE BALLS!
WHAT'LL I DO WITH MY BLANKET?
I'LL HOLD IT FOR YOU
YOU'RE A GOOD MANAGER, CHARLIE BROWN!
SCHULZ

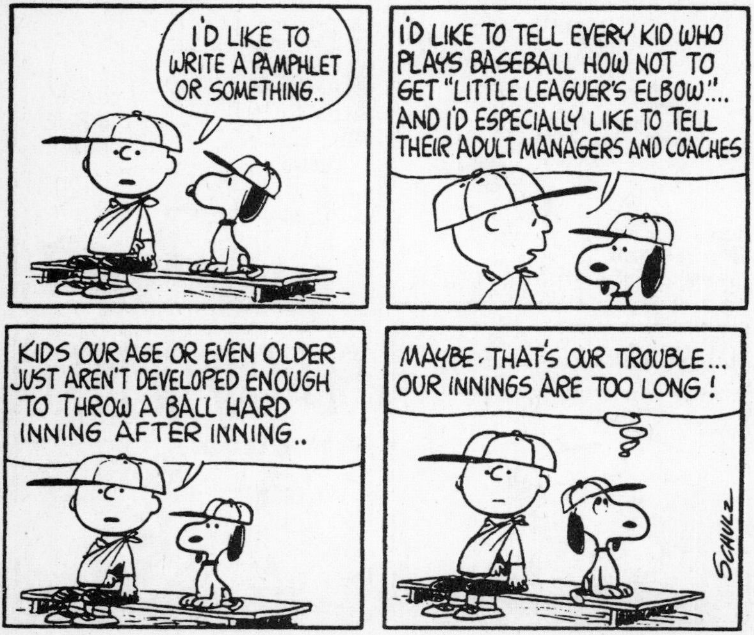
I'D LIKE TO WRITE A PAMPHLET OR SOMETHING..
I'D LIKE TO TELL EVERY KID WHO PLAYS BASEBALL HOW NOT TO GET "LITTLE LEAGUER'S ELBOW"... AND I'D ESPECIALLY LIKE TO TELL THEIR ADULT MANAGERS AND COACHES
KIDS OUR AGE OR EVEN OLDER JUST AREN'T DEVELOPED ENOUGH TO THROW A BALL HARD INNING AFTER INNING..
MAYBE THAT'S OUR TROUBLE... OUR INNINGS ARE TOO LONG!
SCHULZ

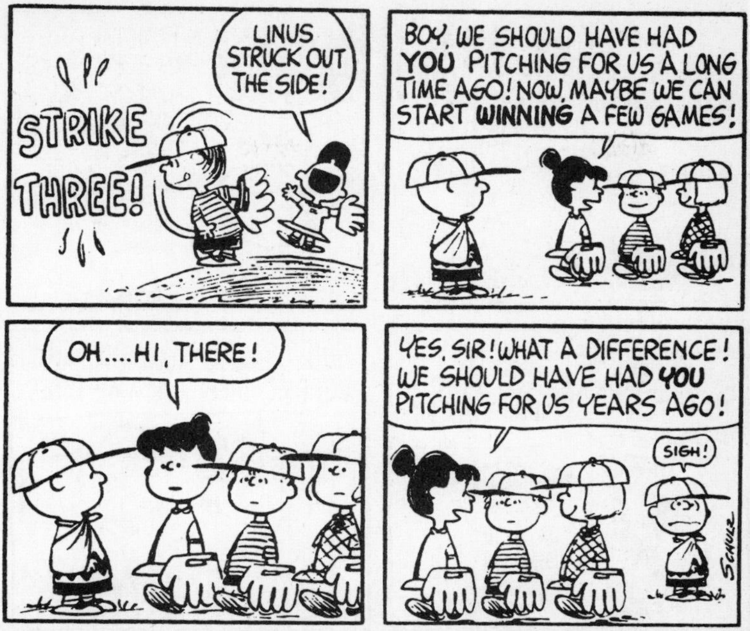
STRIKE THREE!
LINUS STRUCK OUT THE SIDE!
BOY, WE SHOULD HAVE HAD YOU PITCHING FOR US A LONG TIME AGO! NOW, MAYBE WE CAN START WINNING A FEW GAMES!
OH....HI, THERE!
YES, SIR! WHAT A DIFFERENCE! WE SHOULD HAVE HAD YOU PITCHING FOR US YEARS AGO!
SIGH!
SCHULZ

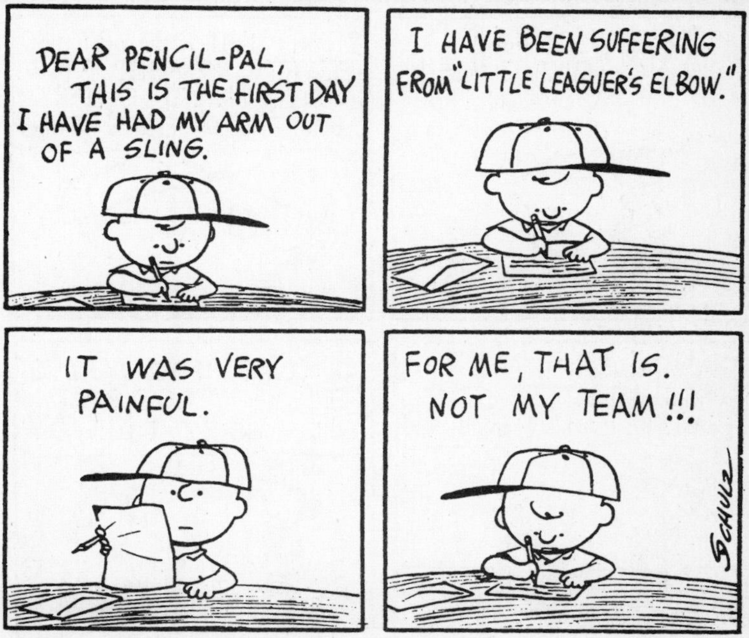
DEAR PENCIL-PAL, THIS IS THE FIRST DAY I HAVE HAD MY ARM OUT OF A SLING.
I HAVE BEEN SUFFERING FROM "LITTLE LEAGUER'S ELBOW."
IT WAS VERY PAINFUL.
FOR ME, THAT IS. NOT MY TEAM!!!
SCHULZ

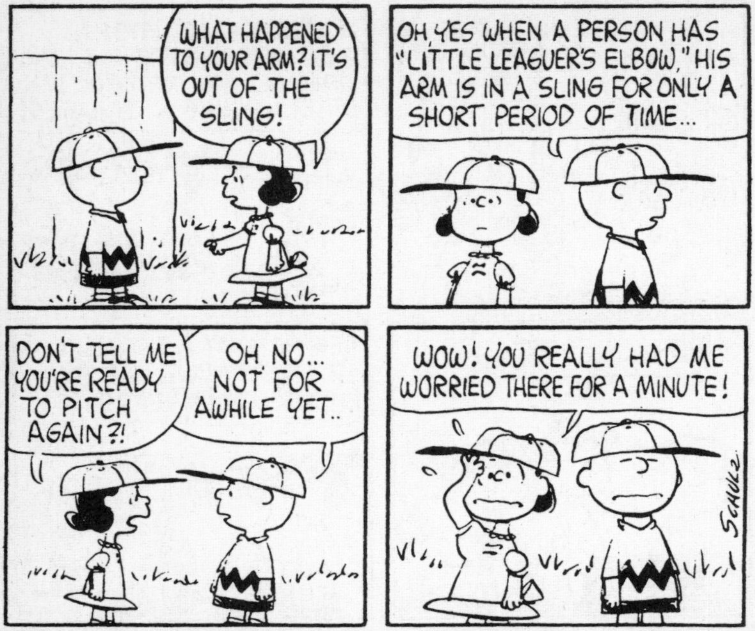
WHAT HAPPENED TO YOUR ARM? IT'S OUT OF THE SLING!
OH, YES WHEN A PERSON HAS "LITTLE LEAGUER'S ELBOW," HIS ARM IS IN A SLING FOR ONLY A SHORT PERIOD OF TIME...
DON'T TELL ME YOU'RE READY TO PITCH AGAIN?!
OH, NO... NOT FOR AWHILE YET..
WOW! YOU REALLY HAD ME WORRIED THERE FOR A MINUTE!
SCHULZ

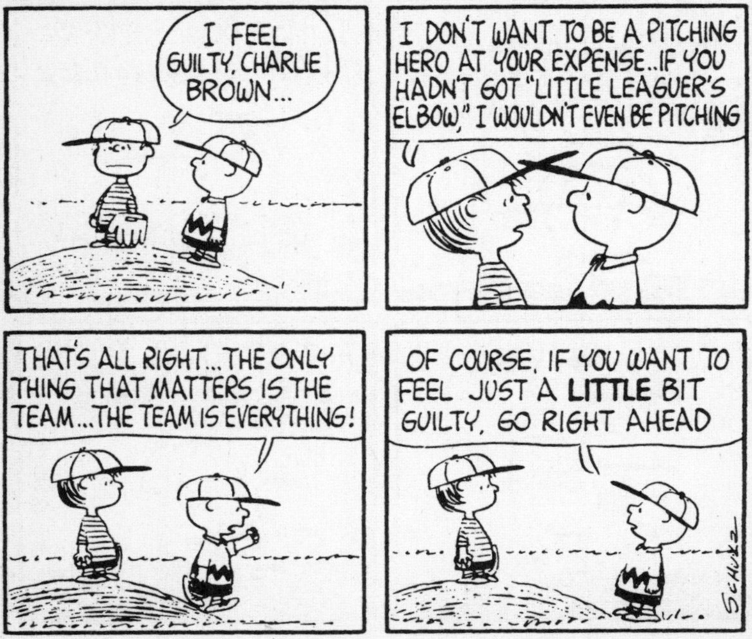
I FEEL GUILTY, CHARLIE BROWN...
I DON'T WANT TO BE A PITCHING HERO AT YOUR EXPENSE..IF YOU HADN'T GOT "LITTLE LEAGUER'S ELBOW," I WOULDN'T EVEN BE PITCHING
THAT'S ALL RIGHT... THE ONLY THING THAT MATTERS IS THE TEAM... THE TEAM IS EVERYTHING!
OF COURSE, IF YOU WANT TO FEEL JUST A **LITTLE** BIT GUILTY, GO RIGHT AHEAD
SCHULZ

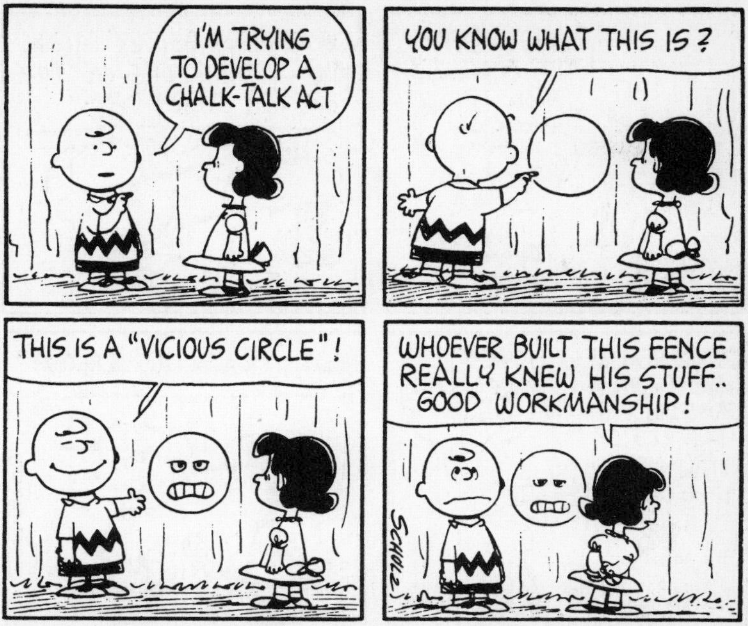
I'M TRYING TO DEVELOP A CHALK-TALK ACT
YOU KNOW WHAT THIS IS?
THIS IS A "VICIOUS CIRCLE"!
WHOEVER BUILT THIS FENCE REALLY KNEW HIS STUFF.. GOOD WORKMANSHIP!
SCHULZ

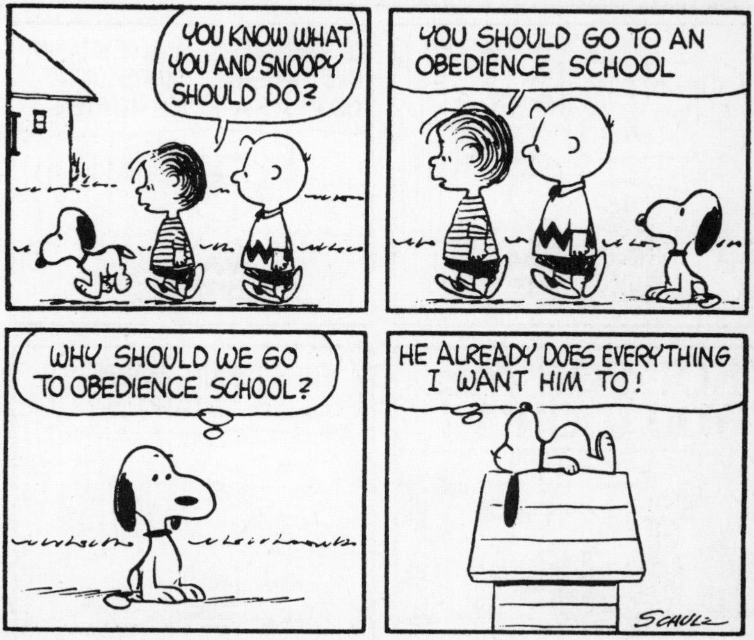
YOU KNOW WHAT YOU AND SNOOPY SHOULD DO?
YOU SHOULD GO TO AN OBEDIENCE SCHOOL
WHY SHOULD WE GO TO OBEDIENCE SCHOOL?
HE ALREADY DOES EVERYTHING I WANT HIM TO!
SCHULZ

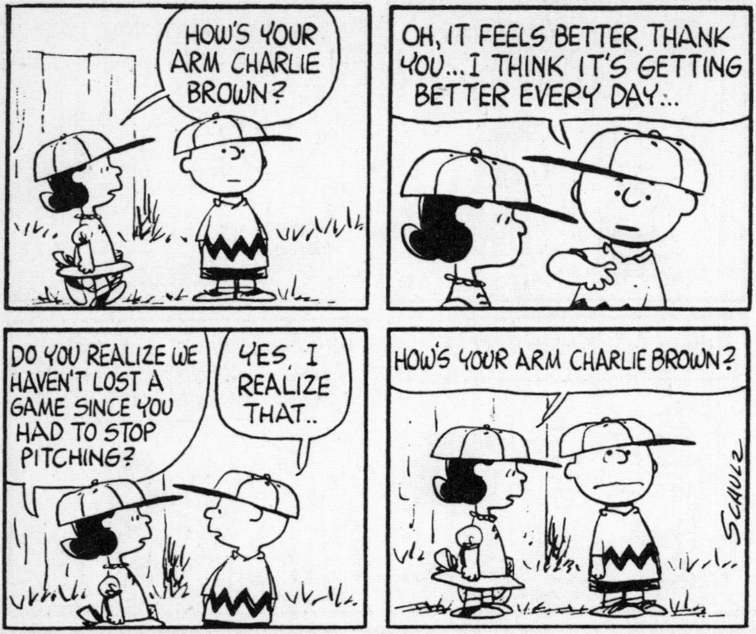
HOW'S YOUR ARM CHARLIE BROWN?
OH, IT FEELS BETTER, THANK YOU...I THINK IT'S GETTING BETTER EVERY DAY...
DO YOU REALIZE WE HAVEN'T LOST A GAME SINCE YOU HAD TO STOP PITCHING?
YES, I REALIZE THAT..
HOW'S YOUR ARM CHARLIE BROWN?
SCHULZ

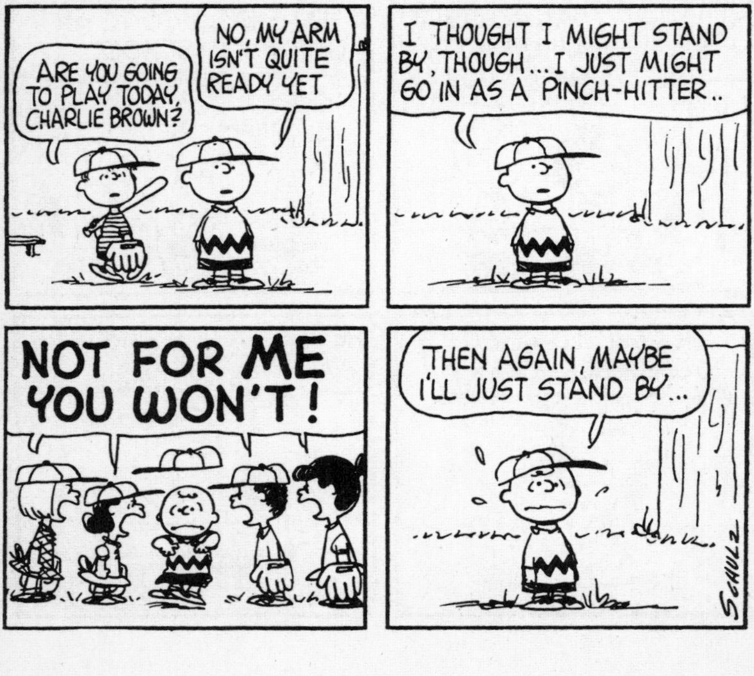
ARE YOU GOING TO PLAY TODAY, CHARLIE BROWN?
NO, MY ARM ISN'T QUITE READY YET
I THOUGHT I MIGHT STAND BY, THOUGH...I JUST MIGHT GO IN AS A PINCH-HITTER..
NOT FOR ME YOU WON'T!
THEN AGAIN, MAYBE I'LL JUST STAND BY...
SCHULZ

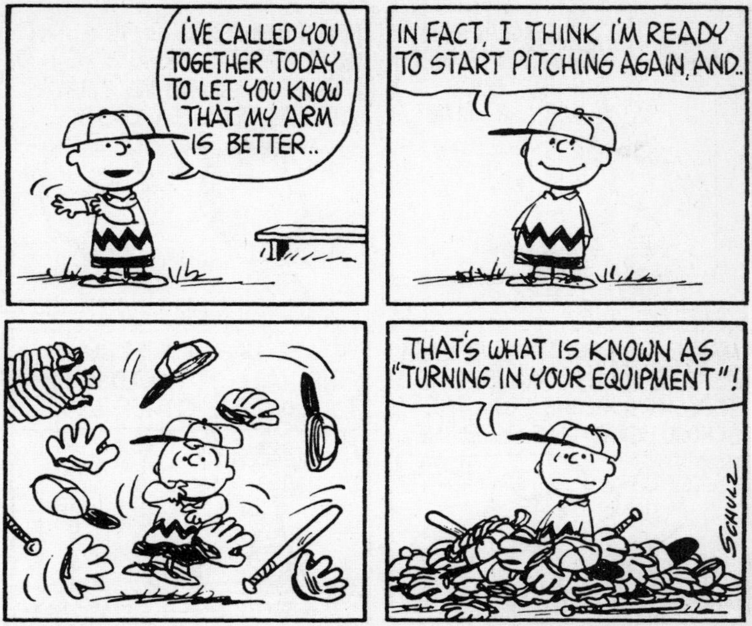
I'VE CALLED YOU TOGETHER TODAY TO LET YOU KNOW THAT MY ARM IS BETTER..
IN FACT, I THINK I'M READY TO START PITCHING AGAIN, AND..
THAT'S WHAT IS KNOWN AS "TURNING IN YOUR EQUIPMENT"!
SCHULZ

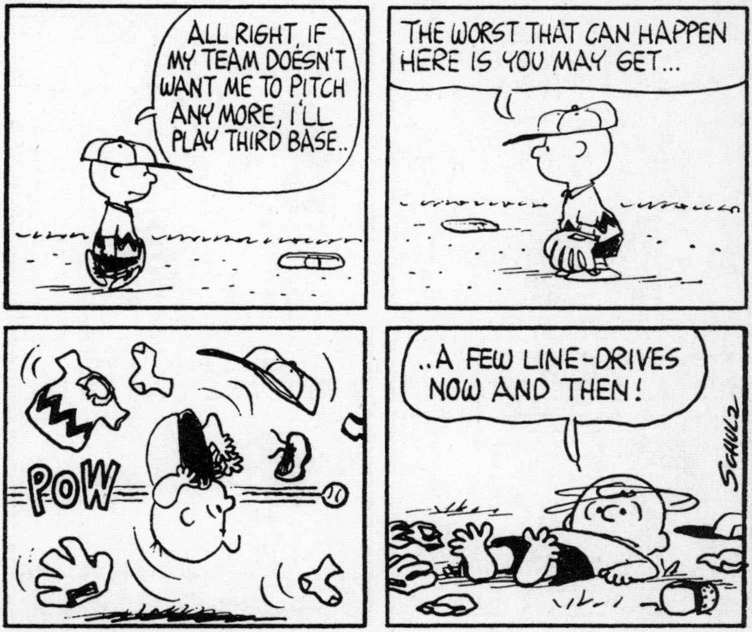
ALL RIGHT, IF MY TEAM DOESN'T WANT ME TO PITCH ANY MORE, I'LL PLAY THIRD BASE..
THE WORST THAT CAN HAPPEN HERE IS YOU MAY GET...
POW
..A FEW LINE-DRIVES NOW AND THEN!
SCHULZ

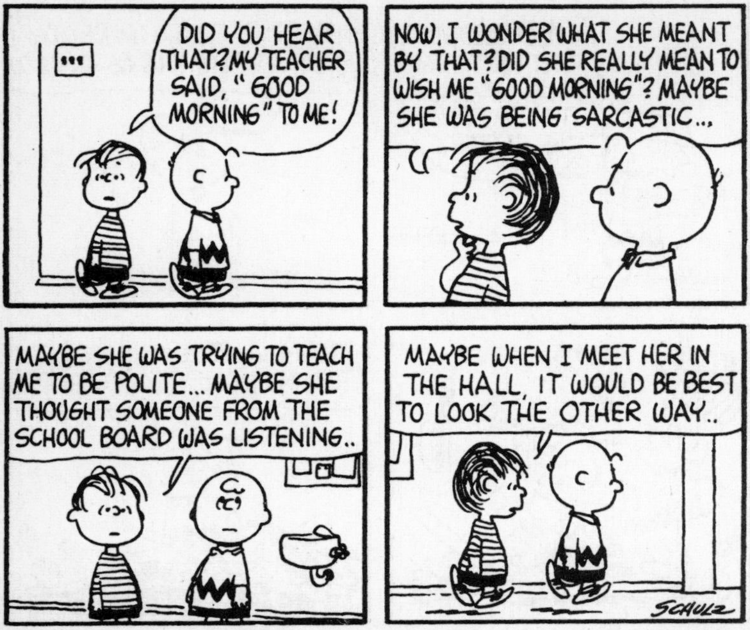
DID YOU HEAR THAT? MY TEACHER SAID, "GOOD MORNING" TO ME!
NOW, I WONDER WHAT SHE MEANT BY THAT? DID SHE REALLY MEAN TO WISH ME "GOOD MORNING"? MAYBE SHE WAS BEING SARCASTIC...
MAYBE SHE WAS TRYING TO TEACH ME TO BE POLITE... MAYBE SHE THOUGHT SOMEONE FROM THE SCHOOL BOARD WAS LISTENING..
MAYBE WHEN I MEET HER IN THE HALL, IT WOULD BE BEST TO LOOK THE OTHER WAY..
SCHULZ

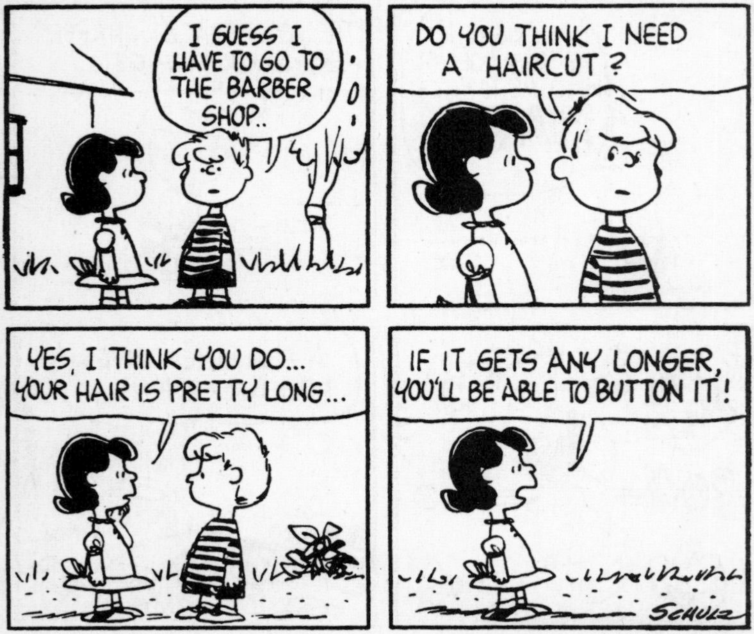
I GUESS I HAVE TO GO TO THE BARBER SHOP..
DO YOU THINK I NEED A HAIRCUT?
YES, I THINK YOU DO... YOUR HAIR IS PRETTY LONG...
IF IT GETS ANY LONGER, YOU'LL BE ABLE TO BUTTON IT!
SCHULZ

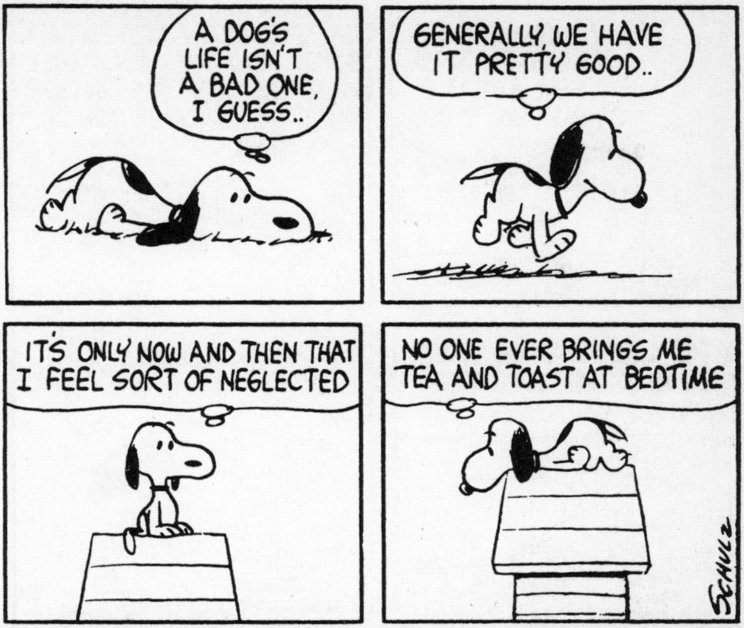
A DOG'S LIFE ISN'T A BAD ONE, I GUESS..
GENERALLY, WE HAVE IT PRETTY GOOD..
IT'S ONLY NOW AND THEN THAT I FEEL SORT OF NEGLECTED
NO ONE EVER BRINGS ME TEA AND TOAST AT BEDTIME
SCHULZ

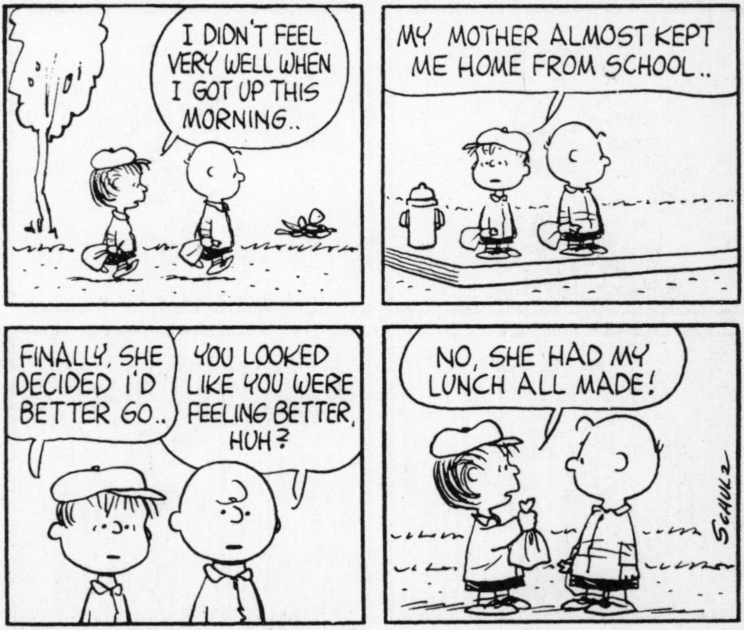
I DIDN'T FEEL VERY WELL WHEN I GOT UP THIS MORNING..
MY MOTHER ALMOST KEPT ME HOME FROM SCHOOL..
FINALLY, SHE DECIDED I'D BETTER GO..
YOU LOOKED LIKE YOU WERE FEELING BETTER, HUH?
NO, SHE HAD MY LUNCH ALL MADE!
SCHULZ

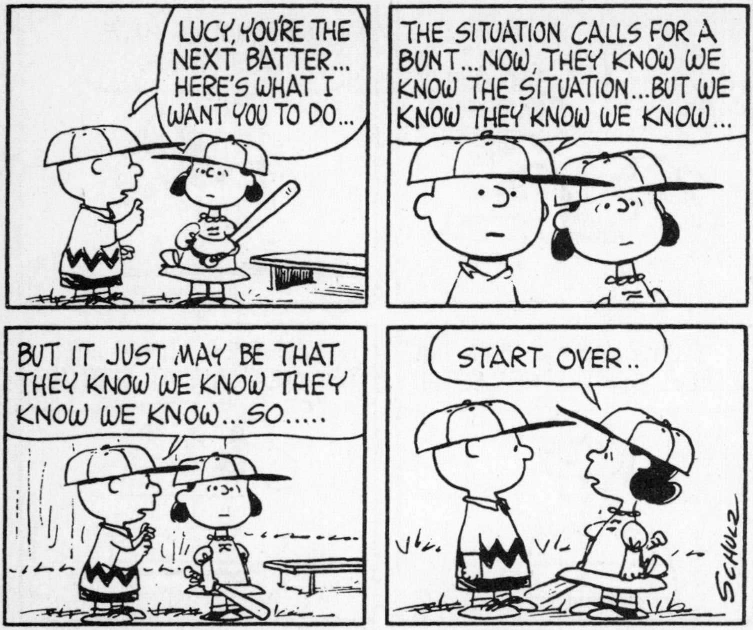
LUCY, YOU'RE THE NEXT BATTER... HERE'S WHAT I WANT YOU TO DO...
THE SITUATION CALLS FOR A BUNT...NOW, THEY KNOW WE KNOW THE SITUATION...BUT WE KNOW THEY KNOW WE KNOW...
BUT IT JUST MAY BE THAT THEY KNOW WE KNOW THEY KNOW WE KNOW...SO.....
START OVER..
SCHULZ

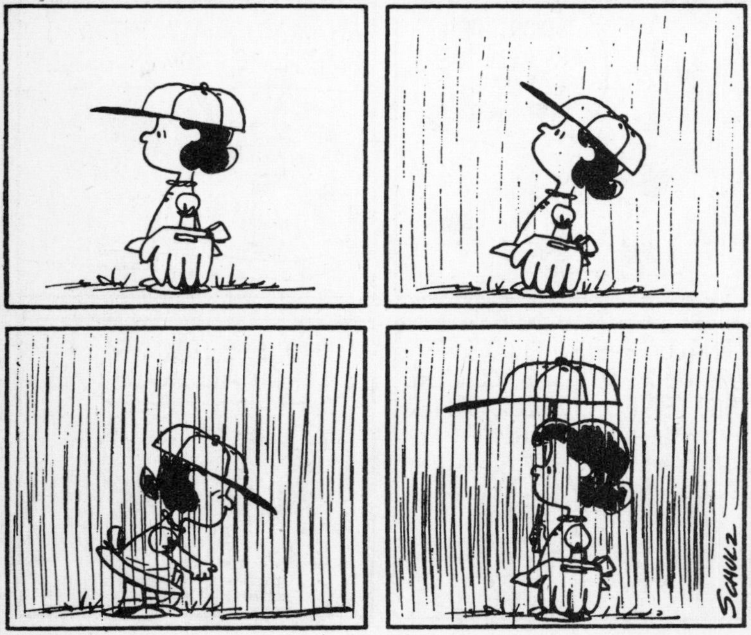
SCHULZ

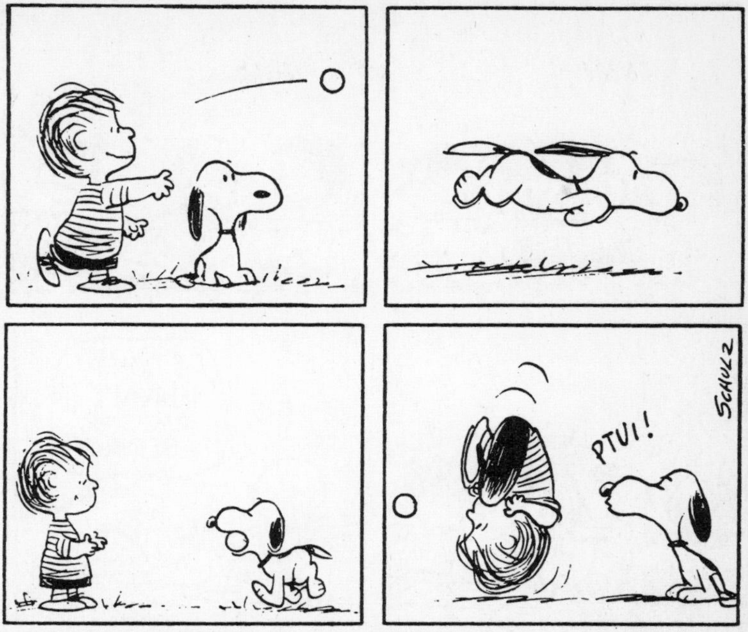
PTUI!

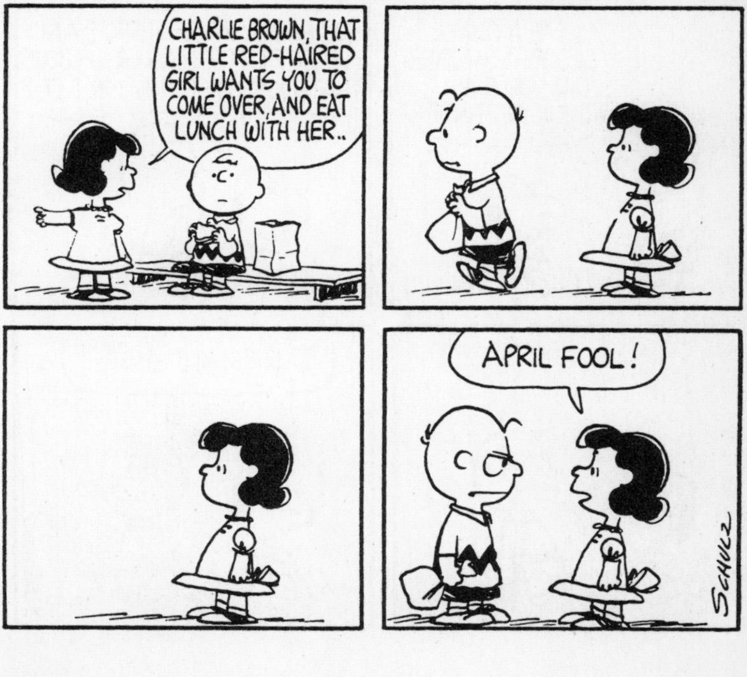
CHARLIE BROWN, THAT LITTLE RED-HAIRED GIRL WANTS YOU TO COME OVER, AND EAT LUNCH WITH HER..
APRIL FOOL!

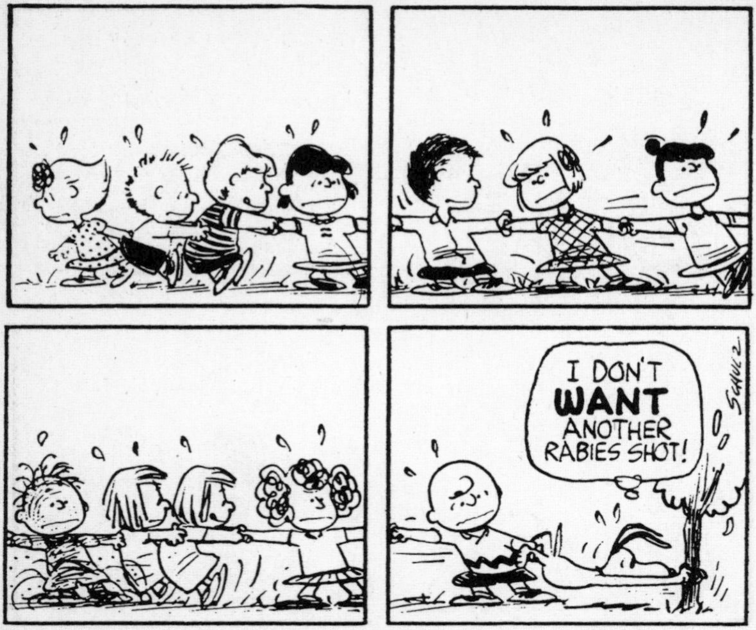
I DON'T WANT ANOTHER RABIES SHOT!
SCHULZ

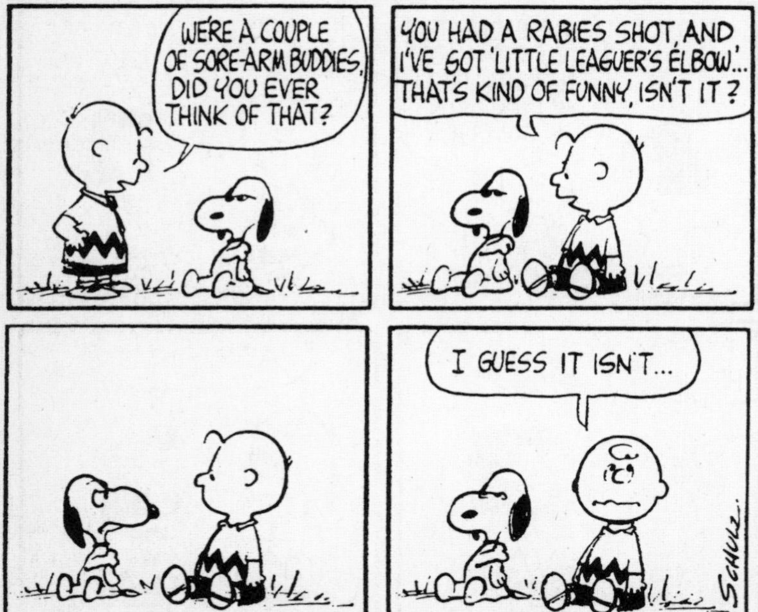
WE'RE A COUPLE OF SORE-ARM BUDDIES, DID YOU EVER THINK OF THAT?
YOU HAD A RABIES SHOT, AND I'VE GOT 'LITTLE LEAGUER'S ELBOW'... THAT'S KIND OF FUNNY, ISN'T IT?
I GUESS IT ISN'T...
SCHULZ

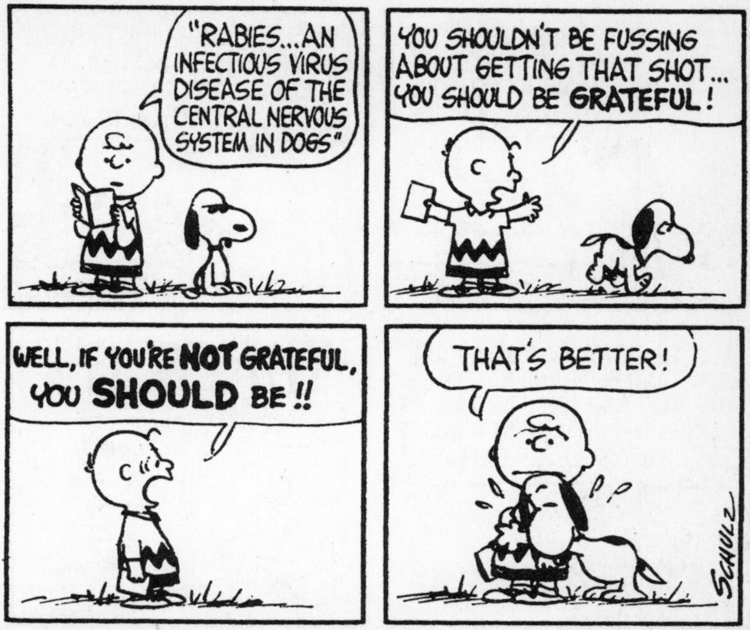
"RABIES...AN INFECTIOUS VIRUS DISEASE OF THE CENTRAL NERVOUS SYSTEM IN DOGS"
YOU SHOULDN'T BE FUSSING ABOUT GETTING THAT SHOT... YOU SHOULD BE GRATEFUL!
WELL, IF YOU'RE NOT GRATEFUL, YOU SHOULD BE!!
THAT'S BETTER!
SCHULZ

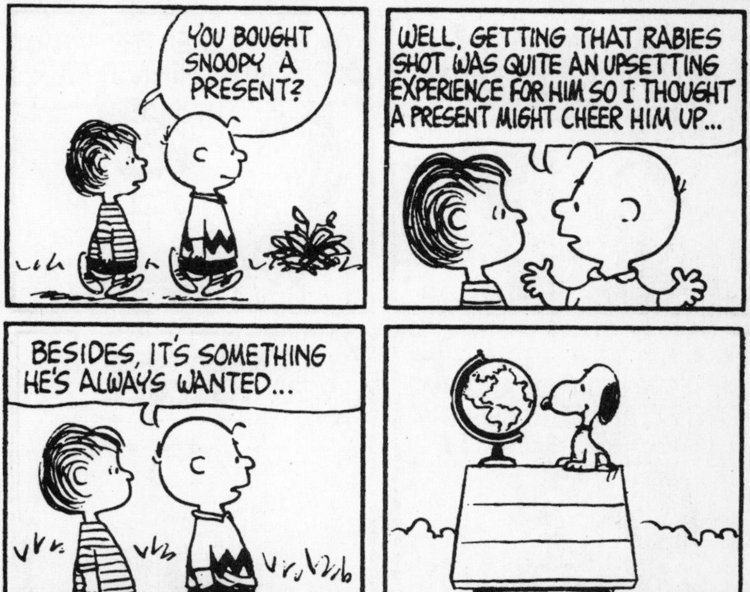
YOU BOUGHT SNOOPY A PRESENT?
WELL, GETTING THAT RABIES SHOT WAS QUITE AN UPSETTING EXPERIENCE FOR HIM SO I THOUGHT A PRESENT MIGHT CHEER HIM UP...
BESIDES, IT'S SOMETHING HE'S ALWAYS WANTED...
SCHULZ

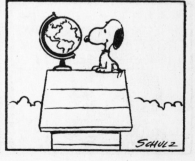

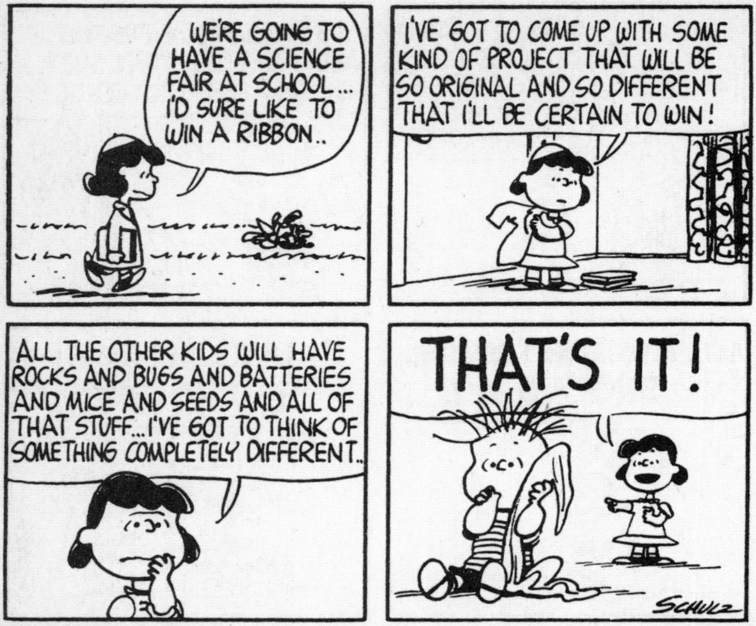
WE'RE GOING TO HAVE A SCIENCE FAIR AT SCHOOL... I'D SURE LIKE TO WIN A RIBBON..
I'VE GOT TO COME UP WITH SOME KIND OF PROJECT THAT WILL BE SO ORIGINAL AND SO DIFFERENT THAT I'LL BE CERTAIN TO WIN!
ALL THE OTHER KIDS WILL HAVE ROCKS AND BUGS AND BATTERIES AND MICE AND SEEDS AND ALL OF THAT STUFF... I'VE GOT TO THINK OF SOMETHING COMPLETELY DIFFERENT..
THAT'S IT!
SCHULZ

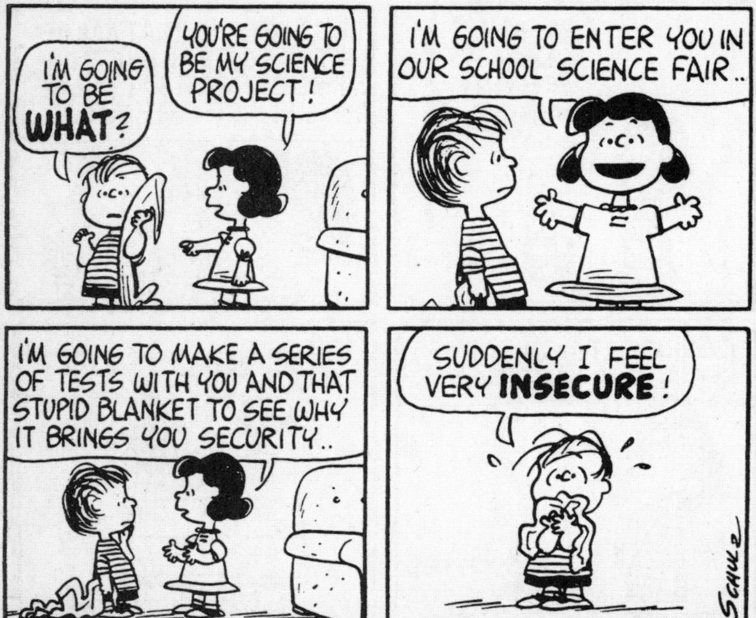
YOU'RE GOING TO BE MY SCIENCE PROJECT!
I'M GOING TO BE **WHAT**?
I'M GOING TO ENTER YOU IN OUR SCHOOL SCIENCE FAIR..
I'M GOING TO MAKE A SERIES OF TESTS WITH YOU AND THAT STUPID BLANKET TO SEE WHY IT BRINGS YOU SECURITY..
SUDDENLY I FEEL VERY **INSECURE**!
SCHULZ

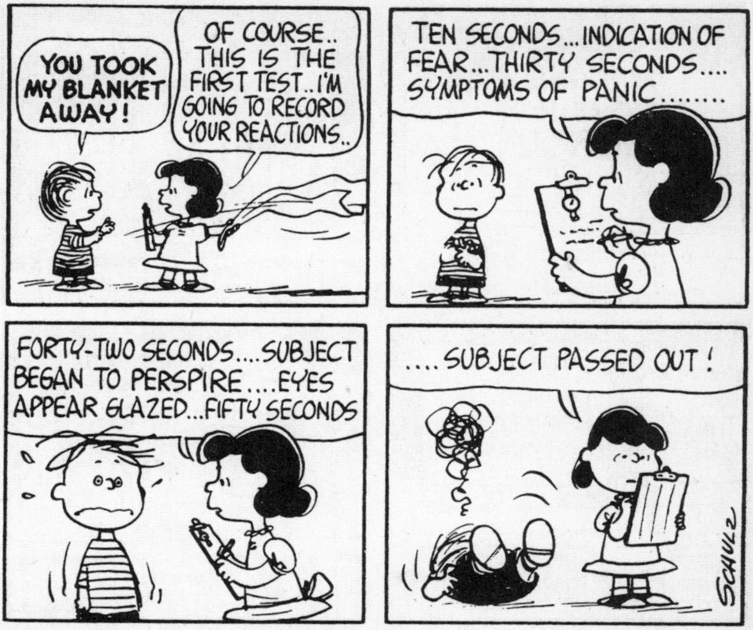
YOU TOOK MY BLANKET AWAY!
OF COURSE.. THIS IS THE FIRST TEST..I'M GOING TO RECORD YOUR REACTIONS..
TEN SECONDS...INDICATION OF FEAR...THIRTY SECONDS.... SYMPTOMS OF PANIC........
FORTY-TWO SECONDS....SUBJECT BEGAN TO PERSPIRE.....EYES APPEAR GLAZED...FIFTY SECONDS
.... SUBJECT PASSED OUT!
SCHULZ

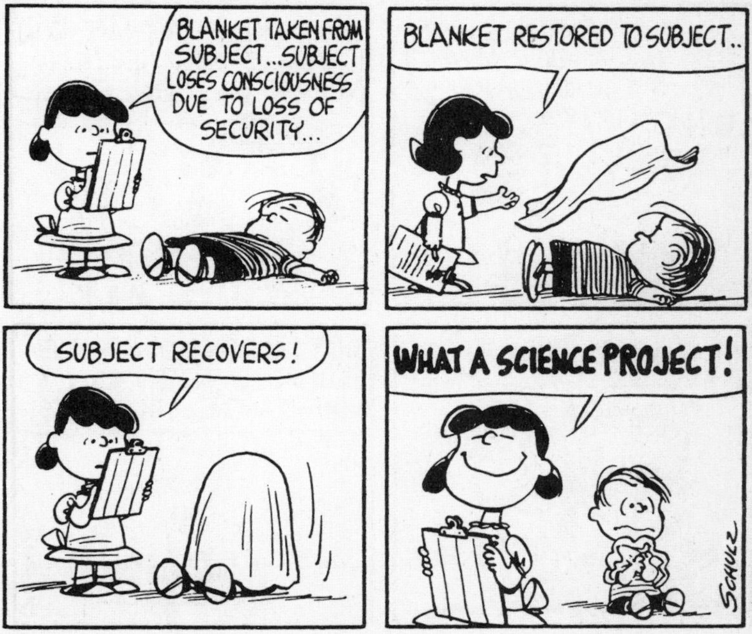
BLANKET TAKEN FROM SUBJECT...SUBJECT LOSES CONSCIOUSNESS DUE TO LOSS OF SECURITY...
BLANKET RESTORED TO SUBJECT..
SUBJECT RECOVERS!
WHAT A SCIENCE PROJECT!
SCHULZ

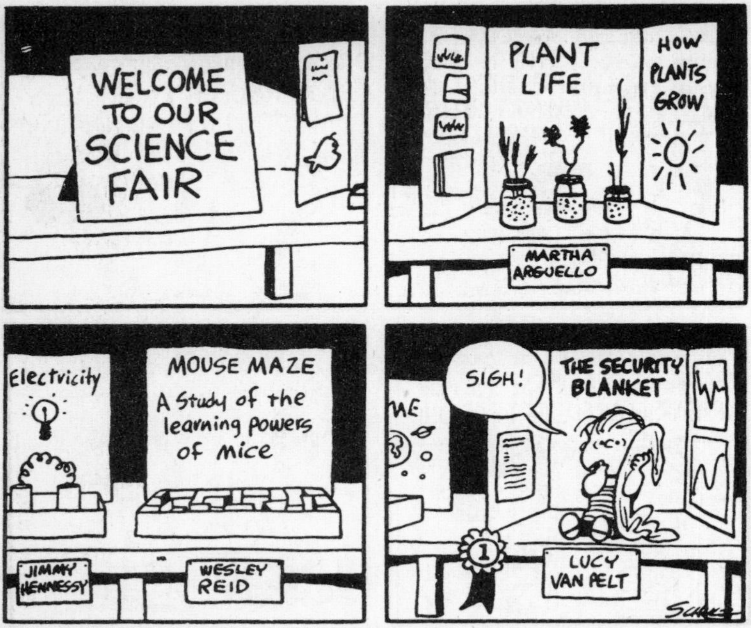
WELCOME TO OUR SCIENCE FAIR
PLANT LIFE
HOW PLANTS GROW
MARTHA ARGUELLO
Electricity
MOUSE MAZE
A Study of the learning powers of mice
JIMMY HENNESSY
WESLEY REID
SIGH!
THE SECURITY BLANKET
LUCY VAN PELT
SCHULZ

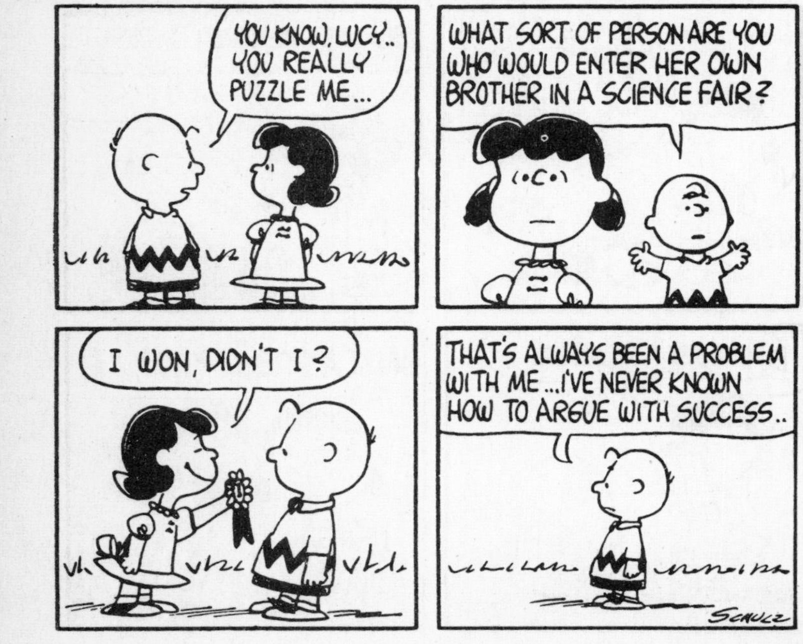
YOU KNOW, LUCY.. YOU REALLY PUZZLE ME...
WHAT SORT OF PERSON ARE YOU WHO WOULD ENTER HER OWN BROTHER IN A SCIENCE FAIR?
I WON, DIDN'T I?
THAT'S ALWAYS BEEN A PROBLEM WITH ME...I'VE NEVER KNOWN HOW TO ARGUE WITH SUCCESS..
SCHULZ

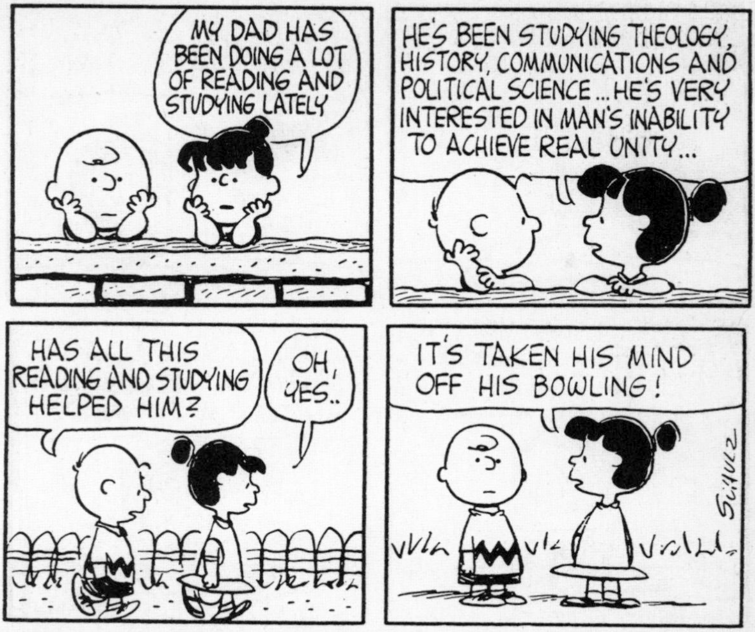
MY DAD HAS BEEN DOING A LOT OF READING AND STUDYING LATELY
HE'S BEEN STUDYING THEOLOGY, HISTORY, COMMUNICATIONS AND POLITICAL SCIENCE... HE'S VERY INTERESTED IN MAN'S INABILITY TO ACHIEVE REAL UNITY...
HAS ALL THIS READING AND STUDYING HELPED HIM?
OH, YES..
IT'S TAKEN HIS MIND OFF HIS BOWLING!
SCHULZ

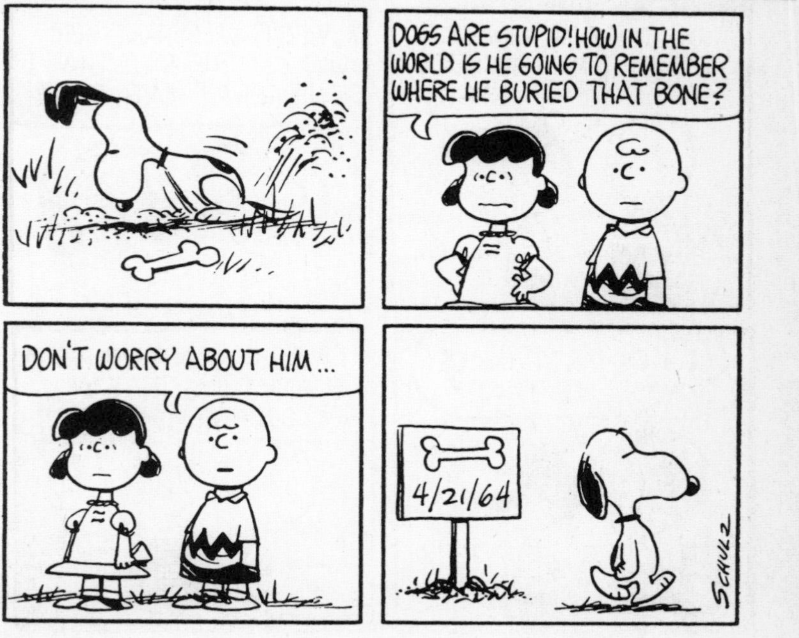
DOGS ARE STUPID! HOW IN THE WORLD IS HE GOING TO REMEMBER WHERE HE BURIED THAT BONE?
DON'T WORRY ABOUT HIM...
4/21/64
SCHULZ

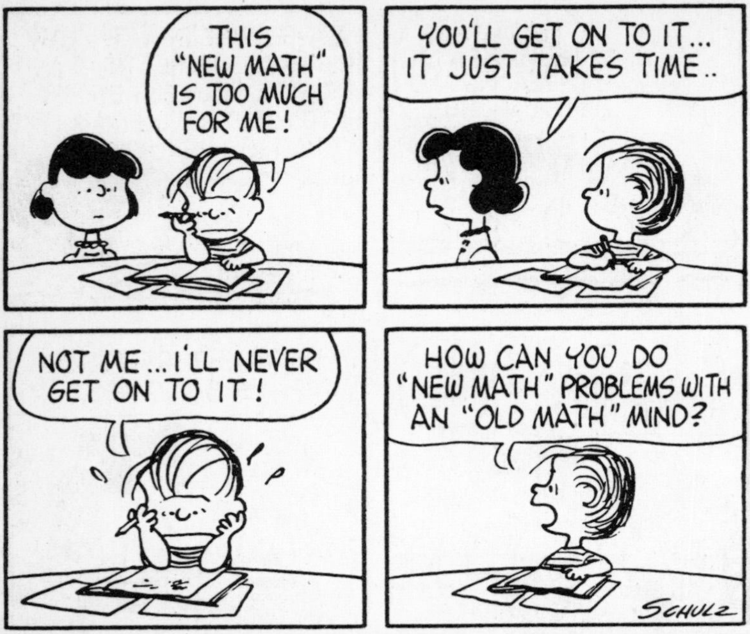
THIS "NEW MATH" IS TOO MUCH FOR ME!
YOU'LL GET ON TO IT... IT JUST TAKES TIME..
NOT ME... I'LL NEVER GET ON TO IT!
HOW CAN YOU DO "NEW MATH" PROBLEMS WITH AN "OLD MATH" MIND?
SCHULZ

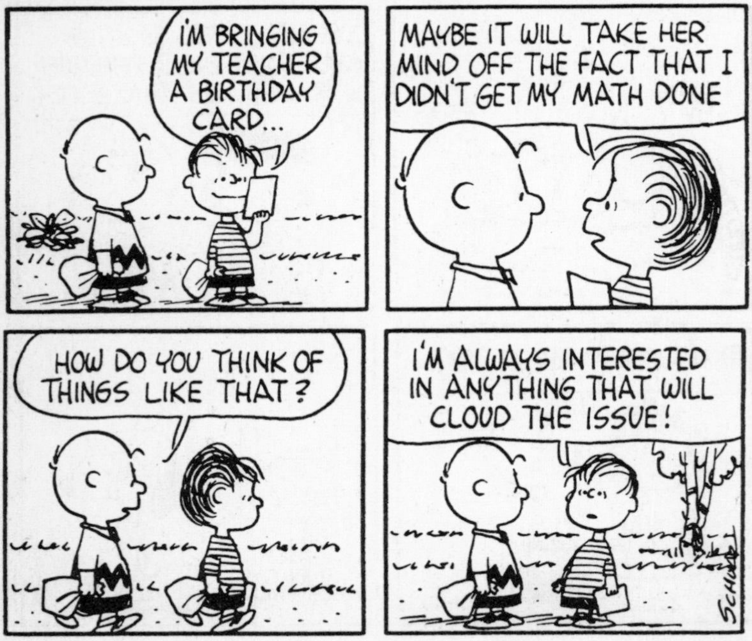
I'M BRINGING MY TEACHER A BIRTHDAY CARD...
MAYBE IT WILL TAKE HER MIND OFF THE FACT THAT I DIDN'T GET MY MATH DONE
HOW DO YOU THINK OF THINGS LIKE THAT?
I'M ALWAYS INTERESTED IN ANYTHING THAT WILL CLOUD THE ISSUE!

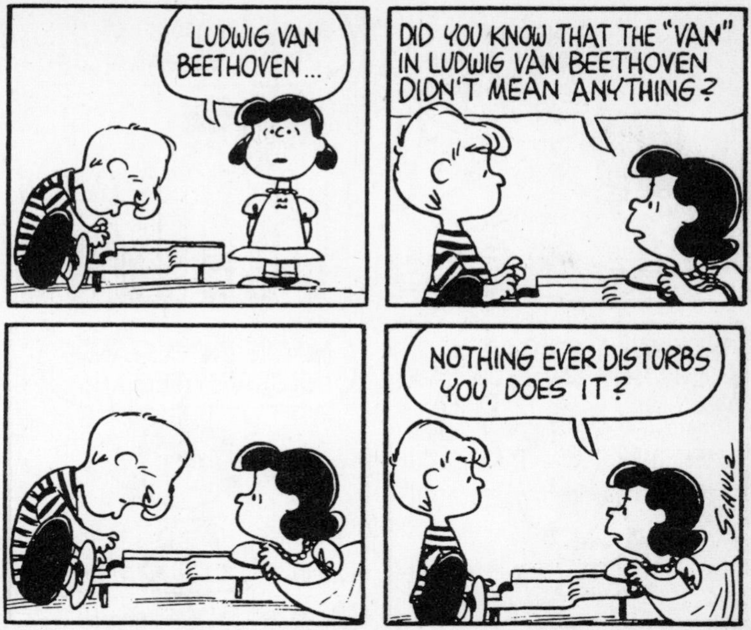
LUDWIG VAN BEETHOVEN...
DID YOU KNOW THAT THE "VAN" IN LUDWIG VAN BEETHOVEN DIDN'T MEAN ANYTHING?
NOTHING EVER DISTURBS YOU, DOES IT?
SCHULZ

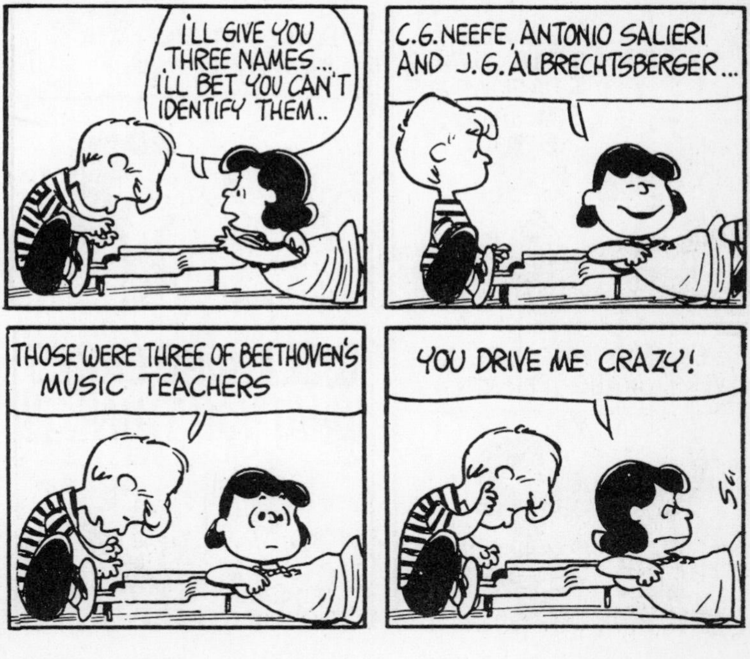
I'LL GIVE YOU THREE NAMES... I'LL BET YOU CAN'T IDENTIFY THEM..
C.G.NEEFE, ANTONIO SALIERI AND J.G.ALBRECHTSBERGER...
THOSE WERE THREE OF BEETHOVEN'S MUSIC TEACHERS
YOU DRIVE ME CRAZY!

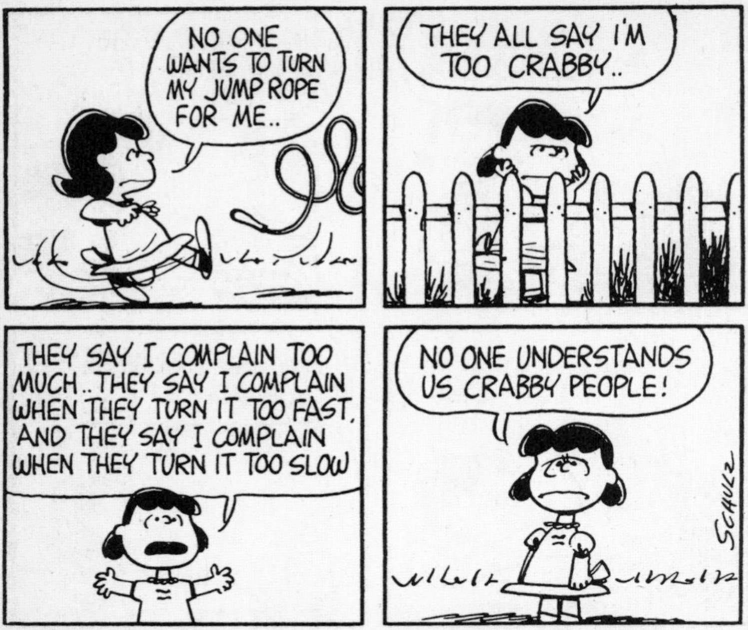
NO ONE WANTS TO TURN MY JUMP ROPE FOR ME..
THEY ALL SAY I'M TOO CRABBY..
THEY SAY I COMPLAIN TOO MUCH..THEY SAY I COMPLAIN WHEN THEY TURN IT TOO FAST, AND THEY SAY I COMPLAIN WHEN THEY TURN IT TOO SLOW
NO ONE UNDERSTANDS US CRABBY PEOPLE!
SCHULZ

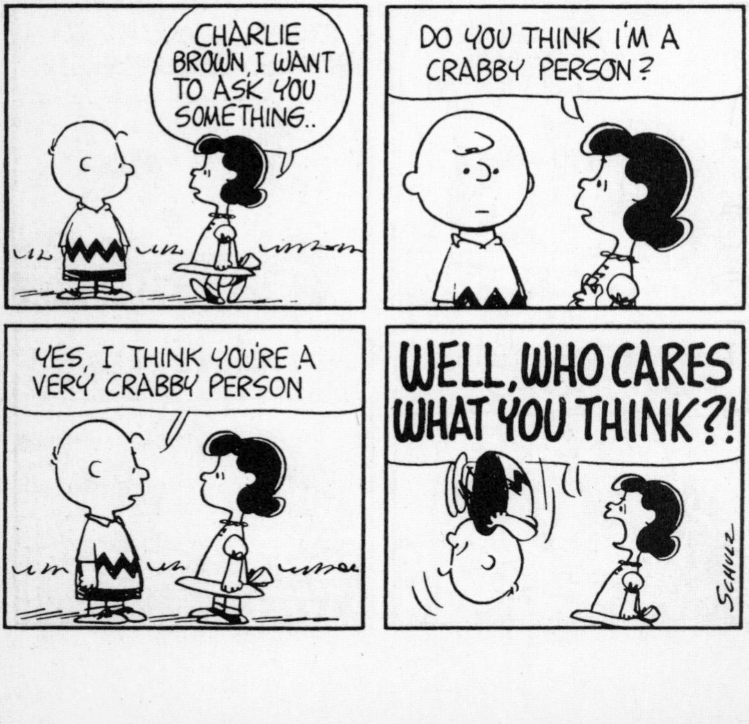
CHARLIE BROWN, I WANT TO ASK YOU SOMETHING..
DO YOU THINK I'M A CRABBY PERSON?
YES, I THINK YOU'RE A VERY CRABBY PERSON
WELL, WHO CARES WHAT YOU THINK?!
SCHULZ

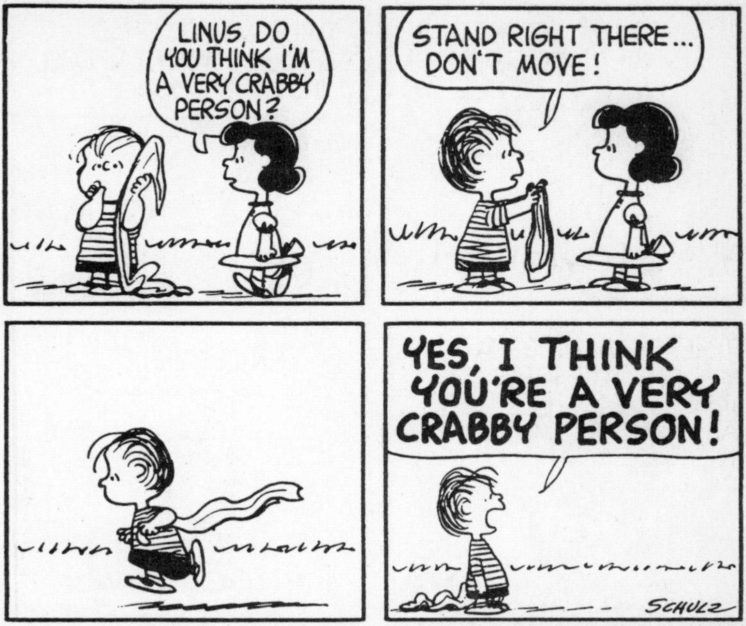
LINUS, DO YOU THINK I'M A VERY CRABBY PERSON?
STAND RIGHT THERE... DON'T MOVE!
YES, I THINK YOU'RE A VERY CRABBY PERSON!
SCHULZ

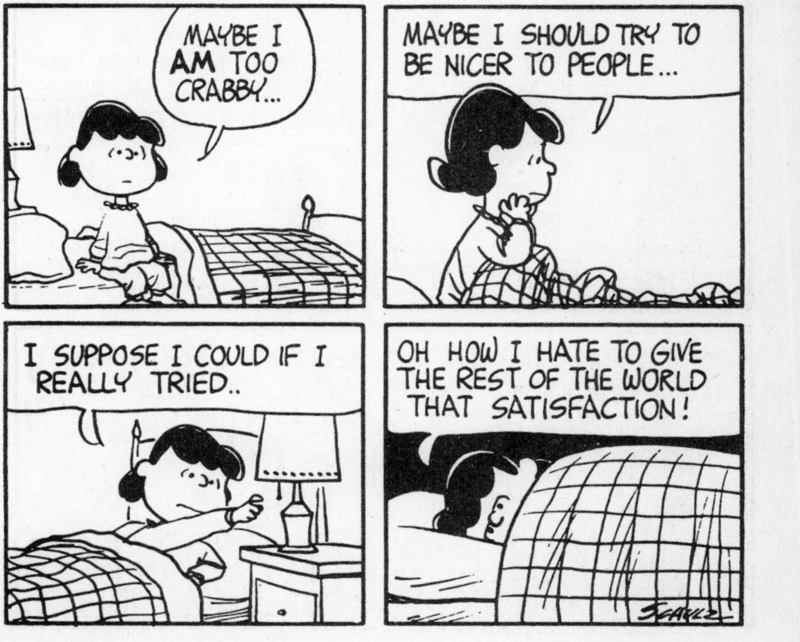
MAYBE I **AM** TOO CRABBY...
MAYBE I SHOULD TRY TO BE NICER TO PEOPLE...
I SUPPOSE I COULD IF I REALLY TRIED..
OH HOW I HATE TO GIVE THE REST OF THE WORLD THAT SATISFACTION!
SCHULZ

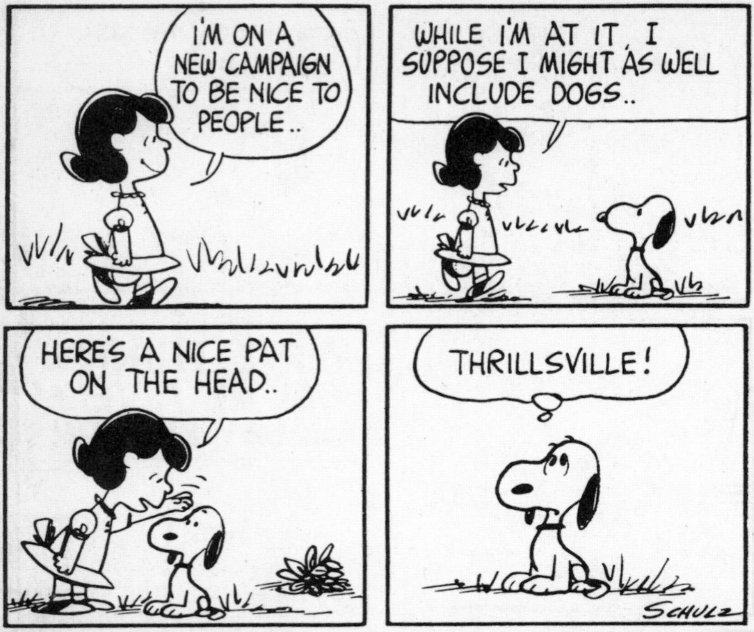
I'M ON A NEW CAMPAIGN TO BE NICE TO PEOPLE..
WHILE I'M AT IT, I SUPPOSE I MIGHT AS WELL INCLUDE DOGS..
HERE'S A NICE PAT ON THE HEAD..
THRILLSVILLE!
SCHULZ

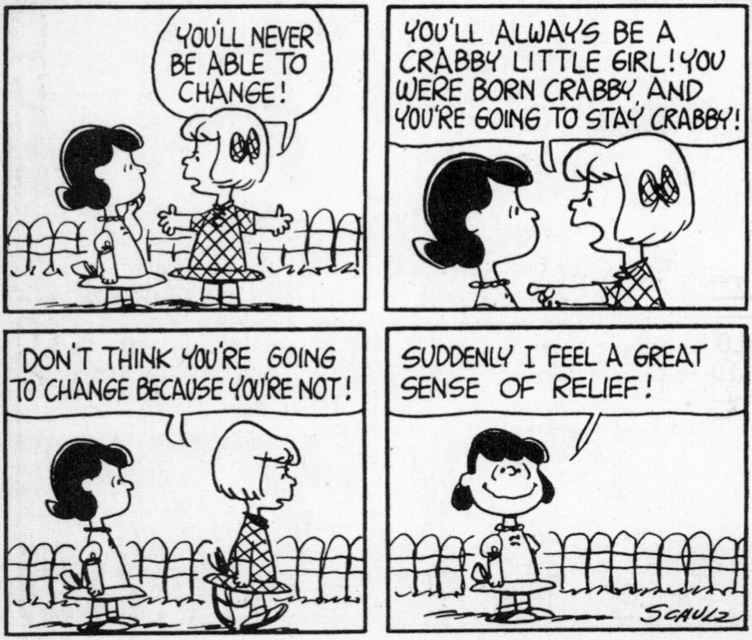
YOU'LL NEVER BE ABLE TO CHANGE!
YOU'LL ALWAYS BE A CRABBY LITTLE GIRL! YOU WERE BORN CRABBY, AND YOU'RE GOING TO STAY CRABBY!
DON'T THINK YOU'RE GOING TO CHANGE BECAUSE YOU'RE NOT!
SUDDENLY I FEEL A GREAT SENSE OF RELIEF!
SCHULZ

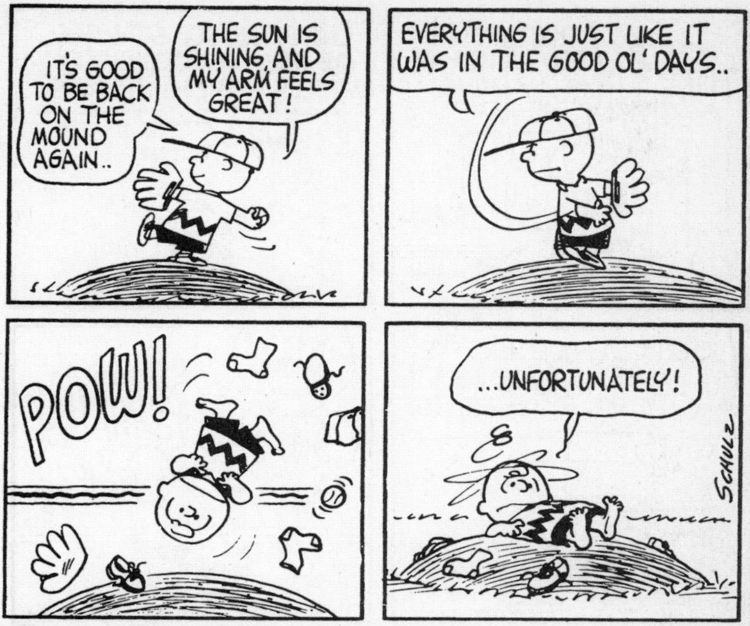
IT'S GOOD TO BE BACK ON THE MOUND AGAIN..
THE SUN IS SHINING, AND MY ARM FEELS GREAT!
EVERYTHING IS JUST LIKE IT WAS IN THE GOOD OL' DAYS..
POW!
...UNFORTUNATELY!
SCHULZ

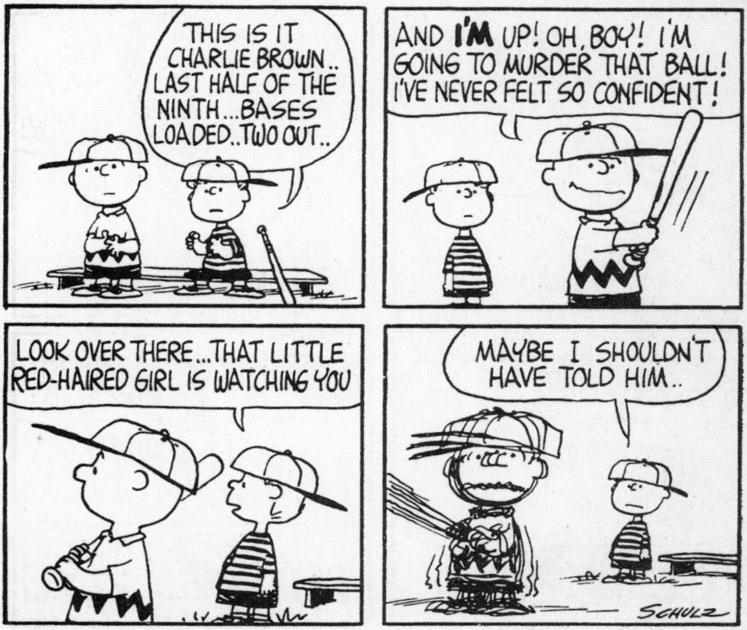
THIS IS IT CHARLIE BROWN.. LAST HALF OF THE NINTH...BASES LOADED..TWO OUT..
AND I'M UP! OH, BOY! I'M GOING TO MURDER THAT BALL! I'VE NEVER FELT SO CONFIDENT!
LOOK OVER THERE...THAT LITTLE RED-HAIRED GIRL IS WATCHING YOU
MAYBE I SHOULDN'T HAVE TOLD HIM..
SCHULZ

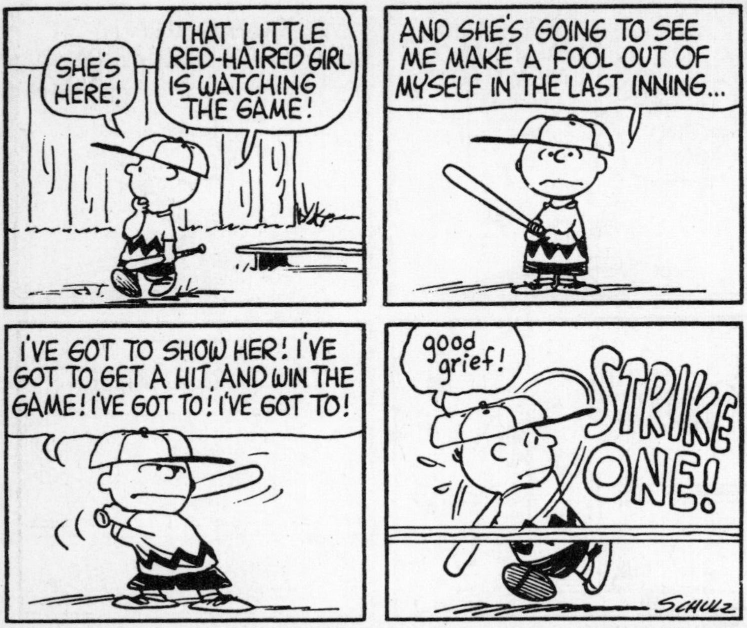
SHE'S HERE!
THAT LITTLE RED-HAIRED GIRL IS WATCHING THE GAME!
AND SHE'S GOING TO SEE ME MAKE A FOOL OUT OF MYSELF IN THE LAST INNING...
I'VE GOT TO SHOW HER! I'VE GOT TO GET A HIT, AND WIN THE GAME! I'VE GOT TO! I'VE GOT TO!
good grief!
STRIKE ONE!
SCHULZ

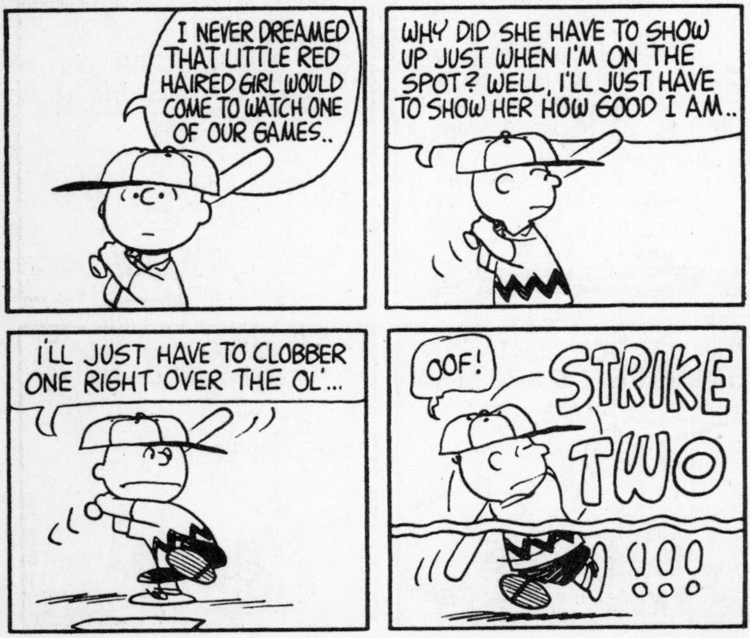
I NEVER DREAMED THAT LITTLE RED HAIRED GIRL WOULD COME TO WATCH ONE OF OUR GAMES..
WHY DID SHE HAVE TO SHOW UP JUST WHEN I'M ON THE SPOT? WELL, I'LL JUST HAVE TO SHOW HER HOW GOOD I AM...
I'LL JUST HAVE TO CLOBBER ONE RIGHT OVER THE OL'...
OOF!
STRIKE TWO
!!!

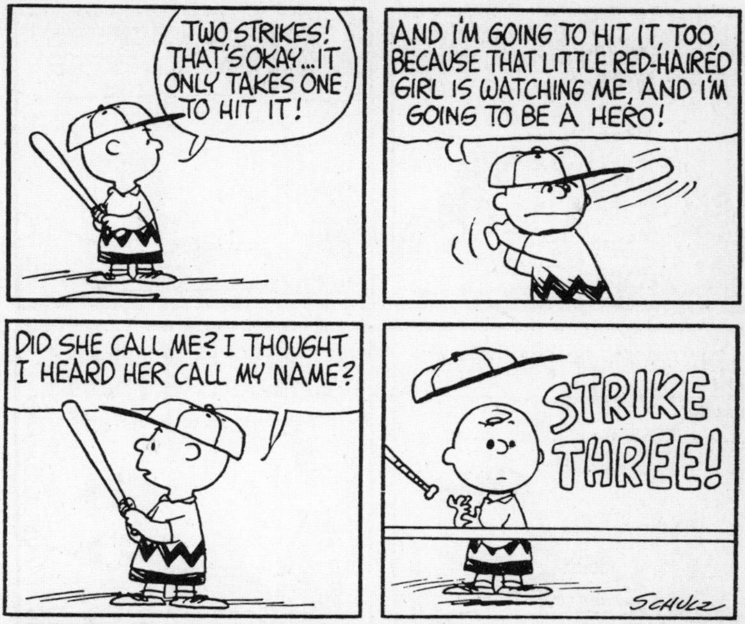
TWO STRIKES! THAT'S OKAY...IT ONLY TAKES ONE TO HIT IT!
AND I'M GOING TO HIT IT, TOO, BECAUSE THAT LITTLE RED-HAIRED GIRL IS WATCHING ME, AND I'M GOING TO BE A HERO!
DID SHE CALL ME? I THOUGHT I HEARD HER CALL MY NAME?
STRIKE THREE!
SCHULZ

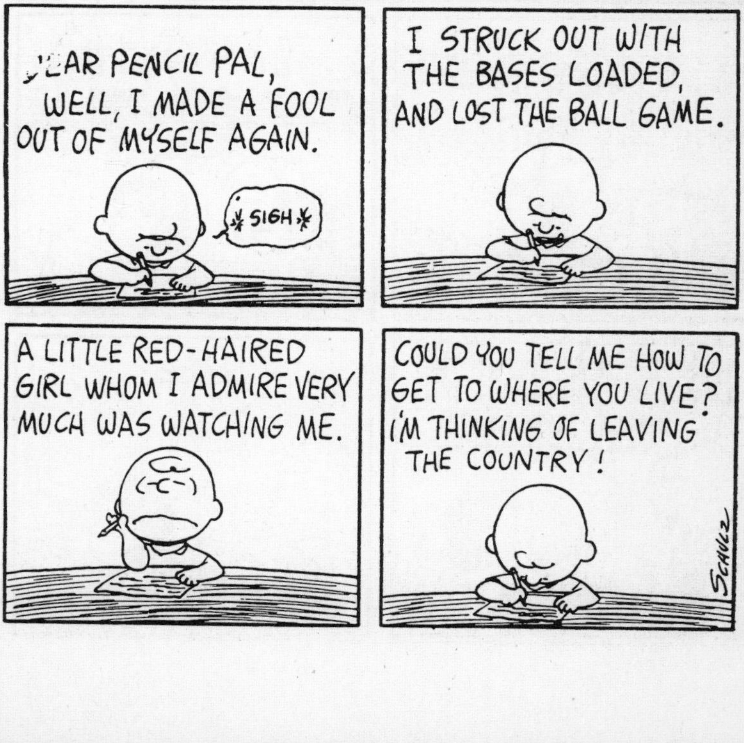
DEAR PENCIL PAL,
WELL, I MADE A FOOL OUT OF MYSELF AGAIN.
SIGH
I STRUCK OUT WITH THE BASES LOADED, AND LOST THE BALL GAME.
A LITTLE RED-HAIRED GIRL WHOM I ADMIRE VERY MUCH WAS WATCHING ME.
COULD YOU TELL ME HOW TO GET TO WHERE YOU LIVE? I'M THINKING OF LEAVING THE COUNTRY!
SCHULZ

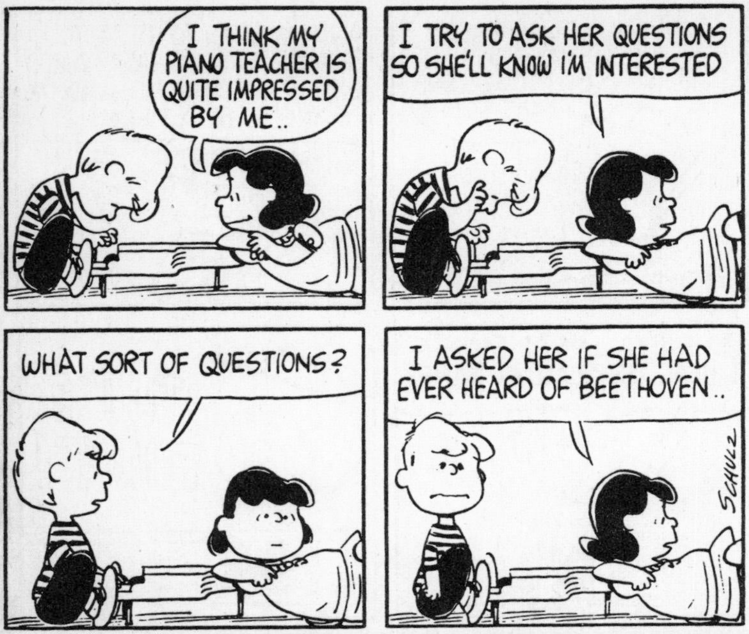
I THINK MY PIANO TEACHER IS QUITE IMPRESSED BY ME..
I TRY TO ASK HER QUESTIONS SO SHE'LL KNOW I'M INTERESTED
WHAT SORT OF QUESTIONS?
I ASKED HER IF SHE HAD EVER HEARD OF BEETHOVEN..
SCHULZ

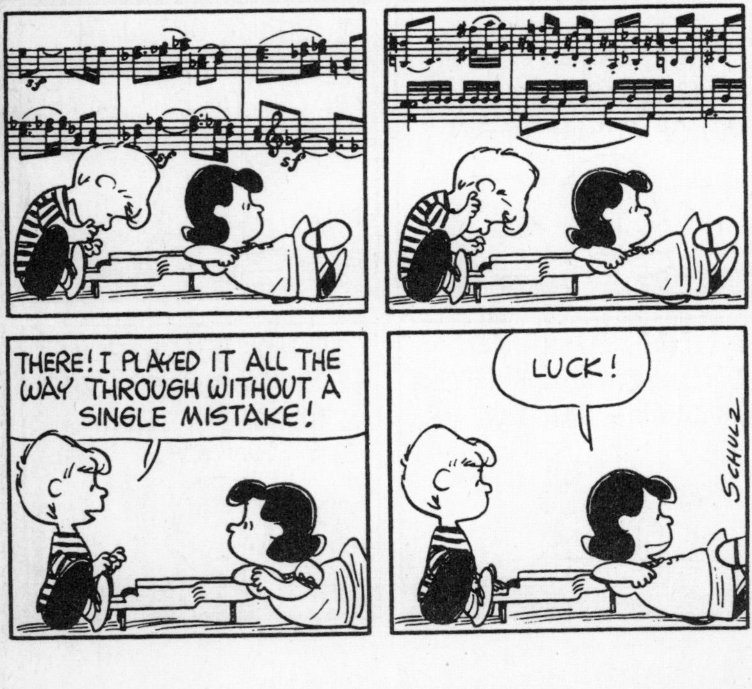
THERE! I PLAYED IT ALL THE WAY THROUGH WITHOUT A SINGLE MISTAKE!
LUCK!
SCHULZ